CODE AND COUTURE

CODE AND COUTURE

KRISTI ANN HUNTER

Oholiab Creations
Georgia, United States

Oholiab Creations, LLC

Code and Couture

Published by Oholiab Creations, LLC

110 Walter Way #1065

Stockbridge, GA 30281

ISBN 978-1-959589-17-4 (Paperback) ISBN 978-1-959589-18-1 (eBook)

Library of Congress Control Number: 2025917778

Scripture quotations marked CSB have been taken from the Christian Standard Bible®, Copyright © 2017 by Holman Bible Publishers. Used by permission. Christian Standard Bible® and CSB® are federally registered trademarks of Holman Bible Publishers.

For more information and questions, contact Kristi Hunter at KristiAnnHunter.com.

The story, all names, characters, and incidents portrayed in this production are fictitious. No identification with actual persons (living or deceased), places, buildings, and products is intended or should be inferred.

Cover Design by Angie Fisher of WTX Labs.

To the God who uses anything and everything for His glory.
Colossians 3:23
To Wally/Warren who will probably never read this book but was the
first to show me ministry wasn't what I thought it was.
And to Jacob, for showing me that God can use my authentic self and I
don't have to be anyone else.

AMY

At four years old, I proudly stomped into my pre-K classroom to show off my brand-new, light-up, sparkly unicorn high-tops, and the other kids let me have the first choice of squares on the color carpet. I learned the value of confidently walking into each and every space like I own it. I've never slunk in through a side door or been pushed or carried into a building, but if I can't make it through those glass double doors on my own steam today, I'm going to have to break down and ask for a piggy-back ride. The inelegant absurdity of being observed in such a position will probably be enough to get my feet moving across the parking lot, but it remains to be seen if it will sustain me through actually entering the premises.

Normally, my schedule is full of places to go, doors to enter, events to attend. I've made a life of it. Not once in my twenty-eight years do I remember having to give myself a step-by-step action plan to walk inside a building. Creating a goal to get a coveted invitation? Absolutely. Making a plan to arrive at a meeting at a specific time and with a certain impressive accessory? On more than one occasion.

I am adept at making detailed plans to achieve a greater goal for my career, my finances, or my personal ambitions. Never have I ever created a series of small targets to build up to the incredible feat of opening a door.

Yet here I am, doing just that. And right now, I'm working hard to convince myself I can't push back the next of those miniature milestones.

Again.

I've already moved it three times.

Today, I cannot call simply making it onto the property a win. I cannot hide in the back row of the parking lot. I cannot climb into the backseat and huddle under a blanket while I connect remotely on my phone.

Today, I'm going inside.

Before I can lose my resolve, I drive past the shaded, out-of-the-way side lot I've been parking in and follow the brightly colored signs directing me to the visitor spaces, right up front, only a matter of steps from the three large sets of double glass doors.

If I don't get out of my car now, there are people everywhere who will notice and wonder, and if one of them approaches to see if I'm all right, it will be more embarrassing than anything that could happen inside.

On the other hand, if I get out and walk with purpose, keep my head down, and don't talk to anyone, I can make it through those doors without drawing the notice of any of the people milling around on the sidewalks outside. Unless, of course, someone sees me getting out of a car parked in a visitor spot, but who really pays attention to things like that?

I grab my purse from the seat, nearly falling out the driver's door at the lack of weight. I'm accustomed to carrying a large bag filled with everything I'll need for the day, but the sedate black bag the size of a box of granola bars is closer to everything I saw when I looked up outfit inspirations online a month ago. In the name of fashion, I crammed the basic necessities into the smaller space and dropped everything else into a Bogg bag tucked behind the driver's seat.

My confidence grows with every step I take away from my sporty red Mercedes. Who knew just getting out of the car was going to be the hardest part? After five steps, I feel certain diving back into the vehicle is no longer a danger.

Now I can set my sights on accomplishing my next goal. Get in. Get out. Don't talk to anyone. Don't draw anyone's attention. Don't linger after the meeting is over.

A small group of people is making their way through the middle set of doors, and I try to fall in behind them, merging with the flow. It takes effort not to swivel my head around and take in everything to be found in the enormous, two-story church foyer, but ogling the decorations is an obvious sign you're new.

I don't want to look new. I want to appear like an insider who belongs here and has come and gone so often that whatever is in this room has become totally mundane. I am as forgettable as the flooring, as innocuous as the wallpaper, as ignorable as the—

"Hi there!"

It would seem a tall woman in a deep violet-colored shirt and hair curled high enough to make a 1980s grandmother proud is going to ruin my plan. She smiles down at me, clearly oblivious to the startle she gave me that has my already nervous heart auditioning for a heavy metal band.

"My name's Betsy."

Her enthusiasm is almost enough to send me back to my car. I can drive to the back of the parking lot and no one will be any wiser.

Especially me because I'll feel like a veritable idiot.

The bubbly woman steps around three other people to stand in front of me, her hands clasped together at her chest as if she is having to physically hold herself back from hugging me. "Is this your first time? I don't think I've seen you here before."

I blink at this woman and her shoulders that are broad enough to inspire the desire to poke at them to see if someone has started fitting

T-shirts with shoulder pads. Across the cavernous space are more double doors. Wooden ones, propped open to reveal an enormous auditorium-style room that has to contain at least a thousand people with more walking in every second. How can she possibly know I've never been here?

I turn my head to look out the doors I just entered, but the visitor parking isn't visible from here. Is there a guy on a security camera relaying the description of everyone who parks there to a special team of people? Discreetly, I try to see if Betsy is wearing an earpiece like a spy, but her giant purple earrings and puffed out curls could be hiding anything.

More people are entering the foyer area from hallways that jut off toward the sides of the building. Why didn't I think to check for side doors? Probably because I didn't realize a church would recruit their welcoming committee from the front of a Wal-Mart. Or are these the greeters that Wal-Mart rejected for being too aggressive? I haven't been to one of those big box stores in years. Maybe all the greeters tackle people at the door these days.

Are all the entrances being guarded by people like Betsy? If I try different doors, they'll think I'm new every time I arrive. Or, with the luck I've been having lately, I'll accidentally choose the door that has me wandering onto the stage.

All of that is a concern for next week, though, assuming I can work up the nerve to make a second attempt at attendance. For now, I need to deal with Betsy.

I give her my best smile, which is normally wide and engaging and all things personable. Right now, it feels tighter than extra strength shapewear. "I'm just . . . going in there." I vaguely point toward the room filled with lots of people and blessed anonymity.

"Of course you are." She loses the battle with herself and one hand lands on my arm. I barely feel it through the cable-knit sweater I settled on wearing. "But you don't want to go without your gift."

"My gift?" My sister, Emma, gave me a long list of things I simply had to do at church. A very long list. An intimidating, suffocating list. Nowhere on it was receiving a gift.

"Your first time visitor gift." Betsy waves the hand not clutching my sleeve toward a counter set up on the side of the large foyer. Purple must be the color family for the newcomer brigade because an enormous banner in indigo hangs over the counter. Large gold letters read "Welcome, Visitors."

More smiling people stand beneath the banner and large brown paper gift bags stamped with the church logo line the edge of the counter. Their shirts are more of an iris color. All these slightly different shades of purple in the same room make my eyes burn.

The logo on the bags appears to be stamped in green instead of purple, though. This color combination is not acceptable unless you're catching beads and getting drunk in New Orleans.

Wait. I should not be thinking about getting drunk while standing in a church. Probably shouldn't be thinking about getting drunk at all. Not that I was ever a fan of that activity. Such a loss of control often leads to unflattering stories that follow you around for years.

Betsy is wanting me to follow her now, as she tries to guide me toward the counter and its small army of paper greeting soldiers that must contain the aforementioned gift.

Oh, no. No, no, no, no. I am not carrying one of those bags around. They practically scream, "Come talk to me. Pretend you're happy to see me. Convince me I belong here."

On the average day I'm a sucker for anything that makes me the center of attention, but I'd rather fade into the background today.

I try to smile again. "That's really not necessary, I'm—"

"Of course it's not necessary." Betsy laughs and the flouncy curls on her head bobble. "That's what makes it a gift."

She continues walking toward the counter with her arm hooked with mine. My choices are to rudely extract myself and run away, follow her to the table and rudely turn down their gift, or fake a smile through it all and rudely ditch the paper bag in a potted plant.

I may be new to this whole Christianity thing, but I'm fairly certain being rude in church is not on the approved behavior list. Maybe I shouldn't have been so determined to figure this out myself instead of letting Emma tell me what to do.

I make one more attempt to get out of more unwelcome welcoming attention. "I should go . . . that way." The excuse that I was meeting someone had been on my tongue, but I know for certain that lying is unapproved behavior.

And I am very deliberately not meeting anyone. My sister and her boyfriend attend this church, but they attend the second of the Sunday morning services. I know because Emma invited me to join her.

Repeatedly.

But I don't want to come with Emma. Our relationship has changed over the past few months, grown deeper and stronger and turned into the real version of the close relationship I'd once thought we had. I'll be forever grateful to her for guiding me to the massive, life-changing decision of salvation, but now . . . Well, now I need to do it myself. I need to figure out who I am and what I do, and I don't need Emma hovering over me and telling me her version of the answers.

So, no, I don't want to find Emma.

Still, I can't keep my desperate gaze from searching through the foyer for some sort of escape. Church would be the most likely location for a miracle, wouldn't it?

My gaze snags on a taller than average man with a head of dark, well-groomed curls. He looks as comfortable in this church as I feel in a Neiman Marcus, and I doubt he had to give himself a pep talk to get out of the car this morning. He's dressed in faded jeans and a plaid button-up and has a small smile that looks unconsciously formed for no apparent reason.

Until his eyes meet mine. He takes in my situation and his smile turns into an amused grin.

I can't look away even as my feet keep following Betsy. When she pulls me to a stop, I tear my attention from the handsome stranger to the counter we've arrived at. Betsy is catching the attention of a middle-aged man holding one of those dreaded gift bags.

"There you are!"

I blink because that sentence did not come from the man now looking at me as if he found an employee's hidden stash in the corner of a boutique sample sale.

The three of us and a few others turn to see the dark-haired man crossing the foyer. I know for certain I have never seen him until thirty seconds ago—I would absolutely remember anyone that attractive—but he's acting as if we're long-lost besties. His smile is as excitedly welcoming as Betsy's, but it doesn't feel like a lure trying to make me the victim of an attack hug.

I press one hand to my chest, curling the tips of my fingers into the thick, soft wool. "Me?"

"Of course, you." He nods toward the doors to the auditorium. "We saved you a seat."

Betsy squeezes my arm. "Why didn't you tell me you were meeting friends? You're in good hands with this one, even if he doesn't know he should meet his guests at the door." She reaches up and pats the man on the cheek.

People actually do that in real life? I thought it was something old grandmothers did in TV shows or movies on the Heartfelt channel.

The man chuckles. "I'll do better next time, Betsy." His blue eyes lift to a point over my shoulder, and he shifts to reach out an arm. "Thanks, Jeff. I'll give this to her."

Jeff is trying and failing to hide his disgruntlement at my would-be rescuer's interruption, but he hands over the gift and finds a smile for the next visitor. My knight in muted plaid takes the bag and brings his bright, questioning gaze my way.

He's clearly asking me a question, but I'm not sure what it is. Do I want the bag? Do I want him to walk away? Do I want to meet Jeff? The answer to all of those questions is no, so I give a small, discreet shake of my head.

He skillfully manages to settle the bag at the end of the row of gifts and guide me away from the counter in a single smooth move.

As we walk away, his smile turns a bit sheepish. "I'm sorry. You can tell me to go kick rocks if you want, but you looked like you could use saving."

I swallow and nod my head several times. "No, I . . . thank you. She seems sweet but, um . . . a little much. At least for me. Today."

He chuckles. "Betsy means well."

I sneak a glance back at the counter where Jeff is handing a bag to a young mom and smiling down at the toddler by her side. "And Jeff?"

"Also means well." He clears his throat. "Mostly. He likes to be the first to know about new, potentially single young women." One hand lifts to run through his dark curls. "It's not as creepy as it sounds."

"I'll take your word on that." As I have no intention of even seeing Jeff again in the near future, much less dating him, his creepiness is irrelevant. If I were going to wade back into the dating waters, which I've avoided ever since I spent an evening upending everything I know about life into a carpet full of tears on my sister's living room floor, it would be with someone like the guy beside me.

Unless I'm supposed to avoid men that are physically attractive now? Ugh. This confusion is one of the reasons I'm on a dating hiatus right now. Almost an entire social life hiatus. My friends don't know what to do with me anymore.

Half the time I don't know what to do with me.

I'm determined to figure it out, though. My mother has been telling me who to be since I was born and now, with this new creation business, I'm left wondering how much of me is, well, me, and how much of it is her. That's why I'm doing this personal discovery on my own.

Two seconds after I'd said amen and opened my eyes to stare at the framed video game posters on Emma's wall, she was telling me all the things I needed to do next. Come to church, meet her pastor, get baptized, join a study group. Not to mention the list of veiled suggestions that might have been from Emma and might have been from some weird form of guilty conscience in my head. The list of things I needed to change or add in my life seemed endless and full of things I definitely wouldn't have had any part of before.

Stepping into a room of people who all know a whole lot more than I do about church and pretending I belong there? Far from ideal.

Submerging myself fully clothed in a vat of water in front of two thousand people in a room and who knew how many more online? No thank you.

Meeting with a complete stranger and sharing how my world is upside down, my confidence is in shambles, my future path is entirely obliterated, and yet somehow none of that undermines the secure feeling of rightness I have over my decision, even though I wake up each morning and spend ten minutes having an existential crisis because I don't know who I am anymore? There aren't words to describe that level of not happening.

My rescuer nods toward the open doors through which instrumental music drifts along with the murmur of hundreds of voices. "Do you have people you're meeting?"

"Um, no."

"Well, I don't actually have seats saved, but you're welcome to sit with me if you'd rather not be alone. We can find a row in the back, and I'll chase all the greeters away." He swings his arm like he's fending off an attacking army.

I can't help but smile at his antics. "I don't want to be a bother. You can just point me toward a quiet corner and go sit wherever you normally do."

He shrugs. "This isn't my normal service so I'm sure someone else is occupying my usual spot."

There's another person in a purple shirt standing by the wooden doors, but he simply looks from me to my escort and smiles and nods.

I've walked into a lot of public buildings in my life and never had so many people want to talk to me. I deal with strangers almost every day in my work, but this is more than a little daunting. My sister wasn't kidding about the level of friendliness in her church.

The possibility of dealing with one person who seems fairly understanding and dozens of people who want to bombard me with some weird form of a love bomb seems like a great reason to alter my *do this on my own* stance. Especially since he's cute. I pinch myself on the arm because, once again, I don't think that's supposed to be something I'm thinking about right now.

I give him a smile I hope is friendly and not flirty. "Lead on."

"Is this your first time here?" My rescuer walks into the auditorium and immediately turns left toward an area of short rows of chairs that are mostly empty.

"What gave it away?" My voice is thin and flat or perhaps that's just the way it's echoing in my head. I don't normally have a problem being in crowded spaces or among people, but being here, in this room, in these back rows, feels like the final admission that I have completely and irrevocably destroyed who I was prior to two months ago.

He chuckles. "The wide-eyed panic, I suppose."

"That would do it." I swallow several times as I lower the seat and slide into it, trying to fix the dryness in my mouth. I've been to the theater, the symphony, the opera, and numerous meetings, talks, and award presentations so the style of seat is familiar and a little comforting. It's also disorienting.

Never have I sat in the back row. The front rows are far more visible and public spaces are for being seen as much as they are for seeing.

Never have I sat in a seat with the intention of actually participating in the show that is about to be put on. Because it's not a show. It's . . . something else, something I'm supposed to be a part of and not just appreciate.

Never have I ever stepped out of my house in a cable-knit sweater, long flowing skirt, and less hair and makeup effort than I would put in for going to the grocery store. This is the look that came up repeatedly when I spent two hours combing the Internet for "church girl outfit," though.

Finding the appropriate look for each occasion has been a crucial part of my life and it would seem it's still a part of who I am. Looking around, though, I'm not certain that the dress code is as set as Pinterest led me to believe.

The dryness in my mouth isn't going away and I can't do anything about it because I don't have my water bottle with me. All the pictures of the girls in the sweaters and long skirts had tiny bags that don't hold all of life's necessities, so I, too, brought a small purse. I should have brought my big leather hobo bag.

The man settles into the seat beside mine, placing his Bible and phone on the arm away from me. "First time in a large church?" He chuckles as he looks around the room where people are wandering about or collecting in groups. Some are taking their seats. "I grew up in a large church, so I forget what it can feel like sometimes."

I wince. "I didn't grow up in church at all."

"Oh, yeah?" He turns partially in his seat to give me his full attention. "When did you start attending?"

Shouldn't the service be starting now? I tried to time my entry so I wouldn't endure much exposure to the social aspect, but obviously I miscalculated. I turn my wrist to check my watch, then almost immediately jerk the sweater sleeve back down.

The watch is a nice one, a gift from a jewelry designer I met when I showed my first clothing collection in New York. That I'm wearing it at all only underscores how scattered my mind is today. Normally I think of every aspect of an ensemble, from the hair accessories to the toenail polish, but I must have grabbed the watch out of habit when I was dressing this morning. It certainly does not fit the low-key, modest vibe I was going for.

I clear my throat and decide to ignore the man's question. I don't know his name and at this moment I can't remember if he told it to me earlier, so I'm not about to ask. Still, in my experience, most personal questions can be diverted by asking the other person a different personal question. As long as that person isn't also avoiding talking about themselves, it works nicely. "Did you grow up in this church?"

"No, though it wasn't too far from here. Morning Glory. Have you been there?"

"Ah, no." The name vaguely resonates, but I don't know that church. I don't know any church, not specifically.

I want to, though. There's a lot of things I don't know anymore, but I have read enough books . . . well, parts of books . . . okay, AI recaps of books and watched enough online services to know that I do want to learn how to worship.

This outfit is comfortable, but I feel exposed. My usual armor is the latest trends in fashion, makeup, hair, and jewelry, all folded into a classic style with a touch of personal flair.

Of course, these days, my usual armor feels as much like a mask as it does a security blanket. Maybe this exposure thing will be good for me.

And maybe, if I tell myself that enough times, I'll start to believe it.

JASON

The lights dim once and the screens to the side of the church begin displaying the five-minute countdown to the start of the service. A distressed squeak comes from my seat neighbor. She must not have known that the service actually starts at three minutes past the hour. Her hands clutch the armrests, and she looks like she's about to bolt from the worship center and maybe even out of the building.

I don't want her to.

Not just because I'm somewhat intrigued by her, enough that I risked great embarrassment and even a slap on the cheek by pretending to know her, but because I don't want anyone to feel like they don't belong here.

Church has always been the one place I felt comfortable in my life. Growing up, there were a lot of other places, including my own home on occasion, that I felt out of place.

This woman looks like she feels that way now.

There's something familiar about her, but I don't think we've met. Maybe it's because she looks like at least a dozen other young women in the singles group, with her simple hairstyle, clean face, and flowy skirt. Still, there's something about her I can't put my finger on that makes her different. It could be the nerves, but whatever it is, I'm glad she's here.

Perhaps she needs to know that.

"I'm glad to have you here."

She blinks at me, waiting for something else, but I can't think what it would be. I'm not about to ask her out or even flirt with her, not when she's new to this church and, if I have to hazard a guess, new to church in general. This is a girl that needs to focus on God, not me.

But if she keeps coming back, I might find myself not much better than Jeff. She's cute. And it's been a long time since I thought a girl was cute in anything more than a passing, observational manner.

"That's it?" Her voice is tight and quiet, like a squeaky whisper.

"I . . ." I give her my most charming, self-deprecating smile. It works on all the other women in my life, except my best friend. "I'm not sure what else you're expecting."

"You're just . . . glad I'm here?"

"Yeah. I'm always glad when people are in church, worshipping God, learning how to live more like Jesus."

The lights dim again as the countdown flies by. I pick up my phone to ensure the volume has been turned down all the way.

"You did a good job."

I look up into the gray eyes that somehow seem to shine in the shadows of the lowered lighting of this back corner tucked under the outcrop of the balcony above. "I'm sorry?"

Her fingers fiddle with the hem of her sweater. One sleeve rides up and I catch a glimpse of a watch that looks similar enough to my mother's favorite timepiece that it pulls part of my attention.

She clears her throat and waves one hand toward the stage. "You know, the whole welcoming thing. Showing newcomers your interest without, I don't know, quizzing them over their credentials."

I forget the watch as I fight the urge for my eyebrows to climb upward. Last week's sermon had been on accepting people—especially visitors—as they were, without expecting them to know about church or

God or the Bible. If God receives people without judgement, so should we. A small laugh escapes as I settle back in my seat, suddenly sad that the countdown is rapidly approaching zero. "I thought this was your first time here."

"I've been watching online."

I nod, prepared to tell her that I think that's a smart, safe way to check out a church, but she's not done talking.

"On my phone."

If I had to guess, the nerves are settling in and they've taken over her mouth.

"From my car."

I can't stop the surprise from showing on my face.

"In the parking lot."

My gaze swings to the back of the room, as if I could see through the walls and out into the parking lot. I never would have guessed this woman to be in that position, but it could happen to anyone. And she's trusting me with that information. I have to step up.

"I'm . . ." I have to pause to clear my throat as emotion clogs it. "Thank you for trusting me. We have a ministry team that can help you. I can introduce you to the coordinator after the service. She's very discreet."

The woman frowns. I can't believe I didn't ask for her name earlier. Did I even offer mine? I don't think so. It feels awkwardly late to do so now.

Suddenly, her frown clears, her entire body seems to lighten, and she starts to giggle. It's a soft giggle, drifting through a wide smile to land softly on my ears. "I'm not homeless."

This declaration brings me back to the exchange and I feel heat gathering at the back of my neck. Fortunately, the shadows should hide any blush I actually form.

Her soft giggles continue as she shakes her head and relaxes into her seat. "It's just taken me a . . . while . . . to get up the nerve to walk into the building."

I shake my head, clearing out the misconceptions I'd been building and fighting a laugh of my own at the picture she's painting. "So you've been driving here, parking in the lot, and watching the service from your phone?"

"Only for the last two weeks." Her smile turns sheepish. "Before that, I couldn't even make it here and had to watch from the Target parking lot down the street."

I can't help it. My laughter joins hers. "How long has this been going on?"

"Four weeks ago, I didn't even make it out of my parking space at my apartment."

"In that case, maybe next week you can move one section up? Work your way to the front of the room?"

She winces and pats the arm of her seat. "This is working fine, thank you."

The music changes and the lights dim down for the final time as the praise band fills the stage. I stand and realize my seat mate has lost her sense of ease and is getting to her feet with a confused look on her face.

She may have been watching the services online, but I have a feeling this isn't just her first time at this church. It's her first time at any church. We don't show the congregation on the livestream, so she'd have no idea of knowing what the people are doing if she hasn't been in the building.

I lean in to whisper in her ear. This close to her, I catch a delightful scent I couldn't begin to identify and need to not think about. I have a more important job right now. "We usually stand for the singing. People are more engaged that way. And those that prefer to sway or raise their hands can comfortably do so."

"Oh." She nods slightly, her eyes flying around the room as her lips barely move.

I nudge her shoulder and point to the side screen where they are broadcasting a close-up video of one of the singers but also displaying the words to the song. "The words are up there. We don't all know it."

Her shoulders relax a little as her gaze glues to the screen. It stays there until someone steps out to give announcements and people are sitting once again.

All the ease she'd gained before the service is gone as her fingers once more wrap around the ends of her armrests with a grip tight enough to make her knuckles stand out and turn white.

I don't know what's bothering her about this moment as everyone laughs at a joke made by the minister, but I want her to know she's not alone.

Following the same instinct that had me crossing the foyer to come to her rescue, I let my hand lay gently on top of hers. My thumb grazes the side of her hand, and I have to will myself not to notice how soft her skin is.

When the next song starts, I don't get up. I stay seated, letting the people in front of us stand and do their thing. Wide eyes turn to me, staring for several seconds, before she lets out a deep sigh and settles back into her chair.

Her fingers release their grip on the armrest and her hand starts to shift beneath mine. I go to move my hand but before I can, she's flipped hers over and threaded her fingers between mine. Her palm is pressed to mine, and I can feel how cold it is.

She's gripping my hand with the same intensity she held the arm rest moments before. There's nothing flirtatious or romantic about it. This woman has decided she needs a lifeline and my hand is it. I might walk out of here with a bruise, but it will be worth it.

Everyone sits and Pastor Brian comes out to start his sermon. The lack of congregant participation must make it feel more familiar, because my companion slides her hand from mine and takes out her phone, opening a notes app.

Occasionally, she types out a question related to the sermon. I'm guessing it's something she wants to look into later. If she didn't have anyone to come to church with, though, I doubt she has someone to answer her questions.

I slide a piece of paper from my Bible. It's an old flyer for a gathering of the singles' ministry, but the back is blank. Then I open up the Bible app on my phone so I can look up things I don't remember with specificity.

Part of my attention stays on the sermon, but most of it is given to sneaking glances at the woman's phone and making a list of verses she can utilize to find her answers.

I don't get to give her the paper though, because when everyone stands for the closing song after the sermon, she bolts from the room.

Grabbing up my things, I move to follow her, but she's already going through the glass doors to the parking lot by the time I slip out of the worship center.

There are several people milling around, volunteers, security, other people who left the service early, and those coming out of small groups that meet during this first hour. It's far too many people for me to call out for her, even if I did know her name.

I can't do anything except put the page of notes back into my Bible and pray I'll see her next week. This isn't my normal service. I'm usually sitting in a small group Bible study right now, but this morning I'd been asked to help in the teen group that meets during the second service, so I'd rearranged my schedule.

Looks like I'll be rearranging it again next week, or possibly even lurking in the foyer before every service, because it's been a long time since I was this intrigued.

I'm still thinking about her an hour later as I make my way from the building and across the parking lot to my car. It figures that the first girl to catch my eye in almost a year is one I need to stay away from in anything other than a brother-in-Christ sense. She's clearly got more important things to straighten out right now.

Once in my car, the feeling of disconnection I've been battling lately washes over me. I don't know what to do with myself. It's disconcertingly similar to the feeling I had as a teenager when I didn't know what to do with the expectations or even the opportunities around me.

Except now I'm a thirty-year-old adult and have the responsibility of creating expectations and opportunities for myself. I have friends, my own business, and enough hobbies to keep me from working eighteen hours a day like I did right out of college. Over the past five or six years I've created a routine and it's a good one.

So why do I feel . . . itchy?

I'd like to blame the experience of seeing church through the eyes of a newcomer, but this discomfort has been popping up more and more over the past few months.

Ever since Emma started dating Carter.

It might be time to admit to myself that this change has disturbed me more than I'm willing to admit.

My phone vibrates and I unlock it to read the message from Emma letting me know our group of friends is meeting for lunch at a nearby Mexican restaurant. I drive over there, my mind bouncing between contemplating my very existence and replaying every moment of my morning with the unknown blonde woman.

Most of my friends are already seated, snacking on the chips and salsa. There isn't an open seat next to Emma. Her good friend Trina is on one side and her boyfriend, Carter, is on the other. That's the place that used to be mine.

Carter's a good guy and, even more importantly, he's good for Emma. I'm glad they're together. I even suppose it's appropriate that he displaced me from my usual location instead of bumping out Tamera, but I miss my best friend a little.

I take the seat next to Carter and snag one of the chips. I've been here often enough that I don't need a menu. Lunch special number 4 order is my go-to here. They have the best chile rellenos.

It's easy to join in the conversation floating around the table and by the time we're giving the server our orders, I've more or less pushed the mopey thoughts out of my mind.

Life isn't supposed to be stagnant. Everything shouldn't always stay the same. But whether it's the fact that our group is consisting of more and more couples—including one that ran off and eloped a month ago and another set to tie the knot in March—or the way my apartment seems more and more empty, it's become very clear to me that the life I've been building isn't exactly a full one.

Now, if only I knew what to do about it.

AMY

Tuesday morning me is not happy with Monday morning me. Yesterday, while I was riding the high of having finally accomplished the feat of attending a church service, I convinced myself that I was on my way to taking charge of this new life and finding where I am meant to be.

I was delusional.

And in my delusions, I made an appointment.

Now I have to keep that appointment, and I am not certain I'm ready for it. Not completely anyway.

On the one hand, I'm very excited to meet my twin sister's mysterious best friend who I actually thought was imaginary until her boyfriend mentioned having gone to the guy's home for dinner.

On the other hand, attending a church service is a far cry from defying my mother. She may not know where I'm going for my client consultation this morning or the fact that I'm the client instead of the consultant, but I know she wouldn't approve. It's obvious even if she has never explicitly said, "Amy, do not take your styling and design business that I thought was part of my boutique, but you secretly formed under a different business entity, and go in a direction that attempts to bring in something other than exclusive, designer, high-end clientele."

If she'd known saying that sentence was an option, she absolutely would have done so.

I can't hide the official business arrangement much longer. Her suspicions are growing as I keep landing more and more clients, but she isn't seeing the boost in her profit margin. That's because the rent for my office space is a set number and all that extra profit is going into my business bank account. Not hers.

The next steps of my business plan need to already be in motion when she figures everything out so that she can't convince me to change direction and come under the fold of the boutique after all.

Unfortunately, my business plan has undergone an abrupt adjustment in the past few months, and I feel more than a little unsure about my new choices. Since I was in high school, the vision has been the same. Become a high-end, couture designer and a stylist to celebrities and important figures.

Part of me still wants that, but a larger part of me wants to help more people. Everyday people.

A sense of utter failure has plagued me since I learned my own sister was so uncomfortable with the clothing Mother and I expected her to wear that she hid huge parts of her life from us. The habits and clothing she needed to be able to build the life she wanted didn't fit our aesthetic, so she kept them away from us.

That was the day I realized there is more to fashion than appearance.

The experience has made me a better stylist, but I can only take on so many individual clients and, if I'm honest, most of the people who can afford my services aren't suffering from a fashion emergency. They want to go from good to great.

There needs to be a budget version of my services if I want people like my twin to be able to curate a wardrobe that doesn't hurt other people's eyes while still fitting their needs.

As much as people don't like to admit it, what we wear and the way we look affects how others think about us and treat us. Even Emma has admitted that she has had an easier time in public since I went through her wardrobe with her a few months ago. She doesn't have to look frumpy to be comfortable, even if she has weird requirements for that comfort.

Unfortunately, custom wardrobe makeovers take a lot of time and money. In order to make a budget-friendly styling service, I need to replicate myself, and I only know one way to do that.

Which is why I made this morning's meeting.

I didn't sleep well last night as the bravado from Sunday was already giving way to nerves, so I take extra time to put cold compresses and hydration masks under my eyes this morning. When I think I'm ready to go, I grab my mascara and give my lashes one more flick of extension to overcome any lingering dullness from the rough night.

The face staring back at me in the mirror is familiar. Properly contoured foundation, perfectly winged eyeliner, and bold, red lips framed by loose, bouncy blonde curls is a look I know. The makeup skills have been honed since I was eleven, the hair since I was nine—though my discovery of heatless curls in the past few years has been a game changer.

Everything looks more me than the girl who attended church two days ago.

I don't feel like me, though.

Of course, I didn't feel much like me on Sunday, either.

At least, not mentally or emotionally or whatever *-ally* options there are aside from physically. I turn left, then right, inspecting myself in the mirror. The loose-fitting black slacks, white chiffon keyhole blouse, and wedge heeled half boots are professional and stylish.

It's actually not that different from some of the outfits I saw at the church. There were certainly enough people dressed similarly to the "church girl outfits" I saw online that I didn't look out of place, but I don't know that this version of me would look completely strange either. I think I even saw one or two pieces of clothing from my mother's boutique in the audience.

I try to imagine going to church in my normal clothes and with my normal hair and makeup. Would I still feel the need to hide in the back corner or flee from the people who want to greet me?

Frequently when I walk into a room, people notice, and they look at me. Whether it's the hair, the clothes, or the way my mother taught me to walk with purpose, I have no idea, but it's not something I'm ready to experience at church. I have too many things to figure out about myself before drawing that kind of attention.

Besides, I think drawing attention at church may be a bad thing in the rule book.

My phone buzzes with an incoming text as I leave my room to gather my needs for the day.

> EMMA: Would you rather be totally covered in hair from head to toe or be completely bald?

I roll my eyes but can't stop a smile as I read the question. About five months ago, when I discovered Emma had an entire wardrobe and therefore life she'd been actively working to hide from me, we had a fight. The biggest fight of our lives as far as I remember. It was obvious that we'd grown far apart as adults.

As hurt and angry as I was about that, I didn't know what to do. Fortunately, Emma did. She started texting me get-to-know-you questions every day, re-establishing our connection in little bits and pieces.

Three months ago, I told her she was not allowed to ask my favorite of anything anymore when she stooped so low as to ask which foot I preferred to start with when clipping toenails. I also took her to get a pedicure after that one because she makes enough disposable income to not be clipping her own toenails when she could be indulging in an hour of pampering at my favorite spa.

By that point, texting me every morning was a habit, and she fell back on Would You Rather questions when she couldn't think of anything else. To be honest, I like the daily connection. Most days we don't have much to talk about, but it's easier to say things or ask questions when the conversation is already started.

I set today's lipstick on my kitchen counter so it can be added to my bag for the day and unlock my phone to type out an answer.

> ME: Easy. Completely bald. There are fabulous wigs and false eyelashes. There're even false eyebrows.

Because I enjoy making Emma cringe over all things beauty- and style-related, I immediately send another message.

> ME: I don't even want to think about the time and money involved in removing that much body hair. Waxing would mean growing out the stubble too often and laser removal is expensive.

> EMMA: Laser removal? Doesn't that burn?

> ME: No. I had my underarms done years ago.

I've thought about doing my legs but waxing and shaving haven't been enough of a pain for me to spend the money. I glance at my watch and start moving about my kitchen, gathering the things I need for the day with one hand while texting with the other. Emma has informed me I don't actually save time doing this as it makes both tasks slower, but I figure if I'm doing them simultaneously, the overall time spent is less.

She wants to time me to see if that's true.

I would rather not know.

> **ME: Are you working from home today?**

> EMMA: <<GIF of Robert Downey, Jr rolling his eyes>>

> EMMA: Yes. There's no need for a fit check.

I laugh as I shove my water bottle and a package of organic granola bites into my bag. Emma using the term *fit check* in any sort of unironic way is something that never would have happened a year ago.

Normally, when I ask if she's going into the office, it is because I want to see what she's wearing. My sister is a fashion nightmare, but we've been working together for the past few months and have found a look that keeps her comfortable but not dowdy.

Today, though, I have an ulterior motive.

I don't want her in her office because I am going to be in her office.

I do realize the irony of wanting to find myself on my own and be my own woman but utilizing all of Emma's contacts and spaces to do so. But there are an overwhelming number of different types of churches within twenty minutes of me and I don't know of another company that does what Emma's employer does.

So, I'm going into Emma's spaces on my own and I'm counting it as independence. The good thing about not telling anyone is no one can contradict me.

> **ME: Are you planning to see anyone today?**

> EMMA: No.

ME: Not even Carter?

EMMA: Carter doesn't count.

I shake my head even though she can't see me. How can she possibly say that Carter doesn't count? Yes, the man is head over heels in love with her, but they've only been dating like six months. That's longer than any relationship I've ever had, but that's still in the make a good impression phase.

Isn't it?

ME: How can Carter not count? You haven't landed a ring on that finger yet, so you still need to maintain a good impression.

EMMA: You sound like Mother.

ME: You say that like it's a bad thing.

EMMA: Well, it's not a good thing.

Emma and our mother don't have the best of relationships, especially not recently. You would think having one of her twin daughters in a committed relationship with a world-renowned artist would make the woman happy, but it hasn't seemed to. I think it's because Emma isn't willing to ask Carter to attend a lot of social events.

Even I have to admit Mother is a little obsessed with her social standing and reputation. I get it, though, as until a couple months ago it was my top priority as well. In the space of single evening, it suddenly became . . . unimportant.

ME: Mother knows a thing or two about fashion, you know. She and Aunt Jade have one of the most successful boutiques in the southeast.

EMMA: That might matter if Carter wanted to marry a socialite.

ME: Does he want to marry a gamer nerd?

EMMA: I certainly hope so.

ME: Just tell me you aren't going to see him today while wearing cartoon-printed pajama pants.

EMMA: I promise.

My sigh of relief is cut short by another incoming text.

EMMA: They're sweatpants.

EMMA: <<Picture of Emma's leg sticking out from her papasan chair, wearing gray sweatpants with a cartoon donkey on the leg>>

ME: NO.

EMMA: They were a gift. It'd be rude not to wear them.

ME: From who? Carter?

EMMA: No. Jason. But Carter was there when I opened the bag, and he approved.

Meeting the mysterious Jason is the only part of today's meeting that I'm still excited about this morning. I've never understood the relationship he seems to have with Emma. For years I thought either he didn't exist, they were secretly dating, or Emma was indulging in a very long unrequited crush. As it turns out, none of those are true because my fraternal twin sister is in a very serious dating relationship and still mentions this other man on a regular basis. Even her boyfriend has mentioned this guy in a positive light. The even stranger part of this concept is that her best friend is also her boss.

Which means there's a good chance she'll learn about today's meeting. I don't know if tech companies have client confidentiality, but I'm going to ask for it. I'm not ready for Emma to know what I'm doing. Maybe once I've committed with a contract. She knows my business is separate from Mother's, but she doesn't know I've been planning a redirection, and I don't want anyone talking me out of it—or into a commitment before I'm ready.

It needs to be my choice alone.

> ME: Whatever. Just keep them in your apartment.

> EMMA: Can do. Carter's bringing dinner over here tonight.

> ME: <<GIF of David from Schitt's Creek saying *I give up*>>

I set my phone on the counter and finish gathering my things. My tablet and earbuds are removed from the charging station, my prepacked lunchbox cooler complete with my indulgent can of Diet Dr. Pepper comes out of the fridge, and I pull my fitted black peacoat from the closet by the door.

With the strap of my large leather bag thrown over my shoulder and my car keys in hand, I pause at the door of my apartment to say a prayer. I'm still new to the idea of praying in a genuine sense. Growing up in the southeast, it was always easy to toss off a casual plea for God to let a pair of jeans be on sale or hold off the rain for another hour. Genuinely asking Him to guide me through my decisions for the day is an unfamiliar and odd feeling.

Still, I want to do this right and it's getting a little easier to remember He actually wants to hear from me every time I do it. And I really do think He wants this conversation to go well today. That, or I am the absolute worst at hearing spiritual guidance and direction. As a pretty new believer, there's an awful lot for me to learn, but I'd hate to think I was so bad at listening that I made up the idea of completely pivoting my livelihood.

"There's only one way to find out," I mutter as I reach for the door-knob.

I start some music on my phone and set it to play through the car speakers, then turn up the volume as I drive out of the apartment complex. Loud rock music has always been my go-to method for lifting my spirits when I'm feeling unsure of myself. Emma gave me the names of several Christian rock bands, and I've been testing them out.

Today, though, I click on a list of old stand-bys. Every now and then I become uncomfortable with some of the lyrics I'm singing and I press the button to advance to the next song, but it doesn't make sense that I would need to abandon everything I used to enjoy in the face of my new beliefs and mindset.

I can keep my confidence-building playlist as long as I use discretion. Maybe that same idea can extend past music?

Once again, my thoughts turn to what my outfit will be for next Sunday. I doubt my church attire is meant to consume this much of my mind, but my first thought about any event in my life is what I'm going to wear.

My nails tap against the steering wheel as I wait at a traffic light. I applied the red lacquer Sunday night, but maybe I don't have to remove it this week? I mean, if I can roll down the road screaming out the lyrics to "Born to be Wild" by Steppenwolf, then maybe I can wear nail polish to church.

A sigh shudders out as I consider the idea. Maybe I'll change it out for pink polish instead. Or a sedate French tip. A compromise of sorts.

I hate feeling like this. A lack of confidence wasn't a problem until I started this whole faith journey thing. Now I'm second-guessing everything except for the fact that I look like a consummate professional this morning.

If only I were as confident about the topic of this morning's discussion.

I slide into the parking spot and check the time. Fifteen minutes early. I can finish the song.

The last of the lyrics pour from my speakers and I sedately mouth along, even though in my head I'm punching my arms in the air and swinging my hair back and forth. Car windows are clear and there is every possibility that someone can see me parked in the visitor parking of this office building. I do not need to leave the impression that I am anything other than reliable and competent.

Once the song ends, I turn off the car and head inside. The wide strap of my heavy leather bag is comfortable on my shoulder, an assurance that I am prepared for whatever situation awaits me. Emma says I'm going to hurt my neck if I keep carrying a bag of this size, but I figure that's what chiropractors are for.

I stride into the building as the picture of confidence. Only I am aware of the rapid beat of my heart and the millions of butterflies swirling in my stomach.

God, I don't know if it's a sign of weakness to ask for signs, but I would really like one about now that proves I'm heading in the right direction.

I give my name to the receptionist, who gives me a visitor badge and sends me to the bank of elevators with the instructions that Jason will meet me on the appropriate floor.

The sound of my deep breathing fills the elevator car as I slowly ride up three floors. The doors slide open, and I step into the vestibule. A big sign with the name and logo for Digital World Solutions points me to the left and I turn.

Then freeze.

This is definitely a sign from God, but I don't know if it means I'm going in the right direction or if it's a warning that I should jump back in the elevator and flee.

Because the man standing in the doorway, looking at me with a very confused frown on his face and a backward ball cap on his head that shouldn't look attractive but is somehow incredibly hot, is the guy who rescued me at church.

JASON

As a boy, I had my share of scrapes and bruises, and as an adult I know what it's like to have my neck hurt because I slept on it funny. However, I have never experienced a stroke or an aneurysm or any other type of brain-injuring anomaly. Not even a concussion.

My pristine cranial health must be coming to an end, though, because as I look at the woman getting off the elevator I feel like my brain is splitting.

This is the woman I expected, of course. I was the one who received the meeting request that came through our website and followed up to set the schedule. I knew I'd be meeting with Emma's sister—there can't be too many people in the area named Amy Trinket that work with clothing, after all—so seeing the blonde woman with styled hair, impeccable clothes and bold makeup is not a surprise. Emma's shown me a hand full of pictures.

When I was not expecting was for her to look like the woman I met at church on Sunday.

The makeup is different, but the eyes are the same gray-blue. The hairstyle is different but it's the same pale golden shade. The clothes are certainly different but the bold, rolling gait that strolls off the elevator is the same one that made a beeline to the exit after service.

They can't possibly be the same person, though. Amy would have attended church with Emma, wouldn't she?

I've thought about the woman from Sunday off and on for the past forty-eight hours, so I refuse to be the first to mention the church encounter. My brain might be playing absurd tricks on me. Instead, I clear my throat and shift my expression into a professional smile as I step aside and hold the door to my business open. "Good morning, Ms. Trinket."

Her answering smile is bright and perfect, with white teeth somehow enhanced by the red lipstick instead of standing out starkly against the bold color. I've heard my mother and her friends talk often enough to know that finding such a shade is a considerable undertaking.

"Please call me Amy. I'd have a difficult time calling you anything other than Jason after hearing Emma talk about you so much." She gives a self-deprecating laugh. "I was going to say it's nice to meet you, but I believe we had our first encounter Sunday."

There is so much information in those few short sentences and the implications aren't minor.

1. Emma's vow of silence appears to have only gone one way. Until recently, she avoided telling me about her family to the point that I thought they were estranged, but she has apparently told them plenty about me.

2. This is the woman I met on Sunday. She'd been cute and intriguing then, but she is knock-me-over gorgeous this morning. I don't think it's all about the makeup, but I confess to liking the hair. Maybe it's the attitude?

3. Amy is keeping her attempts at going to church from her sister. Emma was lamenting at lunch yesterday how Amy doesn't seem to be doing all the things she should be after accepting Christ, but in reality, Amy's been pretty much crawling her way to a Sunday service.

4. Emma is almost never in the office on Tuesdays, and I didn't tell her about this meeting. Whatever we're about to talk about, Emma doesn't know, and I have a sneaking suspicion Amy is going to want to keep it that way.

The attempts at sisterly bonding have only gone so far, it would seem, and my life is probably about to become very complicated as the person stuck in the middle.

I try to laugh and keep it natural, aware that while more than half of the company chooses to work from home on Tuesdays, there's plenty of people who, like me, prefer coming into the office to work. I discovered about two years into this business that if I worked from home, I wouldn't stop for the day until I fell over from hunger or exhaustion.

This visit is eventually going to get back to Emma and I don't need anyone telling her stories that make my keeping the secret more uncomfortable than it needs to be.

Because I will be keeping the secret. I don't know why Amy felt the need to come to church on her own, but she wasn't faking the nerves or the difficulties. Whatever her reasons are, I'm not going to scare her off by breaking her confidence, even if she didn't know who I was when she trusted me Sunday.

I need to feel out how deep the secret goes, though. "If I'd known who you were Sunday I could have texted Emma. She'd have been happy to come sit with you."

Amy winces. "I'm glad you didn't. I'm not . . . ready for that." She takes a deep breath and shifts her enormous leather satchel—a bag that somehow suits her better than the little purse she had Sunday—onto her other shoulder. "I'd prefer you don't tell her about this meeting either."

There was a time when Emma and I told each other practically everything. Or I thought we did. Learning she wasn't sharing huge portions of her life with me had been something of a shock and that revelation came about the time Carter was taking the position of ultimate knowledge. As he should. Still, I'd be lying if I said a petty little thrill didn't roll through me at the idea that I know something Emma doesn't.

That thrill is immediately knocked down by concern, though. "Is everything all right? Are you sick or something? Need help?" I lead her into my office and hasten her toward one of the visitor chairs. "Nothing's wrong with Emma, right?"

Amy's eyes widen for a moment, before she all but collapses into the chair in genuine laughter. She shakes her head. "No, nothing like that." Her satchel slides to the floor and she tilts her head up to blink rapidly at the ceiling while waving her hand in front of her face.

I know that move. She doesn't want watering eyes to mar her makeup.

With a little less concern, I round my desk to sit in my own chair. "Does that mean you actually are a new client? I wasn't exactly clear about the objectives from your message."

"I would like to inquire about your services, but . . ." The words trail off as her eyes dart around the office. They land directly on me and I'm glad I put the desk between us instead of sitting in the other visitor chair like I normally do with new clients. I need the ability to prop myself up by putting my elbows on the desk surface. It's been a long time since I was the direct focus of such a pretty woman.

The truth is we don't really have space for a new project. Our wait-list is almost two years long and I've been looking at the budget and considering bringing on more people.

But this is Emma's sister. I'll accept her project even if it means breaking my work-from-home rule and doing the coding myself.

Amy takes a steadying breath. "Emma can't know."

I take off my ball cap and run a hand through my hair. "I'm not sure I can guarantee that. I'm not in the habit of keeping secrets from my employees." Except for that time two years ago when we scraped incredibly close to going under. It was the first time since starting the company in college that I'd had to inject some of my own money back into the business. I never told anyone about that. Except Emma. "And I really don't keep them from Emma."

Her eyebrows shoot up. "You tell Emma everything? I mean, you're truly that good of friends?" She shakes her head and looks down, appearing almost hurt. "And yet, we've never met."

I understand her pain. "I can guess how you're feeling. Likely the same way I did earlier this year when I learned she isn't actually estranged from you or your mother."

"She said we were estranged? Why that little . . ." Her arm stabs into her satchel and somehow comes out holding her phone. How did she find such a tiny target that quickly?

I hold my hands up, palms out, trying not to laugh. Laughter seems inappropriate right now. "No, no, she never said as much. I just assumed since she only told me stories about you from your childhood." I lean forward, arm outstretched as if I can cover the phone from this distance, but I chose a desk with an enormous surface on it. "I thought you didn't want her to know you were here?"

"I don't." She sighs and folds her arms into her lap with the phone face down. "I didn't think you really existed until Carter spoke of meeting you."

Years of practice, both as my parents' son and as a business owner, allow me to hold in the desire to laugh. I can only imagine what her family thought of me.

I'm also a little bit nervous about what Emma said. From what she's told me about her mother, sister, and aunt, there are definitely aspects of my life that I'd rather them not know about.

At least, not yet.

Probably not ever.

Amy tilts her head and considers me. "I'm still not sure I believe it."

"Believe what?"

"That you aren't jealous of Carter."

Anything I say here has the potential to get back to Emma, but part of me wants to be open, honest, and vulnerable with this woman. I don't know why, and I don't have time to analyze it right now. I'll have to go with my gut and hope I don't regret it.

"I am a little jealous."

"Ha! I knew it." She crosses her arms and looks a little smug. "You wanted to date her yourself."

I take a moment to imagine dating Emma. I allow myself to consider the idea of holding Emma's hand, of running my hand through her straight brown hair, of leaning in to give her a kiss.

A shudder racks my body as I nearly gag. "Ah, no. I do not want to date Emma. We went on three disastrous dates in college and decided we were better off as friends."

"Then what are you jealous of?"

I shrug. "I used to be the first person she called about things. The social partner. It's no different than any friend when their bestie gets a boyfriend."

She blinks at me. "You just used the term *bestie*."

"What can I say? I'm hip and cool."

She blinks at me a few more times. I grin as I run a hand through my hair, then plop my hat back on and turn it backwards.

Her eyes widen a little and I try not to let my grin turn smug. I've had more than one lady tell me there's something enticing about that move. I can't say that I get it and I'm not sure why I wanted to use it on Amy, but I'm just rolling on instinct at this point.

Because I need something to do with my hands, I grab a notebook and a pen. I rarely take notes when I first meet with a client because it usually takes at least three conversations to narrow down what they are actually looking for. Amy's meeting request had been especially vague and all over the place.

"What can I do for you?"

Her back stiffens and her shoulders set. "I want to build an app."

I nod, writing some nonsense on the paper and angling it so Amy can't see.

"It'd be a stylist app for everyday people, like Emma, who need help putting forth a good impression."

Before I can stop myself, I'm looking up with a frown, ready to defend my friend.

Amy points a finger at me, the deep red of her manicured nail distracting a little of my attention. "You know it's true. At least, I assume you do." She frowns as she considers me. "Men can get away with a lack of fashion sense more easily than women can, particularly if they're athletically built."

I feel a sudden urge to change out my T-shirt that says NERD in big block letters and put on the dress shirt and tie I keep at the office just in case. I'd still be in jeans, but this *is* a tech company.

Her frown clears as she gives a shrug. "If you don't recognize that she is completely doing herself a disservice when she selects her own clothing then perhaps you need the app, too."

The grin is as impossible to stop as the frown was. "No, I can't defend Emma's personal fashion taste."

Amy nods. "That's why she needs an app."

"So, this is a gift for Emma?"

"No, I . . ." She sighs. "There are a lot of people who could do with a better first impression. I'm a stylist but my services are rather too expensive for most people."

"And you want to expand your reach?"

"In a way. I also want to help people. Like Emma. I want the app to take fabric sensitivities and personal comfort issues into account."

I set aside the notebook to give Amy my full attention because my brain is already ticking through the complications and possibilities of what she appears to be asking.

And she's not wrong about Emma. If I hadn't gotten to know her brilliant mind in college, I'm not sure I'd have hired her. She's been looking far more put together lately but I'd assumed it was Carter rubbing off on her. Was it a conscious effort by her sister instead?

If so, the twins' relationship has changed an awful lot in the last few months. Even more than Emma has let on.

What else is my best friend not telling me?

Amy continues trying to spill out her vision, her hands moving in front of her face as if the app were an immersive holographic. "I want to make a virtual closet, tailored to a person's needs and categorized by different areas in their life."

She waves a hand in my direction. "If it includes the reality things you do, the person could sort of see themselves in the clothing before putting it on."

My company specializes in augmented reality programs, using phones, cameras, and other technology to add a little something extra to the real world. The idea of the project Amy is suggesting is very intriguing. We've fallen into the rut of creating a lot of corporate advertising and training modules. They're interesting and keeping the company more than profitable now, but they don't challenge my mind like some of our projects used to.

"You know Emma would make this for free in her spare time, don't you?" I grin, remembering my best programmer's last attempt at app design. "You'd want someone else to do the front end, though."

Amy nodded. "I know she would help me, but . . ."

"You want to be professional." I hadn't intended to interrupt, but I know the look on her face. I know the feeling. "You want this to be a real step forward for your company, taken in a way that no one can doubt when it succeeds."

"I . . . yes. I don't know that I could have put it into words, but that's exactly it." She frowns. "How did you know?"

"Because it's not my father's name on the capital venture proposal that started this company."

Nor was it my father's money that had made the initial investment. I'd used a few thousand of the trust fund left me by my grandfather to buy the equipment when I first started, but I'd treated the rest of the growth like a starving college student.

Those first few years, it had been me, Emma, and Kyle, who now leads my design team, working from my apartment. Fortunately, Emma had still been in school then, so she was working out of her dorm room, but I'd let Kyle live in one of my spare rooms rent free as part of his compensation.

Amy nods. "I've known for a while that I need to grow enough to stand alone, maybe move out of the back of my aunt and mother's boutique. Neither of them is going to be happy when they realize I've only been paying them rent."

"How do they not know?"

"Because I'm the one who talks to the accountant and draws up the contracts." Amy winces. "Mother is very aware of the bank account balances, though. Both she and my aunt receive a base salary and a percentage of the profits. Mother is starting to notice that her profit portion isn't going up as much as it should be considering my increase in clients."

I grin. "I'm beginning to see how you and Emma are related. She can be pretty devious as well."

We spend the next twenty minutes digging into what Amy is picturing and how customizable she wants the app to be. The first significant issue I see is that Amy doesn't have one clear, distinct objective in mind. Sometimes she wants it to be a closet, other times a shopping guide, and some of her thoughts sound more like some sort of counseling app.

From a technical perspective, it's difficult to know how a piece of clothing is going to hang on a person without actually seeing it on them. That's an issue for later, though.

For now, I need Amy to home in on a single direction. This app can't be all things to all people. Not at first, anyway.

I sit back in my chair and pull off my ball cap to run a hand through my hair. Tossing the cap on the desk, I give Amy a considering look. "Walk me through it."

"What?"

"This app. Pretend you are a user getting ready for work. What do you want it to do?"

"Well." She picks up her phone and stands, as if she intends to walk through her morning routine. "I'd tell the app what I'm doing that day."

"Which is?"

"Working in an office."

I scribble *User define locations in setup* on the corner of my sketchpad because no two offices are the same. She clearly dresses more formally for her office than I do for mine.

"Then I'd ask for an outfit suggestion."

I ply her with questions for another five minutes until the frown of confusion reappears between her eyebrows. Then I drop my pen on top of my notes. "I think that's enough for today."

She sits back in the seat and pulls her enormous bag into her lap. "How much is this going to cost?"

I know the concern in her eyes. She's not the first start-up entrepreneur I've had in my office.

It's been a long time since that concern made me want to give up something for free, though.

"It's hard to say until we work up an agreed upon final design, but I can send you an estimate and a basic contract by the end of the week."

She nods. "That will work." Her eyes dart to the glass wall of my office, through which the relatively quiet working space can be seen. One employee is walking around, but for the most part it just looks like any other office workspace.

When her gaze slides back to me, that determination is evident once more. I can't help but notice how it brings life to her eyes and color to her cheeks. This is an absolutely gorgeous woman who's got enough intelligence to start a business and enough foresight to prepare for the future.

I love Emma, but I can see why she developed a bit of a complex about her sister.

Amy straightens her shoulders. "I don't want any special favors."

I can't help but grin as I remind myself how unfair it is to compare the two siblings. I wouldn't want anyone picking apart the ways my brother Robert is better than me. At least, I wouldn't want to hear about it. I know plenty of people think it on the rare occasion they remember I exist.

"Your being here is a special favor. We have a wait-list. I'm hoping to expand later this year, bring on some new people and move those projects up, but . . ."

"Oh. Well. I guess a little special treatment is okay then. But no more."

Her voice is small and, for the first time this morning, I see the unsure woman I met at church on Sunday.

"Hey, it's nothing to be ashamed of. There's a reason friends and family discounts exist." I shrug. "Most success in life is about knowing the right people."

"That doesn't seem a very Christian sentiment."

"Why not?"

She gives a little shrug and picks at the edge of her sleeve. "Aren't all people meant to be equal in God's eyes? The ground is level at the cross and all that?"

"Did Emma tell you that?" I smile because that was something I told her when she was asking questions about God in college. Nice to know it mattered enough that she passed it on to her sister.

"Yes."

"Well, yes, the idea that we are all equal in God's eyes is true. There's no friends and family discount when it comes to sin, no skating in on the faith of your grandmother." I run a hand behind my neck. "But in life? It's a different story."

"Why?"

"Because we're human. Our time, energy, and resources are finite. We have to have some way of limiting their usage to a healthy level." I shrug, thinking about everything I learned about business from my dad and the way I've done my best to separate my public image from my family over the years. "Whether we like it or not, we associate people with the people they connect themselves to. You are connected to Emma. Ergo, special privilege."

She shakes her head. "I think this is the first time I've ridden in Emma's shadow." Her nose wrinkles. "I understand a little more why she complains about riding in mine."

I walk Amy out of the office and allow myself to switch from viewing her as a potential client to thinking of her as a person. It's dangerous, given my initial reaction to her and the way our lives are somewhat entangled. But, pretty or not, she's a person with a soul and is new to being a believer.

"Are you coming to church again Sunday?" I ask. "Need me to save you a seat?"

The elevator doors open. "If I do, I know which corner to hide in. You don't have to do anything." She hunches her shoulders, the confident businesswoman replaced by someone still finding her way. "You're Emma's friend. Not mine."

She looks sad as the elevator doors slide closed, and she doesn't get to hear me say, "I think I'd like to be both."

AMY

I get to the boutique early on Wednesday, hoping to appear too busy for my mother to talk to me. There isn't any way for her or my aunt to know about my meeting with Digital World Solutions yesterday, but I feel like it's written all over my face.

My plan succeeds in the morning as I meet with two new clients, work on putting together some outfit options for an existing client presenting an award at an upcoming banquet, and do some bookkeeping.

In the early afternoon, though, the boutique gets a rush of customers and my aunt requests my help out on the floor. I can't very well tell her that I can't because I technically do work part-time for the boutique. Mother would be concerned if I wasn't drawing some sort of salary.

Customers are almost as good a buffer as my office door, though, and I make it all the way to closing time without exchanging more than simple pleasantries with Mother.

I flip the elegant, scrolled metal sign to Closed and throw the deadbolt on the boutique door. If I slip out while she's still closing out the cash register, I can avoid her for the entire day. Tomorrow it won't feel so fresh, and I won't feel guilty.

I hate that I feel guilty. Logically, I know I have nothing to feel guilty about, but I have been keeping a big secret. Even if I haven't explicitly lied to her, it's going to feel like it when she learns what I've been doing.

"Oh good, you're still here." Mother appears in the door of my office while I'm collecting my computer bag and purse.

So close. But close only counts in slow dancing.

"Yes, but I was just on my way out."

She gives me a sly grin. "Do you have a date tonight?"

Only with my TV and walking pad. I'm not certain if Mother has realized that I'm going out less these days or that my friends aren't calling as much. She still acts as if my social life is the same it's been since high school.

"Ah, no. Just tired." I give her a smile and hope the claim of exhaustion explains any tightness in my expression.

"Well, before you go, take a look at this." She pulls out a magazine and flips to a page marked with a purple sticky note.

I come closer and realize it's not a magazine. It's a furniture catalog. She's marked a page showcasing a table-style desk with scrollwork legs and a surface shiny enough to create a reflection in the stained walnut.

"What do you think?" Mother hugs the catalog and looks over her shoulder to the boutique. "I think it blends well with the decor."

"It does, but . . ." I hitch my bag higher onto my shoulder. "What's it for? You already have an antique counter for the register."

"It's for you."

"Me?" I gesture around me. "There's not room for that in my office."

"It's not for back here. If we move you into the boutique, we could charge for on the spot consultations. You wouldn't look like a normal salesgirl."

"Ah . . ." I trail off, unsure what to say to indicate that when I'm out there on the floor I am a regular salesgirl.

Mother frowns. "You've been spending more and more time back here, but it doesn't seem to be paying off. We need to get you more clients."

And I need to look into new office space.

I take the catalog from her and flip through a few pages. "That's an interesting idea. Can I take this with me and look at it?"

"Absolutely." Mother waves her hand toward the catalog. "There are some other options in there, but that's the one I liked the best."

My groan sounds more like a hum of curiosity, and I move toward my car. I thought I'd have another few months, but it looks like I'll be lucky to make it to the end of the year without a confrontation.

Back in my apartment, I pull up my business financials and consider what needs to happen for me to move out of the back of the boutique. My other option, of course, is to tell Mother and hope she'll be happy to keep renting to me. It's not an insignificant portion of money and if I move, I take it with me.

The options play in my head as I fix and eat a salad for dinner and as I pull my walking pad from beneath the couch and pull up some old *Friends* episodes on the TV.

As Ross tries in vain to get a couch up the stairs, I pull out my phone.

> ME: I'm thinking about telling Mother about the business.

> EMMA: At family dinner? Can I set up a camera?

> ME: You think she'll be that mad?

> EMMA: I think she'll be that dramatic.

I sigh. Emma's not wrong. Even if Mother is somewhat okay with the configuration continuing, she's going to be dramatic about it.

I type out a message asking Emma if she finds me to be that dramatic at times, but I quickly erase it. If I start asking Emma how she sees me, I'll focus on making myself into someone she approves of instead of someone I approve of.

We only recently managed to get her to stop doing that for me. At least, I think we did. The last thing we need is to switch roles.

Besides, while life was easier when I let someone else tell me what to do, I've since learned all they told me was wrong. I don't know how I can trust anyone else. I flop onto my couch and pull out my laptop. I've browsed realty websites several times over the past few months looking for an appropriate rental space. There simply aren't any in the type of area I'd need to be in to maintain the reputation the boutique has brought me. As much as I hate to admit it, renting from my aunt and mother is a pretty nice deal. I don't have to decorate a window or foyer space, don't need to display stock, don't have to arrange for pre-purchases or pay restock fees.

My head flops back onto the curved, upholstered back of the couch. I have no choice but to tell my mother and hope she'll be willing to continue the operation.

If I stay there, though, then she'll want a say in how the business is run. It will reflect on her boutique, after all, as Stylized Trinkets is already connected and will remain so as long as people walk through the boutique to get my office.

But Mother is all about becoming more exclusive, not less so.

Maybe I should cancel the app request. No contracts have been signed yet, no investments have been made. The only people who even know about the idea are me and Jason, and while I know he isn't bound by any confidentiality clause, I don't think he'll tell Emma.

The sensation of failure rides me hard as I open my email. As much as I love high fashion, as much as I love being able to help people put their best foot forward with no concern for budget, as much as I still want to create a business known for beautiful things, limiting those the skills and opportunities to the people who can afford my exclusive attention feels wrong.

Emma would never have come to me, even if she could afford me. But there have to be people like Emma who want to look their best but need help to get there. They would consider paying for an app.

But Mother even resisted the idea of putting custom gown inquiries on the website. I still think the only reason she gave in when I also wanted to add an appointment scheduler was because she thought if there were more computer-oriented tasks at the boutique, Emma would join the family business.

But Emma has always gone her own way. I wasn't jealous of that until recently—in fact I thought her foolish for it—but now I wish I knew what it was like to know myself and what I want enough to have forged my own path. In some ways it feels too late to make that shift this close to thirty.

One of the emails in my inbox catches my eye. It's from Jason Miller. It's only been a day. How could he already have an estimate and a plan of action together? I mean, he probably has a boiler plate contract and a formula for determining a timeline, but a one-day turnaround feels fast.

At least he can't have invested too much time and effort into it so I shouldn't feel bad about canceling everything.

Without reading the recap and thoughts he put into the email, I scroll to the bottom to see what sort of contact information he included. There's an office number and a cell number.

I snatch up my phone, because this is a way for me to repay the man for the time he put into this email. Even if I'm not giving him any business anymore.

ME: Do you have two mobile phones? A work one and a personal one?

JASON: I'm sorry. Who is this?

ME: Amy Trinket. And I'm guessing the answer is no since you are answering a text at 8:00 at night.

JASON: No, I don't carry two phones around. I have an office phone and email. That's enough.

ME: Yet you include your cell number on client proposals.

ME: You shouldn't do that. It lets clients contact you at 8:00 at night.

ME: You need a separation of work and life.

JASON: First, I included my cell number on YOUR client proposal.

JASON: Second, you're looking at your work email at 8:00 at night. Which of us is actually having difficulty with work/life balance?

He has a point, but I'm too thrown by the fact that he gave me his number when he usually doesn't include it to feel much shame about my working hours.

ME: Why would you give me your number?

JASON: So you could text me.

I surge up from my seat on the couch, ignoring my laptop as it tips over to sit on the cushion, poised drunkenly on its side. Stress is easier to handle when I'm moving, and this is definitely a stressful moment.

What is he expecting from me? I mean, he was cute. Really cute. But I'm not looking to date anyone right now. Boyfriends are too demanding, wanting me to be available at certain times and act certain ways.

They are not meant to be accessories of girls entering their independence era.

Or maybe this is because of Emma? More friends and family privilege? That would make sense.

I pace my apartment, striding around my couch and into the kitchen before circling through the dining area and back to the couch. I walk loop after loop, faster and faster, and still I don't know how to interpret his text.

The window for acceptable response time is closing, though, so I need to answer. If I wait much longer, I will be showing him that I'm flustered. If time ticks on long enough, he'll think I'm in the middle of doing something else and want to connect with him badly enough that I'm willing to keep interrupting myself. I have to text now or I'll have to come up with a believable reason to text him again later.

I fingers are trembling as I struggle for something to say.

> ME: Well, now I have done so.

It's a stupid answer and I don't even know what I mean with it, but it resets the response clock.

> JASON: So you have.

His response isn't delayed in the slightest. What is he doing? Just sitting there, staring at the phone? Is he actively texting me and not just stopping what he's doing when the notification comes in?

I grab my shirt and puff the front a few times, working to get some air flowing over my suddenly overheating body. Am I starting to sweat?

It's time to do what I need to do, cut the ties, and move on. Maybe I can find this new me that's forming without creating a new life around it.

> ME: I need to talk to you about the app.

> JASON: Okay. What's up?

I type out the words *I need to cancel* but I can't bring myself to hit send. My feet stumble to a stop and I stare at my phone. Why can't I hit send?

The phone rings in my hand, and I scream, flinging the device from one hand to the other as I try to get a grip on it and keep it from falling to the floor.

Jason is calling me. First he was actively texting. Now he's calling. The man is definitely interested, and I just can't do that right now.

Time to cut everything off.

I slide my thumb across the answer icon and hold my phone to my ear. "Hello?"

"I'm not sure where you live, but you're thinking loud enough that I can hear it in my condo."

A condo? Fancy.

"Do you own or rent?" I nearly slap myself for the question. That is something asked only when trying to determine whether or not a guy is solvent enough to be worth the time and energy of getting to know.

"I own." His low chuckle rolls through my ear making me rethink all my resolve.

I should hang up and go back to texting, but now that I've answered, I'm stuck. I should have sent him to voicemail. "That's nice. Listen, about this app, I don't think I'm going to go in that direction anymore."

"Why not? I was looking through our base programs and I think we have one that might work for your customization. Cuts a lot off the time and price."

I groan. That makes things even more difficult. "As good as that sounds, I'm now wondering if an app is the right way forward for my business. There are things I didn't think of."

He's quiet for a moment or two and I bite my tongue to keep from filling the silence with chatter. I've watched enough cop procedural shows to know the psychological tactic of silence when attempting to get information.

That doesn't prevent the urge to fill it in.

And apparently, I'm weak, because it isn't even five seconds before I'm speaking again. "I mean, expanding is a big deal. As I am the only employee of my company, I have to think about spreading myself too thin."

"The initial setup might take a great deal of your time, but a well-coded app would essentially duplicate yourself."

I grin as I avoid my discarded laptop and curl up in the chair. My head rests easily against the padded back, but the hard metal of the contemporary chrome arms presses against my shins, keeping me from getting too comfortable—a good reminder that I shouldn't be feeling that spark of giddiness that comes right before a potential new relationship.

"Are you saying you could code a replacement me?"

His laughter is warm and deep. "I highly doubt it. For one thing, fashion changes so fast you'll need to be making regular updates to the app's algorithm."

I groan. "Even more reason to wait, I suppose." I snag a blanket and wedge it between my legs and the arm of the chair. "But in all honesty, I've found that there are basic classics that never seem to go out of style. If you build a wardrobe around that, you can supplement a few cutting-edge pieces and accessories and always look fashionable."

"Is that what you do?"

"Most of the time. Unless it's a client that is really set on being part of the trends. Those are exhausting though, because if you really want to be a known figure of the fashion world you have to wear what's going to be trendy tomorrow, not what's already trendy today."

"Are you saying that you're creating trendsetters?"

"No. Trendsetters are always a little out there, looking for new things and bucking the existing system. Contrary to what you might think, they're never actually trendy. Fashionable, yes, but not trendy. The people who copy the trendsetters are trendy."

"I don't think I've ever heard the word trendy used this many times in a conversation. It's beginning to sound wrong."

My laugh feels freeing as I curl deeper into the chair. Comfortable. I haven't felt like this in a long time, as if I belonged in my own skin, in my own mind.

That observation poisons the blissful feeling. I've used males to prop up my sense of purpose since I was a teenager. Whenever I was feeling bad about myself, I'd go out and soak up all the male attention. Then I'd know that I was doing something right.

Even before salvation I knew that was messed up. Now it should definitely not be what I'm doing.

I push out of the chair and start to pace again. "The point is, I don't need an app anymore."

He's silent for a few minutes. "What do you need, then?"

My feet stumble to a halt.

Because I really don't know how to answer that question.

JASON

I don't recognize myself right now. I have no idea what I'm doing.

For one thing, I cannot remember the last time I made a phone call that wasn't professional. Pretty sure if I scrolled through my history, the only outgoing calls I'd have made this month would be to my executive assistant, my doctor, or my mother. And while, yes, my mother is technically a personal call, I don't think it equates to the same thing as hitting that little green icon next to Amy Trinket's name.

Pretty sure Emma would be throwing things at me right now because this phone call almost feels like flirting.

I kinda want it to be flirting.

A psychologist would have a field day with this, because it is not lost on me that I am attracted to my best friend's twin but not to my best friend. Even if they look nothing alike, there's gotta be something twisted in that. I don't want to look too hard to find it.

It's been a while since I felt this bubble of nervous anticipation and even though the relationship isn't going to go anywhere, I want to enjoy feeling alive and connected.

She's taking a long time to answer the question I asked, but she hasn't hung up, so . . .

I clear my throat and toss aside any pretense that this is still about her business and her app. "Do you even know what you need? I mean, I was a teenager when I made the decision to follow Christ and I'd grown up in church, so it didn't exactly throw my worldview on its head."

Her breath blows out in a rush, rattling over the speaker and creating static in my ear. "It's certainly thrown mine."

Conviction lands on me hard, and despite the buzz I'd like to keep feeling, Amy is more important. She needs a friend, not a flirt. She might hate me when I say this, but I'm going in anyway. "I saw you writing questions on Sunday."

"You did?" She snorts out a laugh. "Let me guess. You're now going to tell me all the answers and all the things I need to do next."

"I—"

"I don't even get my hair wet at a pool party, and I'm supposed to get dunked in a pool—in a boxy unisex T-shirt, mind you—in front of thousands of people? And just smile about looking like a drowned rat?"

I'm glad she can't see my grin as I move toward my kitchen to pull a carbonated water from the fridge. "I don't think anyone is thinking about your hair when they cheer for your baptism."

"Still. I wouldn't have thought Jesus was big on humiliation."

"Ah, no. That's not really His thing."

"But you're also going to tell me that I should meet with the pastor I've never talked to before and tell him all about my history and how I'm a changed person now."

"I mean, some denominations do the confession thing, and I can see the merits of it, but Community doesn't—"

"And then you're going to tell me to let everyone in the church know I don't know what I'm doing by attending this special class that's going to tell me all the things I need to do now to be a good little Christian."

"That wasn't on my . . . Why do you think that's what I was going to say?"

She sighs. "It's what Emma kept trying to tell me until I refused to talk about it anymore."

I set my drink aside and rub a hand over my forehead. Emma doesn't always think about how things will sound to other people. And I can't tell her how her sister feels about Emma's push for her to immediately take the next traditional steps because that would reveal I've been talking to Amy.

"I see why you didn't tell Emma you were coming to church."

"You do?"

"Yeah." I move into the bedroom I turned into my home office. I use it more as a game room now because, contrary to Amy's accusation, I am trying to balance how much of my life work takes up. But I also use this room for my personal Bible study. The sheet of paper I'd jotted her questions down on sits in the middle of my desk.

Beside it is the list of verses and resources I thought might be helpful to her. "I was thinking I might help you find the answers you were looking for. I don't know if you're a podcast person or if you prefer non-fiction books and articles, but I put together a few resources and Bible passages you might find useful."

The silence on the phone is heavy. I've been hearing random sounds this whole time, like she's been moving restlessly around her apartment. There's nothing now, to the point that I check the screen to make sure the call is still connected.

"You're not just going to tell me what I should do or think?"

"I mean, I'm happy to answer your questions from my understanding, but I'm not going to tell you that you have to agree with me on every- thing. I hate it when people do that to me." I'd been fortunate that it didn't really happen at home. There were rules, of course, but if I didn't like them or understand them, I was free to debate them with my parents as long as I stayed respectful. Sometimes they even changed their minds.

"Oh. Well. That would be good. And I guess I'm an article person? I don't tend to read large chunks these days. Videos are good, too."

"I'll send you some links then."

"That would be nice."

The conversation has gotten awkward and stilted and I'm suddenly remembering that I hate to talk on the phone.

"So, um." I clear my throat and try to remember I'm a thirty-year-old man and not a sixteen-year-old boy. "Sunday. You coming to church again? Want me to look for you?"

"You said that wasn't your usual service."

"My schedule is changed for the next few weeks because I'm helping in another class." That is only partially true. I am helping to make sure the technology is working in a few small group rooms that are using a video series for their lessons for the next few weeks, but that doesn't take up enough time to require me to change my normal schedule. I could just be a few minutes late to my normal service.

Amy doesn't need to know that, though. Nor does anyone else. It's a pretty convenient excuse.

At least, for anyone other than Emma. She knows these tech support gigs usually only take a few minutes. I shrug. Unless she has a reason to be suspicious, Emma usually doesn't ask.

"Oh." Amy's voice is flat, and I can't tell if she wants to see my Sunday or not. "Well, then, if I see you, I won't run in the other direction."

"But you are planning on coming? I mean, if the possibility of seeing me means you sit in the parking lot again, I—"

"I'm coming." She sighs before mumbling, "I can't keep everything the same."

I don't know what to say to that. She apparently doesn't know what to say either because we're both caught on a phone call, connected by an awkward silence we clearly don't want to participate in.

"Yes. So." I want to knock my head on the desk because what in the world is that supposed to mean? "Sunday then."

"Yeah."

"And Amy?" I ask in a rush before she can disconnect the call.

"Yes?"

"I'm not going to cancel the project yet. Why don't you let me put together some ideas and then decide?" It will be unpaid work for me, but I want to do it.

And it's not just because she's Emma's sister.

It's because the sixteen-year-old boy in me wants to impress the pretty girl and even though it makes me feel like an idiot I'm going to do it anyway.

"Okay."

More silence follows her agreement until she finally blurts out, "Bye."

"Yeah. Bye." She's already disconnected, though, and doesn't hear my words.

I slide into my desk chair and, for the first time in a few months, power on my work computer in my condo. I always bring it home, just in case, but I've been trying to resist the urge to work into the night. It's been difficult, as I've spent fewer evenings hanging out with Emma. I've played an unhealthy number of hours of video games. I even reset the password on my Minecraft account and have been playing around in a collaborative creative world where they've been replicating famous landmarks.

I'm pretty proud of my work on the Eiffel Tower.

Tonight, I pull up the base program I told Amy would be a good starting point for her project, then I start playing with it. This initial program had been designed for a theme park ride. It took the rider and dressed them in the uniform of the squadron they were supposedly joining for the ride.

There are a lot of changes to make, but having a base that scans a person's entire body and dresses them in a different outfit means a lot of the nuts and bolts are already there.

For an hour, I play around with the parameters and appearance of the uniform. In some ways, this sort of code is easier because we are pulling the user into the digital world instead of projecting the digital world into the real one.

By the time my phone alarm goes off to remind me I need sleep before going to work tomorrow, I've managed to make a loose T-shirt cover my digitally-recreated body in a way that makes me look a lot like a rejected character from a children's show about shapes.

The problem with clothing is that it drapes and moves. Sometimes. Every type of fabric has its own behaviors, including the way it moves, adjusts, and even the friction when it rubs together. We aren't talking about making this person move through a game world, so things like friction probably aren't important, but my mother has dresses that look like nothing but bolts of cloth on the hanger. If this app is meant to help people find clothes, it's going to have to handle things like that.

I sigh and close the laptop. The truth is that it's been a few years since I did a lot of in-depth programming. I'm more of a consultant and debugger now. Emma could probably fix this issue in a matter of hours, but I promised I wouldn't mention this to her.

I run my finger along the edge of the laptop. Is there a way to make Emma fix it without knowing what she's working on?

With a shake of my head, I move to bed. I'm getting ridiculous and I clearly need sleep.

Hopefully some that isn't filled with dreams about a particularly con-fused blonde woman.

My brain plays with possible coding solutions off and on until the close of business Friday. I think I've straightened everything out enough to show Amy what's possible. After Monday's team planning meeting, once I know everyone's schedules for the week—including mine—I'll set up a demonstration for her.

It will give me an excuse to see her if I don't manage to on Sunday.

My employees start shuffling out at the end of the day and I close my computer down as well. I pause before sliding it into my laptop bag. I should leave it here because I really don't need to work all weekend, but the owner of the company leaving his laptop in his office feels irresponsible.

Before I can debate the decision longer, I throw the strap of the bag over my shoulder and head out into the large, open collaborative work area filled with cubicles.

Emma is packing up her own computer when I stop to lean in the opening.

"Did you see that the new Japanese restaurant opened last weekend?"

"You want to get hibachi? It's like you're joining the rest of the world and celebrating because it's Friday." She smirks and shakes her head before pulling her phone out of her pocket.

I feel a thrill of success at the gesture. Emma never goes to a new restaurant without checking the menu. "Are you saying you don't celebrate it being Friday?"

"Nah." She scrunches up her nose. "I happen to like my job and my boss, so sometimes I celebrate when it's Monday."

"Sadly, I cannot hire the entire world so the stereotype of weekend celebrations shall remain. So, you in?" I nod toward her phone. "Did you see that they have three sauces instead of just two?"

"Oh." She briefly flips her phone so I can see that it's on the messaging screen instead of a web browser. "I was telling Carter I'm heading out." Her head tips to the side. "I think he's already thawed out some pork chops for dinner. Why don't we all go get hibachi next week?"

My moment of thrill fades a little, but I cover it with an exaggerated groan. Of course she has plans with her boyfriend on a Friday night and of course she wants him to come with us when we try out the restaurant.

They've been together almost six months. I should know this by now. "Ugh." I pull out my phone and open the calendar app. "Tuesday?"

"Sure."

I put it in the calendar and select her as an invitee. "When did we become old? We're making plans and sending calendar invites. Where's the spontaneity?"

"I'm plenty spontaneous."

"Oh, really?"

"Yes. Last weekend I was going to buy Astro Bot at the video game store but instead I came home with Balatro." She grins as she leaves the cubicle.

I fall into step beside her as we head to the elevator. "Look at you, wild child."

We talk about video games as we move to our cars, but part of me is wondering how long we have until I'm always having to schedule time with Emma. I'd be surprised if Carter hasn't at least been looking at rings already. Attending the wedding of our mutual friends, Michael and Victoria, probably put the idea in his head if it wasn't there already.

When he does, that will likely even be the end of our biweekly game nights. Emma and I put a group together years ago to get together regularly and play board games. We've been meeting for years, but lately it seems at least one person has to cancel each month. Two cancel if it's a couple because couples tend to have the same calendar conflicts. Michael and Victoria cancel even more since they got married, which is a change

I don't understand. They go home together now, wake up in the same house, and have a standing daily breakfast and dinner date. Shouldn't they be more available instead of less?

Everything is changing and I don't like it.

The grumpy attitude in my head annoys even me. If my three-bedroom condo had a lawn, I'd be yelling at the neighborhood kids to get off of it. I really am getting old.

As I wave goodbye to Emma in the parking lot, I force myself to acknowledge the discomfort. Maybe some of it is guilt because I know something about Emma's fraternal twin that she doesn't know?

I don't think it was guilt five minutes ago, but it is now, because a petty little part of me is happy about the secret. Emma was keeping her family a secret from me before and now I get to do the same.

It's sick and twisted and not the type of man I want to be.

I also don't want to be a man that sits around in his empty home all weekend moping, and that's what I've been doing more often than not lately because Emma and I were always hanging out before she found Carter.

Honestly, it isn't a surprise that so many people thought we were dating over the years.

My mom hinted that I should get myself a girlfriend now that Emma has a boyfriend and I think even my parents assume I have an unrequited crush on my best friend.

I don't. But I might have an unrequited crush on her sister.

Nope. No. Not going there. I do not need a Trinket woman to make my life fulfilled.

Instead of starting up my car and heading to grab some Chinese takeout on my way home, I scroll through my contacts. As Emma said, who doesn't want to celebrate it being Friday?

I text my friend Trina, who is really more of Emma's friend, but we still hang out a lot.

ME: Got plans tonight? Want to grab some dinner?

TRINA: <<GIF of a cartoon character laughing so hard tears are spraying from its eyes>>

TRINA: Oh, no, you don't. I am not replacing Emma.

TRINA: Y'all's relationship is weird.

I type and erase three different responses before I have to admit she has a point and just me and Trina sitting in a restaurant booth would be a little awkward.

It takes three more attempts, but I finally find a guy from church up for grabbing a burger. The meal is enjoyable, the company fun, but I'm still a little unsettled when I walk into my condo.

Emma is hardly my first friend to couple up. I go to a large church with an active singles group. There's a shared Google calendar for people planning weddings so they don't put them on top of each other.

I don't begrudge my friends finding love and getting married and starting families. I want it for myself one day. But it's always felt like a someday thing. Even as I saw other friends tie the knot and trade long Sunday lunches at the Mexican restaurant for grabbing a quick meal so they can stick to the baby's nap schedule, I didn't feel like I was missing out.

But now Emma's turning down hibachi because Carter thawed out pork chops.

I am the thirdest of wheels.

I snatch my phone out of my pocket and scroll to my brother's contact. I have one set of friends that Emma never really crossed into. Maybe spending more time with them will recalibrate the careful balance I've worked to create in my life. This quiet pressure and grumbling despondency has got to go.

ME: Are you meeting the guys at Clint's tomorrow morning?

ROBERT: Today is Friday.

ME: So my calendar app informed me.

ROBERT: That means tomorrow is Saturday.

ME: Pretty sure we covered this in kindergarten.

ROBERT: You join us on Thursdays.

ME: So, you don't need a fourth?

ROBERT: Nah, a fourth would be great. Just saying I don't want to take you to urgent care later.

ME: ???

ROBERT: Altering your schedule might sprain something.

ME: <<GIF of a little girl in pigtails rolling her eyes>>

ME: Clint's?

ROBERT: Yep. It's supposed to rain tonight so bring your racket.

I smile. When I get together with my brother and the other guys we grew up with, we either play basketball or racquetball, depending on the weather. I'm much better at racquetball.

ME: Same time?

ROBERT: I'll give you $10 to show up late so I can record their reaction to seeing you on a Saturday.

ME: I'm not that bad.

ROBERT: . . .

ME: Did you just text me . . . ?

ROBERT: Yes, because I'm not a thirteen-year-old that sends animated gifs.

ME: <<GIF of a monkey sticking out his tongue>>

I try to tell myself that the itch between my shoulder blades is the remaining response to my earlier angst and not a discomfort with making new plans.

Then I open up Minecraft and spend three hours mining out the cliffs of the Grand Canyon.

I have no problem arriving somewhere late because I was waiting on Emma to find her keys or because I had to stay at the office while someone finished up a little work, but if I'm only responsible for myself, late is not an option. However, Saturday morning, I pull into Clint's driveway five minutes after 10:00AM.

If anyone asks, I'm blaming it on Robert. Ten dollars is ten dollars after all, even if it's not quite enough to buy a combo meal at Chick-fil-A anymore.

Technically, I arrive at Clint's parents' house, but he and his wife live in the basement apartment. It's got its own drive splitting off the main one, a separate entrance, and more floor space than my entire condo, so I don't think either of them particularly mind sharing an address with the parentals.

Nor are they likely to complain about keeping access to the athletic facility Clint's parents built when we were pre-teens to convince us to hang out here rather than get in trouble elsewhere.

It worked, though perhaps a little too well, since we're still hanging out here eighteen years later.

I park my Jeep and grab my racket and gym bag from the back seat. The facility is a large square structure with an outdoor half basketball court surrounded by a tall chain link fence on one side. Today it's dotted with puddles from last night's rain, so I head inside, knowing what I'll find.

A private gym, including weight machines, a treadmill, and other equipment, as well as a small dance or yoga room and a racquetball court. And likely my older brother carrying through on his threat to film the reaction of our two oldest friends.

Truly, I've always thought of them more as Robert's friends than mine, but Clint and Max have never made me feel unwanted, so I claimed the coolness credit of hanging out with the athletic boys who were one year older than me in school.

Goodness knows I needed something to balance out the video-game-playing honor student nerd credentials.

"No way." Clint smacks Max in the shoulder. "Today is Saturday, right? Not Thursday?"

I roll my eyes but let them have their fun. They'll move on to teasing about something else in a few minutes and I'll join in.

"Last time I checked." Max grinned. "Good to see you, man. Doubles is always better than trading out for singles."

We enter the court and spend the next thirty minutes smacking the ball around, bickering good-naturedly over points, and trying to "accidentally" hit each other with our rackets.

Afterward, I grab a sports drink from the mini-fridge and collapse onto a bench outside the court to let the sweat dry before I walk back out into the chilled air.

The other three guys follow suit and soon conversation shifts from racquetball to business. Even though we all work in different industries and in different capacities, we can share tactics on managing employees, clients, and government regulations.

It's an easy camaraderie that has been a part of my life for as long as I can remember. Aside from my family, it's the only part of my upbringing that I've kept. The rest of it was shed as soon as I was able.

Since it's Saturday, the only person with a reason to rush home is Clint and when the other guys trail across the driveway to the basement apartment for lunch, I fall right in step with them.

I don't make it back to my condo until midafternoon. The rooms are still empty and quiet, but it's not as unsettling as it was.

I play a few video games. Eventually I have Korean barbecue delivered for dinner.

It's not a bad day.

It's a nice evening.

If this is what life is turning into for me, there are certainly worse fates I could have. As I farm levels in Pokemon Scarlet, I imagine the Blisseys

I knock out are the grumpy feelings I had before. I'm not lonely. My life is good. Change doesn't have to be bad.

And if I repeat that enough times, I might begin to believe it.

AMY

I'm pretty proud of myself as I pull open the single glass door on the side of the church building. Only a five-minute pep talk in the car this morning. Plus, I'm wearing makeup, earrings, and clothing of my own preference. Granted, the makeup is minimal and the clothing is three years out of fashion, but I'm a subdued version of myself instead of a subdued version of the Internet's "church girl."

Last week it was obvious that there wasn't an unofficial dress code, but coming in the latest fashions somehow feels wrong. I can't stop the idea that I should be sacrificing something important for the honor of walking through these doors and spending time with the Creator. It's like an offering. Not a traditional one, granted, but isn't God supposed to be looking at the heart or something?

There's a display on the wall filled with QR codes about various ministries and services at the church. One of them is for a link to give money online. I point my camera at the code and Venmo the church twenty dollars just in case I've got the whole offering thing wrong. Honestly, I've saved at least that much on my monthly spending by not going out late on Saturday nights so I can get up in time on Sundays.

The door from the small side lot I parked my car in dropped me into a utilitarian feeling hallway. It feels like a shortcut for regular attendees or workers as there are very few people in it and all of them are walking with purpose. The hall isn't very long, though, and a great deal of sound is echoing from the wide expanse that I'm walking toward. I must not be as far from that front lobby as I thought.

One step out of the corridor reveals not only the reason for the noise but the fact that I need to try a different back door next week. I've stepped right into the middle of the children's area. Well, not the middle. The front, maybe? There's a long registration desk in front of a large, carpeted play area that has several doors and two more hallways leading away from it. The bulk of the noise is coming from a group of toddling children strolling into the play area, each of them holding on to a plastic ring attached to a long rope extending from a young woman's hand. All of them are singing about a wee little man at the top of their lungs.

Frankly, it sounds like a song I'd hear in a bar at 2am, but I'm not sticking around to figure out why it's different. I scamper past the desk and the walls covered in vibrant greens and yellow and into a much wider walkway, relieved to find myself surrounded by muted grays and blues once more.

The people in this wide hallway are adults for the most part and are meandering with far less urgency. I fall into the rhythm of the traffic, trying to determine which way the auditorium is. Most people appear to be heading toward a group of classroom-looking spaces that I assume hold the small groups Emma mentioned. I'm not ready to find out.

Other people are moving in the other direction so they must be going to the worship service. I fall in step with them and discover, five-minute pep talk aside, I'm apparently not as ready to attend my next in person service as I thought. My heart pounds harder, sending blood rushing to my ears as I get closer and closer to the foyer and the large auditorium beyond.

It doesn't seem to matter than I was in there just last week, that I have a plan and know where I want to sit. Walking in on my own is still daunting.

I fall back on the time-honored female method of avoidance and move to duck into a restroom, but the closest one already looks overcrowded. Backtracking toward the classrooms, I scan every side hall I pass, looking for a mostly empty restroom. I find one moments later and slip inside, already finding it a little easier to breath.

There are a couple of women having a low conversation at one end of the sinks, so I step into a stall and pretend to do my business. By the time I come out and make myself busy washing my hands, I've been able to determine that one of the women has a massive crush on a guy she's about to see in small group and yesterday she made the mistake of letting him know.

And I thought I wasn't ready to walk into one of those classrooms.

"It's going to be fine," the encouraging woman says. "You look great."

"I look like an idiot." The woman sounds like she's about to cry, an action that would absolutely not help her appearance any. "What was I thinking? I work in an auto-parts store and spend my free time at the dojo. I can't remember the last time I wore a skirt."

That is an impressive sounding life. I inspect her in the mirror. A woman whose days are filled wrangling cranky egotistical men both financially and physically cannot be this lacking in confidence.

Her dress isn't bad, but it's just that. A dress. Contrary to popular opinion, clothes do not make the look.

My hands itch and I can't help myself. I move toward the women.

"I'm sorry, but I couldn't help overhearing and I thought I might could help."

The near-tears woman squints at me. "Do you know Trevor?"

"Ah, no. But I know how to make you look like a million bucks." Okay, maybe a thousand bucks given my limited resources, but her confidence can use a little inflating. "I'm a stylist."

She glances me up and down. "You look amazing."

Since I was deliberately not aiming for fabulousness this morning and I am certain I achieved my goal, the compliment makes me a little uncomfortable. If she thinks this is fabulous, it means I can definitely make this moment better.

"First off, no crying. Crying makes us red and splotchy. Here, put your wrists in cold water." I guide her to the sink and get her situated while I think through my options. She needs a necklace, but my outfit didn't call for one today.

Her friend, however, has a large metal owl on a silver chain hanging from her neck.

"Can she borrow that?" I point to the necklace.

Wordlessly, the friend raises it over her head and hands it to me.

I loop it around the girl's neck, then work on loosening the knot of the scarf draped around my own. The woman's dress is a simple, solid-colored sheath. A few items to break up the large block of color, a touch of makeup, and little attention to her hair and she should feel unstoppable.

I gather the scarf and wrap it around the woman's waist. Scarf belts haven't been in fashion for more than a hot minute, but I don't think she cares.

Muttering to myself, I plop my large, leather hobo bag onto the counter and rummage around to see what makeup I have. This woman is a brunette with olive skin so most of the products I have will be entirely the wrong shade, but some classics might work.

I pick up a blush and hold it to the woman's face before frowning and returning it to the bag.

Her friend comes to the rescue, though, thrusting a tiny pouch with a few basic items in it across the counter. "Will anything in here work?"

Spying the perfect shade of blush, I turn the woman toward me and prepare to make some magic happen. Working with my sister, I've learned the importance of making sure people look like the best versions of themselves and not the version I would dress as, if I were in their body. I keep the makeup light. A couple swipes of blush, a touch of mascara, and a lip gloss I haven't worn in so long it probably should be thrown away.

I hand the tube over to her. "Here. Keep it. You might need to refresh it if you lick your lips when you get nervous or something."

My hair is piled into a messy bun on my head. It's deceptively simple looking, since the knot requires three hair ties and a handful of bobby pins. At the moment, I'm glad because that means I have plenty of hair options at my disposal.

Both women's eyes widen as I harvest pins and hair ties from my own head, creating a small pile on the counter. I give my new friend a loose French braid and pull my own locks into a low ponytail before scooping the remaining tie and pins into the abyss of my purse.

Finally, I spread my arms wide. "Ta-da!"

"I don't . . . how did you . . ."

"Wow."

The previously distraught girl turns to me with a wide grin, all trepidation clearly gone. "Thank you so much."

"You are most welcome."

"I'm Tracy."

Tracy and Trevor. It sounds like a couple from a bad dime store novel from the 1980s, but I'll be happy for her. "I'm Amy."

"Well, Amy, thank you so much." She runs her hands over the scarf at her waist. "How do I get this back to you?"

"Keep it." This is the first time I've worn it in years. I'm frankly surprised it was still in my closet. "Think of it as a good luck charm."

Wait. I'm in a church. Can we talk about luck here?

"Oh no, I can't do that." She pulls out her phone. "I'll get it back to you."

Because it's easier to give in at this point, I put my number into her phone.

She grins. "Thanks. Are you new here? Want to come with us to the young singles class?"

Young singles? Why does everything in this church sound like it belongs in a bar this morning? "Ah, no, I'm . . . meeting someone . . . in the service." I know I'm not supposed to lie in church, but I'm a work in progress, I suppose. I pull out my phone and look at the screen without actually registering the time. "Oh, wow, I'd better be going."

I slide toward the door with an awkward wave. "Go knock Trevor's socks off."

"I will." Tracy and her friend are both grinning as I turn and flee the bathroom.

It might not be the holiest of endeavors, but I feel calmer having helped someone. Yes, it was just a fashion emergency, but those are what I'm good at.

The large corridor has all but emptied by the time I make it back to the auditorium. Music is already playing as I slip inside and find a seat near the place I settled last time.

"I wondered if you were going to skip out today."

I spin in the aisle to see Jason joining me near the back row of seats. He gestures toward them with the brown leather Bible in his hand. "May I sit with you again?"

I have to admit that the idea of having him beside me calms the remaining nerves jangling beneath my skin. "That would be great."

"Did you pick up a set of elements?"

I frown as he holds out a small plastic container that looks like a miniature shot glass with a cracker in a sealed compartment on top. "Ah, no."

"Here. Take this one. I'll get another." He hands me the tiny cup and scoots over to a large basket near the door to grab another one. A sign on the front of the basket reads *Pick up your elements here.* I had totally missed it.

Not that I have any idea what it is I've missed.

Once Jason has grabbed another container and returned to stand in front of the seat beside mine, I lean in to whisper in his ear. "What do I do with this?"

I miss his immediate answer because I'm distracted by the lightest scent of sandalwood.

"I'm sorry, what?"

"They're for the Lord's Supper."

Yep, I'd have been asking him to repeat himself even if I had heard him the first time.

I saw them do this once when I was watching in the Target parking lot, but the pastor was so small on my phone screen that I wasn't entirely sure what he was doing.

Shifting to try to discreetly hide the screen, I do a quick search on my phone. The listings all look like commentary articles and Renaissance art paintings. I've seen the art before, but I don't know how this little shot of red wine pertains to the feast I've seen in those depictions.

The service moves along much like it did the week before with people standing and sitting and singing and talking. Nothing is done with the little cup so I leave it sitting on the arm of my chair.

Things are different right before the sermon, though. The keyboard keeps playing a soft melody as the pastor steps to the front of the stage. He, too, has one of the tiny plastic cups.

As he reads from the passage, I realize this is a re-enactment of the meal from the Bible in the paintings. So I have been given a tiny cup of wine.

Seriously. Who needs a Saturday night at the bar?

A tiny grin is on my lips as I extract the tiny cracker from its container, but it falls as the seriousness of what this represents fills me. Solemnly, I take the cracker and eat it, even if I feel a little silly. It's so small that it's difficult to consume with any sort of gravitas.

It also tastes like Styrofoam.

When he tells us to drink the wine, I toss the dark purple liquid back.

Only it isn't wine.

It's grape juice, and not a very good vintage at that. It's sour, like rejected wine that wasn't allowed to ferment. I fight to keep from reacting to the unpleasant taste.

Beside me, Jason is sputtering, so maybe the juice is usually better. I turn to ask him only to find he isn't choking on the juice.

He's trying not to collapse in laughter.

He turns his head, dark eyes meeting my concerned gaze, and then doubles over into another set of suppressed chuckles.

Finally, he has himself under control and he sits up, grinning at me.

"What?" I whisper because the room is quiet as the pastor finishes praying and moves into his sermon.

"I've never seen someone take communion like a shot of tequila before."

I look down at the plastic cup in my hand. How else are you supposed to drink from this thing? Sipping it seems a bit ridiculous when it can't even hold a full ounce of liquid. Of course, it is meant to be wine, which I've never seen anyone sling back before, but only pretentious people sip from shot glasses.

Nothing I can do about it now. I pull my water bottle from my purse and take a discreet drink to wash the lingering taste of bad grapes from my mouth, then situate my notebook so I can jot down my observations and questions.

A few minutes later I feel a buzz in my lap where my phone is residing. I try to ignore it because, well, church. But a few minutes later it buzzes again. Who could be sending me messages on Sunday morning? Most of my friends are still in bed or are going to one of those brunches that they've stopped inviting me to because I keep saying no.

I nudge my phone so I can see the notification screen.

It's Jason. I glance over at him, and he has one earbud in. His phone screen is split so that the top is displaying the sermon notes provided by the church and the bottom is YouTube.

I open my phone to read the messages. It's links to videos and Bible passages, captioned with the questions I've jotted down on my notebook.

I don't know if God tries to test people's resolve to see if they'll stay committed to their plan not to let a man consume too much of their life while they're trying to figure things out, but if he does, I have a feeling I'm going to fail.

AMY

I make it out of the service without doing something embarrassing, but Monday at 7pm, I'm right back in the danger zone.

The fluttering in my middle is at once familiar and strange. I press a hand to my belly after I put my car in park. Am I trying to make the feeling go away? If so, it isn't working.

It's been a long time since I felt the pull of attraction, since I was interested in a guy. Well, a long time for me. This sensation used to be a near-constant companion. I can admit now, after months of self-examination, that I might have been just the slightest bit boy crazy. Possibly even obsessed. I didn't have a lot of extended relationships, but I had a date whenever I wanted one.

Since that night on Emma's living room floor, though, there's been nothing. Zip. Zilch. Nada. Not even a secret fantasy about bumping into a suddenly single Henry Cavill.

Until I met Jason.

I want to chalk it up to nerves, but we're well past that point. I've seen the guy on multiple occasions in multiple places. We've texted. We've talked on the phone. This excitement can no longer be considered the thrill of finally meeting Emma's best friend.

If I'm going to go all in on this new life idea, I have to be honest with God and myself. And honestly, I really like Jason Miller.

Maybe that's why I'm having a difficult time remembering that I'm an adult and he's an adult and adults have conversations in private places because we have our own living spaces and sometimes it just isn't reasonable to meet at PF Chang's for a chat.

Maybe I should have taken Jason up on his original offer to have me come by the office so he could show me the conceptual idea he wants me to see before I completely give up on the app idea.

Today is Monday, though.

Emma goes into the office on Mondays.

And I'm avoiding Emma.

I can't quite believe she never had feelings for Jason beyond friendship. Has she never seen him in a backwards ball cap with little tufts of his thick, black hair sticking through the adjustable fit band opening? Is she completely blind to the way he keeps his facial hair trimmed in that slightly scruffy length of a beard? Does she truly not notice the way his T-shirt pulls across his muscles when he twists around to pick up something?

Because I am well aware of all those things.

Also the sweetly adorable way he's been helping me to find the answers I need and the way he's encouraging me in my business. Somehow the man just keeps getting better looking every time he speaks.

I've never had that happen before.

Most of my boyfriends became less good-looking when they opened their mouths.

Today isn't a date, though. It's a professional meeting that just happens to be taking place in his home.

My eyes widen and I double-check the address as I pull into the complex. It's really nice, with rock walls, complex landscaping, and, as I circle around toward his building, a pool that would fit in at a 5-star beach resort. Mother always says there's good money in successful technology and she must be right. This isn't the most expensive area of town by far, but it's certainly far from shabby. Plus, he owns this condo.

No. No. I shake my head. This is supposed to be professional, right? It doesn't feel like it.

There's an empty visitor space right in front of his building. All the condo doors are situated for privacy, pointing toward separate sections of the breezeway. I don't even have to pass anyone's door as I take the stairs to the third floor. I knock on his door and take in the view. In the distance, I can see the skyline of downtown Atlanta.

Jason lets me in with a smile on his face. Is it my imagination or his expression just a little too warm for a professional greeting? The butterflies get themselves another espresso and begin their training for the Boston Marathon.

"Hi." He shoves his hands into the front pockets of his jeans. The muscles on his arms tense with the motion and stretch the sleeves of his gray T-shirt that has some sort of emblem on it. I don't recognize it as a fashion brand so it's probably something nerdy. His jeans and the baseball hat on his head—black this time—are the perfect level of well worn. The man should be on the cover of Geek Monthly or whatever the actual equivalent is. Surely there's some sort of magazine for tech people.

An answering smile is on my face before I can stop it. It's not the calculated, professional one I practiced in the car. If my face freezes like this, my cheeks are going to be hurting in about five minutes. "Hi."

We stand there, smiling, staring, silent, until something seems to hit him and his entire body jerks as he looks away and pulls his phone out. I am definitely not the only one experiencing this attraction.

Before, that would have been enough for me to act. Now . . .

"Come in. Come in. Do you want something to drink?" He narrows his gaze toward the kitchen along one wall. "Pretty sure I have something besides various flavors of water and energy drinks, but it might take me a minute to find it."

"I'm good." I pat my large leather bag. "Got my trusty water bottle here."

"Right. Well, uh, I wanted to show you some modifications I made to one of our older products so you could visualize the possibilities before changing direction."

How nice of him to say something other than giving up.

"I've also downloaded a few of your competitors so we could make sure we produce something new."

I frown. When I'd had this idea, I scoured the app store for anything that would fill the need already, thinking I could utilize something already made to serve new clients. There'd been nothing. "I have competitors? I thought this was a new idea."

"There's always competitors. In your case, there are a few virtual closet apps, capsule wardrobe systems, and even outfit of the day social media accounts. Anything that would help someone achieve the same end goal is a competitor."

I try not to laugh. I really do. But a giggle escapes. My hand flies up to cover my mouth, but it's too late. The mental image of Jason spending hours scrolling the Internet and trashing his algorithm as he looks over fashion accounts is simply too funny.

He lifts his eyes from his phone, considering me with a half grin, as if my amusement is enough to make him laugh. "What's funny?"

"I'm sorry." This man is simply doing his job. I need to remember that. "It's just . . ." I wave my hand toward his phone. "I'm trying to imagine you scrolling fashion accounts and trying closet apps."

He laughs and shrugs, a hint of a blush appearing along his cheekbones. "I tried the apps, which serve the purpose or helping someone organize their clothing but aren't attempting what you want to accomplish. But I had Stephanie in design locate the other stuff for me." One hand lifts to adjust his cap on his head. "I didn't think I'd know what I was looking for there."

"Makes sense."

Once again, we're standing there, silent, awkward. It feels like the end of a first date when both people are trying to figure out if it's the right time to go in for a goodnight kiss or not.

And just like that, the idea of kissing Jason is firmly in the front of my brain. That is the last thing I need to be thinking about right now. Pretty sure I'm the one on the verge of a total blush now.

He gestures past his C-shaped kitchen toward the living space where a large, upholstered ash-colored couch sits facing two matching chairs. An elegant gray and green rug covers the floor in between and the television is appropriately sized and as discreet as a mounted flatscreen can be without purchasing one of those framing kits.

Unsure of where I should go or what I should do—yet more ideas that feel like first date instead of business meeting—I plop myself onto the center cushion of one of the sofas and pull out my own phone.

When Jason settles onto the cushion beside mine, my heart pounds and the idea of kissing him burns through my thoughts again.

No. I'm being a professional. We're discussing taking my business to the next level. If I were to do this—and when I'm talking to him, it still feels in the realms of possibility—everything would be on the line. My reputation, my family relationships, a huge chunk of my savings. The last thing I need is to screw it all up by making the man creating my app feel a need to start avoiding me. That's the opposite of a friends and family discount. Kissing him when he has given only the vaguest of indications that he would reciprocate the action is a sure way to ruin everything.

Wait. Do Christians even kiss? I know I've heard something about that. Am I allowed to kiss a guy before getting married? What if I never get married? Do I have to go the rest of my life without ever kissing again?

That's not acceptable. I've talked enough with Emma to know I have to give up . . . other stuff, but I really like kissing.

My last boyfriend wasn't good at it. Richie Reynolds cannot possibly be the last man I ever kiss in my life. God cannot be that cruel.

I take a deep breath and try to calm the racing thoughts. I'm being ridiculous. I've seen Emma kiss Carter and there was also a couple saying goodbye in the parking lot after church yesterday that had a little smooch. Of course, they might have been married and just going separate ways for the afternoon, but I don't think so. Slowly, I try to discreetly suck in a deep, calming breath. I'm still okay. Kissing is fine.

Kissing Jason, however, is not.

Especially since he's holding his phone out, showing me something, and clearly waiting for my response to a question I completely missed.

I clear my throat. "I'm sorry. Could you repeat that?"

"Here are some of the accounts discussing fashion in ways that might coordinate with your goals. While not direct competitors, you need to ensure you are providing something they aren't. After all, following them is free and using your app will have to cost."

"They might also be good people to reach out to when we release it. Influencer marketing is important." I scroll down to see a few of the accounts on the list, but since the phone is still in his hand, it's more than a little awkward.

"You can . . ." He extends the phone. "Here."

My hands tangle with his as I take the phone. We're like a couple of teenagers instead of verging on thirty. Well, verging on thirty for me. I don't know how old Jason is, though he has to be around the same age since he met Emma in college.

Holding a phone and scrolling is a comfortable, familiar action. Some of these accounts are ones I follow, and others are intriguing enough for me to send a couple of posts to myself as a direct message so I can add them later.

"You know this is going to screw up your algorithm, right?" I grin at the idea that he'll be seeing posts about choosing a skirt length for the next month.

He shrugs. "I'm rarely on except for work, so having the algorithm connect to my current projects can actually be helpful."

I blink at him. "You don't scroll?"

"Not really." He settles back into the couch. "I don't see a need to live other people's lives."

"It's not about living their life. It's about knowing what's going on."

"But I don't know them."

I blink. "You don't know the president either, but I bet you follow what he's doing."

"That's different. His actions affect my life." He looks at the phone. "EveryWomanFashion isn't going to change my day."

I glance at the phone and straighten my spine, only now realizing how close I'd started to lean. "Well, that's true, but . . ." Suddenly I feel frivolous and ridiculous. I stare at the phone until the picture blurs and my eyes start to cross.

"Hey." He leans forward until he can look into my face. "Hey, what is it?"

"What do you mean?" This time it is my professional smile on my face. The one I give my mother and aunt when they act like I work for them. The one I give my clients when they think a flounce will make them look fat. The one I give my sister when she assumes something about me is the same as it used to be but I'm not so certain anymore.

It's a fake smile, but it's never failed me yet.

"I mean, you just suddenly turned off. There was this glow of . . . of . . ."

Attraction?

". . . excitement around you and now it's just gone."

"Oh."

"What happened?"

"Like you said." I gesture at the phone. "EveryWomanFashion isn't going to change your life. It's frivolous and foolish. I mean, there are far greater problems in the world than clothes."

He leans in further and angles his head until it's covering the phone, his eyebrows are lifted, making his forehead crinkle against the edge of his ball cap. It shouldn't look adorable.

"You got all that from the fact that I don't sit and scroll InstaTok?"

I frown. "I mean . . . yes?"

He shakes his head. "I'm not some noble, screen free advocate. My choice of mindlessness just isn't social media."

"What is it?"

"Video games, mostly."

I can't help but laugh. "You are Emma's friend."

"Yeah, but she won't let me play Wrecking Crew on her Switch because my high scores are better than hers."

The screen goes black, and I see a distorted version of my own reflection on the phone. Jason's hand comes in and blocks the view as he pries the device from my fingers. "What you are trying to do," he says, "what you already do, is going to change lives."

I'm certain he can see doubt on my face because he keeps talking.

"You said it yourself. The way we see people affects what we think of them." He flips the phone around in his hands. "Emma's been spending more time in the office lately, and I think it's because she feels more comfortable relating to people."

"That's Carter."

"Maybe a little. But it's you, too. She doesn't just feel comfortable being herself. She feels confident. That shows."

"And you think I can give that to other people, too?"

"I know you can." He turns the phone back on and pulls up an app. "Here. This is one of the things I wanted to show you." From a storage table beside the couch, he pulls out a set of glasses with a thick, black frame. After pushing a few buttons on both the phone and the headset, he hands it to me. "Put this on."

I recognize these glasses from a project Emma did for the local art museum. The glasses can augment reality, showing the viewer a combination of real world and digital items.

"This isn't what I planned to show you, but..." He hops up from the couch and begins shoving the chairs and end tables to the wall to make a large, open space in front of the sofa. "Look over here."

I stop trying to see what he's doing on the phone and look into the cleared area. Suddenly the space is filled with people.

"Go on. Walk around."

I stand and move amongst the people. I'm not interacting with them, as they stay in the same place they were, but I can shift around, feel like I'm where they are. "What is this?"

"It's an app we're working on with a mental health group. It connects to a monitoring device to track your vital signs while experiencing a scenario such as a party, a work meeting, or public speaking. It can help diagnose anxiety and trauma, particularly in non-verbal patients."

I look back at him on the couch. The mix of digital people around him make him stand out as even more special, more authentic.

More attractive.

"It's cost prohibitive at the moment, unfortunately, but we're working on it."

"What does this have to do with me?"

He hits a few buttons and the scenario changes to an office setting. People are working at desks, and from the audio transmitters in the glasses, I can hear the sounds of typing and even the buzz of overhead fluorescent lights.

"My point is that there's a need for people to feel comfortable in different environments, for them to be confident stepping out in life."

I pull off the glasses as Jason starts fiddling with his phone again.

"Okay. Stand there." He points the camera at me for a moment and then he pushes more things on the screen.

I sit back on the couch to see what he's doing, surprised to see myself on the screen wearing . . . "What is that?"

He winces. "A Space Cadet uniform from Galaxy Defender Gliders?"

I can't stop a small partial grin. "I see. And why am I wearing it?"

"Because I already had this coded. But I've put a couple other things in there, too."

He punches a couple of options and then I'm wearing a snug pink T-shirt and jeans.

"That . . . isn't much better." I can't stop a giggle from escaping.

"I am not the fashionista here." He's laughing, too. "And this is simply a basic prototype. An idea we can build on."

"I don't know."

"I'm not sure I'd have said this before seeing a change in Emma, before hearing you talk about clothes, but I think what you're wanting to do is important. It's more than just fashion advice. It's . . . life advice. Potentially life-changing advice. And it's pretty admirable that you want it to be more available."

"You really think so?" I'm not proud of how small and quiet my voice sounds right now, but I like this guy, and he's complementing something other than my hair or my body. The butterflies I'd temporarily tamed into a semblance of order start fluttering around again.

"I do." His head lifts until his gaze meets mine. "I didn't know you before—" He waves his hand around. "Well, before."

What would have happened if I'd met Jason before meeting Christ? It's hard to imagine, because I wouldn't have had a reason to seek him out to begin with. I'd have assumed he was as awkward and out of touch as Emma was. I never would have thought her mythical best friend was the epitome of the hot, smart, techie dude on an action television show.

Unaware of my musings, Jason continues, "But the version of you I've been getting to know has a huge heart that is going to make a lot of people's lives better."

"How do you know?"

"I follow Trevor on InstaTok."

I blink as Jason once more pokes at his phone screen. He then turns it so I can see a photo of a thin guy with brown, shaggy hair and glasses smiling as he takes a selfie in front of a movie theater poster with his arm around the girl I helped in the church restroom the day before. My scarf is still belted around her waist and her hair is still pulled back in a braid, though she's taken off the owl necklace and forgotten to replenish her lip gloss. She's smiling with utter joy into the camera lens.

He takes the phone back with a grin. "What you did for Tracy's been making the rumor rounds."

I shake my head with a low chuckle.

Jason runs a hand over his jeans. "I have to admit that I've been giving my wardrobe a little more thought since I met you."

"You have?"

He nods and darkens the phone screen before leaning back against the couch to look at me. "You have a gift, Amy. It's unique and I'm honored to help you share it."

I look into his eyes. His posture is soft and relaxed and angled toward mine. His eyes are dark and fixed on mine. I am not misreading this situation. The fluttering butterfly attraction is not one sided.

Professional or not, I want to see where things could go with Jason. I want to try a relationship on this side of life.

There are no words in my head, though, only the butterflies that have escaped my middle to flow through my veins and fill my brain. I cannot go one more minute without seeing if there could be something between me and Jason.

I may not know how to navigate a church service, but I'm well-versed in navigating boy-girl relationships. At least some of that experience has to be applicable here. My mouth can't form the words to ask him out, but I know one other way to get things moving.

Before I can talk myself out of it, I lean forward.

And I kiss him.

JASON

There's a woman's lips pressed to mine. An attractive woman that I've thought about kissing more times than is appropriate considering our professional and personal connections, not to mention the short length of our acquaintance. It's hardly the first time in my thirty years that I've been in this position. It's not even the first time the lady has initiated.

Yet it feels like it might as well be.

I can't remember a kiss that felt this good, tasted this sweet, or scrambled my brain quite this much. The ability to form a complete coherent thought is beyond me. My world is a haze of sensation.

Until the woman lands in my lap.

Suddenly, I'm aware of every single aspect, cataloging the moment in crystalline detail with the speed of an overclocked supercomputer. Not a single one of those details is unpleasant. They are, in fact, the definition of pleasant and I am all too aware that this situation is already one step past trouble.

I surge to my feet and cross the room, shoving my hands into my hair and pulling the strands in an attempt to ground myself into the moment. My hat is gone, but I'll find it later. Right now, I need my heart to slide back into position in my chest and my breathing to regulate down to something that won't cause me to hyperventilate.

A whimpering squeak has me spinning around and everything in me freezes as my heart plunges to my toes.

"Amy, I'm so sorry." I rush back across the room to the elegant woman in a very inelegant heap on the floor.

Where I apparently dropped her in my haste to leave the couch.

I have never considered myself a very suave man, but dropping a woman on the floor because her kisses were a little too enthralling for my peace of mind is far clumsier than I've ever despaired of being.

It's also more than a little embarrassing.

Instinctively, I reach out to help her up. As soon as my hand reaches around her arm, feeling her warmth and resilience, it is only sheer willpower that keeps me from pulling my hand away with alarm and dropping her back to the hardwood. As I step away after helping her back to the couch, the frown directed my way tells me I still let go with an insulting level of speed.

I run my hand over my face and pace back across the room, putting several feet between us.

She clears her throat. "No, I'm the one who's sorry. I thought . . . I thought . . ." Her laugh is cold and short. "It doesn't matter. We can just forget that ever happened."

Forget it? I'm going to be remembering that kiss when I'm forty. Maybe longer.

"Wh—" I stop to clear my throat as the words come out strained and scratchy. "Why would we want to do that?"

Her gaze, which has been bouncing around every corner of the room, slowly settles on me as she pulls her feet up onto the cushions.

I don't need a doctorate in psychology to read her posture as defensive. My feet move automatically in her direction, my gut inclination to offer some form of security or comfort, but I pull myself to a halt because the last thing I need right now is to touch her again.

Her lips twist into some form I can't identify but know isn't good. "Why would we want to forget about it? Oh, I don't know, maybe because it's pretty embarrassing to have a guy literally dump me before we've even gone on a date." She shakes her head. "I can walk away from this project, but you're still going to be in my life, at least a little, because of Emma."

I wince because I really want to laugh at the reference to my dumping her, but while the wording is funny, the concept isn't.

She clasps her hands around her raised knees. "It's best if we just pretend this never happened."

Time and space have brought my body back in line and re-established my ability to reason, but the logical conclusions I'm coming to aren't pleasant. I frown. "You can do that? Just put this from your mind and move on?" The dismissal is more than a little painful. "Why did you kiss me, then?"

A little of her discomfort seems to fade into confusion as she frowns at me in return. "Why does anyone kiss anyone?"

Now that is an interesting philosophical question. "In my experience, it's because they're in a romantic relationship and wish to demonstrate their feelings for each other in a tangible way."

She blinks at me. "Well. That." She flops a hand through the air. "That's why."

"We aren't in a romantic relationship."

"I know."

I keep watching her, waiting for something more, something explanatory.

Finally, she sighs and drops her gaze, reaching out to fiddle with a loose string on the edge of the couch cushion. "I thought perhaps you would like to change that. Obviously, I was wrong."

My eyebrows shoot up before I can stop them. Because while I didn't have a lot of precise, clear thoughts during that kiss, I know I wasn't a passive recipient. "You have many uninterested men kiss you back like that?"

One side of her mouth kicks up. "Men will kiss a frog if it's enthusiastic enough."

"I think I'm insulted on behalf of the male population."

Her arms cross tightly across her chest. "You shouldn't be. Most of the men I know don't consider a relationship a requirement for kissing, so clearly, you're of a higher caliber."

How am I meant to respond to that? This is the strangest post-kiss conversation I've ever had. And possibly the longest. Most of the time it's a simple good night. "Amy, are you trying to indicate that you'd like me to ask you on a date?" I run a hand through my hair again. "I'll admit I'm not always the most adept at picking up on clues and cues, but this one would be pretty obvious."

"I . . . yes . . . I mean . . ." She braces her elbows on her knees and buries her face into her hands. "This is impossible. I have no idea what I'm doing."

I cough, unable to stop myself from stating, "That kiss would indicate otherwise."

Her head flies up, mouth gaping open as color floods her cheeks.

I slap a hand over my mouth, "Oh, man, that sounded . . . I didn't mean that . . . I mean, I did, the kiss was amazing, but I didn't mean to imply . . ."

Didn't mean to imply what? Where in the world am I going with that sentence? It can't be anywhere good.

The embarrassment seems to fade as she starts to giggle. The heat disappearing from her cheeks spreads over to mine. It would appear that I am the one who has no idea what he's doing.

Her giggles slide into full blown laughter. It's beautiful, but I can't enjoy it because what about this situation is actually that funny?

Her forehead drops onto her raised knees as her shoulders continue to shake.

With a great deal of caution, I move closer to the couch. "Amy?"

"Yes?" Her voice is shaky with laughter, though it seems more controlled than a few moments earlier.

There are two, no, three choices before me right now. Four, if one considers crossing back to that couch and kissing her again an option. Which I don't, now that I'm far enough away from her for my mental faculties to be in control. I find it a lot easier to trim my beard in the mornings if I'm willing to look at myself in the mirror.

Instead, I can continue bumbling along on this weird conversation about kissing and hope that Amy eventually pulls us out of it. I can go all in and ask her on a date. Or I can do as she asked a few moments ago and pretend this never happened and return us to a client-centric equilibrium.

I know which one I want to do, but the rush of static in my ears, the constriction in my throat, and the heavy sense that it's the wrong next move keep me from committing to that path.

She's starting to mumble again but I can't make out all the words. I catch the words *couch*, *ridiculous*, and *turtle* but haven't the faintest idea how those all go together.

"Are you busy Friday night?"

Her mouth is hanging open as her words stop mid-sentence.

I want to crawl in a hole. While it is true that it has been a while since I dated anyone, I know this is not how I ask women out on dates. After licking my lips, I plunge on, rewording before she can formulate an answer. "I mean, I'd like to take you out sometime. If you are amenable to that idea, my Friday is available."

Pretty sure I just made things worse. Still, the idea has been stated, the inquiry is made.

And I know in my gut I made the wrong decision.

What I don't know is how to take it back.

We stare at each other for several moments before her lips curve into a smile. "You're smooth."

"Yeah." My voice is gravelly and low as I drag the word out. "Like crunchy peanut butter."

Her giggle this time is one of those cute, flirty ones girls give when the boy they like makes a joke. I never know if it's genuine or not. The pink gloss on her lips catches the light as she smiles, making her whole face appear lit from within. "You're sweet."

My knees threaten to give out and leave me the one sprawled inelegantly on the floor.

"But . . ." Her smile fades and her teeth bite into her bottom lip, cutting off the reflection and revealing she, too, has significant misgivings about the idea, now that she's given it clear consideration.

"I told myself I wasn't going to date for a while and this entire interaction is only confirming that decision." She adjusts her position on the couch to hug her knees tighter. "Have you done that before?"

"Not dated? Yeah. It's my normal state of being." Who lives below me? Would they mind if I sink through the floor and hang out in their condo for a while?

Her face twists as if she can't decide whether to laugh or frown. "I meant, have you ever asked out a girl who . . ." She waves her hands around as if trying to pull the words from the air. "Has a history?"

My throat tightens as I take time to contemplate her meaning. The truth is . . . I don't know. I don't think so, but if I have, I've never gotten serious enough to have that discussion. Most of the girls I've dated were met through church or some sort of Bible study. While there are people there who don't hold the same commitment I have to save intimacy for marriage, they aren't usually very open or vocal about it.

"I, uh . . ."

Her legs move restlessly until she's sitting crisscross on the couch cushion as she smooths her hands over her thighs. "I don't know everything, of course. I mean, there's still a lot of Bible for me to read, but I do understand from Emma that there are a few . . . mistakes . . . in my past that make me a little less of a catch for a man like you."

"She said that?" My hand is already reaching for my phone, ready to tell my friend off and make her apologize to her sister.

"Not directly, no." Amy shrugs one shoulder. "But I've heard her talk about Carter enough that I know God meant all that physical stuff for marriage and well—" Another single shoulder shrug. "My ship has already sailed."

My body and brain are flooded with a variety of thoughts and emotions, but none of them will settle long enough for me to find the correct response to her statement. While I shuffle through the myriad of words available to me, I cross the room and sit beside her on the couch. I may not know what to say, but I know she's feeling untouchable right now, and Jesus always reached out to those that felt that way.

My hand lands on her knee and I have to fight the less noble feelings and ideas that immediately try to surface. That internal struggle helps me decide what to say. I can only hope it's the right thing. "My first kiss was with Mary Sue Gramble in sixth grade."

Her lips quirk into a tilted smile. "Oh, yeah?"

I nod. "Behind the gym at our church's youth summer camp."

A delighted gasp leaves her as she bounces her shoulder against mine. "Scandalous."

"My parents seemed to think so."

"How did they find out?"

"Well, Mary Sue told her friend, and they were overheard by one of the counselors who told our youth pastor who had a talk with me and Mary Sue about following the camp rules."

"And he called your parents?"

"Actually, no. But word got around to the other campers, and the facility was owned by a friend of my parents, and he sent them a capture from the security camera."

"That sounds . . . invasive."

It's my turn to shrug. "Probably would be for some parents. Mine just thought it was funny. The picture has its own page in that year's family photo album."

Amy's voice is quiet when she speaks again. "Delightful as that story is, you do realize I wasn't talking about kissing?"

"I do." I take my hand from her knee and twine my fingers between hers. The press of her palm to mine doesn't cause a lurch of sensation or a flood of hormones. Instead, a warm glow of simple caring spreads up my arm. "But I wanted to let you know I have a history, too."

Her eyes widen. "Are you telling me that you and Mary Sue . . ."

"No. My gosh, I'm doing this badly." My free hand lifts to press fingers into my eyes.

"Maybe." I can hear the smile in her voice. "But your efforts are cute."

I take a deep breath and turn until I'm facing her on the couch, her hand still wrapped in mine. "Okay. Listen. I'm just going to say it. I'm going to infer from this conversation that you have more experience on the physical side of dating than I do."

"Yes." Her gaze drops to her lap where her unencumbered hand is tracing the side seam of her pants. "I don't know how else to show affection or interest or whatever this is."

"It is an exceptionally efficient method."

Her laugh sounds resigned. "Stop making this a joke."

"Why?"

"Because you don't really want to date me."

"I don't?"

"Why would you?"

Let me count the ways. Telling her she's beautiful is on the tip of my tongue because what woman doesn't want to hear that they're gorgeous? But that would only reinforce what she's already worried about. "You are smart and courageous enough to have your own business. You care for your sister. You're funny, easy to talk to. Oh, and beautiful." I can't not say it. "I've gone on dates with fewer initial attractions before."

"And if the date goes well?"

I take a deep breath because here's the heart of the matter. "I take you home, walk you to the door, ask if I can see you again, and then leave without kissing you goodnight."

She frowns. "Without kissing me?"

I nod. "You're afraid of the kissing."

"Oh, I'm the one who's afraid? Who dropped who on the floor earlier?"

I grin, because now that we're past it, the idea is a little funny. "I'll own that one. I'll also own that I can't say the idea that you've known other men won't be an issue for me to get over later. But that's on me. Not you."

"I am the one that slept with them."

"And Christ is the one who makes you a new creation, so all that old business is already forgiven."

She blinks at me. "Just like that?"

"Just like that. And anyone who tries to make you feel different has their own issues to work out with God."

"That sounds too simple."

"The gospel is simple. Doesn't mean it's easy."

She stares at me a while and my heart settles into a deep, slow thud as I lose myself in the stormy, gray-green depths.

I know what I have to do and I'm hoping I can do it the right way. My chest stretches against the tense muscles as I pull in a bracing breath. "Amy, I'm rescinding my request for a date."

AMY

I try not to let my disappointment show on my face, but there's no denying that a full truckload of bricks has landed in my stomach.

Without a doubt I will be picking up the good ice cream and a pack of bonbons on my way home tonight.

In fact, I should probably go ahead and leave.

"Right. I understand."

His arm shoots across my shoulders, holding me to the couch with more strength than punching the buttons on a video game controller would create. Since he didn't let go of my hand, my arm is also stretched across my front, keeping me on the couch. I lift inquiring brows in his direction, but the man is frowning at something only he can see, unless he's suddenly acquired a strong dislike for his wall paint color.

"It's not what you think." His voice is firm and confident, but his face . . . isn't.

"What is it I think?"

"That I don't want to date you because of . . ." He waves his hands about in the air, dragging mine right along. My arm is some awkward puppet in this farce of a conversation. " . . . Stuff."

"And you're saying that's wrong?"

"Yes."

"I don't believe you."

"I know you don't, because I am doing my best impression of a bumbling idiot."

I cock my head to the side and try to consider him without any of my own ideas getting in the way. He certainly looks like a man dealing with a lot of irritation and it doesn't seem to be aimed my way. My throat is dry but swallowing almost hurts. "Why don't you just say what you're trying to say?"

"You don't need a boyfriend right now."

Of all the things I was expecting him to say, that wasn't it. I mean, he's not wrong, but . . . "Why do you say that?"

"You have business decisions to make, you're still working to understand the new belief system that you've taken on, and what you need in your life more than really, really good kisses"—His voice gets a little rough, and I can't stop a small smile—"is a friend."

"And you want to be that friend?"

His single nod is sharp. "If you'll let me. Unless there's someone else better. I understand if you don't want anything to do with me right now. Not only am I truly terrible at this conversation but you're also . . ."

"Attracted to you?"

His throat jerks as he, too, takes a moment to swallow. His voice is dry and gritty when he chokes out, "Yeah."

He pops up from the couch. "Do you want some water? I'll get us some water."

I have my water bottle in my bag and he has a pink can of grapefruit-flavored carbonated water on the table, but I don't remind him of that as he paces to the kitchen. Instead, I shift so that I can fold one knee onto the couch and watch him over the backrest. "Are you trying to save me from myself?"

"Oh my gosh," he groans. "Don't say it like that."

"How else should I say it?"

"I'm a . . ." He chugs down half a glass of water. "Friend. Doing what friends do and supporting another friend."

"So you want to be my friend?"

"Yes." Another of those single, sharp nods that I'm beginning to think are as much for himself as they are for me. "That."

My heart melts a little because the truth is, I could use a friend. Most of mine are barely talking to me anymore because they don't understand the changes I'm making in my life. I don't even completely understand them.

"I could use a friend," I whisper.

His gaze meets mine across the room and we have a silent conversation. I don't know what we're talking about or what's being decided, but by the time he blinks, the situation feels settled. At least for now. As he lifts the glass to drink the rest of the water and his arm tenses against the sleeve of his T-shirt, I mentally reserve the right to revisit this conversation at a later date.

Once the glass is empty, he sets it aside and snags my gaze again. "As your friend, I want you to tell me why you don't want to go forward with the app." He points to his phone sitting on the end table. "Clearly we've got a good head start."

I lay my head on the back of his couch. The cushy upholstery of the chunky couch feels way more conformable than my sleek leather and chrome seating. My sofa is prettier, though. With a sigh, I start to talk, telling him all the pros of staying connected to the boutique instead of stepping out on my own.

"And she won't let you stay there if she knows?"

"I'm actually not sure, but I have to be prepared for that possibility."

"Don't you have to be prepared anyway? You said she could find out any day just by getting curious about the books."

"True." I sigh. He has a point, and I hate that. I wanted to just step back and have everything be safe. "All right, I'm in. What is the time frame on this app and what do you need from me?"

The rest of my week is a strange mesh of interactions that don't feel like they have the same person participating in them. Is this what Emma was trying to tell me all those months ago when she talked about feeling the need to be different people in different situations?

It's exhausting.

At the boutique, I'm doing my best to act like I always have, chatting with customers and my mother and aunt about the latest gossip and upcoming events.

It doesn't all feel fake. For instance, I am truly excited about going to see the Nutcracker this year. Even though Emma is trying to be herself when she spends time with all of us instead of who she thinks we want her to be, she's still committed to attending a certain number of cultural events with us. I haven't given up on getting her to appreciate the fine arts. She's dating a painter, for goodness' sake.

Helping people find the perfect look hasn't gotten uncomfortable either. I still adore and appreciate finely made clothing, still get a thrill from watching a woman look in the mirror and see herself as beautiful.

Pretending it's the most important thing in the world, though, is draining. When Mrs. Bradley bit her lip in indecision after peeking at the subtle price tag on a particular blouse, I gently provided another option that I knew to be less expensive.

Mother gave me quite the side-eye as I rang the middle-aged woman up at the register. Fortunately, I had a client arrive around that same time so Mother couldn't ask me about it.

Then there's my ongoing text conversations with Emma. On the surface, they don't look any different. She asks me random questions, and I tell her not to wear sweatpants in public.

They feel different though.

Probably because it's a stark contrast to the conversations I'm having with Jason. Sprinkled amongst the exchanges that are nailing down the terms of my project contract are links to videos or online posts. Some of them are about my faith questions, but others are simply cute or funny things that must be appearing in his InstaTok feed since he added all those fashion influencers. Most of them are ones I've seen before, but it's still sweet that he saw them and thought of me.

My phone buzzes on the desk beside my computer as I work on balancing the week's accounts for both my business and the boutique. I stop to see the latest message and laugh as I look at a video that went viral at least a year ago.

ME: Are you just now seeing this?

JASON: You've already seen it?

ME: I've seen most of what you send me already.

JASON: I told you I didn't get on social media much.

ME: Then why are you on it now?

JASON: Looking for videos for you. You said you preferred shorter ones.

I groan as I flop back in my desk chair. The man is not making the friend zone an easy place to live. Especially since I'm not sure which one of us put us there. Maybe it was unspokenly mutual or orchestrated quietly by God. Whichever it was, it's likely the best place for us to be. I can't imagine what the week would have been like if I'd been anticipating going out with him this weekend instead of attending a gala with my aunt. He would have been all I thought about.

Since we're just friends, he's only half of what I'm thinking about.

The clock ticks over until it's time for me to start getting ready for the event. I grab the gown I procured for tonight, lock up the office, and head to my car. As I drape the dress bag across the backseat, I can't help but contemplate what Jason would think if he saw me in it.

The thought concerns me as I settle into the front seat. Instead of reaching for my keys, I reach for my phone.

ME: Can Christians be boy crazy?

EMMA: I mean, I think it looks a little different, but yes?

ME: Different how?

EMMA: I don't know? It's always about dating and marriage and stuff? At least at our age, anyway.

I blink at the phone.

ME: Marriage?

EMMA: Yeah, I mean. That's where dating goes, right?

I hadn't really thought about it, but what she's saying makes sense. It also makes me even more grateful I didn't accept Jason's request. Or that he took it back. If the idea of dating is to get married, then I'm definitely not ready to date.

But Emma's been dating Carter for a while now. And she's not a flighty girl who doesn't know what she wants in life.

ME: Oh my gosh, are you getting married???

EMMA: Not yet, but I think he's the one.

I squeal and bounce up and down in my car. This is not a conversation to be having over text. Practically vibrating with questions, I start the car and wait impatiently for the Bluetooth to connect so I can place the call.

Emma answers but she isn't happy about it. "Ew. Why are you calling me?"

"You said you're getting married!" I ease out of the tiny employee lot behind the boutique and start the drive home. Despite this excitement, I do need to get ready for the gala.

"I'm not getting married."

"You said he's the one."

"Yeah, but he hasn't asked yet."

I pause for a little longer than necessary at a stop sign to calm the pounding of my heart. "Do you think he will?"

"I don't know . . . probably?" Emma's voice gets a little higher, a little breathier.

It's the girliest sound I've heard her make in years and I can't help squealing again. "Oh, sweet Chanel, have you been dropping hints about what sort of ring you want?"

"Um, no? Am I supposed to?"

How did we come from the same upbringing? "Of course you are! Otherwise he might get something you don't like."

"I'd like to be getting married to him."

"Obviously. But the ring! Oh, and have you been thinking about dresses? Will it be a short engagement? If so, I don't know if I'll have time to make it for you." Especially not if I'm going to focus on expanding the business. "We may have to start with something off the rack and customize."

"Did you hit your head?" There's both amusement and exasperation in her tone. "He hasn't asked."

"Yet."

"I can't start planning a wedding without a ring."

"Sweetie, women plan weddings all the time without even having a man." I've even gone to try on wedding dresses. A group of friends made appointments at boutiques all over town and we traded off pretending to be the bride because those gowns are seriously gorgeous.

I haven't seen those friends in a while. Maybe they'd like to get together for dinner or something? Usually we would go to brunch or a club together, but we're all approaching thirty. Surely something mature like a nice dinner would be just as appealing.

Emma sighs. "I don't want to jump the gun. Sometimes I still have to pinch myself that he's real."

The line goes quiet as I pull into my apartment complex. I don't say anything until I've parked and can give my sister my full attention. "Do you think he's going to break up with you?"

Emma scoffs. "If I did, I wouldn't be thinking he'd give me a ring."

That's true, but . . . "It's only been six months. Are you sure you want to marry him?"

"Yes. What else would I do?"

"I don't know. Move in with him?" There's a pause while my thoughts catch up with what I just said. "Never mind. I know you wouldn't do that."

The fact that Emma doesn't lecture me or berate me for suggesting she act like most of the other people I know is a sign that our relationship has come a long way. Her voice is soft when she says, "But I'm ready to. I'm that committed. I'm that all in. That's how I know I want to marry him and build a life together."

A suspicious burning sensation hits my eyes, and I blink rapidly to keep any wayward water from escaping. "Well, then, we'll need to get together so I can teach you how to leave hints about what type of ring you want."

"Seriously, Amy?"

"Yes!" I turn off the car and jam my phone to my ear as I gather my bag from the passenger seat. "Even if you're too obvious, if you think he's thinking about it, he won't be surprised."

"No, that's not it." She's laughing now. "Between me and Carter, who do you think would have a better eye for choosing a ring?"

I sigh. "You have a point."

Still, there has to be something I can do to make sure she gets something she'll actually wear. Emma would be the kind of girl to shove it in the jewelry box and only bring that diamond out on special occasions.

"Of course I have a point. I always have a point. Hey, did you know the tradition of wearing white wedding dresses is less than 200 years old? In Ancient Rome the bride wore red."

"Ha!" I shake my keys in the air in victory as I enter my apartment. "You've been listening to wedding planning podcasts!" For Emma, that's the equivalent of thumbing through bridal magazines or making a dozen Pinterest boards for different ceremony style inspirations.

"Of course I have. When it happens, I want to be prepared. I doubt either of us will want a large ceremony or a long engagement."

I hate that she's right. Emma and Carter are both fairly private people. We will not be spending a year planning an epic themed event for 500 guests. "Just promise me you won't elope. Planning even a small wedding will be better than nothing."

"I had no idea you had a desire to plan a wedding."

"Hello, cake tasting. There is no other time in life where you can go into a bakery and spend the afternoon sampling all of their best offerings."

Emma groans. "Okay, yes, even if we elope there will be cake."

"And a dress."

Her groan turns into a laugh. "And a dress."

We wrap up the conversation and I get ready for the gala. While the act of choosing the right dress, shoes, bag, and accessories is familiar and the hair and makeup second nature, looking in the mirror feels different than it used to. I look just the same as I usually do with bold lip color, shadow and liner that make my eyes appear larger, and perfectly formed curls that seem to defy gravity and humidity as they fall down my back. The dress fits me to perfection, and I've never been one to show a lot of skin, believing that sophistication is sexier, so it could easily be one I wore a year ago.

Except it's not, because wearing last season's fashions would be detrimental to my business reputation.

So, if it's not the outside that's different, it has to be the inside. There haven't been as many events in the last several weeks, as people are saving their time and money for the upcoming season of holiday parties, but for the past eight years of my life, I've gone to events like this at least once a month. In some seasons it was almost once a week.

Some of them were events I bought a ticket for because being seen as part of high society makes those women more comfortable hiring me as a stylist, but others I went to as a guest, trading my services to the coordinator for a ticket. Some I went to as a date. Always, I had an objective of people to see or be seen by, introductions to acquire, or connections to deepen so they could later be turned into opportunities.

I finish applying my lipstick and slide it into the tiny evening bag I'll be carrying into the venue with me. Looking in the mirror, holding the winter white leather clutch tight to my high-necked, bronze chiffon evening gown, I know what tonight's difference is.

This time, I don't have any idea why I'm going.

AMY

The event space lobby is filled with people. People I know, people I've worked with, people I've talked about in hushed, quiet whispers and followed in local gossip blogs and society columns.

And yet, I'm standing in the corner, behind some sort of modern art sculpture, giving myself a pep talk as if I haven't been seeing many of these people regularly since I was nineteen.

I know how this all works. Nothing I've learned about the new life I want to lead has altered my understanding of how business works. I need to network, need to make a good impression, need to be seen as an expert, need to be relatable to potential clients.

Business is not what I'm afraid of though. I think I'm afraid of myself.

I haven't been to a gala in a little over a month and the last one did not leave me feeling great about myself. Granted, I've done a lot of study since then, conquered some pretty large personal obstacles, and started building the next phase of my life.

What if I walk in there and forget all of it? What if, once I'm surrounded by indulgence and glitter and potentially powerful connections, my thoughts become superficial? What if I calculate who I talk to based on who can help my business or my personal reputation? What if I spend the entire evening judging other people by what they're wearing, like the woman who passed me five minutes ago in a shade of salmon pink that made her look positively ill?

What if all of the people who've been supporting my business don't like who I'm becoming and stop using me to do their styling and image consultations and I truly do have to end up working for my mother in her boutique?

My stomach lurches and I duck into a bathroom which looks more like a lounge. I fish my phone from my clutch and text the only person I know who's had to psych themselves up to attend a gala.

> ME: I don't think I can do this.

> EMMA: Do what?

> ME: <<Photo of the bronze skirt with layers of chiffon in the center and the toes of gold heels>>

> EMMA: I'm not the best at fashion advice, but I think it's pretty.

> ME: The outfit is pretty.

> EMMA: Where are you?

> ME: The women's bathroom at the Grand hotel.

> EMMA: <<GIF of a cartoon man saying *Ooooh, fancy*>>

> ME: Not helping

I think about calling her but there's at least three other women in this bathroom. If I continue texting, I can perch on this uncomfortable piece of art pretending to be a chair in the bathroom lounge and look nonchalant. Speaking aloud will give away the utter panic in my chest.

EMMA: I don't know what you want from me?

ME: How do I do this?

EMMA: This is a gala of some sort, I'm assuming?

ME: They don't call you the smart twin for nothing.

EMMA: No one calls me the smart twin.

ME: Everyone calls you the smart twin.

EMMA: Carter says to go in there, smile at the first person you see no matter what and that will help you remember they're all people.

The idea has merit. If all the attendees are people instead of business opportunities or potential social landmines, then I can spend time talking to whomever I wish and I don't have to worry if the conversations are beneficial or not.

ME: Tell Carter thank you. I'll text him directly next time.

EMMA: He is closer to that world than I am.

That world. The words bump around in my brain as I slide my phone back into my clutch. I know Emma doesn't mean anything derogatory, but it still leaves me feeling alone. I know I won't be the only one in the room who has prayed for forgiveness and given God control of their life. This is Georgia, after all, and there's a church every forty-two feet. At least a handful of people in the room are likely to be genuine in their faith.

I just wish I knew who they were.

It hits me all of a sudden that such thoughts are almost as bad as the ones I used to have. Wanting to find the people that will help me be a good Christian feels just as calculating as wanting to find the people who would bring the best image to my business.

They're all just people. Talk to the first person I see and remember they're all just people.

I have a crazy moment of wishing Jason was walking in at my side as I leave the bathroom and walk toward the ballroom doors. Not that he'd be any help. He doesn't know anyone behind those doors and there's a good chance the man doesn't even own a suit, much less a tuxedo. He's probably a sport coat and jeans kinda guy.

After giving a nod and a smile to the woman at the door, I step inside. I assume employees don't count as the first person I see, though, because I wouldn't be doing them any favors by asking them to abandon their job and talk to me so I can remember they're a human being.

No one else is near the door, so I have to walk further into the room. Desperately, I try not to look around, because if I make my choice of direction based on who I see then I'm not following instructions.

Of course, if I look at the floor I can't make eye contact with any people.

With a sigh, I make my way toward the bar. My head is swimming, and I could really go for a nice glass of wine.

I make my request and turn to find a man with a straight nose, square jaw, brown hair cut to lay in perfect layers across his head, and blue eyes so light they almost look gray. We've never been introduced, but I know who he is. Robert Miller. Son of a very powerful investment businessman, local philanthropy's poster boy for everything good in this world, and quite possibly the most eligible bachelor in the entire Atlanta area, maybe even the whole state.

Is it a sign? He shares the same last name as Jason, but so does my favorite barista down at my local coffee shop. It's not an uncommon name in this area of the country.

Robert is a very uncommon man, though.

If my mother sees me talking to him, she'll be torn between giddily pointing it out to everyone and having a panic attack that I'll mess this up.

Prime catch or not, this man is a human being. That's what I'm supposed to be remembering right now.

"Hi." I give him what I hope is a sedate, friendly smile and not something that looks creepy and desperate.

He smiles back, so I must have done something right. "Hello."

That went well enough. Now I just need to remember how to make small talk without an agenda.

Actually, I don't think I've ever made small talk without having an agenda.

"What brings you out here tonight?"

He gives me a quizzical look. "Helping children?"

I nod because, of course that brought him out.

He shrugs and smiles. "Also rubbing shoulders with some of the people my father and I do business with."

I blink up at him. "How very frank of you."

He shrugs. "It's not like we don't all know. It's just like the golf course except the clothes are less comfortable, the food not as good, and the spouses are in attendance."

Imagining a gala like a golf game has me grinning. Fortunately, there aren't many fashion decisions made on a golf course, so I have never had to learn. "I don't think we've met. I'm Amy."

"Robert."

I stop myself from saying *I know* as we take our respective drinks and step away from the bar. The peasantries are done and he could easily end the conversation here. I'm not someone beneficial for a man like Robert. Then again, he's probably the man most people are angling to get to in this room, so he might not be worried about finding the right conversation before the speeches start.

He chooses to prolong the conversation. "So, what brings you here tonight?"

With the reminder that he is a human being, not some sort of mythical social deity, I give him a smile. "Business. As important as it is to help children learn social and emotional skills, I'm afraid rooms like this are my golf course."

He glances down, taking in my hair, gown, and shoes. It doesn't feel creepy though. I've had men check me out before, but it feels like Robert is actually looking at the dress and not my body inside of it.

"You're a stylist, aren't you?"

I'm glad I haven't just taken a sip of wine because why does he know that? "Why do you know that?"

He raises his eyebrows. "I make it a point to know who all the regulars are."

"Oh." I don't know how I feel about being a regular.

His examination continues for a few silent heartbeats. "Have you seen the information boards?"

"I . . . the what?"

He lifts the hand holding a lowball glass filled with ice and a clear liquid of some kind and gestures toward a set of open doors not far from where we're standing. "The boards that tell you about tonight's cause."

I start walking that way, mystified. Robert follows. The doors lead to a small conference room adjacent to the ballroom. There are displays along the walls showing the work that the funds raised tonight will be put toward. I stop at the first one, taking in the colorful pictures of children from non-traditional home situations play and learn together.

"Are there always displays like this?" I can't remember ever seeing one.

"Usually. Here, look at this one." He leads me across the room to a table filled with pamphlets and information cards. The charity helps children being raised by single parents, grandparents, aunts, uncles, and adoptive parents learn the social and emotional skills to help them stay children and become healthier adults.

"Wow. You really do like this cause."

He nods. "This one is special to me because I know what a difference growing up with my parents made. I won't lie, I've attended many events just for the networking options, but this one . . ." He looks around the room with a soft expression. "It's special."

"Why are you telling me this?" This conversation is more personal than any I've had during a first meeting before. No one lets their guard down this fast at events like this.

He looks at me, eyes roaming with consideration around my face. "I don't know, actually."

It hits me, then, that Robert the human being is a very attractive man. His brown hair is perfectly cut, the custom tuxedo is doing him all the favors, and he seems genuinely nice. He's even in one of the pictures on a nearby board, playing with a child in a photo that looks very candid and not at all staged.

If I were going to start dating, this is type of man I should go for. Yet when I try to imagine lunging across the space and planting a kiss on his lips, the picture isn't enticing. It's funny.

I have to work not to giggle.

"Is that you?" I point to the photo that caught my eye earlier and Robert turns to look as well.

He laughs. "Yeah. I haven't seen that one."

We talk about the cause for a little while, circling the room to read all the boards and look at all the pictures. Our glasses are empty when we return to the ballroom, and we leave them on a table designated for just that purpose.

"Would you care to dance?"

There are a lot of benefits to dancing with Robert, but they only flit through my brain without landing. The main thought I have as I take his hand and we join the other couples is that this meeting doesn't feel like a business interaction nor is it making my insides jump in attractive excitement. It's . . . easy.

Talking to Robert is easy, being comfortable in his presence is easy, remembering he's a person is easy. If pursuing the volatile attraction I have to Jason is a bad idea, then maybe it would be a good idea to consider a relationship with a man who is easy to be with.

Not that I need to be dating, but . . .

Maybe it's the conversation I had with Emma, or maybe it's the reminder that I don't seem to be spending as much time with my old friends, but how long do I have to do the Bible study and church thing before I'm allowed to not be alone anymore?

When that day comes, maybe a man like Robert would be a better idea than Jason.

Six months ago, Robert would have absolutely been the preferred choice, though for entirely different reasons. Does the fact that those benefits would still exist mean I shouldn't even consider him? Not that it matters because he hasn't asked for my number, much less a date.

When the dance is over, Robert and I part ways, and I find myself chatting with ladies who barely gave me a passing greeting before. If even a quarter of them seek out my services, I'll be a large step closer to moving my business out on its own.

Imagine what being seen with Robert again would do.

I almost groan as the thought comes through my mind. Maybe I'm not ready to date a good guy after all.

JASON

This is not a good idea. I know it's not a good idea, yet I'm doing it anyway. In the grand scheme of things, my going to view the environment in which a client would utilize the app and learn more about the business they're asking us to help with is not a bad idea.

What is a bad idea is that I've brought lunch with me and I'm blurring all the lines between business and personal with a woman I should be keeping firmly in the client zone. Or at least the friend zone.

I don't want her in the friend zone. I want her in the go-on-a-date-and-see-where-it-leads zone and I'm so attracted to her that I've deluded myself into thinking that my lack of judgement is a sign that this relationship would be more real than all the reasonable ones I've attempted in my life.

It's possible this is what the Bible is talking about when it says the heart is more deceitful than anything else but there's also the chance this could become a love covers a multitude of sins situation. The fact that I haven't told Emma about it is an indication that it's the former rather than the latter and I should therefore turn around and run.

But I already bought the soup and sandwiches, and I hate wasting food.

Besides, Amy and I already decided that it was a bad idea and surely both of us won't have a weak moment at the same time. Now that she's had a moment away from whatever inspired her to kiss me last week, she's probably remembered I'm not the kind of guy she dates. Even if Amy adjusts her standards, she's not likely to change her style and from what little I've heard from Emma over the past few months, I am not what Amy prefers.

At least, the part of me I show the world isn't.

So I'm safe. I can indulge my little attraction, help a new client, and endear myself to Emma's family should we ever decide to blur those boundaries.

Only one of those is a good thing.

I am an idiot.

I also know this is likely my last chance to indulge in that idiocy. Amy sent over the signed contracts for the app yesterday which means I can't keep the project out of the scheduler anymore.

By next Monday at the latest, Emma will know.

And only when I'm lying to myself can I believe she won't be unhappy about it. This is the woman who has gone to great lengths over the ten years I've known her to keep me and our friends separate from her family. As far as I know, only Carter gets access to every corner of Emma's world.

And the fact that I'm enjoying knowing something about Amy that Emma doesn't know just proves I have a problem with that idea. Do other friends struggle with feeling displaced when a serious relationship comes along or is this saved for weird situations like mine in which I've been the man in Emma's life for the last several years?

Yeah, I don't really want to think about that one.

The boutique window display is a work of art, with clothes spilling delicately out of an old steamer trunk and a tall candelabra draped with scarves and belts. The store beyond is elegant and tasteful, as would be expected in this part of town. I don't normally come here unless I'm meeting my mother for lunch, at least not anymore. As a child and teen, I walked these streets and shopped in these stores because everyone else I hung out with did, but now I'm better at snagging what I need from Target and ordering everything else from Amazon.

I pull open the door and step inside, suddenly feeling ridiculous that I took the time to put together one of my nicer casual outfits this morning. Since most of the racks around me are filled with women's clothing, I don't know if they'll be able to see the difference between Levi's and 7 for All Mankind jeans, but I wore the ones Mom gave me for Christmas last year just in case. The hoodie is Peter Millar instead of Champion, but the nicer wrapping isn't making me more confidant.

If anything, I feel more like an impostor.

"Good morning. Well, I suppose it's just rolled into afternoon, hasn't it?" An elegant older woman with a sleek blonde bob approaches from the antique table that holds a slim, delicate register.

I give her my best smile. From Emma's pictures I know this isn't Amy's mother, so it must be Aunt Jade. "Hi. I'm looking for Amy?"

Her professional, welcoming smile warms into one of curiosity. "Amethyst? She's in her office in the back."

I wait, hoping she'll give me an indication of whether or not I'm supposed to go back on my own or wait for her to call Amy forward.

She doesn't look as if she's decided which to do yet either. Instead she asks, "Did you bring her lunch?"

The bag in my hand crinkles as I lift it, as if this woman will be able to see through the thick brown paper stamped with a large Randall's Deli logo. "I brought lunch for all of you, unless you don't like soups and sandwiches."

"Soup sounds lovely. Why don't you bring that back to our break room?"

As I move further into the store, I feel a lot better about this idea than I did walking down the sidewalk. This is good. I can see Amy at work, see how she's currently communicating with clients, see her.

I don't know why I was so worried about this.

Another sophisticated, older blonde woman is in the back room when we enter. This is Emma and Amy's mother. I can't see Emma in the woman's features, but the eyes are an exact match for Amy's, as is the smile she bestows upon me when I enter.

"This man brought us lunch." Jade's lips are curved into a mysterious smile.

"Oh? Did we order a delivery?"

"No. He's here to see Amy."

She looks me up and down and I have the sneaking suspicion that not only can she identify the brands of my jeans and hoodie, but she's figured out my socks are Hanes and my Nike shoes were bought on the clearance rack.

"Are you a client?" Amy's mother asks. "I didn't know she was branching into menswear. How exciting."

"Ah, no. I'm just a . . . friend."

"What's going—Jason!"

I whirl around to find Amy in the door of the break room and the last of my trepidation melts away. Coming to see her today was a fabulous idea. As was the food. Because no matter how well-to-do people are, they love getting free food.

"I brought you lunch." I hold up the bag again. "Soup and sandwiches."

The aunt takes the bag from me and begins to unload it on the table. They open the lids from the Styrofoam soup containers and the wonderful deli smells fill the air of the small break room. I can't seem to stop looking at Amy with my tongue stuck to the roof of my mouth until I see them starting to unwrap the sandwiches.

"Oh, wait." I turn to the table and snag up the one with "Special, JSN" written on the wrapped in bold marker. "This ones mine."

All three women stare at me.

"It's an avocado, bacon, and pastrami sandwich with honey-glazed onions. They make it special for me."

Amy's face breaks out in a grin. "You have a special sandwich?"

"Yeah. We maintain their online ordering app, so . . ." Randall was one of my first clients. Back when I was building a general tech and website company and before we'd grown large enough to specialize in augmented reality.

"Oh, are you here to fix our website?" Amy's mother looks at me with raised eyebrows, but she darts a speculative glance at her daughter before returning her smile to my direction.

I'm glad I've just taken a bite of my sandwich because chewing and swallowing gives me time to get my thoughts in order. "I . . . can." I turn my attention to Amy. "What's wrong with the website?"

"Nothing," Amy grumbles. "We just have a few people"—her eyes cut to her mother—"that can't seem to understand the online scheduling portion. We pay a support team to help us straighten them out."

Her mother sniffs. "We wouldn't have this problem if your sister would just join the family business like you did."

Wow. I thought Emma had been exaggerating the issue, but she wasn't. Since I also know Amy's styling work is not actually part of the family business since we signed the contract with Styled Trinkets, LLC, I can only assume that both twins are rebelling in their own ways.

As someone who knows how hard it is to buck the family norm even with parental support, I can only imagine how difficult this has been. If I'd been on the fence about helping Amy expand before, I'm fully on board now. Personal conflicts aside, she needs help to find the next steps in her life, and I am in a position to do that.

Is it sacrilegious to use the excuse of Christian brotherly support to get closer to a woman I'm interested in?

No. She came to me and even if this attraction goes nowhere as it probably should, I'm still her brother in Christ.

I take a deep breath and focus on eating my sandwich.

Eventually my silence gives the women permission to discuss the latest gossip and fashion news. I tune out what the aunt and mother are interested in discussing, but I home in when Amy joins the conversation. Anything she finds intriguing, I want to know more about.

I'm like a child who can't stop poking at a bruise on their leg.

The trending length of sleeves might be beyond even my ill-fated budding interest, though.

At one point the bell rings in the boutique and the older women step out to help their customers.

Amy considers me as she idly swirls a spoon through the half container of minestrone sitting in front of her. "You brought me lunch."

The toppings that have dropped from my sandwich to land on the open wrapper are excessively interesting all of a sudden. "I did."

"Why?"

"Because understanding how your business currently works is essential to building the most beneficial app for your expansion."

"So this is a business call? Do you bring all your client's lunch?"

I can't quite bring myself to say yes, because with any other client I'd have made an appointment, and I almost never initiate work meals. I hate doing business over food.

"Ah, no. The lunch is . . . personal." I want to leave it there, part of me wanting to boldly return to the conversation about dating with yet another reversal on my position, but when I look up to gauge her reaction, I'm not encouraged. She's biting her lip and looking at the wall behind my head.

"Jason—"

"Because of Emma." I cut her off because I know that tone. It's the one women use when they intend to let the guy down gently. I've already been friend-zoned, at least in part by myself, and she needs to know that I remember that.

Also, I need to work harder at remembering that.

Emma is going to throw a pillow at me if she learns I used her as a buffer though. Partly because she hates being a pawn but also because she'll know that means I was at least thinking about shooting my shot with her sister. And I don't need my best friend verbalizing all the reasons I know I'm currently being an idiot. Then I won't be able to ignore them anymore.

"Because of Emma?" Amy asks slowly, reminding me that I need to focus on the tricky conversation I'm currently in the middle of instead of worrying about one that's yet to come.

"Ah, yeah. You know she and I are good friends."

"So she says."

"And you're her twin sister."

"So our mother says." She gives a shrug. "I don't remember Emma being born. I was too busy doing the take-my-first-breaths thing."

I grin. "But you've seen the video, I presume? Emma says she's been tortured with it on many occasions."

Amy folds the wrapper from her chicken sandwich with precise care. "Ah, yes, I have seen the video. In all its gory glory." She shakes her head. "Normally my mother is the most fastidious of women, but when it comes to that . . ." She shudders.

"Anyway," I say as I crumple up my own wrapper to toss into the trash. "It just seems like the connection removes some of the normal barriers I would have with a client."

She considers me. "Does it remove some of the price, too?"

I wince because I did indeed discount the quote I gave her because of Emma.

"You didn't." Her features shift into an expression of stunned irritation. Despite having the opposite coloring from her sister, the glare is eerily familiar to the look I get from Emma from time to time.

I blink. "Wow. You look just like Emma." I wave one hand toward her hair in a wavy motion that indicates the large curls rolling over her shoulder and down her back. "I mean. Not the hair. Or the clothes. But that expression. Exactly the same."

"Is this the look she gets when you do something foolish?"

"Our friends and family discount isn't foolish. Lots of companies do that."

"But I didn't ask for it. Skipping to the front of the wait-list was supposed to be it."

"That's a bigger favor than you think." I wince again. "The wait-list is a couple years long."

She opens her mouth but stops to really process what I just said. Everything from her posture to her attitude deflates as she sits back in her chair. "Oh. Thank you, then. I guess."

We need to change the subject before she starts poking too hard at my reasons for bringing her lunch again. "So." I look around the break room. If I hadn't come in through the boutique I'd think I was in a recently remodeled suburban kitchen. "Is this where you do your work?"

"No, I have an office across the hall."

I stand and clear up everything except the older women's half-eaten lunches. "Let's see it."

AMY

My breathing isn't quite steady as I lead Jason from the break room to my office. Having seen his office, I'm not concerned that he'll think mine is messy or shabby. There's a bigger chance he'll think it's snobby or pretentious. I'm a stylist working out of a high-end fashion boutique though. I can't exactly allow my space to look unpolished.

Still, Emma makes fun of the impracticality of my French antique desk. Will Jason?

It's the first thing he walks over to when we step into the office. He runs his hand along one of the curved legs with awe. "Where did you find this piece? It's in excellent condition." He lowers one knee to the floor and sticks his head beneath the surface. "Original finish?"

I nod, even though he can't see me. "A little bit of refurbishing and an extra coat of protective varnish since I use it as a desk, but yes."

"My mother likes to drag me antique shopping. She says it's either clothes or furniture." He pulls his head out and grins up at me. "I always choose furniture."

I look over his outfit, which is far nicer than anything I've seen him in to date. "Did she buy those clothes?"

"Ah, yeah." He stands to his feet with a sheepish expression. "It didn't feel right walking into a boutique in my normal T-shirts."

"It's still jeans and a hoodie."

"Yes." He smooths the front of his shirt down with one hand. "But it's expensive jeans and hoodie. At least, I'm assuming so since my mother likes to scour the sale racks at Neiman Marcus for me."

I try not to laugh but it comes out as a snort of surprise. "Has she met you? I mean, you look fabulous." I don't pass up the excuse to look him over. His mother certainly knows her son's size because those designer jeans fit him perfectly. The hoodie is still a hoodie, but the look suits him. "But Emma put her foot down about shopping there and your average outfits aren't well . . ."

He chuckles. "I will only step in the store under duress, but a gift is a gift. Who knows? Maybe she truly did land a good bargain on these."

"So it's a price thing for you? You don't think quality clothes should be expensive?"

"I think there's a point at which they cross over from costing what they're worth to costing what the name is worth."

I can't argue with him on that one, but it still makes me itch beneath my skin as I spy the subtle vision board on the corkboard in the corner of my office. It's a collection of local important figures I'd wanted to work with and photos representing various social goals and things I wanted to acquire. One of my ambitions was to be one of those names that could charge a premium price for my work. I wanted my name to be impressive when people wore it.

Part of me still wants it, but I'm not sure if I should.

Jason is noticing the corkboard, too, and the only thing keeping me from ripping it down in shame is the fact that he probably doesn't know who those women are or what the photos might represent.

He gives the corkboard one last look before turning his attention back to me. "Tell me about your business."

"What do you want to know?"

"Pretend I was a potential client. What would you tell me about your services?"

I pull out a binder from the short bookshelf by the door and cross to the desk to lay it open. "I offer several packages, but my premium styling service is a full closet Look Book."

"Is that what you want to recreate on the app?"

He doesn't wait for my answer as he lays the binder on the table and flips it open. Down the side march tabs labeled with purposes such as Evening Out, Day at the Office, and Day Wear. Just about every clothing requirement is covered. There's even a Special Occasions tab in the back that has suggestions for a funeral, a wedding, or a parent-teacher conference.

"This is a copy of the book I made for one of my most inclusive clients. She wanted to make sure she looked her best in each and every situation."

"Even sleeping, it seems." Jason flicks a finger against the *Loungewear and Pajamas* tab.

I swallow. "There could be a fire alarm."

His smile is crooked as he lifts his gaze from the book. "Was that her concern?"

"Firefighters are cute." I flip to the Day at the Office tab. "Her words. Not mine."

He shifts a little, turning to face me more than the book. "You aren't one of those girls who has a thing for a man in uniform?"

"No." I speak without truly thinking through my answer. I've had this conversation with girlfriends before. "Uniforms may indicate noble and brave sacrifice, but they usually come with a pitiful paycheck."

My hands fly from the pages to cover my mouth. I can't believe I said that. I mean, it's true. And I do think I would have difficulty dating a man whose financial security prospects were so slim. I'm not, however, nonchalantly proud of that truth. Not anymore.

Jason doesn't seem offended, though. In fact, he's laughing hard enough that he's taken a step back and pressed his hand to his midsection.

Heat crawls up my neck and I'm almost thankful for the interruption of my vibrating phone.

It rattles against the desk, indicating a new text message. Before I can even pick the phone up, it rattles again. A third message comes in as soon as I pick up my phone.

Jason's mirth fades as he watches my face grow concerned. Then he's reaching for his own pocket as his watch lights up with the indication that he, too, is getting messaged.

It doesn't take twin premonition to know who might be messaging the two of us at the same time and I'm more nervous than concerned as I look down at my screen.

> EMMA: Why is Jason at the boutique?

> EMMA: How do you know him?

> EMMA: How long have you known him?

I start to look at Jason to ask how he wants to play this when another message pops onto the screen.

> EMMA: Please tell me you aren't dating him. You said you weren't dating anymore because you were looking for something new. How does that translate into going after Jason?

Going after Jason? As if I'm trying to lure him in and use him up like a sample of premium shampoo?

It doesn't matter how Jason wants to play this. My sister needs a talking to.

ME: Jason is a big boy and can handle himself. Just because you found your HEA doesn't make you the expert on dating.

EMMA: So you ARE dating him?

ME: I didn't say that.

EMMA: So you aren't dating him?

ME: I didn't say that either and the way you're speaking to me doesn't deserve an answer or any gossip

EMMA: Fine. I'll ask Jason.

I drop my phone on the desk and circle around to snatch Jason's phone from his hand. "Do not answer her."

His eyebrows wing upward. "Why not? If I don't, she'll be waiting in the office when I go back this afternoon."

"Sneak in the back."

"There's only one door."

I frown. "That seems like a fire violation."

He grins. "I mean she'll be in my office. Probably even in my chair with her feet propped on my desk as she glares at the door waiting for me."

"Don't you lock your office?"

"Yes."

"She has a key?" I know these two are friends, but I'm beginning to see it's more than just a normal guy-girl friendship. I truly am a romance cliche, crushing on my sister's best friend.

How weird.

"Still." I shake his phone in my hand. "She should have to stew about it. Maybe you can work from home the rest of the day or something. That's what she does a lot."

"I . . . could."

"Good. Do that."

I go to hand him his phone back but my eyes land on the screen.

> EMMA: You carried a Randall's bag into my mother's boutique.

Oh, my goodness, does she have access to the security cameras?

> EMMA: I hope you aren't trying to woo my sister with minestrone.

> JASON: What's wrong with minestrone?

> EMMA: That's the part you're going to respond to?

A partial message is in the process of being entered. It currently says, "Your sister is" and I would dearly love to know what was going to come after that.

Jason clears his throat, and I realize I'm rudely reading another person's messages. "I'm so sorry," I say as I shove the phone back at him.

He takes the device and pockets it even as it starts vibrating again.

My voice is hesitant as I ask. "What are you going to tell her?"

He's looking at me as if trying to read my mind through my eyes. It's disconcerting. "I'll tell her you're a client. That's the truth."

"Right." I think about sitting next to him in church for the past three weeks. I think about all the helpful videos and resources he's been sending my way. I think about our kiss. I think about our conversation about why dating would be a bad idea. I think about what it would be like to close my office door and kiss him again.

Then I think about having a repeat of Jason telling me all the reasons why it's a bad idea. This time Emma will join in because there's a camera covering the door to my office as well and if my sister has access to those feeds, she's probably watching me right now.

My hand itches to flip off the camera, but I'm trying to be a new person and I don't think that's proper behavior in the Christian handbook.

I should also probably stop referring to the Bible that way.

The atmosphere in the office has gotten tense and awkward, so I nod toward Jason's phone. "Who uses the word woo anymore?"

Yeah, I don't think that's the subject change we needed.

He nods to the desk. "Who prints out that much paper anymore?"

I gasp, ready to defend my binder. It's a work of art covered in leather, not one of those plastic and vinyl numbers from an office supply store. His grin stops me, though. He's teasing.

My phone buzzes again and I look at it even as I tell myself I shouldn't.

EMMA: You told him not to respond to me?

I glare at the camera. Does it have sound?

ME: Why are you spying on me?

EMMA: Why are you keeping things from me?

ME: Oh, because you're the world's best example of an open book.

I turn off the screen and lay my phone face down on the desk where it continues to buzz but I don't pick it back up. Instead, I cross my arms over my chest and glare at it until I hear a strange noise from my right.

My gaze lifts and connects with Jason's. We stare at each other for several moments and then suddenly burst into laughter.

I lean back in my chair and he leans back against the wall.

"So." I cross my legs and let one foot bounce in the air as I consider Jason. "Do you frequently woo the ladies with Randall's Deli?"

He actually blushes. "I can't say it hasn't become my go-to first move."

"That's terrible."

He rubs a hand along the back of his neck. "I know. Good thing we've already decided not to do the dating thing, huh?"

I cannot tear my gaze from his face. His words are saying one thing, but his eyes . . . My swallow is loud in my ears. "Good thing. As your friend, I can tell you it's probably not the best opening move."

"Not classy enough?"

"Too risky. Do you know how many women aren't eating bread right now?"

"Hence the minestrone."

"Hence?"

He shrugs. "Goes with the word woo."

The man is simply too cute. The same urge I gave in to a week ago rolls through me again and I want to push my way around this desk and plant my lips on his.

I sigh and drop my head to back to rest on the top of my chair. "I want to kiss you again."

The sound he makes is unidentifiable. A groan? A laugh? A cough? A weird gurgle of emotional turmoil pulled from the depths of his toes?

"I know it's a bad idea." I press my fingers into my eyes. "But I'm still learning how to resist that urge."

"Is that how you used to pick your dates? By who you wanted to kiss?"

I sigh. "That and who would increase my social power if I was seen on their arm."

The silence in the room suddenly feels heavier and I lift my head to find Jason looking at me with something that might be judgement for the first time since I met him.

"Really?" he asks.

"Well, yeah." I run my finger along the seam of my trousers, allowing the fine stitching to keep me grounded. "I had goals in life, and they required I connect with the most important people in the South. Like it or not, those important people like connecting with other important people."

"And you would choose your dates for what they could do for your reputation or what social doors they could open."

"Sometimes." I wrap my arms around myself. "I'm not doing that now." I can't help giving him a pointed look as he stands there in a hoodie and jeans before mumbling, "Obviously."

"Ugh, direct hit." He gives an exaggerated flinch and tries to smile, but I can tell there's something real underneath it.

"I don't . . . I mean . . ." This is why I'm not ready for this.

I snatch up my phone. There're several messages from Emma, but I ignore them as I pound out a text.

ME: I just hurt Jason's feelings and it's all your fault.

I toss the phone back on the desk and look up to find Jason watching me with raised eyebrows. My finger extends to jab at the discard phone. "This is all her fault."

"What is?"

I wave one hand in the air. "This."

"You wanting to kiss me is Emma's fault?"

"Us making it weird is."

"Pretty sure we're capable of doing that on our own."

I sigh.

"For the record, I want to kiss you, too."

"There is way too much kissing talk for a professional conversation."

It's his turn to sigh. "Right. Professional."

"Yep."

He looks at the floor for a moment then drops into the chair I keep for clients and pulls the binder over to him. "Okay. Tell me more about how this works."

As I go through the details of how I do my business and answer his questions about how I choose the clothing, anyone looking into the office would think we were nothing but friendly professionals.

Both of our phones still buzz occasionally but neither of us checks to see how often those notifications are from Emma.

We'll have to deal with her soon enough.

JASON

S ince I have my computer with me, I do as Amy suggested and don't go back to the office. I also don't go home because Emma has a key to my condo as well as my office. I wouldn't put it past her to go looking for me when I don't come back to work.

Instead, since I'm not that far away, I go to my parents' house. I also turn off location on my phone so Emma doesn't know where I've gone.

I don't know that I ever realized how totally connected our lives are until I'm attempting to avoid her.

No one is home when I get there, but that's not a problem since I just need somewhere to sit and a reliable Internet connection. The afternoon flies by as I answer emails, review reports, check in on project statuses, and comment on a few design debates. I work an hour longer than my normal sign off time, partly because I took a longer lunch than I should have, but also because I want Emma to have given up and headed over to Carter's for dinner.

It's almost 7:00 when I let myself into my condo and find Emma sitting in one of my kitchen chairs. She positioned it right in front of the door so there's no way to miss my entrance.

I step aside so the door can click shut and slide my computer bag to the floor as I look around the apartment.

"What are you looking for?" Emma's voice is tight.

"Carter."

"Why would Carter be here?"

"Because you don't go anywhere without him these days?"

She frowns. "That's not true."

I hold up a hand because I did forget one exception. "My bad. You don't go anywhere besides work without him."

Her grunt of annoyance lacks conviction. If she even thinks to challenge me on this one, I'll be the one on the attack instead of the defensive.

"You act like I've abandoned the rest of my life to hang out with Carter."

"I didn't say that." I walk past her and start hunting through my kitchen for what I'm going to feed myself for dinner. I'm not sure if she's staying to eat, but I look for something that can feed two just in case. I can always eat the leftovers tomorrow.

She follows behind, talking as if she didn't hear me agree with her. "I still host our board game club, and you and I still go to dinner and have movie and video game nights."

I stop in the process of pulling out a bag of frozen hashbrowns and look at my friend. Without a word, I drop the bag on the counter and cross to her. One of my arms drops across her shoulders and the other extends to point across my open-plan living space to a corner by the window. At one point I had a life-size Iron Man suit model in that corner. Now, it stands in my home office because I felt bad for the way Carter had to keep moving things around to get the best light for some of the sketches he was doing. He's been experimenting with colored pencils, apparently.

That corner of my home now boasts a chair and a small side table, perfect for holding a drink and a container of pencils. I'll say this for the man, he can happily amuse himself while Emma and I animatedly argue about movies and video games. I don't mind him tagging along with her, but she can't say he isn't always there.

Emma shifts beneath my arm and juts her nose into the air. "So?"

"Really?" I walk back into the kitchen shaking my head.

"If you didn't want him to come, you could have told me."

"If I didn't want him to come, I wouldn't have bought him a chair." I pull out a bag of frozen meatballs. "Are you staying for dinner?"

"No, I—" She stops mid-sentence as if realizing what she's about to say. While Emma and I still hang out a lot—with Carter, of course—one thing that has changed is how often we eat together. She was my takeout partner, my throw something from the freezer into the air fryer partner, my grab a quick bite after work or church partner.

Now she's not.

"Yes." She hoists herself up to sit on my counter. "I'm staying." She grabs her phone and punches out a quick text before sliding it back into her pocket.

I silently put another portion of meatballs into the air fryer and grab a pan to cook the hashbrowns in. I don't remember feeling this awkward around Emma since my sophomore year of college when we went on a handful of dates because it seemed like we should try.

It was an absolute disaster, but I'm glad we did it. Otherwise, we'd always have wondered.

That this moment feels much the same worries me. I understand that Carter being around changes things, but I don't want to completely lose what Emma and I have.

"Are you dating my sister?" she finally blurts out after several minutes of silence.

I'm glad she phrased it that way because now I can answer with complete honesty. "No."

"Oh."

I glance at her as I flatten the potatoes into a single later in the frying pan. "Did you want me to be?"

"No." The hard vehemence of her answer makes me wince, but I doubt she sees it since I'm facing the stove.

"Glad we had this talk."

She sighs. "I just . . . why were you at the boutique?"

"Your sister hired us."

"We have a two-year wait-list."

"I gave her the friends and family privilege."

"We don't have a friends and family privilege."

"Apparently we do because I gave it to Amy."

She can't argue with that because, despite everything, it's technically my company. I can make any policy I want, within legality and reason.

I shouldn't have underestimated Emma's ability to debate. "We don't have the space."

I look at her, eyebrows raised. "I seem to recall we found the space when you wanted to do a special project."

She pouts. "I donated my overtime."

I shrug and turn back to the hashbrowns. "This time I will."

"You're going to work for Amy for free?"

"You would."

"She's my sister."

"Yes, she is."

Her jeans scrape against the solid surface as she fidgets on the counter. "Of course I'd put in some effort for my sister."

"And I'm choosing to put in effort for my best friend's sister as well, or am I still not allowed to touch that part of your life?" I hope she doesn't catch the bitterness that I feel creeping into my voice. It's her right to have privacy after all, even if we did exchange a full set of keys.

"It's a bit too late for you to check." There's no missing her annoyed tone. I don't even think she tried to hide it.

I snatch a bag of frozen steamer broccoli from the freezer and throw it in my microwave with more force than necessary before leaning against the counter across from Emma, arms folded over my chest to glare at the person who probably knows me better than anyone else alive.

At one point I thought that went both ways, but now I'm not so sure. "What are you actually upset about, Emma, because this doesn't make any sense to me."

She kicks her feet a few times while she contemplates my floor. "I'm worried about you."

"Why?"

"Because . . ." She sighs. "There's a reason I never introduced you to Amy. Well, an additional reason beyond the obvious."

"The obvious being your desire to not have anyone see you pretending to be someone else in order to keep your family happy?"

A flush of red crawls up her neck. "Yes."

I give a sharp nod but move on because I don't really care about her masking a different personality in front of her family. I just mind her hiding it from me when I welcomed her into my own complicated family situation. My mother even invites Emma to our Christmas party, though she rarely comes. "What's the other reason?"

"Amy has . . . aspirations."

I want to tease her, to say something sarcastic like *How dare she?* but Emma is being serious right now. Also, I saw the vision board. My mother's picture is in the corner. Has Emma seen it? Will she tell me about it? "And?"

"Amy's image is important to her. My mother raised us to try to infiltrate high society."

I can't help but grin. "Infiltrate?"

"There's not a better word for it. She sent us to the most prestigious private school she could. We were there on scholarship, but she acted like weren't. I didn't even find out until my seventh-grade year. She pretends to have a household staff, but she doesn't. She has a maid service that comes in once a month to do a deep clean."

"This is your mother, not your sister."

"But Amy's just like her. Not when it comes to the fake prestige, but in ambition. She's planning to get there through her clothing and her boyfriends."

Is that the person she is or the one that she was? I think about the woman I've spent time with, the one I've chatted with. She didn't seem consumed with social ambition.

Unless . . .

"She doesn't know who I am." I say it like a statement, but it's also a question.

"No. At least, I don't think so. I've never mentioned it."

I grew up with the address, school, and opportunities Emma's mother would salivate over. The same ones Emma is saying Amy craves as well. The ones I turned my back on because I felt like it removed me from the rest of the world.

The ones Amy admitted she used to look for in a boyfriend.

There are stories of kids growing up in impoverished areas or in the foster system, watching the families on TV and wondering why they couldn't have school experiences like those, Christmases like those, families like those. I was the same way, except for the fact that, when it was just the four of us, my family seemed TV Normal, just with better vacations and box seat tickets to the Atlanta Braves. It was everything else in my life that felt off. I wanted more Malcolm in the Middle and less Gossip Girl. And yes, I watched Gossip Girl in high school. For the year I dated a girl who liked to watch it, at least.

I went to college, determined to make the sort of life I wanted. I stayed in a dorm, got a job as a teaching assistant for a year, ate off the cafeteria meal plan, and basically did my best to look average. I watched commercials for a month and then drove around to stores like Old Navy and American Eagle to buy clothes that matched what others would be wearing.

I met Emma my sophomore year. At the time, she seemed like a bird venturing from the nest that needed protecting. Eventually we became friends.

Now, it appears she's decided I'm the one who needs sheltering.

I don't know how I feel about that.

"If you think Amy only wants status and you think she doesn't know I have access to it, then what are you worried about?" I flip the hashbrowns in the pan.

"I don't want you to get hurt."

I look at her over my shoulder. "Seriously?"

"Yes, seriously. Amy is . . ." She sighs. "Guys like Amy."

Since I like Amy, I can't really refute that statement. "Guys also have brains. I don't let my emotions dictate my actions." If I did, I probably would be dating Amy. That post-kiss conversation was heading into go-on-a-date territory before I derailed it.

Emma groaned. "You took her Randall's Deli."

"I like Randall's Deli."

"It's also your go-to move when you like a girl but you're trying to pretend you're not all in yet."

I scoff and pull the broccoli from the microwave. She's right, but as I've already been informed that this move is lame, I'm not going to admit it. "I do not."

"You so do." She laughs. "Nadia, when she started visiting the church."

"The deli is close to the church and has good outdoor seating."

"What about Carly?"

I frown because that name is not ringing a bell and I usually remember people pretty well, especially if it's a girl I was potentially crushing on. "Who?"

"Zach's sister?"

I roll my eyes. "I wasn't interested in her."

She gives me a skeptical look. "You weren't?"

"No. I was trying to keep her from convincing Zach to take extra vacation days because I needed him on that project."

"Keep telling yourself that."

"I don't even remember her name."

"Which makes you a jerk, not an uninterested party."

I flip off the stove burner and plate up the hashbrowns. "What is this? You lie in wait in my home, attack my past . . . who are you and what have you done with my best friend?"

"Ugh. I'm sorry. You're right." She props her elbows on her knees and drops her head into her hands. "I'm just worried."

"About me or Amy?" I add the meatballs and broccoli to the plates and take them to the table before returning to the fridge to grab two cans of flavored water.

"Both?" Emma pushes off the counter and crosses to plop herself into a chair at the table.

"Why me?"

"Because Amy will chew you up and spit you out."

I frown because the Amy I've been getting to know doesn't seem like that type of person. "Are you sure?"

"Yes. I've seen her do it to guys before."

I pause in the act of picking up my fork. "Before what?"

Emma frowns as she stabs a meatball. "Before today?"

"So, you're assuming she's still the same, that choosing to believe in Jesus didn't change anything for her?"

"I . . ." Emma sighs and puts her own fork down. "I don't know. She won't talk to me about that."

This is a dangerous conversation, because if she starts complaining that Amy isn't coming to church or studying the Bible or whatever else sort of evidence Emma is looking for, I'll either have to lie to Emma or betray Amy's trust.

Best to steer away from it.

"Let's talk about me then."

"Your favorite topic." She resumes eating.

"Not really, but apparently you're obsessing over me these days. Carter must be thrilled."

"Carter is fine." She rolls her eyes. "But yes, I'm concerned about you."

"Why?"

She picks up her fork and toys with it for a few moments before dropping it back on her plate and pushing the whole thing away. "I think Carter is going to ask me to marry him soon."

A flood of different emotions rolls through me. It's not like it's a surprising statement, but still . . . it hits me somewhere. Marriage changes things. Whether we want to admit it or not, it does.

Two years ago, our friends Ben and Charity were dating but never missed a game night. Then they got married. Eloped, actually, and had a huge first anniversary party with their friends. By the time that party rolled around they weren't even pretending to be a part of game night. Now Michael and Veronica are moving in the same direction.

I understand how people tend to drift apart once kids come along, but I've never understood why marriage makes such a difference. Isn't it still like being engaged but you live in the same house now? You should be more inclined to go out with your friends, not less. After all, you get to see each other at breakfast every morning.

Emma and I will be different. At least, I think we will be. We should be. My relationship with her isn't like mine with Michael or Ben. Then again . . .

I take a deep breath. This isn't the time to worry about what might be in a year or two. "Are you ready for him to ask?"

"I think so." She blows out a full breath and smiles. "I know so. But I'm worried about you."

"Are you worried about Trina, too?"

"No, but Trina has . . ."

"She has what?"

"A life."

I snort. "I have a life."

"Yes. One that's twined with mine to a rather unhealthy level, I think. I didn't realize it until I was dating Carter, but we didn't leave a lot of room for anyone else."

"Apparently we did because you're planning to get engaged." I stand and take our plates to the sink. "What sort of ring do you want?"

"Why are you asking?"

"Aren't there best friend duties in this situation? Is Carter going to ask my opinion or something?"

"I . . . don't know? I've never been potentially engaged before."

"Well, I'm happy for you." I scrape the plates and load them into the dishwasher. "And I will be just fine. You are not the only person in my life."

"Really?" She crosses her arms over her chest and leans her nose into the air. "Name one thing you do on a regular basis that doesn't involve me."

I'm glad she only asked for one because I'm not sure I could come up with two. "I play racquetball with my friends from high school."

She blinks a few times and lowers her arms. "You do?"

I nod. "Yep. Basketball, too."

"You play basketball? How did I not know this?"

"Because it didn't involve you."

"What other secrets are you hiding?"

None. Well, none besides Amy. But she doesn't need to know that. "I thought we were supposed to be having more of our own things, not less."

The frown that crosses her face over being caught in her own words almost makes me laugh, but I manage to hold it in. If I laugh, she'll pounce. As it is, I have a small window to redirect her thoughts and if I'm lucky, she'll be home before she realizes we didn't have the conversation she wanted.

"I picked up a new game last week. Want to play?"

"You know I do." She moves toward my home office/game room. "If you've already been playing for a week, I should get an hour to acclimate myself."

"Not a chance." I chase after her, pretending to fight her for her preferred chair. "You can learn as you lose."

Two hours later, she calls it quits and I walk her to the door, good-naturedly ribbing her over getting blown up by her own grenade. I think I've managed to survive the evening when I close the door behind her, but my phone buzzes thirty seconds later.

EMMA: You swear you aren't dating my sister?

I drop my head lightly against the closed door with a quiet groan before answering.

ME: I am not dating your sister.

ME: I am, however, going to bed. Stop texting me.

Then I put my phone on Do Not Disturb.

AMY

I manage to avoid Emma for most of the week—a feat that shouldn't be difficult since we aren't really in each other's daily lives aside from texting, yet somehow the accomplishment feels like a decisive victory. Perhaps it's the effort I've had to put into my responses to the daily get-to-know-you question. Keeping the tradition going without allowing her the opportunity to ask nosy questions took a lot of mental gymnastics.

There's no avoiding her today, though. It's our monthly family dinner at Mother's house. For the first time in perhaps ever, I was the one who attempted to get it moved. After all, Thanksgiving is in three weeks. Technically that's the same month.

In other events that have never happened before, it was Emma who insisted the dinner stay as it was.

Probably because I've been avoiding her.

Mother hands me my normal drink as soon as I walk into the living room. I stare at the Cosmopolitan for several minutes before taking a sip. Am I still allowed to drink alcohol? The Internet seems to be a mixed bag on the topic and I haven't learned enough about Bible studies to feel confident in looking it up myself.

I suppose this is the kind of thing one learns in that new believer class Emma wants me to sign up for, but the description on the online registration form sounded . . . oppressive.

Slowly, I sip the drink. It still tastes good. Does that mean it's okay? I've tried other things I used to do all the time like flirt with men in the clubs or choose an outfit particularly for the way it showed off my physical assets in a tempting way instead of just a flattering way, and they have left me feeling decidedly uncomfortable. So much so that I've stopped doing them entirely.

That doesn't seem like a smart way to determine everything, though.

After all, I was still more than ready to make out with Jason on his living room sofa.

The thought of Jason has me taking a larger sip of my drink. Maybe I can ask him about the alcohol. He's been helpful on other things, giving me multiple sources so I can make up my own mind and encouraging me to do my own thinking.

And maybe I just like excuses to text him.

ME: Are Christians allowed to drink?

I slide my phone beneath my leg to keep it out of sight. Sometimes Mother has an issue with my attention being elsewhere, although she's complained much less since Carter started joining us on the regular.

Where are Emma and Carter, anyway? I would have thought she'd be arriving early so that she could ask me a million questions. I did receive an email from Jason's company that my project has been put on the docket and a design team assigned.

Does that mean I won't be working directly with Jason on it anymore? I hate that I won't have a built-in excuse to talk to him. Perhaps I need to make arrangements to meet with him at church Sunday instead of hoping he'll keep "accidentally" arranging it.

No. No. That is not the point of church. Nope.

My phone buzzes beneath my leg, almost eliciting a guilty squeal from my lips. Fortunately, I've drunk enough of the cocktail that it doesn't spill over the edge when I jump. After taking a deep breath, I slide my phone out.

> JASON: Depends who you ask.

> ME: I'm asking you.

> JASON: I don't drink, but I have friends that do.

> JASON: I'll send you some videos.

I can't help but grin. I've watched more YouTube in the past few weeks than the rest of my life combined. I tried the podcasts—after all, Emma swears by them and can't have a discussion without mentioning them—but I got distracted by the chatter that wasn't over the topic or lost in the depth of the discussion. Plus they are way too long.

Jason sends me short videos.

Emma and Carter arrive and more drinks are passed out in the small flurry of greetings. Theirs are non-alcoholic.

Finally we're settled in our seats. Mother and Aunt Jade are monopolizing Carter. His presence is still something of a novelty to them. To me, he's just become Emma's boyfriend. Still a bit of a new idea, but somewhat less fascinating.

Emma has abandoned her man to the wolves and has eyes only for me.

"An app, huh?"

I glance at Mother. "Shhh."

She rolls her eyes. "You're going to have to tell them eventually."

"That timing is mine to decide, not yours."

She frowns and I know she's thinking about how I said almost the same thing about going to church, meeting the pastor, and getting baptized.

I brace myself for yet another argument, but instead, she deflates with a sigh, slumping back into the couch that is quite comfortable but never allowed to be wallowed in. "I'm sorry," she says.

"You are?"

She nods. "I think, for the first time in our lives, I saw an opportunity to be the one who knew things about life instead of just books."

I can't hide my grin, though I lift my glass to try. "It seems you're doing the life thing pretty well. You're the one thinking about marriage, after all."

"There's more to life than marriage."

"Obviously." I roll my eyes. "Otherwise, I'd probably have at least one ex-husband by now."

The joke makes her shift a little in her seat, but it's true. I could have been married by now. Twice. More than one of my friends from high school has accomplished such.

"I guess I'm just worried that you're going to fill the void in your life with something unhealthy."

"Like a man?"

"Like a man."

I look down into my drink, suddenly glad for the bite it offers when I take a sip. "What makes you think I have a void in my life?"

She pulls out her phone and opens InstaTok. "I dunno . . . maybe the dozen posts you forwarded to me last Saturday night?"

I roll my eyes. "Spending a little time doomscrolling does not mean I have a void in my life."

"You were on your phone on a Saturday night."

"Clearly I'm becoming an old fuddy-duddy." Her statement is uncomfortably convicting though. I do have a void in my social life. As much as I've tried to stay connected to my friends, they don't seem as fun as they used to. Nor do they seem to like it when I turn the conversation to serious topics because they're being more than a little ridiculous.

"You could join my board game group."

I raise my eyebrows. "Your what?"

"My board game group. We're meeting Friday at my apartment."

"Board games?"

"Yes."

"Like what, Monopoly?"

"Okay, Rudolph." She rolls her eyes. "There's a lot more to board games than Candy Land and Pretty, Pretty Princess."

"Do you have a copy of Pretty, Pretty Princess?"

She narrows her eyes. "No."

I grin. "If I bring one with me, will you make everyone play it?"

She groans. "You're making that a condition?"

Emma should hardly be surprised. It was the only way she got me to play anything with her when we were little. I'd trade one game of Pretty, Pretty Princess for a round of Scrabble or Wii Bowling or whatever other game Emma was keen to play.

I don't say anything, just hold her eye contact and sip my drink.

"Fine." She groans. "If you bring Pretty, Pretty Princess I'll make everyone play it."

"Carter will look adorable in clip on plastic earrings." I can't stop myself from imagining Jason spinning the wheel and fighting for his own set of cheap, brightly colored bling. He's probably part of this board game group, but I'm not about to ask for confirmation.

She narrows her gaze at me. "Do you have a copy of Pretty, Pretty Princess?"

I scoff. "Hardly." I lift my phone and wave it in the air. "But the Internet is a treasure trove of random crap that can be sent to your doorstep in 24 hours or less."

"I'll pray it's out of stock everywhere."

"And I'll pray I find it on sale. We'll see who God decides to answer, won't we?"

She frowns. "I don't think that's how we're supposed to use prayer."

I shrug. "Probably not."

The rest of dinner moves along as normal. Mother preens over the latest invitation she's received or the most famous customer of the week. Aunt Jade argues that a senator's wife is more influential than the local evening newscaster. Carter deflects any question aimed at Emma.

And I poke at my food.

There was a time I'd have joined the argument because they are both wrong when it comes to the fashion world and the InstaTok influencer who dashed in when her luggage didn't make it with her to the convention she was attending has way more impact on trends. She tagged me in the video, and I've already gained 400 new followers.

But I don't care enough to correct them. Let them think we still live in the days of Jackie O, when everyone wanted to look like the beautiful political wife.

What I do care about right now is what Emma said earlier. I didn't think I had a void in my life. In fact, I thought the whole point of the ask Christ into my heart thing was to fill the void I had prior to praying on Emma's living room floor.

But if I make myself stop to consider it, I am a little lonely. Maybe a lot lonely. Or maybe I'm not lonely and Emma is just getting in my head. In the nearly thirty years we've been on this earth, she's never been the more socially savvy one. After we exchange our good night pleasantries, I sit in my car and pull out my phone.

A few years ago, my calendar started getting so full that it looked like a solid yellow block when I opened it. The solution was to color code different social groups and obligations. Not only did this make appointments easier to identify, it was symbolic proof that I led a full and varied life.

Looking at my calendar now, there's more than enough space to put another engagement. Instead of three or four colors overlapping on the same Saturday, I've got two or three colors scattered over an entire week. Of course, I won't find any blue since that's the color reserved for dates, but there isn't a single shade of green or purple to be found in the past two months either. Has it really been so long since I've planned a shopping excursion or gone to a night club?

There are plenty of yellows and tans because those are for work and I see a good assortment of pinks for my family obligations. But everything else—what there is of it, anyway—is shades of orange. My social life is now nothing but going out to eat and that's only happening a couple times a week.

No wonder I was scrolling InstaTok at 9pm on a Saturday.

Well, this is easy enough to fix, isn't it? As night clubs are never going to become my thing again since I'd been getting somewhat tired of them even before I chose to throw my life into a blender, I decide purple will now be casual, non-meal oriented social engagements.

I'll worry about a simpler term for it later.

For now, I open up Friday and create a lavender colored appointment for the evening. Then I open up my shopping tool that searches multiple store websites at the same time and type in Pretty, Pretty Princess board game.

Ten minutes later, I'm driving for home, satisfied that the first game I've owned in years will be delivered to my apartment by Tuesday, and Friday I'll take my first step toward making my new life as full as my old one.

JASON

"Tell me again why I had to get here an hour before I normally do? I had to leave work early." I toss the grocery bag holding two bags of chips onto the counter in Emma's apartment and help myself to her stash of flavored waters.

"Because," Emma says as hustles by me with her arms full of random items, "Amy doesn't make empty threats. Can you take those chips out of the bag?"

I'm glad I wasn't actively taking a drink because I'm choking on the air I was in the process of breathing. "Amy's coming?"

I do as I was asked and dump the plastic grocery bag out, sending the two bags of chips sliding across the counter. The barbecue ones come perilously close to tumbling over the edge, but they stop with only a corner of the bag jutting out into space. I'm not quite sure what to do with the grocery bag, though. While Emma and I have spent a lot of time in each other's homes over the years, her kitchen is not a place that usually holds grocery-related activities for us.

I fold up the bag and place it on the back of the counter. If there are leftover chips, I'll need it to carry them home.

Emma swoops through the kitchen area, grabbing the grocery bag and stuffing it into a box beneath the sink. Then she's opening and closing cabinet doors with an air of desperation that I'm torn between finding funny and concerning. I glance at Carter who has a small smile on his face as he shakes his head. Funny it is, then.

When her first tour through the small number of kitchen cabinets doesn't yield what she's looking for, Emma starts over at the beginning.

"What exactly are you looking for, honey?" Carter catches Emma before she can open the third cabinet again and wraps his arms around her.

"Bowls. For the chips."

Both Carter and I look at the chip bags.

"What's wrong with the bags?"

She scoffs. "If you think Amethyst Trinket eats chips out of the bag they came in, you need your head examined."

Carter tilts his head to the side. "I don't know that I've even seen Amy eat chips."

"That's because she doesn't. But if she did, they wouldn't be out of the bag."

I hold my hands up to stop the discussion. "I have questions."

"Of course you do," Emma mumbles. Her behavior this week has been just shy of avoiding me. I'd thought it was just more of the natural changes from her being in a relationship but I'm beginning to think it's something more.

"We'll come back to what you mean by that, but, first off, why is Amy coming tonight?"

"Because she has no life. She's not going out with her friends and her event attendance has more than halved." She shakes her phone at me. "She was texting me at 9PM. On a Saturday."

This is apparently supposed to tell me everything I need to know because she shoves her phone back in her pocket and lunges for the first cabinet again. "Maybe we can just have pretty bowls to eat from and then it won't matter what the chips were served from."

"Oh, no you don't." I cross the room and lift the stack of bowls from her hand and place them back in the cabinet. "Game night rules. Everything has to be disposable. No one's going to be stuck cleaning the kitchen."

"But Amy—"

"Is coming to game night. Apparently." I'm still confused as I why I had to be early, but I'm assuming that will eventually become clear.

"Right. Right." She takes a deep breath and seems to relax a fraction until a brief set of knocks breaks the silence. The door opens immediately after, and Amy steps in.

I've seen her in a lot of different looks so far, all of which have their own attractions, but this . . . this version of Amy might be the death knell for my resolve.

Her blond hair is pulled up into a ponytail that swings down her back in a waterfall of looping curls. She's in a pair of jeans that might just convince me designer labels are worth the price and a sweater that's three large strips of color. Her makeup is somewhere between what I've seen her wear to church and what she wore at the office, with bold eyeliner and a pale pink lipstick.

I could see this version of Amy hanging out on a Saturday. Maybe going for a walk before settling on the couch for a movie. Or maybe going to the pizza parlor or an arcade or even bowling. It would have to be one of the fancier bowling alleys with the leather couches and the shoes that don't look like forty-two people already wore them for a three-day tournament, but still, I could see her there.

It's an appealing image.

Our gazes connect and for a brief moment, she seems to hesitate. But the moment passes, and she walks in with her suitcase of a purse over her shoulder and a mischievous glint in her eyes. We've texted some this week and not all of it has been about her project, but she never mentioned coming to game night.

She plops her purse on the table and pulls out a box covered with cartoon princesses on it. "Ta-da!"

Emma covers her face with her hands and groans. "You found one."

"Did you doubt I would? If there's one thing I know how to do, it's shop."

"Well, let's get this over with." Emma gestures toward the table before looking at me and then Carter.

I ease toward the table, eyeing Carter to see if he has any more clue than I do.

Amy frowns. "I thought you said this was a group thing. I mean, technically three is a group, but . . . I kinda expected more."

"They'll be here in an hour."

Amy narrows her gaze. "You didn't want your friends to play Pretty, Pretty Princess?"

My gaze drops back to the cartoon-printed box. What sort of game is it?

"No, I didn't." Emma pulls out a chair and drops into it with a smile. "Besides, I looked it up and it's a four-person game." She points at herself and then Amy before sweeping her hand in my and Carter's direction. "Voila. Four people."

Amy's gaze connects with mine and her smile turns impish. "Let's play then."

Fifteen minutes later, I have a hunk of plastic clamped onto my left ear, a beaded necklace draped around my neck, and a bracelet hooked over my thumb because it won't fit on my wrist. Carter is doing a little better, seeing as he has both earrings, the necklace, and a ring. There's also a ridiculous plastic crown perched on his head. All he needs is the bracelet. Amy has all her pink plastic baubles but the ring, and Emma has somehow managed to only accumulate the necklace and the black ring that will ensure she loses. Given the simplicity of the game, I'm convinced she's cheating.

Emma flicks the spinner and quickly moves her piece down the board. "Put a piece back." She whips the beaded strand over her head. "I only have a necklace. That's not fair."

With narrowed eyes, I look at the board and count the spaces. "Oh, no, you don't." I nudge her piece one space back to sit on the instruction that she should take the crown. "I can count to four."

Her glare is comical as she puts the necklace back on and allows Carter to move the plastic tiara from his head to hers.

Amy's mouth drops open. "You're cheating in order to lose?" She leans back in her chair and crosses her arms as she purses her lips together. The pink plastic discs stand out against her blonde hair. Somehow she's making the atrocious jewelry look good.

Perhaps because her competition is a guy who has both blue discs clamped to the tops of his ears instead of the lobes.

"It's not that I want to lose, exactly." Emma twirls the black plastic ring around her pinky. "I just want you to win."

"Uh-huh." Amy points an accusing finger at her sister. "I don't think cheating is in the handbook."

"For the last time, the Bible is not a handbook."

"What is it then?"

"It's a book that teaches us about God and how He loves us and . . ." She trails off, probably searching for something to say that doesn't indicate the Bible teaches us how God wants us to behave.

Amy saves her with a shrug. "Fine. I don't think cheating is in the textbook."

I know Emma wants to argue against calling the Bible a textbook as well, but she doesn't. Instead, she takes a deep breath and rubs her hands over her legs. "You're right, it's not." One hand reaches up to straighten her plastic crown. "I apologize for cheating."

Amy reaches out and flicks the spinner. "It's not me you have to apologize to."

Emma frowns. "It's not?"

"Nope." Amy very deliberately hops her piece three places down the board where she lands on the remove-a-piece space Emma had tried to end up on. She slides the bracelet off and drops it back into the pile. "Pretty sure the Big Man cares more about why you'd let me win than I do."

I cover my mouth to keep from laughing at the utter shock on Emma's face. I glance to my right and accidentally meet Carter's gaze. He, too, is trying not to laugh. Hastily I look away to my left.

"Go ahead." Amy waves a hand in Emma's direction. "We'll wait while you pray for forgiveness."

A snicker escapes from behind my hand and Carter is covering a laugh with a cough.

Emma is just blinking at her sister. "I . . . Yeah . . . Okay."

Everyone waits while Emma bows her head for a few seconds. Then she looks up at her sister. "Since I also cheated to get this black ring, should I put it back?"

"No. Your inability to win until someone else saves you from that fate is your penance." Amy picks up the yellow earring. "That, and wearing these earrings for the entirety of game night."

"Oh, no, that's not happening."

"It's not?"

"Nope. God's forgiveness is total. Jesus paid the price so I don't have to do penance."

That's it. There is no holding back my laughter anymore. My bracelet falls off my thumb as my hand lifts to stifle the sound and I accidentally dislodge the earring in the process. By the time I've put everything back together, the whole table is watching me expectantly, waiting for me to take my turn.

I spin the dial, acquire my second earring, and then sit back in my chair. Five minutes later, Carter and Amy are both just in need of snagging the crown from Emma's head, I've lost my beaded bracelet, but gained a clunky pinky ring, and the game play has become oddly intense. Carter moves his piece and groans as he has to take the black ring of doom from his girlfriend.

"I thought you were supposed to give her a ring, not take one from her," I quip but soon find myself to be the only one laughing.

Amy is shaking her head but Carter and Emma both look at the floor as she spins the wheel. I think they might be blushing.

Fortunately, Amy attains the crown on her next turn and the game is blessedly over.

"Kinda sad to win this way because it means I don't get to wear the crown long." Amy adjusts the plastic trophy to sit better on her head.

Emma scoffs as she starts packing up the game. "Dare you to wear it all evening."

"Only if you wear the earrings."

"As if you would approve of my wearing giant yellow discs with an orange top."

"Since it's a hoodie that has a hole in the pocket, I don't think you're in danger of damaging your fashion credentials."

A small smile tugs at Emma's lips as she retrieves her yellow earrings. She'll never admit it, but I think she's actually glad her sister brought this game.

Once everything is back in the box aside from the crown and Emma's baubles, we grab paper plates of chips and salsa and wait for the rest of the gaming crew and the pizza to arrive.

"So," Emma says as she drags a chip across her plate, "when did you start making jokes about forgiveness and the Bible?"

Amy wipes the tips of her fingers on a paper towel. I've never seen anyone look so awkward while eating chips. "I don't know. I've been . . . finding my way."

"Finding your way where?"

"YouTube. A few online study sites." She breaks a chip in half. "Church."

"You've been coming to church?"

Amy is saved from answering by a knock on the door and the entrance of Trina.

Emma's attention is pulled away as Trina teases her about the plastic earrings and Amy uses that moment to take her plate of uneaten chips across the room to the kitchen situated along the wall.

I follow on the premise of loading my own plate full of more chips. "You doing okay?"

Amy nods and breaks the chip again. "I'm nervous. I don't remember the last time I was nervous about attending a party."

"When was the last time you were at a party full of people you don't know?"

"I know you."

"True. And Carter and Emma."

Her gaze tracks to her sister, an almost wistful expression flitting across her features. "Right." The chip is all but crumbs now. "Her favorite fruit is a chocolate-covered strawberry and she would rather eat cereal with chopsticks than eat soup with a fork."

I frown. "How do you eat soup with a fork?"

"I don't know, but that's the sort of stupid things I know about Emma now. Do I actually know her anymore?"

Since my older brother has always been one of my best friends and I've spent the rest of my life keeping a polite distance from anyone I didn't know well enough to consider properly vetted, I can't really relate to how Amy is feeling.

But I can sense that she's one breath away from snatching up her suitcase of a purse and fleeing.

"You won't fix that if you run."

"I'm not running."

"But you're thinking about it."

"How do you know?"

That is an excellent question. How do I know? It's not like she's inching toward the door or making the precursor moves to be able to claim an illness or a headache. But I know she's thinking about leaving. "I don't know, but apparently I'm not wrong."

"And you think I should stay."

"I think you came for a reason, and it probably wasn't to make me and Carter wear plastic necklaces."

"No." She snatches the crown off her head and lays it on the counter. "I don't know why I brought that game. I used to make Emma play it when we were children. I thought it would make me feel like we were close again."

"Didn't it? I mean, you seemed to be getting along."

She doesn't answer me as she pushes the plate of broken chips aside.

I look at the plate of tortilla chip dust. "Not a chips and dip fan?"

"I can't remember the last time I ate chips."

"Why not?"

"It's not exactly sophisticated."

I grab another plate and put five chips and a pool of salsa on it. "Then maybe it's time to remind yourself of the salty, crunchy goodness." After sliding the plate in front of her I pick up the discarded tiara. "And maybe it's time to remember that you are, in fact, a pretty, pretty princess."

Her look of exasperation is tinged with amusement. "I still think Emma somehow cheated to make me win."

"Absolutely. I saw her nudge the spinner, but that's not what I was talking about."

"It's not?"

"Nope." I place the crown on her head, doing my best to arrange it so the prongs don't mess up the sleek hair. "You are a child of God. By definition, the daughter of the King is a princess."

One side of her mouth tips up. "And you think I'm pretty?"

"That goes without saying." I lower my hands and tilt my head so I can meet her eyes. "You're still you, you know. Everything that has made you who you are all your life isn't gone. It's just . . . reoriented."

"What does that mean?"

"It means, you are still special and important and have something to offer. You just have to give yourself space to find where you want to offer it now."

Our gazes stay connected for another few heartbeats and then she slowly breaks a corner off a chip and dips it into the salsa. After she's crunched it a few times and swallowed, she gives a slight nod. "Okay. I'll stay."

"Good." I take my own plate, piled high with chips, and turn away from the kitchen counter, only to find the moment I thought was a private little aside has drawn the notice of someone else in the room.

Emma is staring right at me, and for the first time in recent memory, I can't tell what she's thinking.

AMY

I'm not sure what I thought game night was going to be like, but this isn't it.

My sides hurt from laughing and I'm truly enjoying seeing a side of my sister I've never seen before. She literally allowed herself to get dragged across the table rather than let go of the last spoon in the card game that I'm still not sure I understand.

I got out in the first round, and Jason lost the round after—what is it with these two and cheating to lose?—and spent the rest of the game trying to explain to me what was going on. The effort was an utter failure, but I really enjoyed the way he spoke the explanation into my ear.

Who knew the rules of a card game could sound sexy?

The last round is Emma versus her friend, Trina, and they are both standing, hunched over the pile of cards and the lone remaining spoon. I'm actually afraid for Emma's dining table at the moment.

"She didn't tell me you're all so . . . cutthroat," I whisper to Jason.

"Game night is not a joke around here."

"Clearly."

Suddenly cards are flying and Emma's arm is trapped beneath Trina who is curled up in a ball on top of the table.

After much squealing and yelling, Emma emerges triumphant, hand held high with a bent metal spoon in it.

"And that's why we have a dedicated set of spoons for playing this game." Jason laughs at the shock that must be present on my face.

At this point, months of daily questions aside, I'm not sure that I know my twin at all anymore.

Once the cards have all been picked up, as well as the chips from the plate that got sent flying in the melee, Michael pulls out a box that looks at least a little familiar. It a trivia game so there's not likely to be anyone hauled across the table.

There is, however, a debate over how many teams we're going to play. There's eight of us, so the choice seems to be two large teams or four small ones. Personally, I'm leaning toward the large one. I can hide better.

"I say we make the sisters team captains." Michelle looks from me to Emma with a grin.

"Captains?" Emma groans. "You mean we have to choose our teams like we're in elementary gym class?"

"You know," Trina says thoughtfully, "I never actually saw that done in gym class. It was just something they did on TV to make everyone hate gym."

"Whatever. We're doing it now." Michelle points at Emma. "You're the host, so it's only fair that Amy gets to pick first."

"But she doesn't know anyone." Michael nudges Michelle's shoulder. "Is it fair to ask her to pick her team when she doesn't know everyone's strong suits?"

"She knows Jason."

Everyone's attention flips from Trina to Jason to me and then back to Trina.

"How do you know that?" Emma's voice sounds calm, but I wince at the steely note underneath. A glance at Jason reveals he, too, heard the unease in Emma's question.

"They've been sitting together at church." Trina looks around, seeming confused at the reactions her statement is getting. "I mean, I thought that was why she came tonight. Aren't they dating?"

Oh. My. Goodness. I should have left after Pretty, Pretty Princess. At least I'm not wearing that ridiculous crown anymore as I force myself to meet Emma's gaze without flinching. Or wincing. Or crawling under the table. "We're not dating. Just friends."

"Right." Emma swallows visibly. "Captains. Amy picks first."

"Uh, yeah. I'll take Jason." No one has to move since he's already sitting next to me from having explained the previous game.

"Carter."

"Duh." Michael rolls his eyes at his wife. "Why did you put us through this again? Those were the most obvious first choices ever."

Jason leans in to press against my shoulder. "Pick Trina. She knows history."

I clear my throat. "Trina."

"Michelle."

It's Trina's turn to tell me what to do. "Pick Michael. Keeps things interesting." She smirks and kicks at Michael under the table.

I shake my head. "I can't do that."

"Why not? If Emma gets them both she'll practically be cornering the market on geography."

"But they're married."

"Which means they'll see plenty of each other when they go home tonight." She nudges me in the shoulder. "Come on. Game night is war."

"Obviously." I want to look to Jason and get his opinion, but my connection to him is already causing suspicion—not to mention the conversation Emma is going to want to have later. "Michael."

Which means Emma gets Mia and the game is set.

Twenty minutes later, Emma's half of the table is groaning as my team's piece once more lands on a fashion and culture question. I try not to smile. They may all have their strong points, but it's obvious that none of them have excelled in this category before.

"What furniture style emerged in the late 17th century characterized by elaborate ornamentation and curved forms?"

I bite my lip. I don't know the answer to that one.

"Baroque." Jason's voice cuts decisively through my tension.

"How did you know that?" Emma jams the card into the back of the box.

"My mother is an interior designer. I've heard way too much about furniture in my life."

"Ah." The sound of discovery leaves me before I can stop it, but I'm not about to let the rest of this group know I've been to Jason's home by explaining that I had wondered why a bachelor's residence looked so put together. I grab up the die and give it a roll before anyone can question me.

The game comes down to the very last question and Emma's team is ultimately victorious.

I'm completely drained and exhausted—two things I've never felt at the end of a social engagement before—and I slip out while everyone is cleaning up and putting things to rights.

Footsteps follow behind me on the stairs down to the parking lot and I turn to see Jason has escaped the coming inquisition as well.

I make a noise somewhere between a chuckle and sigh. "It's not going to stop her long, you know."

"I know. But I'm not about to let her corner me without knowing what you want to tell her first."

That's sweet. The man is sweet. He walks beside me as I round the corner to where I parked my red Mercedes. The parking lot directly in front of Emma's building has way too many trees and, despite the crisp briskness in the air, too many birds. I hate cleaning bird droppings off my car.

"Did you park over here, too?"

It's too dark to tell his cheek color distinctly, but he ducks his head a little as if he's blushing. "Ah, no. I'm walking you to your car."

I shake my head. "You don't have to do that."

"It's the gentlemanly thing to do."

"But we decided we're not dating."

"Yeah." He rubs a hand behind his neck. "But I'm still a gentleman."

"Right."

I open the driver's door and toss my bag into the passenger seat before turning to face Jason. He has one hand on the door and one hand propped on the roof, caging me into the space. It doesn't feel confining though. It's almost . . . cozy.

Why did we decide dating was a bad idea again?

He nods his head back toward Emma's apartment. "What did you think of game night?"

What did I think of game night? "To be honest, I don't know. It's . . . odd."

A confused frown slides across his face. "Really?"

"That's not . . ." I sigh, because this is one of those times lately where I feel like my own skin doesn't quite fit me anymore. Or perhaps it's something inside that doesn't work like it once did. Either way, my brain and my body aren't vibing and I'm not certain which one is off.

I lean into the V of my open door, putting a little bit more space between myself and Jason. "I think I had fun?"

"That's a good thing, right?"

"I suppose. But, at the same time, it felt odd. The closest I've ever come to participating in a game night was trivia night at a pub."

Jason winces. "Emma and I tend to get kicked out of trivia nights."

"I could see that." The two of them had definitely gotten heated in the trivia game. It's just one more side of Emma that I've never seen before. At the moment I'm a little too off kilter to think about that, so I pull the subject back to the more important issue at hand. "I don't think my trivia nights were like yours."

"How so? Isn't a trivia night a trivia night?"

I laugh. "Ah, no. I'm betting you and Emma went to a local pizza place or something like that. My trivia nights were at a club. We gave a lot more attention to how good-looking the other teams were than we did to who was in the lead."

"I see." He grins. "I don't think you were checking out the other team tonight. That would have been weird."

I laugh. "Yes." Especially since, for my money, the best-looking guy in the room had been leaning into my space to loudly whisper his thoughts on possible answers. "This was different."

"Good different?"

"Yes, but . . ." I sigh. "These are Emma's friends, Emma's world. I appreciate what she wanted to do, but I can't use her life to fill the void in my own."

"So you agree there's a void."

I lean into the car and snag my phone from my purse. He waits while I pull up InstaTok and thumb over to my friend Heather's stories. I turn the phone so Jason can see the video of three girls dancing. Heather's holding the phone high in the air, so it's easy to see the three heads of perfectly straightened hair, the tops of their snug dresses, and the pink martinis in their hands.

He pulls away a little bit, making a point of looking past the phone to meet my gaze. "What am I looking at?"

"My friends. My former friends? I don't know." I pull the phone back and watch the stories rolls by. "I'd have been in this video a few months ago, but now I can't even tell which club they've gone to. They stopped inviting me after the last time I went and ended up leaving early."

"Are you looking to make new friends, then?"

I turn off the phone and shove it into my pocket. Maybe it's the memory of years of nights at clubs dancing, drinking, and flirting, but I find myself settling into that perfect stance that positions myself to advantage. "I thought you were my new friend."

Despite the platonic words, I know I'm flirting with Jason. I can't seem to help it.

He leans more onto the side of the Jeep, propping his elbow on the side and running his hand through his hair. "Right. We're new friends. So how about you and I try finding you some more satisfactory void-filling activities?"

"What did you have in mind?"

"Ah . . ." The sounds trails off as he looks somewhere over my head. "You like plays and stuff, right?"

"Yes." I frown. "Do you?"

He shrugs. "Not really, but there is one place I like going."

I groan. "It's not some Dungeons and Dragons live thing, is it? Emma convinced us to count that as her cultural event obligation once and I've still not forgiven her for it."

Jason laughs and a shiver of goose bumps run up my arms. "No. Though I do enjoy those." He pulls out his phone and sends his fingers flying over the screen as he searches up something. "My mother is a lover of the arts as well, and when she was trying to expose me to the wonders of that world, there was only one place I actually enjoyed."

"And it was live theater?"

"Not just any live theater." He looks up from his phone with a boyish grin. "Shakespeare."

I'm glad the car is holding me up, because my knees suddenly weaken and wobble. Shakespeare is the only theater I've never found particularly interesting. "Ah . . . really?"

"Not a Shakespeare fan?"

"I mean, it's a little hard to understand."

It's his turn to show me his phone screen. "Have you ever seen it done at the Tavern?"

The picture on his phone is of a small room as far as theaters go. It's full of rough wooden tables and chairs, with a U-shaped balcony hovering over the edges. "Where is that?"

"Shakespeare Tavern. Downtown Atlanta. Much Ado About Nothing is playing this week. Looks like there's tickets available for tomorrow's show."

I bite my lip as he adds two tickets to his online shopping cart. "This sounds like a date."

He shakes his head. "Just going as friends."

"Is that what I tell Emma?"

He glances over his shoulder and then grins at me. "Why do we have to tell Emma anything? Pretty sure she didn't inform you of our visit to the hibachi restaurant a couple weeks ago."

"No, she didn't tell me about that."

"There you have it." He finishes buying the tickets and does something else on his phone that correlates with a buzzing of my own. He's likely sent me the event details. "I'll pick you up at 5:30. They have dinner available at the Tavern."

"Okay. We'll go to the Tavern."

He nods.

I swallow, trying to change the sudden dryness of my mouth. "As friends."

"As friends."

His gaze holds mine for several tense moments before he steps back and taps the side of my car.

I slide into my seat without saying a word and wait for him to close the door and step up onto the sidewalk.

As I drive away, the thought I've been holding off for the past fifteen minutes breaks through, no longer able to be suppressed.

I'm pretty sure Jason and I are both deluded idiots playing with fire and it's only a matter of time before we get burned.

JASON

The Shakespeare Tavern is a strange little place. The door looks similar to a small storefront on a downtown side street. If you didn't know what it was, you'd likely completely miss it. I hold the door for Amy, and instinctively my hand lands on her lower back to guide her through the opening. As if she'd lose her way in the three-foot space.

We're just friends. Dating would be a terrible idea. I could handle the fact that our mutual connection to Emma would make the relationship doomed to be messy, but Amy is still deciding who she is and what her life will look like now.

She doesn't need a boyfriend adding more variables to that.

Not that one date would make me a boyfriend, but it's hard to imagine getting involved with Amy in that way and not having it quickly evolve into something serious. I already think about her more than I did my last girlfriend. Just knowing I was going to be picking her up today had me distracted all afternoon.

She looks around the rather industrial-looking lobby. "This doesn't look like the picture."

"Just wait until we pass through that curtain. It's like stepping back in time. The theater is modeled after the Globe Theater where Shakespeare was originally played."

Her hair floats around her shoulders as she turns her head to glare at me with narrowed eyes. "This is a theater for nerds isn't it."

It's a statement, not a question, but I nod anyway. "Why do you think I like it?"

We move into the theater and go through the food line. I purchase two Cornish pastries and a fruit plate and soon we're sitting at our table. There are only two rows of tables between us and the stage, and Amy looks around with fascination.

"How have I never heard of this place? I thought I'd done everything in the Atlanta arts."

"It's not exactly a refined see-and-be-seen sort of venue."

She frowns and picks at her food. "Is that what you think I want?"

I lift my eyebrows. "I think it's what you did want. Isn't that the point of posting club stories on InstaTok?"

She nods her head sideways in reluctant agreement. "Do you think it's what I still want?"

"I can't answer that for you. Do you think it's what you still want?"

She sighs and sits back in her chair. "I can't say I don't want it. If I avoid that entirely, my business will all but fold. Even now I'm watching the door to see if someone I know comes in."

A flicker of unease worms through me as my gaze also flits to the door. I stopped having to actively avoid the public world I grew up in a few years ago because I'd done such a good job of disappearing that people stopped asking about me. It hasn't been something I've had to think about in a long time, but it's suddenly occurring to me how dangerous it is for me to take Amy out in public to places that have a possibility of drawing an encounter with one of my parents' friends.

Fortunately, the show starts and the lights dim. Anyone who comes in now won't be able to see us sitting here anyway.

As the comedy of errors plays out on the stage, I can't help but wonder if I'm the one who is a fool in this situation, because being friends with Amy is playing with fire. Is it worth the risk of being burned?

The public place might have given me pause, but there's no misgivings when I'm in a space where I can focus only on being with Amy. Conversation has not been an issue all night. Even during the show, she moved her chair closer to mine so we could lean our heads together and whisper about the onstage antics.

My car is filled with chatter from both of us as we talk about what we find worth coming downtown for and what is simply not special enough to bother with the traffic. Conversation moves easily on to other topics, even shifting to business and the ins and outs of managing clients. Amy has insights that I've never considered and thoughts my other business-minded friends would never come up with. We discuss what she's been learning in her Bible studies and the questions she's still struggling with. I share what I've been learning in my own discipleship times.

We talk so much that my throat feels parched, but I don't want to end the evening, so I suggest a stop for drinks before taking her home.

"I thought you were trying to show me a different way to have fun."

"There's more than one location open late to get a drink, you know."

She waves a hand toward the road out my windshield. "Lead on."

Her laughter fills the car as I pull into a 24-hour gas station. The convenience store is large and brightly lit and well known for its wide variety of Icees, fountain drinks, and coffees.

I park and climb out, circling the car to open her door as she continues to laugh. "This is definitely different."

"Not worried about being seen at the gas station?"

"Anyone seeing me is also at the gas station, so no."

We go inside and peruse the drink section. Amy looks like she's giving the selection serious thought. "Which of these options don't have caffeine?"

"Well." I look around the offerings as well, because late-night caffeine has never been too much of a problem for me. It might take me a little longer to settle into sleep, but it's not going to keep me up until three am or anything. "There's decaf coffee."

"Gross." She selects a small plastic cup and fills it with crushed ice and lemon-lime soda.

I do the same because I don't particularly care what I drink and the topic of caffeine and mental health doesn't seem to fit the evening. Why that feels too personal and date-like to me while an in-depth analysis of why people rank some sins higher is fair, friendly fodder, I don't know.

Nor do I want to take the time to think about it now.

Instead, I pay for our sodas and we take them back to the car.

The problem with getting gas station drinks instead of hitting up a late-night piano bar is it doesn't really prolong the evening. The parks are closed and unless I want to sit with Amy and watch the parking lot of late-night Wal-Mart shoppers, there's not much to do but continue toward her home.

So I take the long way.

If she notices the number of times I turn in the wrong direction, she doesn't mention it. She just keeps sipping at her soda as the conversation rolls easily from topic to topic. I can honestly say I never saw myself enjoying a conversation about the draping properties of silk jersey, but here I am. Not that I could pick silk jersey out of a lineup, but Amy is obviously excited about the experiments she's done with it.

And that's enough to make me care.

Because that's what friends do.

Even if I did tell Emma to stop yammering about puzzles the other day. It wasn't that I didn't care about what was obviously important to her. It was simply the fact that she had moved past the somewhat interesting part—whether or not it was more efficient to start with the edges instead of the more distinctly recognizable portions of the middle—to a lengthy dissertation on her favorite types of pieces. I could have gone my whole life without knowing that a piece with one tab and three blanks is called a little man. I also didn't even know the bumps were called tabs and the indentions called blanks.

Of course, I could probably also go my whole life without knowing silk jersey is both lightweight and breathable while still looking smooth with a light sheen, but my head is full of useless information I gathered at various points in time. Amy's monologue is just more interesting than Emma's.

Which is fine because they're both my friends.

Finally I turn into Amy's apartment complex because to keep driving I'd have to start repeating my path. I pull into a parking space, turn off the car, and hop out to round the car with the intention of opening her door before I can think about it. Have I ever done this for Emma?

I can't remember doing it for her but I also don't let myself think on it too hard. Amy and Emma are not the same person so my friendship with each of them will be different. I can open a door for Amy even if I don't do it for Emma.

Probably shouldn't kiss her goodnight at her door though. Even at my most self-delusional I can't pretend that's a thing friends do.

So I won't think about it.

I carry my drink in my hand as much to keep it occupied as to try to look casual. The ruse feels like it's working until we get to her apartment door. Then casual is the last thing I appear. Amy gives me her drink to hold while she digs her keys out of her bag. If I look even half as awkward as I feel right now, it's a wonder she isn't collapsed against the building in laughter. I don't know where to put my hands, despite the fact that the options are limited given they're both wrapped around cold plastic cups. I don't know where to stand or what to say or even how to leave.

"I, uh, had a good time tonight." I wince at the date-like words.

Amy smirks at me as she slides her key into the deadbolt. "Me too. We should do it again sometime."

Our eyes meet and the teasing laughter in her gaze somehow breaks the tension of the moment. Self-deprecating laughter escapes me as I hold her drink out for her to take after she gets her door open.

"Thanks." She shrugs one shoulder. "For everything. I really did need a . . . friend."

"Glad I could help." I take a step back before I can bring the awkwardness back by doing something else non-friend-like. "See you tomorrow?"

She takes a fortifying breath. "Yeah. Tomorrow."

As I walk back to my car, I suck up the last of my drink and pray. I'm not even certain what I'm praying for. Wisdom? A change in circumstances? A change in myself? Fortunately, even if I'm clueless, God knows.

A small sense of peace comes over me as I approach the car and hit the button to unlock it. It lasts until I settle into the driver's seat and shut the door. The interior of the car still smells like Amy. My eye drops to the disposable essential oil diffuser attached to one of my air vents. I'm fairly certain it ran out of the smelly stuff several weeks ago, but just in case, I snatch it out and drop it into my empty drink cup. As I drive from the complex, I toss the cup into the drive-by trash bin.

AMY

I've never considered myself a coward. Wily and creative at avoiding getting caught or having a confrontation, yes, but not afraid of moving forward. Ever since I did the whole accepting Christ thing, I find myself terrified of even picking out my groceries wrong.

Jason had me reading the passage about Fruits of the Spirit last week and I'm pretty sure cowardice was not on the list, so this fear of making a misstep thing is of my own making and not God's.

That doesn't make it any less debilitating as I sit in my car in the church parking lot on Sunday morning.

> JASON: Your sister found me this morning.

> JASON: She's waiting on you.

> JASON: Just wanted you to be prepared.

If I go in, I'll have to face something much scarier than Betsy's enthusiastic greetings and Jeff's weird attempt at flirting.

I'll have to face my sister.

Because she now knows I've been coming to church and sitting with Jason in the earlier service.

That is a terrifying prospect.

Our sisterly relationship is finally becoming something solid and warm, reminiscent of what we had as teenagers. What if she starts laying in with telling me all the things I need to be doing again? I don't want that.

And if I don't go inside, it won't happen.

I toss the phone into my bag before he has time to answer.

Except I have to be on my phone if I'm going to watch the service. And while I've stopped parking in the visitor parking, I haven't reverted back to hidden sections of the parking lot, either, so people will likely notice me lurking in the car.

I jab my key into the ignition and start the car, pulling out of the space before I can change my mind. Since I don't put it past Emma to come searching the parking lot, I leave the church behind. I can just watch it from home.

Of course, by the time I get home, they'll be a good twenty minutes into the service, so I'll have to watch the replay to see the whole thing.

And if I'm going to do that . . .

My gaze drops to the clock as I join a line of cars stopped at a traffic light.

I'm only ten minutes from the brunch place I used to go to on the occasional Sunday morning. Are my friends there? Keeping an eye on the red light, I glance at my messages. There is an unread one from Jason and another from Emma, but I don't click on those. Instead, I open the group thread labeled Mimosa Mamas. I'm barely active enough for them to keep me in the group anymore, and I wouldn't be surprised to learn they've already made a separate thread that they're slowly shifting over to, but for now, I can still see if they're meeting this morning.

They are.

When the traffic starts moving again, I change direction and head to the restaurant. Heather is just getting out of her car when I pull into the lot and park beside her.

"Amy Trinket, you live!" She laughs and gives me a hug as I shut the door and lock the car.

"Got room for one more?" I hate that I have to ask. There was a time when I would be the one making sure we had enough seats at the table.

She rolls her eyes and tucks her dark hair behind her ear. "Of course. Glad to see you come to your senses."

"My senses?"

"Yeah." She nods to the restaurant. "Only someone who's lost their mind would think anything in the world is better than this place's eggs benedict."

I laugh and bump hips with her. "You're the one who has lost her mind. This is the only place that makes Belgian waffles worth the carbs." And since I haven't been here in months, I can indulge without guilt. At least, without guilt over eating the waffle. I'm fairly certain there's another type of guilt just waiting to consume me when I allow myself to pay attention to it.

Heather loops her arm into mine as we enter the restaurant. Sadie and Jessica are already at a table along with a girl I don't know.

Have I been replaced?

"Look who I found, ladies!" Heather drags me to the table and waves her arm like a game show model.

"Amy!" Sadie salutes me with her mimosa. "Welcome back."

"Please tell me you've been avoiding us because you have landed a big fish of a man." Jessica waggles her eyebrows. "Heard you were rather cozy with Robert Miller at the Children Stay Children function."

The new girl gasps. "You're dating Robert Miller?"

"I . . . no, we're not dating." I slide into the seat and ask the waiter to bring me a water and a mimosa.

"But you were with him at the gala?"

I swallow and resist the urge to fidget in my chair. "Yes, but we met there."

"He never talks to anyone as long as he did you, not any lady at least." Heather sips her drink and gives me a pointed look. "You should absolutely be fanning that flame, my friend. Even just a few dates with him would do wonders for your reputation."

"Has he ever dated anyone more than a few times?" Sadie picks up her phone and InstaTok fills her screen with a blur of color as she expertly flicks to Robert's profile and begins scrolling down the pictures. "He never posts about a girlfriend."

Jessica rolls her eyes. "He never posts about anything but work. Honestly, he strikes me as a rather dull guy. I never hear of him doing anything fun. It's always charity functions or going to the opera. I've never heard of him popping up in the VIP section at a concert or anything like that."

"True." Sadie gives up on finding documented answers to her question and closes the phone screen. "If he didn't have money, looks, and power of the social, political, and monetary variety, he'd be an absolute nobody."

The rest of the table laughs and I smile and sip my drink to appear part of the moment, but I'm not comfortable with the way they're talking about Robert. Is this how they've been talking about me? I haven't been going to concerts or clubs, VIP section or otherwise. I haven't been showing up to brunch or posting outlandish moments on InstaTok.

I spent the last two evenings playing board games and attending a hole-in-the-wall theater.

And I had fun doing both.

More fun than I'm having at this brunch, if I'm honest. I would absolutely rather be sipping gas station sodas with Jason again than nursing this six-dollar mimosa.

The new girl, whose name I still don't know leans forward. "Please tell me he was dull and boring. It is seriously unfair for a man to be that rich, that successful, that good-looking, and have a good personality."

I set the drink down and twirl the glass slowly with the stem. "I didn't think he was boring." Shrugging one shoulder, I do my best to look and sound nonchalant. "The conversation was good, actually."

"Oh my gosh, do you like him?" Jessica leans toward me.

"Are you secretly dating him?" Heather leans in.

The new girl looks at me over her glass with a raised eyebrow as Sadie also leans toward me. "Is that why you've been ditching us?"

How do I answer that? I can't say I haven't been ditching them because, well, I have. I've been turning down their invitations, taking way too long to reply to text messages, and avoiding our normal hang outs. It isn't them pulling away from me that's the problem, it's that I'm pulling away from them.

As much as I don't want to be the kind of person that turns her back on her friends, I don't know how to be with them anymore. I don't want to speculate over Robert's social life or pick apart how he could improve my social standings. I don't want to calculate ways to be seen with him or stalk his preferences so I can appear like the perfect girlfriend.

Because I've done all of those things and I've done them well. Even now my brain is pulling together all the right things to say and all the right moves to make it happen. But some other force inside me is telling me I will absolutely regret it if I act on any of those options.

"I, uh..., the thing is I've been... reprioritizing."

As one the girls lean back in their seats. Heather frowns. "Reprioritizing? As in, we aren't important to you anymore?"

"No, no, it's not that." I'm saved from having to say what it actually is by the arrival of our food. While the waiter lays out plates and fills last-minute requests for particular sauces, more utensils, or a fresh drink, my mind scrambles for what to say.

It's possible they'll forget the topic and move on to a new one, but even as everyone lifts up their forks, all eyes are turned back to me.

"I've been attending church."

Four sets of unnatural lashes blink at me.

I stab at my egg. "With my sister." Okay, that one's sort of a lie, but it's not a complete stretch.

Still, no one moves as I cut my first bite and slide it into my mouth. I can't answer if my mouth is full, so I chew very, very thoroughly.

"Like . . . you're going to church every week?" Sadie takes her own bite and chews slowly as she gives me a thoughtful look.

My food is all but obliterated now so I swallow and smile as if I haven't said something foreign and unusual. "Yes. Every week." I poke at my food. "Except this week."

"Why not this week?"

Why not this week? Because I'm avoiding my sister. Who I said I was going to church with.

This must be why God tells people not to lie.

Well, this and the whole being honest and trustworthy and reliable thing.

"I . . . was late." This is more of a stretch of the truth than an outright lie. I was later than I wanted to be and I would have been late signing on to the livestream.

"Do they like lock the doors or something when it's not a special Sunday?" There's nothing but curiosity in Jessica's face as she cuts into her own food. "I went with my mother at Easter and there were people slipping in and out the whole time. Of course, I don't know which church you're going to, but maybe that's just a special service thing."

"No, they don't lock the doors, I just . . . didn't want to be a disturbance. I can watch the service online later."

More slow sweeps of the fake lashes.

Heather breaks the silence this time. "Why?"

Why indeed. I haven't had to verbalize this yet, but I need to. If I don't tell these girls they need Jesus like I do, they might not ever hear it. "I like taking the time to focus on worshipping God and the sermon is helping me learn to study the Bible better."

"What are you studying it for? Is there a test?" Jessica doesn't give me a chance to answer before turning to the others at the table. "Did you hear that Mary Bell Stanton failed her driver's test?"

"Why was she taking a driver's test?" Sadie turns her attention from me to Jessica.

New girl shifts in her seat, looking coy and important. "Because she'd been using her old California license but she let it expire because she was trying to convince that one guy that she was only twenty-seven instead of twenty-nine and she's been living here in Georgia for three years so, really, in some ways the license expired three years ago instead of three months ago and honestly the woman is a mess."

It's my turn to blink. Seriously, who is this woman? I need to be exceptionally careful what I say around her for the rest of the meal.

The truth is I don't say much at all for the next hour. I let the conversation flow around me, saying just enough to not appear like a snob who thinks herself too good to chat with the rabble or something like that. Part of me knows I should be disappointed that the conversation turned and didn't stay on the topic of why I've started attending church, but most of me is just relieved. I know that what I believe now is the truth, but that doesn't mean I fully understand my place in it. I don't know how to tell someone else yet.

It'll come, though. Today I didn't back down from talking at least a little bit about my new faith to these women who clearly gossip with enough frequency and vehemence that my professional reputation could be shredded in a matter of hours. That's a baby step of a win and that's got to count for something.

When I get home to my apartment, I change into a matching set of light green cotton loungewear and settle onto my couch to turn on that morning's recording. There are seven unread messages on my phone, but I've been ignoring them. As the recording loads, I open them up.

> HEATHER: So great to see you today! Let's go shopping next weekend. I NEED some new shoes.

> MOTHER: Jade has an appointment to get her hair done tomorrow. Could you open the boutique?

Those two are simple enough to answer, so I send off the messages and add a few notes to my calendar. Then I move on to the difficult ones.

> JASON: I understand why you skipped out.

> JASON: Emma is giving me the third degree but I'm staying strong.

> JASON: Let me know if you want to get together to discuss the sermon later.

I snort out a laugh at that last message. As nice an offer as it sounds, it's really him holding me to my promise to attend online. In order to talk about the sermon, I'd have to watch it.

> ME: Recording is loading now. I'll let you know if I have questions.

> JASON: Where'd you go?

I bite my lip, wishing I were listening to him ask this question instead of reading it. Is he judging me? Is this an accusing inquiry or a curious one?

> ME: I went to brunch with some old friends I haven't had a chance to speak to in a while.

> JASON: How'd it go?

> ME: It was a little weird to be honest.

> JASON: We can talk about that later, too.

I can't help the smile prompted by that response. It's so very . . . Jason. I've never met anyone willing to support me as unquestioningly as he does. Finally I take a deep breath and open up my thread with Emma.

> EMMA: Jason says I scared you off.

> EMMA: Are you avoiding church so you don't have to see me?

I don't know how to answer. There's a good chance that she's preoccupied for the afternoon and won't notice that I've read the message for a while yet, so I turn my phone face down onto the couch cushion beside me. I'll answer her after I watch the service.

An hour and twenty minutes later, I'm staring at the church logo on the television screen. I have a question or two but mostly I'm just . . . confused. It wasn't the same. There's an emptiness to it that I don't understand. It's not like I interact with anyone while I'm there, well, aside from Jason and random women that I consult in the bathroom.

My phone buzzes and I flip it over to see a text from Emma.

> EMMA: Milkshakes and fries. ETA five minutes.

AMY

I meet my sister at the door with arms crossed over my chest. Am I going to let her in? Probably. Am I going to leave myself the option of shutting and bolting the door? Absolutely. It won't keep her out for long because she does have an emergency key to my apartment, but it will make a statement.

She's got a drink carrier and a brown fast-food bag clutched in one hand as she approaches my door. Her face is as impassive as I think I've ever seen it, giving me no clue as to what she's going to say when she gets here. Milkshakes and fries are her break up food, so I'm a little concerned at her declaration that this moment needs them.

"Are you going to let me in?" She comes to a stop in front of me and raises her eyebrows.

"I haven't decided."

Her mouth gapes open. "I'm your sister."

"You're a pain in the neck."

"Most people would consider that an element of the job description."

I roll my eyes. "What do you want to talk about?"

She shrugs the shoulder of the arm not holding the food. The scent of French fries reaches me and even though I rarely let myself indulge in fast food, I'm tempted to snatch the bag from her and slam the door so I can eat both servings.

As she lists the possible topics of conversation, she draws the words out as if she's having to work to come up with options. "We could discuss work . . . or church . . . or boys."

Ah. She wants to talk about Jason. Did he say something when I didn't turn up at church? Was he sorry I wasn't there or glad he didn't have to nurse me through the service?

Do I want to know either way? Both are devastating in their own right.

Which might mean I need to talk about it with somebody. Goodness knows I can't talk about it with Heather or Sadie or the other brunch girls. Maybe hashing it out with Emma will help me clear my head.

I step back into my apartment and hold the door open. Emma slides in with a grin that looks just evil enough to make me think about changing my mind.

But she does have French fries.

I close the door with a sigh and follow her into my living room. After we settle ourselves on opposite ends of my couch, she hands me my milkshake and container of fries. The sweet chocolate and salty potatoes become my whole focus as I wait for her to start a conversation.

Jason's name will not cross my lips first.

"So, tell me about this app."

I blink and almost drop the fry from my mouth. We're starting with work? She actually wants to talk business? "Can't you see it? It's supposed to be in the system, whatever that means."

Emma sighs and slumps deeper into the corner of the couch. "Jason blocked me from the folder."

I smother my laugh by taking a long drink of milkshake. "Why?"

"That is an excellent question. Why don't we ask him? My phone is almost dead. Can I text him from yours?"

"Nice try." I think about tossing a fry at her, but if I'm going to indulge I'm not going to waste any. I toss a throw pillow at her instead.

She snags the pillow and tucks it behind her. "Thanks. Your couch is exceedingly uncomfortable."

I don't even dignify that with a response. She's never liked my couch even though it pulls together the decor of my open living space perfectly.

"Can we talk about Jason yet or should I pretend I have another topic of conversation first?"

"Your issues with your boss are not my concern. If he won't let you see a project, I'm sure he has his reasons."

"Oh, I'm sure he does." She waggles her eyebrows. "And I bet they're personal."

"What happened to the girl who didn't want me to have anything to do with him?"

She takes a long slurp of her milkshake and pokes around in her fries before saying. "I still think it's a bad idea, but I should stay out of it."

I'm glad I'm not chewing or swallowing at that moment because I'd have choked. As it is, the air I'm breathing is almost too much to handle. "I'm sorry, what?"

"I think," she says slowly, dragging the words out like she needs to use them to provide enough coverage for a Met Gala stair train. Then she sighs and spills the rest of the sentence out in a rush. "I think that maybe I know too much about both of you to see the situation clearly. And I was probably overstepping when I told him to stay away from you."

"You told him to stay away from me?"

"Yes."

I snort out a laugh. "Clearly he doesn't listen to you."

Her eyes widen. "Is there more I don't know about? Are you two secretly dating?" She sits up so quickly that a scattering of French fries fly from her container.

Rolling my eyes, I quickly move to scoop up the fallen potatoes before they can leave grease stains on my couch and floor. "No, but we're . . . talking."

Her face screws up into a thoughtful frown. "Isn't that like, pre-dating or something? I seem to recall that when I read a pop culture lingo article."

I narrow my gaze at her and scrunch up my nose. "You know that most people get pop culture lingo from, you know, the culture."

She waves a hand in the air. "Whatever. So, is it like that?"

"No, it's not." I drop back down to my side of the couch. "I mean, yes the word can mean that, but in this case, it just means that we, well, we talk."

"Oh." She's quiet for a moment. "About what?"

"What do normal friends talk about?" I shake my fry container. "We talk about our jobs, the things we did that day, what existential observations we've been having."

Her slurp of milkshake is long, thoughtful, and noisy. "Family?"

I roll my eyes. "No, weirdo, we don't talk about you." My head lolls to the side as I try to look casual. "We just talk about friend stuff."

She frowns. "So you don't like him like that?"

I don't want to answer this because I don't know what was said when I didn't show up at church this morning. Did she quiz Jason like this? Did he say he only saw me as a friend? Was he lying if he did so? I never used to exhibit such shows of anxious insecurity, but maybe that's because the other person's opinion didn't matter enough.

Even thinking about how the girls from brunch are probably talking about me on a separate group chat doesn't bother me right now. Wondering if Emma and Jason talked about me this morning, though? My insides feel like they're shaking.

I clear my throat. "I wouldn't say that."

Emma has no compulsion about throwing food and chucks a fry at me. "What would you say, then?"

I pluck the fry from my shirt and drop it onto the napkin holding the other ones I picked up a few moments ago. "I would say that the attraction is there. I mean, he's a nice guy. He doesn't talk down to me or think my ideas are silly. He's . . . supportive. He's not the best kisser I've ever encountered, but he—"

"Wait!" Emma spreads her arms wide as she jerks upright, balancing atop the couch cushion on her knees. Fortunately, her milkshake has a top on it and her fry carton is all but empty now. "Wait, wait, wait, wait."

"I'm waiting."

"He's kissed you?"

Oops. I shouldn't have mentioned that. "Technically, I kissed him."

She lowers down to sit on her heels. "Why would you do that?"

"Because I like him?" I shrug. "How else do you show your interest in a guy?"

"A smile? Extended eye contact? A little note that says do you like me, check yes or no?"

I snort out a laugh. "Is that what you did for Carter?"

"I, well, no. I threatened the sanctity of everything he holds dear, but that's not going to work for everyone."

"No, I would think not." I sigh and stand up, gathering the trash from our indulgence. "I guess you have your method and I have mine."

She follows me to the kitchen area of the living space. "But your way doesn't work because y'all aren't dating."

I toss the trash and turn to face my twin. "Do you honestly think my dating is a good idea right now?"

"Dating Jason? No. Dating in general?" She sighs. "Maybe?"

"I'm not willing to bank on maybe." I take her containers and toss them into the trash can as well. "Besides, he apparently agrees with you on our not dating being a good idea. He isn't exactly trying to convince me to change my mind."

Memories of our "outing" the night before push against my statement. Still, the man didn't try anything when he walked me to the door, even though I'm pretty sure I was giving off every unspoken invitation I could.

"And there's only him? You aren't interested in anyone else?" She pulls out her phone. "Maybe I can help with that."

"What are you doing?"

"Texting Trina to see which guys at church are currently single."

I snatch the device from her and breathe a little easier when I see the text is mostly written but not yet sent. "If you send that text, I'll tell Mother you miss her and want to take her out for lunch next week just the two of you."

"You wouldn't."

"Oh, I would." I fumble with the unfamiliar phone but manage to delete the unfinished text eventually. "And she just got off the wait-list at that country club so she's got more than enough stories to keep you entertained for a lengthy mealtime."

"Fine. I won't text her." She swipes the phone back. "But no matter what happens, I want you to know I'm on your side. I want what's best for you."

"Why would you think I thought otherwise?" Even when we had that big falling out earlier this year, I never doubted that my twin sister wanted what was best for me. Was I wrong? Has there been a time she didn't care about me that way?

Color tinges Emma's cheeks and my stomach seizes tight. Does she know something I don't know?

I can't stand the questions anymore. "Did you and Jason talk about me this morning?"

She sighs. "He might have pointed out to me that I've been a bit . . . demanding lately. I've been trying to make you do what I wanted you to instead of allowing you to move forward at your own pace as God worked with you."

My insides relax and a warm glow passes through me. It's possible my cheeks are now turning pink, but Emma's looking at the toe of her atrocious Converse sneakers, so I don't have to worry about it. "Did he say it that way?"

"Ah, no, I believe his exact words were, 'Why would she tell you she was here and risk having you haul her off to join the choir?'"

I frown. "Does your church have a choir?"

"Our church has one for special occasions like Christmas and Easter, so yes, there is currently a group meeting for choir practice because it's almost December."

"I don't sing."

"Neither do I, but Jason was making the point that I was pressuring you to implant yourself like someone who was comfortable with every-thing." She frowns. "I don't think I ever thought about how strange church would look if you weren't familiar with it."

I snort. "Don't you remember? I mean you weren't raised under a steeple so it should have been strange to you once."

"I started at a college ministry. By the time I went to regular church the ideas were less foreign."

"Oh."

She straightens her back and gives a soft huff of determination. "Here's the deal. From now on, I will not push you into doing anything you aren't ready for. I hate that you've felt like you couldn't ask me questions or even let me know you were in the building. I still can't believe you hid for that long."

"It's a big building."

"But we're twins."

I squint at her. "We shared a womb, not DNA. You do know what fraternal means, don't you? You were the one who got the smart genes after all."

"You're smart, too."

"If you say so."

"No really. Just because you don't do math in your head or know the chemical compound for salt doesn't mean you aren't smart." She fluffs at the layer of thick bangs on her forehead. "These were your idea." She waves a hand down her body. "And I'm not in cartoon pajamas, am I?"

I glance down at her tunic blouse and the stretch trousers that I had to scour the Internet to find for her. "Isn't that what you wore to church this morning?"

She, too, glances down at her clothes. "Well, yes."

"Did you previously wear cartoon pajamas to church?"

"No." She crosses her arms over her chest. "That's not the point."

"Oh, I believe it is." Mostly because I'm tired of having this conversation.

"No. The point is that God blessed you with other smarts and I should follow your lead on using those smarts to do the faith thing."

I smile at the flustered look on her face as she fumbles with the phrase *do the faith thing*. "Like you followed my lead on the pants."

"Well, okay, different kind of lead. It's not . . . I'm not going to copy you, I'm going to support you. And—" She stops talking as I fail at restraining my giggles. One short-nailed finger points at me. "You know what I mean."

My giggles fade into a smile. "I do. And I thank you for it."

"Now." She crosses the room to pick up her bag. "I'm going to go home, put on my cartoon pajamas, and play video games."

I walk with her to my door. "Will Carter be there?"

She shrugs. "Probably."

I shake my head. "If the man can stand to be around those awful pajamas, it truly must be love."

Her grin is enormous as she looks over her shoulder. "I know."

Once she's gone, I flop back onto my couch, lying along the cushions as I stare at my ceiling and contemplate what she said about being blessed with my own smarts. It seems to be the key I was missing all this time. Maybe it isn't so much about finding all my own answers as it is applying them to my specific life and situation.

My phone dings with a text message and I unlock the screen, expecting Emma to have some last-minute thought before she drives away.

But it isn't Emma. It's the girl from the bathroom several weeks ago.

> TRACY: Can you work magic for job interviews, too?

> TRACY: I have a friend who just got her degree online and she's got a corporate interview Tuesday.

> TRACY: I just saw her planned outfit and even I know it's bad.

I grin as I press the phone to my stomach and look back at the ceiling.

I've been blessed with my own smarts, and I think God is telling me how to use them.

JASON

"Yo." Robert draws out the word long enough for the me to close my car door and make it to the open gate to the half-court enclosure. "This is becoming a habit, little brother."

"Seems to be a habit for you guys, too." I'd gotten the text about an hour after church this morning that the guys were getting together at Clint's this afternoon. As far as I knew, Sunday wasn't a regular time for them. "Or have you always gotten together this often?" I shut the gate behind me.

"We don't all have pseudo-girlfriends taking up all our time." Clint tosses the basketball in my direction, and I use one arm to catch it against my stomach while my other hand keeps a grip on my small gym bag. "Now that Emma has a real boyfriend, he's able to come play with us more."

I toss my bag into the pile by the fence. It lands on top of Robert's and then rolls to the side, landing in a heap of crumpled green canvas. "You do remember that you have an actual wife, don't you?"

He grins. "Well, yeah. Why do you think we meet in my backyard?"

Robert snorts out a laugh. "We've always met in your backyard."

With a little more force that necessary, I throw the ball back at Clint. "And Emma is my real friend. Not my pseudo-girlfriend."

I can't say that he isn't wrong about my free time though.

Max scoffs as he dribbles the ball in a figure eight between his legs. "She was your platonic girlfriend, dude. You have to admit that."

"Otherwise known as a friend, dimwit." I dart across the court to steal the ball from Max before tossing it to Clint, unofficially starting a casual game of two-on-two.

"Nah, I don't buy it." Max shakes his head and blocks me from getting a pass with moves that would be considered illegal in actual gameplay given the way his elbow is digging into my ribs. "What are your default plans on Friday nights?"

Clint shoulders his way between me and Max and bounces the ball in my direction. "Who is the first person you call when you have a problem?"

Max wraps Clint in a bear hug, giving up all pretense of fair play. "Who accompanies you to any and every social outing requiring a plus-one?"

Robert raises his arms and tries to get between me and the basket, but his gaze is on my face, not the ball. "She's a part of almost every story you tell when someone asks about an update on your life."

"See?" Clint grunts. "Girlfriend."

I misjudge my dribble and the ball bounces off the toe of my foot to roll across the court and hit the fence. While part of me knows the answer to these questions is, or at least would have been, Emma, she isn't the person floating into the forefront of my mind.

Instead, it's Amy's face, smiling at me from the passenger seat of my car as she sips on a gas station soda. Amy, slinging back the communion grape juice like a shot of whiskey. Amy looking at me like she wants to tackle me to the floor and kiss me again.

Max and Clint stop wrestling and Robert drops his arms, but none of us go after the ball. The three of them watch me while I prop my fists on my hips and breathe heavily. It isn't the exertion taking all my air right now. It's the idea that they might be on to something, but also that things have changed.

My first thought isn't to call Emma and see what she thinks.

It's to text Amy. Or go by and see her.

And the anticipation of having something to talk to her about isn't the same excitement I ever had when talking to Emma.

My effort to be Amy's friend doesn't seem to be succeeding completely.

"And there it is." Robert slaps me on the shoulder before jogging to the fence to collect the ball.

All the guys are grinning at me as if I've finally seen the light, but I doubt they realize the revelation I'm having to face right now.

"I think it's why you stopped dating." Clint shrugs. "You didn't need a girlfriend for anything but kissing, and that's pretty pointless if you aren't looking for someone to marry."

I wouldn't mind kissing Amy again.

Does that mean I'm contemplating marrying her?

Max slams his body into my shoulder. "Look alive. Your existential crisis can wait for the next water break."

But when we do stop to grab water after twenty minutes of trash talk and mediocre ball handling, I don't bring the subject back up. No one else does either. Instead we talk about business.

Of the four of us, I'm the only one who struck out on my own.

Robert is our father's right-hand man, working his way through the different areas of business so he can take over one day. Most people don't believe that I'm more than happy for him to take it. The intangibles of the business management consulting world make my head hurt.

Clint is in a similar position in his family, though his sister is working alongside him. Technically speaking, Max has his own business but everyone knows it will one day be merged with his uncle's company when the old bachelor is ready to step down.

Still, we all work with customers, manage employees, and have to think about taxes and government guidelines. There's plenty of conversation and speculation to fill the time.

We play a few more rounds, working up a sweat and trying to stave off the softness that comes from working a desk all day. I don't have a visible six-pack or anything because I like my health enough to stay hydrated and actually eat. Still, for a guy rolling over the age of thirty, I'm in pretty good shape.

Good enough shape to attract a woman who's accustomed to pretty things, anyway. I push the thought away as I attack the court once more.

The sun is lowering in the sky as we scoop up our bags and leave the chain-linked enclosure.

"What we need to do is get Jason a date." Max throws his gym bag into the seat of his McLaren 570GT and then leans against the door. "Who's up for dinner at that taco place while we discuss some options?"

Robert shakes his head and climbs into his car. "I'm out. I have just enough time to get home, shower, and heat up dinner, and get on a conference call."

"California?" I ask because that's what I remember Dad talking about last time I was home.

Robert shakes his head and starts the car. "Vancouver."

I raise my eyebrows. I didn't know he'd taken the business international.

Before he shuts the door, he grins at us all. "Besides, I've only met one nice girl lately and if I'm setting anyone up with her, it'll be myself."

Before any of us can press him for more details, he shuts the door and drives away.

"My mom's all but given up on getting Max to date my sister. Want me to tell her she should consider you now that you're free?" Clint slings the shoulder strap of his bag higher onto his shoulder. I'm not even certain why he brings a bag out here since he lives mere steps away.

Max squints as he looks up at the house. "As much as I want your mom off my back, I can't in good conscience sic her on a friend to do so."

"Man, my mom's a socially-conscious family seeker, not a police dog."

"What your mom is, is relentless. She would recognize my car when it pulled in the drive and run outside to flag me down before I could drive around to the back." He shakes his head. "I had to buy a new car to throw her off the scent."

I look at his sporty luxury car. "I thought you bought a new car because your name finally come up on the wait-list."

"That too, but it's not as fun of a story."

"Fun as it would be to play matchmaker with you two, I have already won the marital game and have a dinner date with my wife." Clint gives us a salute and crosses the pavement to enter his basement apartment.

When Amy didn't show up to church this morning, I had to admit that I missed her. I also practically attacked Emma on Amy's behalf. Why would I do that unless my feelings were already more involved than I wanted to admit? It's always been me and Emma against the world. Never me against Emma.

Before I got here, I'd all but convinced myself that not dating Amy was the wrong decision. But what if the guys are right and I'm trying to use Amy to replace Emma? Oh, none of them said as much but that's because they don't know Amy exists.

Do I like the person Amy actually is or am I projecting a version of Emma onto the sister I'm more physically attracted to?

A pulse of pain starts to prick the back of my brain.

"What about you?"

I blink as I realize Max has been trying to catch my attention. Clint is long gone and the sun is barely visible over the trees.

"Ah, what about me?" I slam the back door of my car closed and circle to the front.

"Tacos?"

I look down at my sweaty shirt. "We aren't exactly presentable."

He shrugs. "They've got a screened patio." When I don't immediately agree, he sighs. "Fine. We can both go shower first."

"I live half an hour away."

"You're only fifteen minutes from me."

"Because you speed like it's your job."

He grins. "It is my job."

I roll my eyes. Yes, Max's mechanical design firm makes components for luxury custom vehicles among other things, but he never built the engines.

"Fine." I open the door and climb in. "Tacos. My place. You're buying. And delivering."

An hour later, Max is opening takeout containers on my kitchen table.

"You really okay with Emma dating that guy? It's gotta be pretty serious by now." Max pries open a taco to dump a line of salsa on top of the meat, cheese, and vegetables.

I nod. "I imagine he'll be proposing. If not over Thanksgiving, then over Christmas."

"How do you feel about that?"

"I'm not sure." I know what Max is after and I string him along for a bit because it's fun. "I mean, what do I say if she asks me to be in the wedding? Do I stand up on her side or his? Do I have to wear a dress?"

He rolls his eyes as I laugh.

"Okay, okay," he says, holding up a hand palm out. "But if you are such good friends explain the look on your face earlier. I thought you'd had some earth-shattering revelation. If you weren't reconsidering your relationship with Emma, what was it?"

I take my time carefully folding up the wrapper from my second taco. "Emma has a sister."

"No."

"Yes. A twin."

"Dude. That's messed up."

I ball up the folded paper and throw it at my friend. "Not a twin twin. A fraternal twin. It's not like a carbon copy or something."

"And you like the sister?"

"I . . ." I want to hedge, to say I don't know what I think, to say I'm on the fence, to say it's just attraction, to say I'm only interested in helping her find her new foundation. All of that would be a lie and I'm a little tired of lying to myself, much less to other people. "I think she could have the power to hurt me."

My breath stops and I blink at my partially unwrapped third taco and then at my friend across the table. He's quiet, eyes glued to my face. "You look like you didn't know you were going to say that."

"I didn't."

He pops the last of the taco in his mouth and takes his time to chew and swallow. "I'm not an expert, mind you, but it seems to me that the only way a woman could be important enough for you to love like a wife would be if she was close enough to rip your heart to shreds."

"How romantic."

He lifts one shoulder and lets it drop. "You don't pay me to be romantic."

"I don't pay you at all."

"That's what you think. I slid your copy of NBA 2K into my jacket pocket when you weren't looking earlier."

I laugh because I absolutely believe he did and that he has no plan to return it. I also know he'll have a new copy express delivered to my house tomorrow. "Jokes on you then, I was pre-playing it before giving it to you for your birthday."

He tsks in solemn disappointment. "My birthday's not until June, man. You have so little faith in your ability to beat it that you think you'll need seven months?"

After clearing the rest of the trash, he grabs the game from his jacket and heads toward my office. "Come on. Let me show you how it's done."

We spend the remainder of the evening playing video games and I truly am as trash a player as he was claiming I'd be.

Because I'm not thinking of digital basketball. I'm thinking about what he said about a woman worth loving being one who could rip your heart to shreds.

There might be truth to that statement, but it seems like the smart thing to do would be to choose a woman who isn't likely to do that.

And I'm not so sure Amy, who is still learning how to commit to her faith walk, who is tightly connected to one of the most important people in my life, who has a vision board dedicated to attaining the life I specifically walked away from, fits that qualification.

AMY

There's a paying client's file open on the computer in front of me, but I'm not thinking about it. I'm not even really reading it. My thoughts are entirely on the person due to arrive in an hour. She's not a client, but I can't think of her like a charity case. She's a person who needs help.

And I can provide that help.

I mean, it's not one of the necessities like food or shelter or something like that, but it's still important.

Isn't it?

I blink several times and focus on the account in front of me. Colors and fabrics are noted, links to various online stores and inspiration pictures are organized in neat lists, and the client's life has been broken up into seven different categories.

My gaze drops to the vision board I've grown increasingly uncomfortable with since Jason visited my office. I made it two years ago, when I hit twenty-seven and started panicking that I was on my way to being old with nothing to show for my life.

If I try, I can still remember what it feels like to truly crave everything on that board, to think attaining those goals would make me satisfied. I was convinced they were what life was all about.

I know better now, but part of me still wants to achieve some of those milestones. The urgency is different, but the desire is still there. They are more of a means to an end now instead of the goal itself.

Is it wrong to want that?

I grab my phone and open the text messages before I can stop myself.

> ME: Is fashion frivolous?

I wait, staring at the blank screen, wishing he had the same type of phone I do so I would know if he hadn't yet seen my message, was busy typing, or was ignoring my ridiculous question.

He is at work, after all. And Emma has mentioned an all-staff morning meeting. Maybe he won't be able to answer until—

The phone vibrates.

> JASON: In what capacity? I mean, I still don't understand the point of purchasing jeans that already have holes in them.

> ME: It gives them character. But I mean, in general.

> JASON: Why are you asking?

> ME: That shouldn't change the answer.

> JASON: The why always changes the answer.

> ME: Do you consider people's appearance when you hire them?

> JASON: Honestly by the time I see a new hire, it's about how the team thinks they'll fit and how they did on the skills test.

Why did I think Jason would be helpful in this situation?

> ME: I think we judge people by how they look whether we intend to or not.

> ME: A job interview wouldn't be any different.

> ME: So helping people present themselves well during an opportunity is a somewhat noble endeavor.

I know I haven't given Jason space to answer, but my thumbs keep flying over the screen, throwing my thoughts into text as fast as possible because they refuse to stay inside.

> ME: It'd be lovely if we lived in a world where it didn't matter but that's not the case.

My thumbs aren't fast enough, and I hit the voice-to-text button after a glance at my office door to ensure that it's closed.

> ME: That verse you sent me last week about God dressing the lilies of the valley or something means He sees the advantage of visual appeal but then there's that other verse about being hands and feet, so that means God isn't dropping a suit in someone's closet because He's got people that follow Him who can make that happen instead.

> ME: In a way, that makes my helping someone look like an offering.

I stop and read through the word vomit I just threw over text message. My fingers shake as I send one final message.

> ME: Right?

> JASON: Sounds to me like you've figured this out on your own.

> JASON: Proud of you, Amy.

Those four words slam into me so hard that I all but throw my phone down on the desk.

Has anyone ever said they were proud of me? I mean, Mother has been proud of my work, proud of my reputation, proud of my ability to socialize with a variety of people.

But this feels different. Jason is proud of me for being a better human. He's proud of me, not my accomplishment.

And he agrees with me. I figured it out on my own. I applied verses to my life and thought about showing God's love to people on my own.

Just like I wanted.

It feels like a goal that should have taken a lot more time and effort to get to. Does God really just come in and start using and teaching and loving a person because they ask? I haven't even attended that new believer training Emma was bugging me about.

Not that I don't think there's more to learn, but there's not a degree I have to earn or a license to practice that I have to take a test for. God's just . . . here.

My phone buzzes against the desk surface and I scoop it up, wondering if Jason has more to say.

But it's not Jason. It's Sydney. Letting me know she's closing out from her breakfast shift at the restaurant she currently works at and then she'll be coming to the boutique.

I had her send me a picture of herself in the outfit she was planning to wear, and I scroll up to it now.

There's a sloppiness to the clothes that looks like a woman who has either lost weight or gotten hand-me-downs from someone of a larger size and she's doing the best she can to make them fit. Her hair is limp and her makeup is every shade of wrong for her coloring. I zoom in on the earrings and I'm pretty sure they are some form of painted plastic.

The hair is a matter of technique, the makeup solved by a couple purchases at the drugstore. The clothes though . . .

Her interview is at 9:30 tomorrow morning and I have an afternoon full of client meetings. Taking her to some secondhand shops isn't an option even if she has the funds. Not that I have any idea where a decent secondhand shop is.

I make a note in my planner to visit several in the area so that next time I'll know where the best places to go are.

For now, I'll have to make do with what she has.

Or something I already have.

I slip from my office and into the closet where we store the items for our semi-annual resale. We don't carry a lot of professional clothing, but some of these pieces could be put together in a businesslike way.

A strange peace comes over me as I dig through the racks and stacks, pulling options that should work with her body type and coloring. By the time she texts me that she's parked her car, I have three options I'm feeling confident about. Some of the pieces might be from the last-season sale rack in the store instead of the resale closet, but Mother and Aunt Jade won't notice their absence. With a thrill of excitement, I leave my office for the main boutique.

Sydney comes in slowly, her eyes wide as she steps carefully into the store. The door barely has room to shut behind her as she looks around at the sophisticated displays, artistically arranged clothing racks, and elegant customers.

Everyone including Sydney can tell she is not our normal clientele, but I don't care. I rush across the store and greet her, warmed by the grateful smile she gives me when she sees my face.

I usher her back to my office and grab my first choice of blouse. "Now, most people don't think bright colors are good for the workplace but trust me when I say this blue is not going to look obnoxiously bright on you." I scoop up a dark gray blazer. "Especially if you put this on top of it."

She reaches out and lets her fingers graze over the fabric. Her face slides into that blissful expression so many women get when they imagine themselves in fine clothing. Sydney's smile soon turns sad, though, as she pulls her hand away and tucks it behind her back.

Her eyes don't meet mine as she whispers, "I can't afford anything in this store."

"These items are only ten dollars per piece." I'm glad my office door is closed so Mother and Aunt Jade can't overhear me. They'd faint away. "If that's too much right now, we can work up a store credit that won't be due until you've been at your new job for a month."

I want to just give them to her, but I know that I never feel as confident in clothes that were gifted to me or part of a business deal. I imagine charity would feel even worse.

Sydney looks from me to my office door. Beyond that door are racks of clothing with prices that contain three or four digits per piece.

"These are from our out-of-season stock," I continue. "We can't sell them on the floor."

"Really?" Her eyes are wide once more, but this time they don't look fearful. "Are you sure?"

"Positive. Why don't you try this on?" I push her toward the screen in the corner that I have set up for occasions just like this when clients need to try on items.

It only takes thirty minutes to give Sydney a brand-new first impression. I was absolutely right about the blouse and blazer, but it seems best to pair them with a pair of black slacks that she already owns. Once we take away the ill-fitting top, they hug her frame nicely.

Teaching her a new hairstyle takes only minutes, and she readily agrees to buy new blush and lipstick on the way home, sticking to the list of shades I provided.

As I walk her back through the boutique, we're talking easily about funny videos we've seen on social media. I hand her the bag with the clothes at the door and wave her off, just like I do all my high-end clients.

When I turn around, I'm met with the concerned face of my aunt and the disapproving frown of my mother. Both of them switch to confident smiles as they help one last customer with their purchase, but as soon as the woman, leaves the lock is flipped and the open sign turned off.

"Amethyst Jewel Trinket, what on earth are you doing?" Mother crosses her arms over her chest and shudders.

I raise my brows. "You mean with Sydney? I was helping a new friend."

"We cannot have customers seeing undesirable people in our boutique. They'll think we have no class."

Please, God, tell me I was never like this.

That prayer is followed by one pleading for the right words in this situation. There may be a lot of things I don't know or understand about this whole following God thing, but I've got the desperate emergency prayer idea down pat.

"Mother," I say slowly, "please tell me you did not just call a person undesirable."

She rolls her eyes. "You know what I mean."

"No, I'm afraid I don't." Although, actually, I do. I just want to make her say it out loud.

"We have a reputation to maintain. The people who come in and out of our shop are a large part of that."

"So, you wouldn't sell clothing to someone who came in looking like Sydney?"

"Of course we would, dear." Aunt Jade steps in front of Mother, placing a heavy hand on her younger sister's shoulder. "But she didn't buy clothing from us, did she?"

"Yes, as a matter of fact she did." I cross my arms, thankful I charged her that twenty dollars.

"Oh." Aunt Jade blinked. "I didn't see her selecting things from the floor."

"Because I had the items pulled and in my office already. The way I do for most special occasion clients."

While most of my styling services are for overall wardrobe and appearance, I have done several single occasion appointments. Weddings, premieres, galas. People have special events in their life all the time and often need help since they are so far out of people's normal consideration.

"Still, one can only wonder what Mrs. Jenkins was thinking when she saw you with . . . Sydney." Mother smooths her cashmere sweater. "Perhaps your . . . friends . . . can use the back door when they come to visit you at work."

Heat crawls up my neck as I have a sudden recollection of a conversation from a little over a year ago. I suggested that Emma use the back door when she was coming and going. Even when she was doing her best to dress in a way that would make us happy, I was still embarrassed by her appearance on occasion.

I was the one making my own sister feel undesirable and unwanted.

This was what drove Emma to hide her life from me and Mother. This was what convinced her that she had to be miserable to be accepted as a member of our family.

She looked at me like I am currently looking at our mother.

I think I'm going to be sick.

No. No, I'm not going to be sick. I'm going to remember the words Jason told me. I am new. My past is just that—past. Every moment that reminds me of my past is an opportunity to do something different.

"Mother, Aunt Jade." I look from one to the other of them. "What, exactly, is it that you found objectionable about having the boutique associated with Sydney?"

The older women blink at me. Aunt Jade speaks first. "Didn't you see what she was wearing?"

"Yes. Which was why she needed to come see a stylist. If she'd been wearing flattering clothing, she wouldn't have needed my services."

"Yes, but we know what good clothing looks like, Amethyst." Mother presses her mouth into a sour pucker. "She probably got that shirt from Wal-Mart, and did you see how old and warn that jacket was? It probably came from the thrift store."

I, admittedly, have never been in a thrift store. I'm inclined to think that they don't sell items that are already worn out, though. That wouldn't make sense.

"Mother, would you trust me to choose your outfit for next weekend's charity event at the club?" We're scheduled to attend a garden party fundraiser a week from Saturday. There's an idea churning in the back of my mind and I don't know if I can pull it off for a formal event. A garden party, though, should be doable.

"Of course." She pats her pale blond curls as she looks around the store. "What did you have in mind?"

"Nothing from the boutique. I've been experimenting with some new looks and want to try them on you."

Aunt Jade clasps her hands together. "Are you working on a new line? I know you said after your first one that you weren't sure designing was the direction you wanted to go, but you're so very talented at it."

"I haven't decided to create another line yet, but I have been feeling a surge of creativity lately."

Mother preens under the idea. "You should do Jade, too, dear. We are the face of this company, after all."

I nod. "Absolutely."

Having forgotten all about Sydney as they imagine what I'm going to do for them next weekend, they set about performing the closing routine of the store. I never thought about it before, but it now strikes me as the height of irony that my mother will sweep and fold clothes in the store but considers doing those chores in her own home as a sign of being a less-valuable individual.

And I had been on a path to be just like her.

On the one hand, I'm both humbled and happy to see a real measure of the growth God has worked in me. On the other, I'm willing to acknowledge that I still have a long way to go, because what I'm planning now could be considered more than a little petty.

I pull out my phone and open the messaging app. My conversation with Jason is sitting on top, with Emma's right beneath it. My finger hovers over the screen, shifting from one name to the other.

Biting my lip, I select a conversation and type out a new message.

> ME: Have you ever been to a thrift store?

JASON

I can honestly say I haven't spent a great deal of time in secondhand clothing stores, whether they are thrift stores, vintage resale shops, or consignment stores. Still, I swing by the boutique to pick up Amy for a morning of touring various options in the area. My office closes for the week of Thanksgiving and everyone works lighter remote hours, so I've got the flexibility to join her this morning.

It's a toss-up whether I'm more curious about the different types of businesses or about why Amy wants to check them out. The most important thing is that this isn't the sort of event I'd classify as a date so I shouldn't have the same issues I had with our outing to the theater. All week, the conversation from Sunday has played in my head and I'm halfway convinced that my reasons to not date Amy were either unfounded in the first place or no longer apply.

The other half of me is more certain than ever that a relationship would be a terrible idea.

I pull up to the curb outside the boutique and throw the car into park so I can get out and circle around to open her door. It's a courtesy I don't always give Emma, admittedly, but I do it for the other women in my life. Mostly.

Amy exits the store as I get to the passenger door. Her enormous leather bag is thrown over her shoulder, one hand clutches a small stack of sticky notes and a to-go coffee from the bakery down the street, and her other hand is holding her phone and a pair of sunglasses. She slides the glasses into place and then unlocks her phone, using her thumb to search for something as she settles into the car.

"Good morning," I say with a grin. This is obviously a girl on a mission, and I feel honored to have been included in the adventure.

She looks up and a soft laugh escapes through a brief smile. "Yes. Sorry. Good morning."

I close the door and jog around to get back in the driver's seat. "I'm guessing you have a plan?"

"Yes." She places her coffee in the cup holder and holds up the stack of colored squares and her phone. "I have a few options for routes, depending on how the first experiences go. I have to be back for an appointment at 1:00 this afternoon."

"No problem. I'm meeting my mother for a late lunch this afternoon as well." I put the first address in my phone and pull into the light traffic of a Tuesday morning before a holiday. "Why the sudden desire to shop secondhand?"

"Well, twice a year our boutique does a resale event. We always offer customers a discount if they bring in a previously purchased item in good condition and then we keep them stored in a back room until the next event."

"For PR purposes?" I'm well aware of companies doing things that make them look better to those who criticize the basic company model. In this case, the idea that people tend to toss perfectly good clothing away when they buy new or how the high boutique prices are too far out of reach for most people.

"Yes. It was Emma's idea, actually. Mother and Aunt Jade were a little resistant until a blogger heard about the idea and couldn't sing the boutique's praises high enough."

I nod. All of that makes perfect sense but doesn't explain this morning's mission. "So, you're checking out the competition?"

Her head swings toward me and even though she's wearing dark glasses, I can practically feel her blinking at me in confusion in the same way Emma sometimes does. Amy's cuter, though.

Man, I am sunk. I might as well admit it.

"No," Amy says slowly. "If we made an entire store for resale we wouldn't get the advertising from the events."

"Right. So, why are we here?" I pull up to a store with signs in the window about consignment inspection hours and store credits. Rack upon rack of clothing can be seen as well. If she intends to work her way through all of that, we won't be getting to any of the other places on her list.

"Because I can't keep pilfering from the resale stock or we won't have enough to hold the event."

Amy doesn't wait for me to come around and open her car door. She pushes her way out and is opening the door to the store before I've even locked the car behind me.

Once inside she frowns at the racks. Some are separated by designer label, other racks are by general sizing. I trail after her as she wanders up and down the aisles, occasionally pinching a piece of clothing between her fingers. She stops to pull a shirt that is way too large off the rack and holds it up to admire. Then she looks back at the racks she's already passed.

"Do you think they have this in a smaller size?"

I sputter out a laugh. "Ah, no."

"Why not?"

"Because that would require another person to have brought in the exact same shirt at a similar time so both items could be in the store at once." I shake my head. "You should know this from your sale."

"We frequently have the same items in multiple sizes." She sighs and places the hanger back on the rack. "I'm not supposed to be shopping for me anyway."

"Who are we shopping for?"

"Sydney. Or rather, people like Sydney." She grins. "And my mother."

I only know one Sydney. She's in the singles group at church. While it's unlikely that's the Sydney Amy is referring to, I have to admit that the woman does not wear the most flattering clothing choices. Amy's mother makes absolutely no sense.

"Are you branching out your styling services?"

She mumbles as she practically dives into a rack of dress pants. "Maybe."

My eyebrows rise but I say nothing as I trail her around. She does end up buying a pair of jeans and a blouse with a giant pink flower on it and then we're on to the next location.

This one is a thrift store, and Amy's eyes widen as she looks around the warehouse-like space. While I've never bought clothes at a store like this, I visited several in college with friends looking for furniture or old electronics. I still hit them up sometimes when I'm looking for old video games, though most of that searching is done online from the comfort of my office chair.

Amy has clearly never set foot in a place like this because she's come to a full stop about three feet past the door. Gently I nudge her to the side so people can pass us.

Looks like she's going to remain stuck in some kind of shock unless I provide assistance. We'll start with the furniture. There's a large couch positioned next to a dinette set that's missing a chair. A wooden china cabinet is sitting back-to-back with a large, particleboard corner desk. In the center of the section is a bean bag chair and a wooden end table with a built-in lamp that looks about four decades old.

"What do you think?" I fight back a laugh because Amy looks adorably confused.

"I . . . how can you ensure everything matches if you buy your furniture like this?" She looks from the lamp table to the couch as if trying to imagine the items in the same room.

"That's not the point of thrift store furniture."

"What is the point then?"

I think about one of the frat houses I occasionally visited while in college and the downstairs game room that didn't have a single piece of matching furniture but boasted enough cheap couches that it wasn't a big deal if people got a little too rowdy and broke one of them. "Cheap, mostly."

"Oh." I can tell it's a foreign concept to her. Based on what little she and Emma have told me of their upbringing, it doesn't surprise me. A highly image-conscious social climber wasn't likely to shop at a thrift store. Or, at least, wasn't likely to admit it to her daughters that she was trying to raise in a socially-elite setting.

I point to the couch. "There's two reasons to buy cheap."

Her eyebrows lift. "And they are?"

"Budgetary reasons."

She winces and I have a feeling she's either running close to the limit of her budget or God's been convicting her about some of her expenses. Either way, I'm not trying to lecture her. I'm trying to get her to loosen up, so I press on. "And option two is for fun."

"Fun?"

"Yep. If the clothes aren't expensive, they don't matter as much. Come on, let's play a game." I saw this on InstaTok when I was looking for accounts that related to Amy's business. It's similar to a game my friends and I played in college where we took five dollars into a thrift store and had to purchase our gift for the name we drew in the Christmas party gift exchange.

With an arm thrown over her shoulders I lead her toward the clothing racks. The warmth of her pressed into my side is more than a little distracting, but I stay focused on the prize at the end of this little jaunt.

"Now I've only seen this game played online, but normally I would be the one choosing your outfit."

She looks from me to the racks of clothing, a mix of skepticism and fear on her face. "You are choosing me an outfit? From here?"

"No, I figure I'll be gracious and let you do the choosing." I grip her tighter to my side when she starts to head for a rack. "But there are rules."

"Okay." I almost feel the change in her body as she shifts her focus from whatever brought us here in the first place to whatever this relationship is with me. "What are the rules?"

"No looking."

She blinks at me and then looks at the racks filled with every fabric and color and style imaginable. "No looking?"

I shake my head. "Nope. I will let you feel the clothes with one hand, but you have to keep moving down the aisle. Once you fully grip an item of clothing, that's it."

"And then I have to find other things to go with it?"

A grin pulls at my cheeks as I shake my head. "Same process for shirt, bottoms, shoes, basically anything you need to make an outfit."

"But that's going to look terrible. What do I do with such an outfit?"

"We go out to dinner in them."

"You're going to do this, too?"

"It's no fun to make you do it alone."

Her gaze meets mine and she stares into my eyes for several moments. The store ceases to exist for me. There's nothing but Amy and a desperate hope that she takes this challenge. Because if she doesn't . . . If she doesn't then I've become infatuated with a girl who doesn't exist instead of with the woman God is forming out of her prior self.

"I have stipulations."

My eyebrows raise. "Okay."

"Dinner is somewhere weird. Like . . . Emma says there's a little diner in Appleton I should try sometime."

Appleton is a really small town about an hour away from here. She's not likely to run into any of her clientele there. I have to give her that because being seen in mismatched thrift store clothes would not help her reputation any.

I nod in agreement. "Anything else?"

She opens her mouth then closes as she shrugs. "No, I think that's it."

"Okay then. Close your eyes." Her dark lashes sweep down, cutting off her gray gaze, and I guide her toward the shirts first. I place her hand on the first hanger. "Your size starts here and goes down this whole row and half of the next."

"And I have to keep moving?"

"Right."

Her pace is so slow a glacier could beat her in an uphill race, but she is technically moving forward as her fingers dance along the edges of the garments. Finally, she frowns slightly and backs her hand up two shirts. I bit my tongue to keep from laughing. I'm sure it feels like a nice shirt, but the portion I can see is splashed with bright neon colors.

"This one." She dutifully keeps her eyes closed while I grab the shirt and hold it up to guess whether or not it will fit.

"Okay, do you want pants or a skirt?" I wrap my arm around her shoulders and guide her toward another row.

"Pants." She sighs. "They're more likely to be neutral."

"Almost makes me want to take you to the skirts instead."

She grins up at me, eyes still firmly shut as she leans into my guidance. "Should have thought of that before you gave me an option."

Fortunately for my amusement, she doesn't choose a neutral pair of pants. It's a pair of wide-legged trousers with some wild sort of fringe running down the front and back seams of the legs. She couldn't feel that when dancing her fingers along the hangers.

Next, we hit shoes and, since next week is Thanksgiving and the air is occasionally thinking about being cold, the jackets. I stash her atrocious bundle with the clerk at the front of the store and then we repeat the process with the men's clothing. As much as I'm tempted to cheat when she selects a bright green corduroy dinner jacket to go with the plaid shirt and blue pants, but I dutifully take the whole lot to the register.

With the collective outfits in two different bags, we leave the store and briefly visit one more shop on her list where she finds several items to purchase before heading back to the boutique.

If she didn't have an appointment to get back for, I'd be tempted to keep her out all day. My mother would be beside herself if I canceled so I could go out on a date.

But this wouldn't be a date. Because we're just friends.

I fake a cough to cover a sigh because it's time I admit it. I don't want to be Amy's friend. I want to be her boyfriend. I want to hold her hand as we walk into church. I want to assume she'll keep me updated on her weekend plans. I want to cook her dinner and pretend I'm teaching her how to play video games while we snuggle on the couch.

I want to introduce her to my parents.

That last impulse terrifies me into holding my tongue because I'd been on the verge of suggesting we change our relationship after Thanksgiving. Maybe it would be best to let things lie as they are through the new year. Christmas is such a hectic time and there are so many family events that I'd have to invite her to, and I just don't think my family's Christmas party should be the first thing we do together as a couple.

Still, when I park the car I notice we both have a little time before our different obligations. I walk her into the boutique.

Her mother is watching me, so I give her a little wave. Hopefully she won't judge the fact that I'm not in designer clothing this time.

Back in Amy's office, the first thing I notice is the blank space on the wall where the vision board once was. I can't see much of the blank space, granted, because she had the board fairly well blocked from a client's perspective, but I can see that it's gone.

Is there a way to delicately ask why?

"I had fun today." I jab my hands in my pockets and stand awkwardly in the middle of her office.

"Me too. I didn't think I would, but it was fun. I'm especially excited to tell my mother she wore secondhand clothing to a garden party." She drops her purse on her desk and clasps her hands in front of her, mirroring my awkward swaying. "And now we have an atrociously dressed dinner to look forward to."

"Oh, yeah, we do." I look over my shoulder. "I forgot your bag in the car."

"That's okay. I probably shouldn't see it until the last minute anyway so I don't chicken out."

We grin at each other. Make eye contact. Look away.

We might as well be at her door after a date. Seriously, who do we think we're fooling? This wasn't a standard date-like outing. This isn't a standard drop off location. But these feelings? These actions? I know this dance. I haven't done it all that often, but I've done it enough to know that most of the time the awkward is at least partially an itch to run away.

This awkward is all about keeping myself from kissing her good night. Er, good afternoon.

And I appear to be failing because I think I just took one step closer to her. That or the world's tiniest earthquake just jostled me across the floor.

"If you, uh, ever need another shopping buddy . . ." My voice is low and quiet.

"I'll find one who lets me shop with my eyes open." She grins up and me and then slides her eyes shut. "This is only good for sleeping, scary movies, and kissing."

"Kissing, huh?"

Her eyes open and she takes a deep breath. "Yes."

"You prefer to kiss with your eyes closed?"

A slight frown mars her forehead. "Doesn't everyone?"

"I honestly don't know that I've ever paid attention." And then my head is leaning down, and my eyes are certainly not closing. Until our lips meet and then my eyelids slide closed, shutting out everything but this moment.

I meant it to be a brief kiss. Actually, I didn't mean it to be a kiss at all, but once it became inevitable, I intended to keep it short.

But I don't want to stop.

And she's not showing any signs of putting on the brakes.

It's either I pull away or things are going to be really weird when her client arrives.

The effort required to step away fills me with a sensation something like guilt as I realize that, before Amy, I've never had to be the one to stop an all-consuming kiss. I've always dated good Christian church girls that shared my views of intimacy and marriage and they've always been the ones to hold up a hand or break the connection.

Not that I tried to push them or anything, but I certainly hadn't taken the lead in keeping things in check.

Now it is falling to me because while Amy may be planning on waiting now, she doesn't have the years of experience in holding back. I realize how unfair I was to those previous girlfriends.

I take another step back and avoid Amy's gaze while I try to give her a smile. "That was not what I intended."

"Me neither," she chokes out.

"So . . . I should go."

"My client will be here soon."

"Right."

I take two steps toward the door then stop, run my hand through my hair, and allow the sense of guilt to convict me into apologizing. "I shouldn't have done that. I'm sorry."

Her eyes widen. "You're sorry?"

"I . . . yeah. I'm sorry. It's not fair to you to be . . ." I wave my hand toward her and then run it through my hair again.

Her surprise hardens into a mask of indifference. "Kissing me?"

I swallow hard. "Yeah."

One perfectly-groomed eyebrow arches. "Dating me?"

"Yeah, I—Wait, I haven't been dating you." I frown.

Her head cocks to the side as she inspects me.

I have to admit that the last couple of outings we've been on felt very date-like, but they weren't official so I don't think they should count against me. "They weren't dates. They were . . . date adjacent."

She rolls her eyes, which is a welcome break from the icy expression she was wearing. "You sound like Emma."

"That is rather to be expected." I shrug one shoulder.

Her face scrunches up. "That doesn't make this any less weird."

"Right." I sigh and take another step toward the door. "So . . . we'll just go back to being friends and I'll do a better job of keeping my lips to myself and that will give you time to figure out this new you and I'll prove to my friends that my life isn't missing something because Emma has a boyfriend."

And I probably shouldn't have said that part out loud.

Amy sits slowly in her chair. "Have I been a substitute for Emma?"

I snort out a laugh. "No. I have never thought about kissing Emma."

"Not even when you dated?"

"Not even when we attempted to date." I shake my head. "Today's shopping adventure was more date-like than anything Emma and I ever managed."

"Right. But your Saturdays are free because Emma's with Carter."

"Life is all about changes, isn't it?" This is getting uncomfortable, but I can't be the one to end the conversation. I don't know why, but I feel like if I don't close this conversation correctly I'm going to lose something precious. I still want to wait until after Christmas, but maybe giving her a hint would be a good idea? "We really need to talk about this."

"This?"

"Us."

There are words—important words—in her eyes but I never learn what they are because her mother barges into the office at that moment.

"Oh my, I didn't realize your guest was still here."

Ms. Trinket is a terrible liar. She was hoping to walk in on something more like what we were doing three minutes ago. Still, the way we're standing across the room looking at each other isn't exactly innocent.

Amy closes her eyes for a breath and then looks at her mother. "Can I help you, Mother?"

"Your client is out front, dear. I stalled her for a few minutes by having Jade show her the new arrivals." The older woman looks from me to Amy. "You know, in case you needed a minute."

And on that note . . . "I'm gonna go." I back out into the hall and turn, fleeing the scene like a man with way too many things to figure out. I consider bailing on my lunch with my mother anyway, but it's a monthly thing and she's probably already at the restaurant.

Besides, I could definitely use the distraction.

And maybe the reminder of why I didn't want to date a socialite.

AMY

The Thanksgiving holiday has never been a very important one for my family. Mother would, of course, purchase a small catered dinner for us and we would gather for a picture-worthy meal, but given the busy days ahead of us at the boutique, the day has always been low-key.

It's one of the few weekends I still work full-time for my mother and aunt. Even the well-to-do like to think they're getting a good deal by going shopping the weekend after turkey and dressing. We only put a few items on sale—and those are only 15% off—but it doesn't stop our customer traffic from almost quadrupling.

In fact, I'll be working on Sunday morning and I'm thankful for the excuse to miss church again this weekend. I might need a break from seeing Jason for a while. The aftermath of our shopping outing has been plaguing my mind for several days.

But no more. With my family obligations seen to and no other responsibilities until the boutique opens in the morning, I have taken a self-care afternoon. There is a clay mask on my face, a collagen mask on my hair, and aloe masks on my hands and feet. Episodes of Designing Women, an old show I discovered in my teens, are playing one after the other on my television and a Diet Dr. Pepper is sitting on the table with a long straw sticking out so I can sip without disturbing the clay.

My phone, which has lain eerily silent on the couch for hours, buzzes. Then it buzzes again. And again. The notifications come so close to each other that the phone starts moving along the couch cushion from the constant vibrations. I watch helplessly as it tumbles over the side.

Fortunately, I have a plush rug underneath so I'm not worried about the screen, but I am worried about why so many people are contacting me. Or why one person needs to contact me that many times.

It will take too long for me to dispose of the thin aloe-soaked gloves and wash my hands, so I drop to the floor, the plastic grocery bags keeping my aloe-soaked socks off the carpet crinkling ominously.

Of course, my phone is face down, so I lower onto my elbows, carefully keeping my hands raised, and wedge the phone up until I can grip it with my teeth and flip it over. For not the first time in my life, I am so glad I live alone because I would have to start living underneath my couch if anyone saw me in this position.

Although if someone else were here I wouldn't have to resort to such lengths to see my notifications.

Once the phone is flipped over, I use my elbow to activate the screen then position my face for the ID unlock. It takes three tries before I admit the camera isn't happy about my clay-covered face and use my tongue to trace out the unlock sequence.

And then my heart stops.

Because there are fifteen text notifications from Emma.

Fifteen.

I stab at the screen with my nose. I open my email, a makeup tutorial app, and my maps before successfully getting the texts open. My stomach is in my throat the entire time. If I thought my slimy fingers would work, I'd rip off these gloves and deal with the mess on my rug later, but I know from experience that they would do nothing but slide across the screen if I touched it, so my nose is all I have for now, even if it is leaving thin streaks of clay on the glass.

The trepidation flows out of me as I realize no one is in the hospital or the police station or considering shaving their head.

The news is just as life-changing though, because it would seem that Carter has proposed.

I flop onto my back as another buzz sounds from my phone. My eyes slide closed as I wait for my breath to return to normal. Once I feel in control of myself, I push up from the floor and shuffle to the bathroom to clean my hands. I'd like to take the time to get rid of all the masks, but it is imperative that I respond to Emma as soon as possible.

My messages will just have to come from the part of me that is squealing and excited—at least on the inside because doing so on in the outside would have this mask flaking off and leaving clay chunks around my apartment. The part of me that feels a little panicked about news that I knew was coming is just going to have to wait for a better time to get attention.

I return to the living room to grab the phone, then wander back toward the bathroom as I feel my smile growing. If I'm going to have to clean up the clay, it'll be easier to do so in a place where the floor is tile.

EMMA: GUESS WHAT?!?!?!

EMMA: You'll never guess.

EMMA: Carter asked me to marry him!

EMMA: I said yes, of course.

EMMA: Look at the ring

EMMA: <<Picture of her hand with a gorgeous, simple engagement ring on her finger>>

I flinch at the clean but unpolished and unshaped fingernails. She keeps them trimmed short because she spends so much time typing, but they aren't entirely even. Her skin could also use fifteen minutes in a set of the gloves I just removed.

The ring is pretty, though. At least, pretty for Emma. The band is silver and sort of swirls around a tiny chip of a diamond. Carter could afford a bigger ring, but he went with something Emma would prefer instead. I'd be willing to bet that tiny diamond is perfect in cut, clarity, and color, though.

I scroll to the next message.

> EMMA: Would you be my maid of honor???????????

> EMMA: I know I'm supposed to ask in some cutesy way, but I can't wait.

> EMMA: I also know you're going to say yes because you've been saying we'll stand up in each other's weddings since we were three.

That's true, though usually I pictured me being the first to get married. Especially once we hit our teenage years and I had way more dates than she did.

> EMMA: I can't believe I'm getting married!

That makes two of us.

> EMMA: Mother is going to freak out about it. Maybe I'll wait to tell her.

I wince because that is a no-win situation. If she tells Mother now, the woman will want to be all up in the event planning, trying to turn it into something that will help her social standing. On the other hand, if Emma waits and Mother finds out from someone else, their already strained relationship might take a killing blow.

> EMMA: Ugh. No. I can't. At least not long. That would be mean.

> EMMA: I'll tell her tomorrow.

> EMMA: Maybe I can plan the whole thing this weekend before she has time to give any input?

Another notification comes through and I shoot off some private messages to Emma before checking it.

> ME: <<GIF of Julia Sugarbaker from Designing Women saying *Congratulations*>>

> ME: The ring is beautiful. Tell Carter I approve.

> ME: Of course I will be your maid of honor. Do I have time to design your dress as well or are we hopping on a plane to Vegas?

> EMMA: Oh my gosh, how did you know?

I blink. Is she truly planning to elope?

> ME: You aren't serious.

> EMMA: No, but I wish I could see your face right now.

> ME: It's covered in a clay mask so you wouldn't be able to see much.

> **EMMA:** Pics or it didn't happen!

> **ME:** Guess it didn't happen then.

I exit out of our chat and see what else is in my inbox.
Emma has also added me to a group chat. It's me, her, and . . . Jason.

> **EMMA:** Greetings dual honor attendants!!!!!

> **EMMA:** I'm starting this group chat because, while I know I should probably wallow in the happiness of being engaged for a while, I simply have to get moving!

> **EMMA:** I cannot wait to spend the rest of my life with Carter and the sooner I plan the wedding the sooner that can happen.

> **JASON:** <<GIF of Elvis singing *Viva Las Vegas*>>

> **JASON:** You could even charter a private plane. It'd be cheaper than a wedding.

> **EMMA:** My mother would never speak to me again.

> **JASON:** Tell me what you need. I'll get my mom to help me.

> **EMMA:** You don't need your mom. You have Amy!

I freeze. I know she means that I'm part of the honor court, too, and
can therefore help with decisions, but just seeing it phrased that way
makes me think of other things.

What is Jason going to say to that? The messages had been coming fast, but now the whole bathroom is quiet. My feet are beginning to tingle, the clay is so dry it's starting to crack, and I need to rinse out my hair before I discover if one can do too much of a beauty treatment.

But I need to see what Jason says first.

My phone buzzes and I open the screen.

> JASON: Sounds like I can get out of planning then and just show up. Isn't that what a guy does?

> EMMA: That's what the GROOM does, theoretically.

I close the screen and put the phone down. It buzzes a couple more times. Probably Emma stating that Carter is going to have opinions about the colors and the decorations and the photographer and a whole lot else. The guy is an artist after all.

Responding to all of that can wait. I need to take care of myself right now.

Maybe that's in more ways than one?

As I work my way through rinsing and cleansing and lotioning and sealing, I think.

I think about how I've spent so much time trying to be perfect and make everything perfect from my hair to my job to my new faith. I think about how many opportunities I've let pass me by because I didn't know for absolute certain that I could do them all perfectly. And yes, I think about the fact that I'm almost thirty and my sister is getting married.

My whole life has moved at glacial speed because I had to be sure of every step. The only impulsive thing I've ever done was make Jesus my Lord and Savior as I cried on Emma's floor. I didn't know what that would be like before I did it. If I had, I don't know that I'd have made the jump. Now, of course, I fully accept that my relationship with my old friends has changed and my idea of a good time isn't what it used to be.

But life isn't going to wait for me to put everything together with this new perspective. Business rolls on, the rent is still due every month, and premature wrinkles must still be combatted.

What had I read this morning? I've been working my way through the Gospels in the Bible and got to a passage with the subheading The Great Commission. It read like a graduation speech to believers, but instead of being sent out into the world at the end of our studies, we were being commissioned at the beginning.

Even that one guy, Paul, said he didn't have it all together. The study aid Jason had pointed me to had clarified the translation of the verse in Matthew to mean *as you go*. Meaning we are supposed to figure this following Jesus thing out *as* we walk.

It's not going to be possible for me to learn everything and be a perfect Christian before moving forward.

And that is a seriously terrifying thought.

Once I'm dressed and my hair dry, I pick up my phone to read the rest of the messages. It's buzzed off and on during my process, but the flurry of messages slowed down while I was in the shower.

As expected, there's several messages about Carter planning on being involved in the wedding planning. He knows photographers and what colors will best flatter Emma in the pictures. I'm sure he knows which colors will flatter him, too, but he's a smart man and is going to make sure my sister shines brighter than anyone.

I resign myself to looking slightly green because what works for Emma does not work for me.

JASON: Please tell me I don't have to go dress shopping.

EMMA: No, I won't do that to you.

EMMA: But you are going to have to help with the tuxedos.

JASON: What's wrong with putting the guys in jeans and sport coats?

I smile. Totally called that one.

EMMA: I'm saving the wrath of my mother for more important things.

JASON: Like?

EMMA: Like the date. We're thinking Spring.

I blink at my phone and reread that. Spring as in a few months from now? I don't know a single wedding that was planned in less than a year. Usually longer, in all reality, because so many women research themes and dresses and plans for years ahead of time.

While I haven't let myself look at it in a while, I have a board or two of wedding ideas on my Pinterest account.

JASON: That's fast. You'll barely have a chance to get used to being engaged.

I let out a laughing scoff. They've barely had time to get used to dating.

JASON: Makes sense though. Why get used to a state you're not staying in? Might as well spend the time and effort learning how to be a married couple.

There's more conversation but I lower the phone as Jason's statement. He's putting a lot of effort into accustoming us to being friends. Does that mean it's a state he intends to stay in?

Tears blur my vision at the thought. Yes, I'm learning how to be a Christian, but perhaps I'm too far behind to ever be of real interest to him. Is he just having to work his way through being attracted to me? Because I'm experienced enough in relationships to understand that reality.

But the only reason not to follow an attraction is because something in your mind knows it's a bad idea, knows it's something you shouldn't have. Like a triple fudge brownie sundae that's meant for two, but you scarf it down all by yourself and later feel sick to your stomach for a day and half.

Am I a triple fudge brownie sundae?

I open my phone again and send a couple of replies to the wedding conversation so Emma doesn't think I'm upset about this turn of events, then I switch over to my conversation with Jason.

> ME: We never did plan our thrift store outfit dinner.

> JASON: No, we didn't. I think your bag of clothing is still in my car.

He said we'd go to dinner as friends, but then he kissed me and honestly, this is the first time in my adult life I haven't felt like I needed a man, but that doesn't mean I don't want one. Despite not knowing all the ins and outs of God and the Bible, becoming a Christian has slid my view of myself into focus. I'm still me.

Why should I become accustomed to being a single version of that woman if I'm ready to be part of a couple?

I take a deep breath and plunge on.

> ME: We should make it a date. I'm free next weekend?

> JASON: What do you mean by make it a date?

My fingers tremble as I type.

> ME: Just what I said.

There's silence for an excruciatingly long time. Finally a message comes through.

> JASON: I think that's a conversation we need to have in person.

> JASON: But I can't next weekend.

> JASON: In fact, I'll be out of touch most of next week. I have a family obligation.

> JASON: I'm sure your December calendar is also full, but we'll find a time.

> JASON: Maybe we should wait for the new year.

I send back an *Of course* because what else can I do? As I just reminded myself, people are still people when they come to Jesus, and I've dealt with enough people to know a gentle let down when I see one.

My concerns that Jason wanted to be nice to me but didn't want to be attracted to me are certainly well-founded.

I send one last message to wish him a happy Thanksgiving.

Then I go curl up on my couch, press play on another episode of Designing Women, and cry.

AMY

Monday morning, I slide in the back door of the boutique, hoping to make it to my office without having to speak to either Mother or Aunt Jade. All weekend it's been nothing but wedding and business talk. I was happy to hide behind the statement that it was Emma's wedding so I'd wait to see what she wanted, while Mother planned the society gathering of the ages. The truth is I was jealous. I never thought seriously about getting married, but I always assumed I'd tie the knot before Emma did.

And the business talk? That was worse. Mother and Aunt Jade want to freshen the brand in the Spring—I'm pretty sure she plans to tie it into Emma's wedding somehow—and I didn't participate in any of the discussions. When Mother pressed, I said I was focusing on my own stuff.

What followed that announcement was a hushed rant over my lack of initiative, ownership, and commitment. She all but told me I was riding on her coattails and if I wanted to make something of myself one day, I needed to push a little more. Her lack of belief in my abilities still stings even though I've done my best to keep my initiative from her. Perhaps that proves her point. Look at how I started my business. In shadows and beneath her established branding.

The raw emotion uncovered Thursday night was rubbed with sandpaper and doused in lemon juice throughout the weekend. While part of me was grateful for the excuse of work to keep me away from church Sunday morning, mostly I'm just tired. Between the holiday and a lack of what had become my weekly reset anchor, my mind and body are ready to succumb to the onslaught of all the emotions and just wallow for a while.

I'll have to settle for losing myself in work. I go to my office and push the door closed behind me with a sigh of relief. My relief at having made it is premature as someone knocks lightly on my door before it can completely latch shut.

Fortunately, I know how to pretend to be happy. That's one talent I didn't lose with this whole faith adjustment. I may not be enough of a strong woman of faith for Jason or enough of a businesswoman for my mother, but I refuse to allow myself to believe I'm not enough, period. The last three months of working on my faith have taught me that.

"Come in." I put a smile on my face and give my attention to the door as I place my bags on the desk.

Mother walks in, appearing to be full of genuine joy and excitement. Obviously she's put our disagreement behind her or she's as good at faking it as I am.

In truth, she's probably better. I had to learn the skill from somewhere.

"What are you doing this weekend?" Mother clasps her hands in front of her, energy all but rolling off her in waves. If she were a less appearance-conscious woman I think she'd be bouncing on her toes.

"I have no plans yet." Not going on a date with Jason, at least. Probably not even talking to him. Because he's got family obligations that he didn't invite me to. Not that I should have been included, but he seemed to be very deliberately not telling me what those plans were. He knows all my family. If he were hoping to change things between us, wouldn't he want me to meet his or at least know about them?

"Good. Then your Saturday is now taken." Mother crosses to a rack of evening gowns in the corner. "I just received tickets to something you've been dying to attend for years."

My heartbeat picks up, trying to remember if one of the Broadway plays I particularly like is in town or if there's a concert I don't know about. No matter what the event is, I'm going to attend. This is a sort of peace offering from her and I know I need to keep a good relationship with Mother. I *want* a good relationship with my mother. For the fore-seeable future, we're sharing a workspace and even when that ends, we'll still be family. I can give an evening to make peace.

"Excellent." I pull my computer from my bag and set it on the desk followed by my sketch pad. "What is it?"

"I want to keep it a surprise." She pulls a gown off the rack and spins it to examine the front and back. "Just dress for elegance and be ready at 5:00."

"Elegance?" I look from her to the gown I pulled for a client to consider wearing to a hospital Christmas gala. "As in formal?"

She shrugs. "I suppose it doesn't have to be." Her smile slides into a youthful grin as she hugs the gown to her chest. "But wouldn't it be fun?"

Fun? We dress formally more often in a single year than a normal person does in their entire life. Which means doing so again isn't a problem if it makes Mother happy. "Yes, it would. Should we match color schemes?"

Our coloring is similar so there are plenty of shades that look amazing on both of us. Fortunately, our body shapes are different enough that we can't wear the same gowns. Given the level of giddiness with which she agrees with my idea, I wouldn't put it past her to suggest such.

For the rest of the week, her excitement only grows. I'm amazed that she can keep our destination a secret, especially since Aunt Jade apparently knows and is obviously upset that Mother wasn't able to procure three tickets instead of two. She's so distraught that I'm tempted to offer her mine since I won't know what I missed until it's over and done, but the tension between Mother and I reveals she hasn't put this weekend's discussion as far in the past as I'd hoped. I can't risk making things worse.

Mother wants to go shopping for new dresses, but the idea of doing so makes my chest tight, so I help her find one that coordinates with my favorite blue evening gown from the collection I launched earlier in the year. She accepts the excuse that I absolutely love this dress and want to wear it again before it goes out of style, but she frowns in surprise at the same time.

I don't blame her for being confused. I've never turned down an excuse to go shopping before, especially for formal clothing. Evening gowns are some of my favorite things. I can't help but think about Sydney, though, who couldn't even afford a new suit for an interview that might change her life. I'll have to text her soon to see how things went.

On Saturday, when I pull out the gown and drape it across my bed, the tightness caused by the unfamiliar thoughts and Jason's quiet rejection starts to ease. I may not have this whole being a Christian thing figured out, but I do feel like I'm relearning who I am and, more importantly, learning to accept that it may not make sense to everyone else.

The process of curling and styling my hair and applying my makeup is relaxing. I try a new eyeshadow tutorial, but I don't like it better than my usual evening look, so I cream off the makeup and start again.

By ten to five, I'm ready to go, waiting by my door and scrolling my phone until Mother arrives.

Jason is as radio silent as he predicted he would be, and no matter what he said the reason was, I can't help but feel it's him pulling away from me.

I asked for something more and he doesn't actually want that from me. There are a dozen plausible reasons why he wouldn't want a relationship with me even though he likes kissing me, and my brain plays them all on repeat.

I open our texting thread and frown. The last exchange was from Monday, when he'd sent me a picture of a baby koala after I let him know I'd watched the recording of Sunday's service like I promised.

After that, there's two more messages from me—a question about a popular Christian TV show that I tried to watch but simply couldn't get into and, after that question went more than a day without an answer, a funny meme about the weirdness of the English language.

At this point it's been so long that one of us is going to need a reason to text the other. We've gone far too long between messages to send anything general or purposeless. In fact, I can't be the next person to text him at all. At least, that's the rule I used to operate under.

Biting my lip, I open up my message exchange with Emma.

> ME: Are the messaging rules the same if you are dating a Christian guy?

> EMMA: Error. You have sent a social etiquette inquiry to a number that does not accept such questions. Please look at the number you sent this to and try again.

> ME: I'm being serious.

> EMMA: So am I.

> ME: It's been days since I got a text from Jason. I'm afraid if I text first, I'll look desperate.

I wait for a return message. And wait. And wait. And wait.

ME: This is an etiquette question. Not a Jason question.

EMMA: It's Jason adjacent. And I thought the two of you weren't dating. Did that change?

ME: No. But I want it to.

EMMA: Why?

ME: I don't know. Because I like him?

EMMA: You're going to need to be able to answer that question.

ME: Did you have some deeper meaning behind accepting a date with Carter?

EMMA: No.

ME: There you go then. Can we pretend we're back in middle school when I made you go ask Billy Jenkins if he thought I was cute?

EMMA: Wow. Desperate much?

I drop my head against the wall and the immediately straighten. This is not worth flattening my curls.

ME: Yes. I am.

EMMA: Didn't he tell you he's busy this week?

ME: Yes.

EMMA: It's true. He hasn't even been in the office since noon on Tuesday.

I sigh. At least that part is true. But to not text at all? After we'd been near-constant communicators for weeks on end?

EMMA: If you want to text him, text him. If you want to send him pictures of your breakfast, do it. You won't get to know him better if you don't talk to him.

While her advice seems sound, I have trouble trusting it. There's no strategy to her suggestion, no intentionality or management of expectations.

ME: What if he doesn't want to get to know me better, but he feels some sort of strange obligation.

The minutes drag on and when Mother knocks on my door, Emma still hasn't answered. I squeeze my phone into my clutch, grab my wrap, and leave the apartment. All the ease I gained while getting ready stays behind the door when I slide the lock into place.

My suspicions that we're going to a show downtown increase when I learn Mother hired a driver and town car for the evening. She hates trying to park downtown and since I don't know where we're going, she can't ask me to drive. We don't head downtown, though. We head out to the North Benton area instead.

The houses get larger and then move out of sight, hidden behind enormous hedges and decorative fencing. The gates get further and further apart.

I want to ask where we're going, but I doubt she'll tell me. She's kept it a secret this long, she's not about to spoil it within miles of our destination. The only events that happen at houses like these are parties and there's very few that are regular enough, important enough, and exclusive enough that I would want an invitation.

Or would have wanted an invitation.

While I will admit to a growing excitement over the idea of whatever gathering we're driving to, I think I'm more excited about seeing inside one of these gorgeous homes than I am about appearing to be one of the exclusive people who live in them. That realization makes me glad I'm sitting down as everything in me turns to jelly.

It's been a couple of years since we came over here, but Mother, Aunt Jade, and I used to drive these streets, dreaming of one day being important enough to count ourselves among the residents.

For years, gaining access to this social circle was my main objective. To style exclusive society matrons like Abigail Lee or Camille Miller would boost my reputation enough to potentially catch the eye of celebrities and political figures. To design for them or style their looks would get me posted on fashion blogs and in magazines.

I don't think I'd turn down those opportunities now, but I haven't thought about ways to attain them in a couple of months. How odd, as I used to contemplate how to make it happen at least once a week.

The car slows and joins the traffic moving toward an open gate. A glow of light comes from behind the hedge, indicating the house and grounds have been lit brightly for tonight's gathering. I can't help craning my neck, trying to determine which house we're at and by extension which party we're attending. My brain rolls through what I know of the social calendar and as I stumble over what the answer must be, my breath picks up.

It can't be.

I turn to Mother, my eyes wide, and my excitement for the evening real for the first time all week. "We are not going to the Miller's Ornament Exchange."

Mother produces two small gift bags from where she's been hiding them beside her seat. "Oh, but we are."

An ornament exchange might sound like a mundane event. Churches and schools and community groups around the country—and possibly around the world—will be participating in a similar event.

They are nothing like the Miller Ornament Exchange. While yes, every attendee brings one ornament and leaves with another, what happens between those two occurrences is the most exclusive and legendary party in the city. It's not a social event or a charity gala. It's an invite-only gathering of the Millers' family and friends. Granted, the definition of *friend* is fairly loose and likely includes political and businesspeople they want to have a firmer connection to, but if formal could be done casually, this would be the event.

Getting an invite to this is the ultimate indication of having successfully climbed the social ladder.

"How . . ."

She gives a one-shoulder shrug. "I mentioned you, of course."

"Me?" Mrs. Miller knows who I am? She's seen my work?

"Frankly, I was surprised you hadn't already gotten an invitation, because she made it sound like she'd wanted to have you on the guest list already."

I can't speak. I can't think. Apparently all I can do is blink and breathe in shorter and shorter gasps.

The car eases up to the gate and Mother shows our invitation to the security guard. Then we're flowing up the drive with the other admitted guests, rolling slowly toward the front of a large house. It looks almost like a castle with the bow windows extending all the way up to the third floor and the stone facade blending into the landscaping as if the house grew in the garden.

A man in a tuxedo opens the car door and extends a hand to help us out and I feel like I'm stepping onto the red carpet at some movie premiere or arriving at a high-end club or restaurant. I glance around, half expecting to find reporters or paparazzi standing in the bushes but there's nothing but three-foot Christmas trees in gold pots covered in twinkling lights and red and green ornaments.

Of course there's no press, no paparazzi. In fact, I've never seen pictures from this party. Not even personal ones. It's known that if you want to be invited back, you keep this evening private.

I peak in the bag Mother handed me and see an ornament of a dressmaker's dummy. An elegant gown is in the process of being draped on it and I have a feeling the shiny metal portions of the frame are covered in real gold.

Another security guard—this one dressed in formal wear to blend in better with the surroundings—checks our invitation before admitting us into the house.

Beyond the door is a large foyer and we're directed through one of the arched openings into an honest-to-goodness rotunda. A staircase spirals up through the multi-floor opening topped with a tiered chandelier and swagged with ropes of green garland and white Christmas lights. A massive Christmas tree reaches well past the handrails on the second floor, though the ribbons and decorations stop about five feet from the floor. On the bottom section of the tree, guests are hanging the ornaments they brought. As I pull mine from the bag, I take in the ones that have already been hung.

There's an intricately carved wooden Santa, a beautifully painted frog wearing a red and white hat, a star made of blown glass, and a few dozen other exquisite offerings. No matter which one I leave with tonight, it will be a keepsake memory I will always treasure.

Mother hangs an ornament beside mine, a delicate seashell with a detailed painting of the beach on the inside curve.

There seems to be an unspoken flow directing people on toward a large open area. My guess is that this would typically be the living space and the wall blocking off the kitchen area is temporary, along with the lack of furniture currently gracing the room. I doubt anyone rings their living room with high-top cocktail tables on a regular basis.

Mother immediately moves deeper into the room, grabbing a glass of champagne and trying to look like she knows everyone here and exactly what she's doing.

I take a moment to get my bearings.

People are crowding toward one corner of the room and I'm guessing our host and hostess are over there. That needs to be my first stop because I need to thank her for the invitation and hear for myself that she likes my work.

I'm waylaid, though, by a familiar face.

"Amy?"

I stop, my smile widening until my cheeks hurt. "Robert, hello!"

After our animated conversation about the children's charity, I didn't know if we'd ever cross paths again. It hadn't seemed right to exchange contact information when we had no legitimate reason to keep in touch. At the time, I'd been sure that Jason and I had a connection I needed to respect even though we hadn't defined anything.

In the past, I still would have exchanged numbers, even started a deliberate flirtation. Accepting a date from another man would have been my way of making sure there wasn't a better option and encouraging the guy I'd already been seeing to make some form of exclusive commitment. It was all about playing the field and locking down the best option.

I hadn't wanted to do that this time. I wanted to devote all my romantic energy to seeing if Jason was the right guy, to slowly grow the spark into a flame.

Of course, that only works if both people are tending the spark and the combination of that silent text exchange and his pushing off any relationship discussion for a month is saying something else pretty loudly.

If Jason isn't interested, or is only going to date me if he loses a battle with himself, perhaps I should entertain other options.

Robert's enthusiastic greeting is something of a balm. If I'd known where we were going, I would have, of course, expected to see Robert here. It's his family's party, after all.

"I must say you look exquisite in that dress tonight."

"Thank you." My cheeks heat in pleasure at the compliment because no matter what the situation with Jason is, I'm still a woman.

Unlike Emma, I've never gotten the idea of being friends with the opposite sex. Every man has been evaluated on a datability scale. Except I hadn't thought about whether or not I wanted to kiss Robert during that our lengthy conversation. Nor did I consider the fact that he'd have access to good reservations or be a good asset on my arm at functions.

Unlike Jason, though, Robert is showing all the signs of being an interested man. Maybe I need to try to change how I think about him, too.

I work to keep away the frown thinking of Jason tries to inspire and put on a perfect smile instead as I give the skirt of my gown a little swish. "I designed this one."

Robert's eyes widen as he steps back to give the gown another slow perusal. "Really?"

I nod. "I haven't decided yet if I want to design an entire line, but this one in particular was a pleasure to create. I think it's my favorite dress I've ever owned." My nose wrinkles as I realize what I've said. "My goodness that sounds egotistical, doesn't it?"

"Not at all." He reaches out and grasps the fingers of my left hand. "You should be proud of your work. And you should enjoy it. I'd be more surprised if your favorite dress wasn't one you made." He shrugs with a small laugh. "You know, if you're making clothes. If I made a tuxedo, it certainly wouldn't be my favorite since it would be rather ill-fitting."

I laugh, remembering his earlier description of a regular day involving a number of spreadsheets and financial reports.

Robert nods toward the Christmas tree in the foyer. "What did you bring?"

I smile. "Are we supposed to share that information?" I fight to maintain the curve of my lips and not show my desire to wince. Yes, I'm veering very close to flirtation but I'm a single woman. I have no reason not to flirt.

Even if I'm not sure I want to.

"Mine is the rocking horse."

"Oh?"

He nods. "I always bring a rocking horse."

"This is my first year."

"I've been attending since I was sixteen. The rocking horse was a joke my younger brother suggested since I would be the youngest person in attendance." He gives a little shrug. "I've done it ever since."

I didn't realize Robert had a brother. Whenever I've seen his family out in society, it's just been the three of them. I don't mention it in case there's some tragic reason the younger brother isn't around and Robert keeps up the rocking horse tradition.

Instead I keep my response light. "What has been your favorite ornament to receive?"

He frowns. "Mother always makes us select last, so I'm afraid I normally end up with something rather unimaginative. I have a lot of glittery glass orbs."

"Orbs?" I can't help but grin.

He nods. "They are far too fancy to be considered Christmas balls."

"Such a shame that you couldn't choose first." I lean forward. "I'm tempted to make my escape early just so I can get my hands on the dog ballerina I saw as I came in."

He laughs. "Mother says that since we're the hosts, we have to take what's left."

The blatant reminder that Robert is what my mother calls established society makes my thoughts squirm. He's firmly rooted in the upper echelons and capable of opening any and every door he—or I—could desire.

He's exactly the sort of man I would have drooled over three months ago.

Whenever I look up into his face, though, something makes me think of Jason. I can't really picture the tech nerd walking around in a tuxedo at a party like this, though. He wouldn't be able to wear his ball cap and the froth of fake, formal politeness being spouted in most of the conversations would annoy him.

This conversation with Robert isn't like that though. It feels genuine, if simple, and I want to prolong it, if only to delay the polite simpering that's bound to come my way later in the evening.

We select glasses of champagne from a passing waiter and wander through the rooms, chatting and sipping the bubbly liquid. It's easy. Comfortable. And Robert is obviously intrigued, if not fully interested. He pauses at one point, seeming to consider something deeply before asking, "Can I call you sometime?"

It's not a request for a date but it is an indication of interest. I haven't fully decided to give up on Jason, but if I do, I'd be an idiot not to consider a nice guy like Robert. This is a game I know how to play, though. I know how to keep a connection open without signaling any sort of confirmation or commitment to future entanglements.

I smile. "Do you have your phone? I'm afraid mine is so wedged into my clutch that only an emergency will have me pulling it out."

"Of course." He reaches into his pocket and pulls out his phone. His thumb moves over the screen a few times before he hands it to me.

The screen is open to a blank text message. He knows how to play this game as well.

Quickly, I send myself a text message and then delete the message from his history. Now the ball is firmly in my court to decide if I want to have any further conversation with Robert.

Once his phone is secured back in his pocket, we keep walking through the library and across the foyer. Conversation turns to favorite Christmas movies. Eventually we wander under an arch into a room where beautiful Christmas carols are being played on stringed instruments. The quartet of musicians is tucked into an octagonal space created by the turret-like architecture. This room has also been cleared of its normal furniture and a temporary parquet dance floor has been set up in the middle of the room and couples are slowly filling the space.

Robert smiles at me. "Would you like to dance?"

"Of course." We set aside our empty champagne flutes, and I let him lead me to the floor.

As soon as his arm comes around me to settle against my upper back, I know I'll need to part ways with him after this dance is over. If he actually is interested, I need to make sure this fledging flirtation goes very slowly. I need time to prepare myself to give Robert a real chance.

And I should probably be a mature woman and have an actual conversation with Jason instead of just assuming things. We aren't dating, but I still feel like I need to break up with him before going out with anyone else. Hearing him say he was never going to date me will hurt, but it will help with the idea of moving on.

As we float around the floor, our discussion remains easy. Robert is an exceptional conversationalist and not once does he try to steer me toward the shadows of the softly lit garden. He's just . . . nice.

If Jason were here, though, I'd be taking over this dance, nudging him toward the door so we could step outside and have some privacy, even if all we were doing was talking. I can't help but feel like everyone is watching me dance with Robert, and I'm okay with that because there's nothing intimate about our interaction.

As the song comes to an end, I step back and smile. "Thank you for a lovely dance. I should circulate through the rest of the guests now."

He offers me his arm to escort me off the floor as if we were in some period piece drama. "I'd be happy to take you around."

"I'll be fine on my own."

He nods. "I hope you text me back so I can have your number this time. I'd love to see you again."

"No worries, brother. I can give it to you." I jerk around, recognizing the voice but not the cold hardness that runs through the middle of it.

Jason.

He's standing at the edge of the dance floor, and though I couldn't picture him dressed to the nines in a tuxedo earlier, he more than carries it off. The man is simply hot, that's all I can say.

But he's also . . . hurt? Wait, what did he call Robert? His brother? But that would mean . . .

His eyes land on me, grooves of anguish pulling at the corners. "You're more her type anyway."

JASON

They say those who don't learn from history are doomed to repeat it and here I am, fulfilling the prophecy. There's the girl I'm interested in, the woman I'd let my guard down around and begun to consider letting fully into my life, hanging onto my brother's arm with a wide smile on her face.

To say the sight is painful is an understatement.

At least this time it isn't cheating. Not really. While I haven't been able to think of anyone but Amy since I met her, we haven't come to any sort of agreement. In truth, I've insisted on the opposite of one because I don't want to rush her into a relationship when she's so focused on learning how to stand alone.

Everything with Amy has been backwards. I guess that should have been an indication that it wasn't meant to be.

I nod to my brother, who's looking from me to Amy with a stricken expression. He knows. And just like the last time, he is absolutely horrified. I can't be mad at him. This is all about Amy.

Even though, logically speaking, I know I can't be upset with her, either, I can't label the burn in my gut as anything other than anger. If I can't direct it at someone else, I'll have to aim it at myself.

I knew from Emma's stories of her family that social position was important to them. I knew Amy worked with high-end clients. I knew she was a frequent attendee at galas and charity events. I knew my family's position was her greatest ambition.

I knew all these things and still I allowed myself to believe she was different.

Robert steps closer to me, Amy trailing along with him as her hand is still snugged in the crook of his elbow. "Are you saying—?"

"No." I shake my head because I can't let Robert feel the guilt that would come from an exact repeat of the past. "We've talked some, but nothing official. Haven't even been on a date."

But we've kissed.

And it absolutely shifted my world.

I swallow hard. "She's free to . . ." I struggle to come up with a word I genuinely believe. Because I don't want to think of Amy dating, flirting, or even considering another man. I finally settle on just repeating, "She's free."

Amy frowns. "Free to do what?"

"Whatever you want." I force myself to shrug.

My mother appears at the edge of our little cluster just then. "Good evening, boys." Her smile is bright and happy, more so than normal. I know it means a lot to her that I pull out my tux and show up at this party every year. I didn't want any part of this life while I was growing up, feeling like I was constantly on display, having to ask my parents if there were pending business deals with the parents of any new friend I made at school, and never knowing how to answer the people who assumed I wanted to step into my family business as soon as I turned sixteen.

Fortunately, my family is different in private. They've completely supported my decision to step out of the spotlight and cut most of my public ties. Some people know there's a second Miller son, but they'd have to dig pretty deep to find out it's me. Miller is a common enough name that people don't immediately assume I'm connected. I show up for two parties a year, the ones my mother likes to think are more personal and less strategic, and that makes her happy since I come around for other truly family-only things all year round.

Tonight, though, she looks almost giddy to see me.

"I have a surprise for you." She leans toward me and nudges my shoulder with hers.

I force a smile onto my face, accustomed to faking my way through this party every year anyway. "Oh, yeah?"

She nods. "Why didn't you tell us you had a girlfriend?"

My eyebrows lift as I slide my gaze briefly to Amy who looks as shell-shocked as I feel. I slide my attention back to Mom. "Because I don't."

"But she knew . . ." Mom places a hand to her chest and looks around the room as if trying to find someone—presumably whoever claimed to be my girlfriend. The irony of this moment is not lost on me. Mom's claim probably has Amy's mind scrambling if it wasn't before.

"Oh, dear." Mom looks down to the floor, obviously debating what to do next.

"What did she know, Mom?" I ask.

"Well, it was her mother, actually. She saw us having lunch at Alexandra's Bistro last week and spoke to me as I was leaving. She said she was so happy to meet the mother of the man who was making her daughter so happy."

"And you believed her?"

"Well, not at first, because it's easy enough to find your name if someone really wants to, but she said you would bring her daughter lunch, and she knew how you ordered your sandwiches from Randall's."

My breath shudders in my chest as my gaze flies to Amy. Her skin has paled to a concerning level of near translucence, making her previously artful makeup stand out in streaks of bright color. Her mother knows how I take my sandwich and which deli I get it from.

Mom continues, "She said she was looking forward to getting to know me one day because she could see how much you and her daughter cared for each other. It seemed so honest that I added her to the guest list tonight." Mom's voice lowers to a whisper. "She knows what neighborhood you live in. Jason, do you have a stalker?"

I shake my head no, but I look at Amy again and leave my attention on her.

"I didn't know." She swallows visibly, and I shift my weight, prepared to catch her if she passes out. Fainting looks like a definite possibility. "I didn't . . . She didn't even tell me we were coming here. I found out when we arrived. I didn't know it was you."

"You're his girlfriend?" The confusion is clear. "Why were you dancing with Robert—oh, no." Mom's voice hardens, and I can feel her stiffen beside me even though I can't pull my gaze from Amy. "I'm going to get security."

I stop my mother with a hand on her arm. "No, Mom, it's not like that."

"It's not?" Amy's voice is small and the pain in her eyes slams me in the gut.

"Amy and I are . . . not dating." I force myself to continue spilling the truth as if I'd been cut and forced to bleed all over the floor. "We're . . . friends." It almost pains me to say the word because Emma is my friend, and I don't feel remotely the same sensations when I look at Amy.

Amy's body jerks backward a half step at my declaration. How can she be hurt by my casual claim when she was flirting with another man five minutes ago?

Robert gently removes Amy's hand from his arm, and she stares at it as if she forgot she was attached to the slender fingers.

"I think," Robert says in his business manager voice, "that Amy and Jason need to talk. Maybe a stroll through the garden? Mom ordered some amazing light sculptures this year."

Because I want to get out of this room and, no matter what the situation, I don't want to ruin Amy's life by having her bodily removed from the premises, I nod my head in agreement. We aren't far from the door leading to the patio and I turn toward it, straining to hear the light click of Amy's heels on the floor as she trails behind me.

I step outside and walk to the edge of the patio, stopping before stepping out onto the path that winds through the decorative garden. Amy comes to a stop beside me, arms wrapped around her middle as she looks at the ground in silence.

The night air isn't cold but the slight bite I feel on my ears and nose is enough to give a woman in a strapless evening gown a chill, so I shrug out of the tuxedo jacket and offer it to the quiet woman.

She takes it, looks at it for a moment, then whips it around her shoulders like a cape. Her gaze is bright and determined when she looks up at me.

"You haven't asked me for an explanation, but I'm going to give you one. Then you are going to return the favor."

My eyebrows wing up at her firm declaration. I'm not sure what sort of explanation I owe her. We're getting to know each other, and I don't tell people about my family until they become part of my innermost circle. Emma didn't learn about them until a year after she graduated, when we'd worked together long enough that I knew I could trust her.

There's a possibility she'll show up here tonight. She gets an invitation every year but has only attended once. More often, she meets me afterward at Waffle House so I can tell her ridiculous stories. This crowd could be good for Carter's career, though, so I wouldn't be surprised to see them circulating.

That Amy and her mother don't know about that annual invite is proof that I can trust Emma. I have to wonder if I assumed I could extend that trust to Amy.

"I met Robert at a gala several weeks ago. We had an enjoyable conversation about the charity and the food on offer. We shared a dance and debated which items were worth bidding on in the silent auction. I didn't give him my number or lead him on. It was . . . friendly."

I'm the last person who can make the argument that men and women can't be friends. But I know the gala she's talking about because Robert said he'd actually had a good time at it. He said he'd met someone that he hoped to see again sometime.

Emma's also mentioned how Amy doesn't believe men and women can be nothing but friends. So what does that mean for what I saw tonight?

Amy pulls the jacket tighter around her and keeps talking. "I didn't know where I was going tonight, but I won't lie to you. This event has been one we've talked about for years. If you're trying to break into the upper tiers of society in Atlanta, an invite to this party is a sign that you've made it."

"Glad I could help." I can't keep the bitterness from my voice.

She winces. "I thought you weren't going to hold the person I was before against me?"

"Are you saying you aren't still trying to gain access to the upper tiers of society? They'd be advantageous clients." I close my eyes. "My mother is on your vision board."

She sighs. "I'm not saying I'd turn her or her friends away as clients, but I . . . It's become less of a priority. I took that board down, but I'm not sure what to put on a new one." She shakes her head. "My life has a lot of change in it right now. There's a lot on my plate. I don't have the . . . the . . . bandwidth to do society, too."

I can't help the slight grin that breaks through. "Bandwidth?"

"I've been spending too much time with you and Emma, clearly, but at least I can know you understand what I mean."

"I do." My voice is quiet as I debate how to take her story. I don't think she's lying but I also don't know how I feel about her knowing my most closely guarded secret already.

An itch spreads beneath my skin at the thought. I need to move. "Can you walk in those shoes?"

"These are only two-inch heels," she says with a flat voice. "I can walk for miles."

I gesture her toward the stone pavers that create a path through the ornamental garden. "Shall we walk, then?"

We stroll away from the brighter lights of the house and patio into the ambiance of hundreds of Christmas lights strung through the garden.

"Do you believe me?" Her voice is strong, but small. As if I could crush her with my next words, but she's braced to take it.

I do believe her, but I don't think that's the most important thing for her to know right now.

"Five years ago, I had a girlfriend." It was my last serious relationship, actually. "The company had just completed its first solid year, I'd moved into my condo, and life felt settled. I thought I was ready to take that next step in building my future."

"I'm guessing she didn't feel the same?"

My laugh is short and dry. "Oh, she was definitely looking to build her future. I still don't know if she knew who I was before we started dating, but soon after we became official, I brought her by to meet my parents."

"And Robert?"

I shook my head. "He wasn't here that day. But she knew about him."

"Idiot."

I nod. "I know. Even when she started being evasive and trying to pull away, I didn't realize it was because she was trying to create the idea that she saw me more as a brother than a boyfriend."

"Not you, her. How can anyone have met you or your family and believe they could successfully switch brothers?" She snorts in derision and the inelegant noise makes me smile. "I've spent five minutes with your mother—five treacherous minutes, mind you—and I can tell you that no one would accept that."

I nod. "It's true. The worst part is that she managed to connect with Robert, and he was pretty infatuated with her. He brought her to a family dinner and, as you could guess, she tried to act like she and I had never been an item. She was all condolences that I'd been confused and devastated that she'd caused me pain, but didn't I understand love?"

"Please tell me Robert didn't fall for that."

"He didn't. We'd lived our whole lives learning how to be on guard against people who would try to emotionally manipulate us for gain." I glance toward the house. "Makes me surprised my mom believed yours."

"Mother is exceptionally skilled at emotional manipulation."

Some of it is my fault, too. Ms. Trinket had a great deal of personal information about me, information my mother would know isn't public.

"I believe you." My words are soft and I hope they convey everything I don't quite know how to say.

She's quiet for several heartbeats. "Thank you."

"But it still happened."

"And you think I should apologize for something I had no part in?" She shakes her head.

"I'm not ready to bring you into this."

"*This* being your family or your life?" She starts to walk a little faster. "I think you've made yourself clear on the fact that you want me to stay a certain distance away from you."

Then I'm a terrible communicator. Because that's not true.

But if she doesn't have the bandwidth to utilize one of the most exclusive parties of the year to build her business, the goal that brought her into my life in the first place, she certainly doesn't have the space to start a relationship.

Kissing her, wanting to kiss her, thinking about dating her, it's all more out of line than I'd even realized. Before I know it's happening, a tear rolls down my cheek. Can Amy see it in this dimmer lighting? Do I want her to?

We approach the patio once more and I have even fewer answers than when we left it.

"What do you have the bandwidth for? Because it seems to me—"

"Emma?" Amy's voice is full of surprise.

I blink and look over to find my friend.

"Amy." Emma stumbles to a halt. "I . . . uh . . . Robert said you were upset, and . . ."

Amy frowns. "Robert told you I was upset?"

"No, um, he mentioned Jason." Emma winces. "I don't think he knows I'm related to you."

Amy looks up at me. "You invited Emma?"

"I always invite Emma. She doesn't normally come, though."

Emma spreads the skirt of her green evening dress wide. "I have a dress I can stand to wear now. Also, Carter said attending this would get his agent off his back for at least a month."

"Glad I could be of service."

She swats me on the arm. "Don't be like that. We brought two minia-ture canvasses as our ornaments."

"Mom might break her rule about going last for one of those."

"He brought a third one as a hostess gift." She frowns. "I think he feels guilty about getting in here through me."

"As he should."

She rolls her eyes. "Stop it. You're the one who told me to remind him what sort of people would be in attendance."

"So, it's okay for her but not for me?" Amy's question is like throwing a rock through a window.

I know better than to tell her that Emma's been tested and verified as trustworthy while Amy hasn't. Still, I can't not respond to the pointed accusation. "My issue tonight was more about finding you dancing with Robert than trying to sell a service to Abigail Lee."

"Yet you didn't invite me." Before I can respond to that, she turns to her sister. "And it's okay for you to help Carter but not to help me?"

Is Amy more upset at me or her sister? It's hard to say, but she's definitely upset. I suppose I can see where she's coming from. If Amy's been salivating over this event for years and her sister was annually throwing an invite in the trash, it would feel like a betrayal.

But if Emma had told her sister who I was and utilized her privileged information to pull someone into my parents' world, it would have been a true betrayal.

Amy isn't looking at things from my perspective, though. She steps away from me and that extra distance makes me feel cold. Another tear slips from my eye but I don't wipe it away because that would call attention to it.

But Amy sees it. "You are such hypocrites. Both of you. And . . . are you crying?"

I rub a hand across my eyes to prevent more tears. "I appear to be, yes."

She scoffs. "Worried about your precious privacy? Don't worry. I won't tell anyone." After a pause she very deliberately says, "You can trust me."

"It's not a matter of trust." I swallow because that might be a lie. "This . . . thing . . . between us. You're not ready for it. You're still working on committing to a church and even a business model. Where would a relationship fit in there?"

Emma winces. "Jason—"

But I don't let her speak. "You're so determined to do this by yourself, but you aren't going anywhere. Do you really want to have a relationship with me or is that something else you were trying out?"

"At least I'm trying something. You ran away and hid."

"I . . . what?" What is she talking about? "What do you think I'm hiding from?"

"From everything."

"I have a life."

She scoffs. "Yes, you do. One you made by rejecting everything God gave you to start with."

I look at the glowing windows and brightly-dressed people. "You mean all that?"

"I mean all those people. All those connections. All those moments."

"You'd like it if I took my place as the long-lost son, wouldn't you? Then you could say you always wanted a relationship with me and could ride the coattails of my renewed appearance into popularity." My arm waves around, indicating the glitz and glam surrounding us. "I guess this is a point in my favor instead of a burden to take on for you."

As soon as my rant is over, I want to take it back. The hurt I'm feeling seems to be reflected in Amy's face. The jacket she extends toward me without making eye contact doesn't help.

The steadiness of her earlier voice is gone as she speaks to the air between me and Emma. "I need to . . . go. Tell Mother I'll send the driver back for her."

And then she's gone, leaving the patio and disappearing back into the bright lights of the party.

I follow, keeping a distance of several feet between us. Emma trails after me, but I ignore her until I see Amy successfully collect her wrap and security handing her into a town car.

We turn as one and step back into the foyer and stare at the giant tree.

Amy hadn't taken an ornament.

AMY

I don't bother keeping the emotions bottled up on the way home. What does it matter if I get a reputation among the limo drivers of Atlanta? I'm sure they've seen worse and I'm hardly important enough to gossip about anyway.

The funny thing is, I didn't feel like I'd been abandoned and left alone when my friends stopped inviting me to brunch or when fewer guys approached when I stopped giving come hither looks or even when my family looked at me like I was crazy.

But now? Riding home by myself with the knowledge that both Emma and Jason kept part of their lives from me? A part they had reason to think would be extremely important? I'm devastated. And the guy I'd been thinking was an alternative option to the man who seemed to be fighting his interest in me? Obviously no longer an option.

For the first time I feel truly alone in the world.

What am I supposed to do now? I pull out my phone but don't know what to do after I unlock it. Who can I talk to about this?

No one. There is absolutely no one I can share with, no one whose opinion I can ask. Heather would tell me to double down on flirting with Jason, that patience would bring its own reward. Sadie would tell me that everything's fair game since there was never an official relationship and I should try my hand on nabbing Robert.

My mother, who is still at the party, already showed her complete lack of integrity by lying to me and Mrs. Miller to get our invitations. She's clearly ready to sell my emotional wellbeing in the name of social progress.

I open my messages to see if there's anyone I'm forgetting. The top two threads mock me. Emma and Jason. I could text each of them and complain about the other. And the whole time I could wonder if they were secretly texting each other about me. Or maybe even sitting on opposite sides of a couch somewhere in the private areas of Jason's parents' house, discussing what to tell me.

Emma's friendship with Jason is obviously deeper than mine with either of them. Has Jason been telling her about me all along? No. No, Emma wouldn't have reacted the way she did or said the things she'd said if she'd known everything about Jason.

Although her words a couple of weeks ago are suddenly making sense. I thought her concern was for me and the possibility I'd get sidetracked from strengthening my new faith by getting involved with a guy, but now I don't think she was worried about me at all. She was concerned for Jason and what I would do when I learned who he is.

Well, I have learned. And what I'm going to do about it is go home, turn on Designing Women, and cry into my emergency pint of double chocolate gelato. I know it's cliche to bury heartache in ice cream, but sometimes things become associated with each other for a reason.

The limo driver pulls up to my gate and I send the admittance code from my phone. Five minutes later, I'm inside my apartment. I kick off my shoes and stroll to the freezer to pull out the ice cream. I don't care that I'm still in an evening gown that is custom-made couture. I don't care that this is one of my least favorite episodes of Designing Women. I do care, slightly, that I don't have a pint of double chocolate chip and I have to settle for peanut butter fudge.

Two of the characters get trapped in a snowstorm and it's both funny and touching. When the episode ends, it rolls straight into the next. Thank goodness for auto-play. I'd have to put down my ice cream and spoon to press a button on the remote.

My spoon scrapes the bottom of the carton and I give up on getting any more ice cream. The spoon rattles against the edges as I set the carton on the floor and flop onto my side to watch the show. No matter how I turn, I can't get comfortable. This couch was a foolish purchase, obviously. I bought it more because it looked right in the room than because it was comfortable. I didn't even sit on it in the store.

When the next episode ends, I roll off the couch and trudge into my room to trade the dress for pajamas. Habit more than anything has me brushing out my hair and performing my cleansing and skin care routine. I drag the fluffy blanket from the foot of my bed as I return to the couch to curl up in a ball.

I will never let anyone—particularly Emma—see these pajamas, but I pull them out on nights like this. The fabric is impossibly soft, and the entire thing feels like a cotton hug without being unbearably warm. Unfortunately, they are also ugly and ridiculous, covered with dancing breakfast foods and enormous-eyed cats wearing chef hats.

As I wiggle down into the crevice of the couch, I have to admit that my earlier discomfort might have been the dress. Aside from the metal arms, my couch seems to snuggle in rather well. I start the next episode but soon pause it so I can go to my kitchen, dig into the back of my quick snack drawer to pull out a package of microwave popcorn, and wait for the buttery goodness to expand in the microwave.

I dump it all into a bowl and return to my flopped position on the couch. The popcorn bowl sits on the floor, and I hang one arm over the edge so I can feed myself without much effort as I escape into another episode.

My phone buzzes twice and then starts to ring.

I don't answer. I don't even look to see who it is. Chances are high it's either Jason, Emma, or my mother and I don't want to talk to any of them. I don't want to talk to anyone else, either, but I particularly don't want to talk to them.

There is something petty and childish about watching the screen light up and then blink out, sending the caller to voicemail that I rarely check. It's at once satisfying and uncomfortable.

After the fourth call comes in, a niggling thought in the back of my brain starts to consider all the reasons they might be calling that have nothing to do with me. What if one of them got into a car accident? What if someone choked on one of those sausage and olive canapes? What if Carter broke off his engagement to Emma?

Honestly, that last option is the most ridiculous, but once the notions enter my head, there's no getting rid of them. I roll off the couch and crawl across the living room to where I dumped my purse and my phone. The popcorn bowl gets pulled awkwardly with me and I flop onto the carpet, one hand on the phone, one continuing to shovel popcorn into my mouth.

There's a call from Mother and three calls from Emma.

None from Jason.

That silence speaks rather loudly.

There are no text messages from Emma, either, which means she went straight to trying to call me. Well, not straight. I've been gone from the party at least an hour and a half. What has she been doing all that time? Talking to Jason about me? Hobnobbing with people who will help Carter's career? Giggling in the corner with Mrs. Miller because they already know each other?

It takes me a few moments to remember how to get to my voicemail and then I play the message, leaving the device on speakerphone.

"Amy?" There's a deep sigh. "I know you're mad and I guess I know why, just . . . please let me know you're safe at home? The driver said you looked a little wobbly walking into the building. Actually, his description was that you looked drunk, but . . . just . . . send a proof of life selfie when you can and we'll talk tomorrow."

It's a reasonable request, but I don't want her to know I've been wallowing or see my breakfast cat pajamas, so I go into my bathroom, throw my hair up in a messy bun and rub a little of my clay mask mixture onto my skin. It's far too thin to actually do anything but Emma won't know the difference and it will mask any evidence of the tears that might have fallen at random times over the past hour.

I wrap my silk robe over the pajamas, being sure to close it at the throat, and then snap a selfie. After double-checking that no incriminating evidence is visible, I shoot it off to Emma, add the line *Making an early night of it*, then set the phone to Do Not Disturb. I take another minute to wash off the mask and shed the robe, then it once again it's me, my popcorn, and the ladies of Sugarbaker and Associates.

Tomorrow I can figure out what the new me is supposed to do in a situation like this but for tonight, there's comfort in old habits.

I wake up the next morning with popcorn spilled across my floor and an imprint of the fringe on my throw pillow embedded into my cheek. The television has turned itself off, so there's nothing to make my falling asleep in the living room look any less pitiful than it is.

Every joint and muscle in my body protests the way I collapsed on the couch as I try to stand to my feet. Thirty is just around the corner and my back is letting me know it. It takes me three tries to get the coffeemaker going and then I stand there, listening to the hiss and bubble that precedes that first drip of caffeine. The coffee starts to drizzle into my cup, and I continue to stand there, watching the steady flow of coffee as if turning away will make the process stop.

I don't move until I've sucked down half the mug of doctored brew.

I look at my phone, then decide the world can do without me for one more day. Today is Sunday. And despite what Jason may think, I truly do want to get this Jesus thing right.

So, I watch the service. Then I watch more episodes of Designing Women. Then I make myself get up and get dressed because I've never been a girl who thought wallowing for extended periods of time solved anything.

The vision board I brought home from the office catches my eye as I go to the closet to get the supplies for my weekly cleaning session that I didn't manage to do yesterday. My hands cover my face as I groan over the absolute failure my almost-relationship was destined to be. The man's mother is on my board along with the house he grew up in.

No wonder he didn't want to ask me out despite being attracted to me.

I was doomed before we ever got going.

A flash of anger flows through me. Partially at Emma because there are an awful lot of things she should have warned me about, but mostly at Jason. Was there ever a chance he would believe I didn't want his connections? Even if he did believe me, my career means that being in a relationship would push him at least somewhat into the public eye. If he knew he would never be comfortable with that, he shouldn't have done things like take me to see Shakespeare or text me adorable pictures of baby animals.

And he definitely shouldn't have kissed me.

Just friends, my foot.

I take out my anger on the minimal dirt that has accumulated in my small apartment, even going so far as to get out the stepstool and vacuum out the air vents near my ceiling.

By the time I finish and take myself out for dinner to celebrate, I've developed some resolve in addition to the hurt, pain, confusion, disappointment, and anger swirling around my gut. I can't cut Emma from my life because she's family, but I can avoid her until Christmas and only talk to her a family functions.

Everything else can go.

I grab my laptop and start researching churches. Within fifteen minutes I'm so overwhelmed a headache is starting to brew. Why are there so many different types of churches and why are there so many of them within ten miles of my apartment?

When a headache starts to prick behind my eyes, I close the laptop. It's only 8:56pm, but I get ready for bed and tuck myself in with a book I've been meaning to read for several weeks.

Monday morning, I retrieve my phone from the charger and let the world back in.

There are two emails from people on the development team working on my app. They're from Friday afternoon, but I'm assuming Jason won't cancel the project. After all, he knew who his mother was when I hired him.

Though I'm wondering if he should cancel it since I'm second-guessing everything as I flip through the mock-ups they've provided and the preliminary use study notes. I can't tell if the idea isn't working right or I'm just in the mood that sees everything as a dismal failure, but everything they've sent me looks and feels completely wrong.

I close out of my email and brave my messaging app where no less than thirteen text messages are waiting for me. Four of those are from Emma, three from my mother, two from brands I frequent, and one each from my landlord, my eye doctor, Sydney, and an unknown number.

A very glaring zero of them are from Jason.

I quickly clear the ads and the payment reminders, decide to ignore my family for a little longer, and stay far away from the unknown number that I know is me texting myself from Robert's phone. Instead I open Sydney's message.

> SYDNEY: I didn't get the job, but I wanted to thank you anyway. This suit gives me the confidence to apply to more.

> ME: Sorry to hear that. Did they say why?

> SYDNEY: Not explicitly, no.

> SYDNEY: I know I didn't interview very well. They didn't cover that in my night classes.

I wince because, truth is, I probably wouldn't interview well either. I've never experienced a professional job hunt, but I imagine it's a lot like sales except the product you're peddling is yourself. How does one do that without sounding like a conceited troll?

> ME: Maybe we can practice before your next interview.

> SYDNEY: That would be great! I'm sure you've interviewed potential employees before so you can tell me what I'm doing wrong.

The closest I've come to interviewing a potential employee is calling around to get estimates on fixing the weird noise my car was making last year. I know a lot of people, though. Surely I can find someone who's willing to help her. The list of potential people flits through my mind and it is lengthy.

I let Sydney fall from my mind as I set about getting dressed for the day. After showering, drying my hair, dressing, and doing my makeup, I can no longer justify not answering my family's texts.

I start with Mother because part of me is truly curious how the rest of her Saturday night went after Mrs. Miller learned she'd been tricked.

Her messages end there, so I can only assume the woman she saw was Emma and she quickly learned that all was not well in social paradise.

There isn't anything I can say to those messages since the end of them means she likely got home without a problem. We can deal with the fallout from her scheming later today, if I choose to leave the door to my office unlocked. Or decide to go in at all. I could meet my clients at a coffee shop or something.

I take a deep breath and slowly let it out before opening Emma's thread.

> EMMA: I think she was angrier than you that I was invited.

> EMMA: Jason has also left the party early even though he normally stays right to the end.

> EMMA: I'm sorry. I don't know why I told you that. I promised I wouldn't get in the middle.

I turn off the screen and set the phone on the counter. Emma's messages don't require a response either. I can only imagine some of the things Mother said if she learned how long Emma has been getting invitations to that party and not utilizing them.

I'm more upset about the fact that I feel like she set me up for failure with Jason. As soon as she knew there was . . . something . . . between us, or at least the potential of something, she would have seen this day coming. The day when he would be confronted with my former aspirations and have to decide if I liked him for him or for his family.

Since I don't know what to do about any of the problems in my existence, I tackle the ones in my new friend's life. I grab my laptop and search for interview methods while I drink my coffee. There are a lot of posts with suggestions and tips and strategies, but even I know the best plan in the world isn't going to make her look experienced to the next recruiter she talks to.

She needs someone who can tell her what she is doing that makes her look like the less-than-ideal job candidate. I ponder the problem as I get dressed and drive to work and carefully and deliberately avoid my mother.

A few of my clients are lawyers or business owners. Maybe I can reach out to one after Christmas as see if they'd be willing to help Sydney. My phone buzzes and I open the screen.

> SYDNEY: I have an interview Thursday!

So much for after Christmas.

> ME: Great! Let's see if we can set up a practice before then.

I open up my contact list and scroll through, sending out a couple of feelers to people who might be available or know someone who is. Then I do the same with my client list.

Three people respond with interest, but two of them can't do anything until after the new year and the other wouldn't have availability until Friday.

I scroll through my messages, praying God will give me the right inspiration, and my gaze lands on the text from Saturday.

The one from a number that isn't saved in my contacts.

The one I sent to myself.

One long press of my thumb opens the single message thread.

If I send a text, will Robert even answer? By now, he's heard everything from Jason, I'm sure, and might have already blocked my number from his phone.

He's a businessman, though. One who has probably interviewed hundreds of employees in his day and likes to give his time to help others.

I could text him on Sydney's behalf. Chances are he's as unavailable as everyone else is, but for her sake, I have to try.

It doesn't have to have anything at all to do with Jason. No matter how much I want to, I'll refrain from asking if he's doing okay today, given the fact he left the party early last night.

Asking Robert anything personal would feel like a betrayal of Jason's trust somehow. But if he volunteers information about his brother, well, I'll listen. It would be rude to do anything else.

After another deep breath and another desperate prayer, I save the contact and open a new message.

I'm at work, but I don't think I've convinced anyone that I'm actually working. The staff meeting was a complete wash, as I barely heard any of the updates and I tried to tell Daniel in marketing to look into the error being flagged by one of our clients. Emma stepped in to claim the task and more than one staff member sent me pitying looks.

I've been holed up in my office ever since, staring at the dark void of my blank monitor. There isn't a single thought in my head, not even about Amy. I'm literally just . . . here.

The door to my office flies open and bangs against the wall, almost taking out the intruder as it rebounds back toward its previously closed position. Emma slaps a hand on the wooden surface before it can hit her in the face and sends the door careening back into the wall.

"Hi, Emma." I sigh because my best friend is exactly what I need right now. She'll help me sort out the mess that is my mind, give me a little sympathy, and help me make a plan to move forward.

Only comfort and guidance don't appear to be on her mind. Her face is set in a scowl that can only be considered angry. Nor is she acknowledging me. She isn't talking, isn't even looking in my direction. Instead she crosses the small room to the bookshelf along the back wall.

The black wooden case mostly holds manuals and standard operating procedure guides. There are a few mock-ups for clients and some legal filings. Nothing Emma should need to access or be upset about.

She bypasses all the binders, though, and places her hand on the spine of the leather-bound study Bible on the end of the top shelf. The book lands on my desk with a thunk and she starts flipping through it at a rate that leaves me a little concerned for the fate of the thin pages. One hand blindly reaches across my desk toward the pen cup. Her fingers wrap around a green highlighter and pull, knocking the other writing utensils across the wide surface of the desk.

Her teeth snag the top of the highlighter and uncap it. She then blows the lid into the pile of ignored pens and pencils and drags the highlighter over a few lines of text. After flinging the uncapped highlighter onto the desk, she finally turns to look at me.

And she's even angrier than I thought she was. One hand slides the Bible across the surface, pushing several implements out of the way. She jabs a finger at the highlighted verse.

"I've been thinking all weekend. About you and Amy and what I know and what I heard that implies there's things I don't know and . . . just . . . all of it. And you, my friend, are a clanging cymbal." After biting off the words, she flounces from the room, pulling the door closed with a slam.

I stare at the closed door, blinking several times before I let my gaze fall to the Bible in front of me.

Her highlighting is rather crooked but it's easy to determine the verses she wanted to mark.

1 Corinthians 13. The love chapter.

Her parting words hit me as I read the first verse.

If I speak human or angelic tongues but do not have love, I am a noisy gong or a clanging cymbal.

She skipped a couple of verses after that, using her highlighter to sloppily tag all the things love is in verses 4 and 5.

Love is patient, love is kind. Love does not envy, is not boastful, is not arrogant, is not rude, is not self-seeking, is not irritable, and does not keep a record of wrongs.

The pale green color gets darker over the words *does not keep a record of wrongs*, indicating Emma felt a need to highlight the phrase multiple times.

Even though Emma stopped there, my eyes keep tracking down the page, taking in the next two verses.

Love finds no joy in unrighteousness but rejoices in the truth. It bears all things, hopes all things, endures all things.

My first instinct is to say I'm not in love with Amy. I can't be. We never even dated. But even as a part of me isn't firmly sold on that statement, I know that isn't the type of love being referred to here. Whether or not I stay romantically involved with Amy—and, date or no date, even I have to admit that kisses like that indicate a romantic involvement—I am called to love her as a sister in Christ, as another human being created by God.

And while I'll stand by the truth of everything I said to her, there's no denying that I didn't say those things with love. There was nothing kind in my words and I was absolutely throwing around a record of everything she's ever done wrong.

Emma's right. I'm a clanging cymbal. A cracked and hurting cymbal to be sure, but a noisy, wrong one as well.

I contemplate what I should do next as I slowly pick up all the contents of my spilled pencil cup. After recapping the green highlighter and sliding it in to rest with its counterparts, I push to my feet. The problem is that while I feel thoroughly chastised by my best friend, I still don't know what to do.

I slink from my office and make my way to Emma's cubicle, taking the long route to avoid walking past as many other people as possible. I come up along the back side of her space and fold my arms along the top of the carpeted walls as I look down at her bent head. "Hi."

She looks up, gaze narrowed as she takes in my face. I stand in silence while she examines me, hoping she can see that I've heard her, even if she hadn't exactly been kind with her truth either. I guess there's a difference between getting someone's attention and beating them to an emotional pulp.

Finally she sighs and rolls her eyes. "Hi."

"Lunch?"

One side of her mouth ticks up. "It's 10:30 in the morning."

"Brunch, then?" I adjust the positioning of my hat on my head. "I don't really want to talk here."

"Fine." Her tone is grumbly, but she doesn't delay in gathering her coat and purse and putting her computer to sleep. "Let's go."

I circle the cubicle, trying to pretend I don't see a few heads popped up like gophers to peek over the walls of the work area. Neither of us speak as we take the elevator down and exit the lobby. Once we're standing in the parking lot, squinting against the bright winter sun, I realize I have no idea where I want to go.

Emma takes pity on me and unlocks her car with a laugh. "Come on. Let's get milkshakes and fries and watch the geese attack the runners in the park."

"It's 10:30 in the morning."

She shrugs and pulls out her keys. "Doesn't matter. Milkshakes and fries are the best breakup food."

"You have to be dating someone to break up with them."

I can practically hear her eyes rolling as she sighs while climbing into her car. Once I'm settled in the passenger seat, she looks my way again.

"Fine," she says with a huff. "Milkshakes and fries are the best heartbreak food."

There's no arguing with that one. My heart hurts. Even though I had a hand on the knife.

She pulls through a Sonic drive thru, which means we end up with tots instead of fries but I'm not going to complain, before driving to the nearby park. Despite bring the middle of the morning on a Monday, there are several people on the paths that circle a little too close to the lake for the geese's comfort. I grab my milkshake and follow Emma to a bench where we settle in to watch the inevitable show.

"So." She folds her legs up onto the bench in a crisscross position and takes a loud slurp of her shake. "Talk."

Where do I start? "I stand by everything I said to her, but you're right. I said it with the intent to hurt instead of help. I'm sorry."

She snorts and stabs a hand into the bag to grab a tater tot. "It's not me you need to apologize to."

I grunt because I know she's right, but . . . "I don't know if I can talk to her right now."

"Why not?"

"Because . . ." I sigh. How do I tell my best friend, who I couldn't even manage to go on a successful date with, that the very sight of her sister melts my brain. Add in the way I've learned she's smart and caring and adorably impulsive but wholeheartedly committed and I can't guarantee emotions won't take over my tongue again.

And this time it might not stick to words.

I settle on pointing out the fact that no matter how much I wish for a redo, I'm not sure what I would do differently. And I really don't know what to do next. "What would I say?"

"I'm sorry is usually a good start."

"And then what?" I shake my head. "I shouldn't have said things the way I said them, but that doesn't mean I was wrong."

She winces and stuffs two more tots in her mouth to buy her a little time. After she swallows those, she takes an extra-long drink of her milkshake.

"See?" I wave my Styrofoam cup in her direction. "You don't know what to say either."

"You've put me in a tough position, you know." She groans and drops her head back against the bench. "This is why people aren't supposed to date their sibling's best friend." Her head pops up and she points a finger in my direction. "And do not tell me again that the two of you weren't dating. I'm counting every time you played tonsil hockey or even came close to it as a date."

My milkshake is suddenly extremely interesting. But after a couple seconds pass, I can't resist pointing out, "I had my tonsils removed when I was five."

"I will feed you to the angry geese, Jason Miller."

"Noted."

We sit in silence, munching on tater tots and slurping at milkshakes. I have to admit that Emma is right about there being something comforting about the combination of salty and sweet, warm and cold. Now isn't the time to mention it, though, because I'm hoping her brain is coming up with some idea of what my next steps should be.

Apparently not, because she breaks the silence by saying, "Our relationship is changing."

"Yours and Amy's?"

She nods. "But mine and yours, too."

"Because of Carter." I pop my last tot into my mouth. "That's as it should be, Emma. I don't resent it."

"I'm glad." She sighs. "Even with that, though, you are my friend and . . . What do you want to do?"

I want everything to work out. I want Amy to get everything she's worked for and become everything God created her for. I want to be able to date Emma's sister and explore the idea that for once in my well-planned existence I just want to jump. I want to be able to keep my contained, ordered life while I do it.

"I don't think what I want is the most important thing right now."

"Probably true." She sets her cup aside and folds her arms. "Let's talk about what I want then."

"Okay."

"I want to plan my wedding."

I'm not sure where this is going but I also know I don't really want to discuss china patterns right now. "That is usually what comes after an engagement."

She doesn't take the bait. Instead she plows on as if I've said nothing. "I want you to be my man of honor."

I choke on my milkshake. "You actually meant that? I thought it was a joke. Is that a thing?"

"It is if I want it to be."

I suppose that's true. We've had dozens of friends get married over the past ten years and their ceremonies have been as widely varied as one could imagine. None of them had a man standing up next to the bride, though. "I . . . am honored?"

She grins. "That's the idea."

"What does being the man of honor entail?"

She gives a shrug. "Most of the things traditionally given to the maid of honor I suppose. We want a fairly short engagement, so we're keeping the plans simple. And you'll be splitting all the duties of course."

"Of course," I mutter, but the words crack as my mouth goes dry. There's only one person it would make sense for me to split honor attendant duties with.

Her twin sister.

"See my dilemma?" Emma swipes her cup back up, but gestures around with it instead of taking another drink. "I'm trying to plan a wedding and the two most important people in my life aren't talking to each other."

I smirk. "I'll be sure to tell Carter where he stands in the pecking order."

"Since Carter and I are about to become one, as they say, he will still rank above you."

"Does that make me one of the most important people in Carter's life, too?"

Her elbow jabs me in the ribs as she takes another drink. "Focus, man. I cannot have you and Amy fighting during my wedding."

"I can safely promise we won't fight during your wedding." Even if Amy wanted to start something, I care too much for Emma to allow myself to be pulled into a mess that would ruin her day.

"Stop being obtuse. That's not what I mean."

I sigh. "I know it isn't, but Emma, I don't know what else I can tell you. There are things Amy needs right now, and, well, I can't pull her focus from that." I also can't provide what she needs, not without breaking promises I made to myself. It's a realization I've been wrestling with all weekend.

"There are things you need, too."

"Like what?" I hope she's got an idea because right now, I feel a little lost about what to do next.

"Like someone to take my place."

I reach over and grab two tots out of her container and stuff them into my mouth because this is not a conversation I want to have. Unfortunately, keeping my mouth occupied does nothing to block my ears.

"You'll never stop being my friend, but Carter made me admit the other day that my friendship with you isn't going to be able to continue as it was or even as it's become." She pouts. "Life is going to keep changing."

I give her a crooked grin because I can almost guess what prompted this discussion. "Were you ranting about my situation with Amy?"

"Possibly."

I nod because Carter's not wrong. My relationship with Emma is changing. On this point, at least, I can reassure her. "You'll always matter to me, Emma. Carter, too, since, as you pointed out, he's now a part of you. But things will change. We won't be as close as we were. I've seen it with my other married friends. Life is just . . . different after marriage. But it's not a bad different. You're growing, changing, moving forward with your life."

"Are you going to move forward?"

I assume she means move on from my infatuation with Amy, so I answer accordingly. "Eventually. It won't be soon, I imagine, especially since I'll be seeing her regularly with this wedding stuff."

"You haven't known her that long."

"True, but . . . I don't know. I'm not a boy anymore. I'm almost thirty."

"Is your biological clock ticking?"

"No," I say on a laugh. Only Emma could make me laugh when I feel like this. "But I know what my life is and who I am. It's easier to recognize a good thing."

"And Amy is a good thing?"

I nod. "She is. Or she will be. Her heart is chasing God pretty hard right now and even though she'll make a mistake or two along the way, He'll honor that in the long run. She doesn't need me getting in her way."

"Isn't she old enough to know what she wants, too?"

"She is. But there's only room for so much change at a time, you know? Maybe in a few months . . ."

"You're willing to wait for her?"

The idea of waiting for her makes me the most settled I've been since the argument. "Yeah, I think so. But even if I do, I don't know if I can ever be what's best for her. A relationship has to work with the mind as well as the heart if it's going to last."

A runner comes down the path, music blaring from the phone attached to her hip. Emma and I both turn our attention to the pond with glee and sure enough, the gaggle of geese aren't happy about the interruption to their peaceful morning. Two birds start toward the runner, wings outstretched, beaks open to release a string of obnoxious honks.

The runner squeals and leaps into the grass to avoid the first bird, only to have the second jump into the air and flap its wings, nearly taking off the woman's hat. With another frightened squeak, the woman sprints away and the geese soon return to waddling around and pecking at the grass.

"You know what isn't good?" Emma asks, pulling her phone from her pocket.

"What?"

"The trial numbers for Amy's app." She opens up a document and hands me the phone, showing me the charts.

I frown as I read the reviews from the test market. It doesn't sound at all like they were viewing a digital version of Amy's Look Book services. It sounds like they took a lengthy survey and got a confusing list of fabrics and cuts to shop for. "Do you have the mock-up app?"

"Yes. I downloaded it this morning." She frowns as well. "It's not what I expected. What was the goal?"

I sigh. "I don't know. I sort of turned everything over to Stephanie." I can almost guess what happened after that. Amy, who is completely scrambled right now about what direction she wants to go in life, gave Stephanie a very garbled direction for the design.

This I can fix. I've seen what Amy does, know the gifts God gave her that she doesn't know how to use, and I can make this better.

I'm determined to make this better. Because I still want the best for Amy and if this app goes live in its current state, it will all but ruin her reputation.

My mind doesn't change as a text notification shows up at the top of Emma's screen, but the last piece of hope in my heart crumbles.

It's a text from Robert asking for the name of Amy's boutique.

AMY

If I were in possession of a time machine I would go back to the point when Emma wanted to introduce me to the pastor and get me registered as a new member. I would smack myself in the back of the head and tell myself to get it over with because in four months you're going to find yourself setting up a meeting with the pastor anyway and he won't have a clue who you are.

Most likely, the only thing that is going to come from this meeting is that long overdue introduction, an invitation to do whatever people do to become an official member, and more pressure to take a swim in the baptistry pool in front of thousands of people.

I own a fabulous waterproof mascara, but that won't keep me from looking like a drowned rat.

Also, there was a girl who lost her footing in the water two weeks ago and her feet floated up to stick out of the water. The callous on the ball of her foot was broadcast in living color, three feet tall on the side screens.

I'm not ready for that.

But I am ready to admit that God has a use for my skills. It's not conventional and a lot of people might not see its importance, but I have texts in my phone that prove otherwise.

Tracy has a third date next week and Sydney got a request for a second interview. Robert came through with more than just interview suggestions. He met with Sydney in my office and walked her through a practice interview, giving suggestions on how to answer questions and phrase her various experiences as a benefit. I can make her look the part of a woman you would want as the first face of your business, but I didn't know how to make her sound like one.

Robert is actually the reason I made this meeting.

I thumb open my messages and scroll back while I sit in the waiting area of the church offices for the pastor or his assistant to come escort me back.

> ROBERT: I enjoyed meeting with Sydney. She's going to nail that interview.

> ME: Thanks for meeting with her. I'm sorry if my contacting you was awkward, but I don't know a lot of people who would have been willing to do it.

Then a few days later I sent him the update on Sydney's next interview.

> ROBERT: That's great. I don't know why I never thought about helping people this way.

> ROBERT: If you make this a formal thing, put me on the list. I can give a few hours a month doing practice interviews and I know a few other people who would be good as well.

The idea of making this a regular practice rang through my head for days.

It may not look like it on the surface, but this is a ministry. It serves a need many people have, and I want to help more of them.

But I'm enough of a businesswoman to know that structure and support are necessary if I want to maintain my sanity.

Also, there should be people involved aside from myself. As much as I love a well-fitted jacket and a great scarf, there are more elements that go into making a proper impression. Interview skills, etiquette, knowledge of the culture you're walking into whether it's a business or personal setting. I can't be an expert in all things.

Now I just have to convince a man who spends his time telling people about a God who looks at the heart instead of the surface that the church needs a ministry to help people create a better external presentation.

A short woman wearing dark, slim jeans and a bright azure sweater walks through the office toward me. Her smile is wide and welcoming and her fashionable low-heeled ankle boots create muffled thumps against the carpet with her brisk steps.

"Are you Amy?"

I stand with a nod, resisting the urge to rub my hands along my own jeans. We're a complete contrast with my wide-legged jeans and snug-fitting long sleeve shirt. Her curly brown hair is twisted up in claw clip while mine is down in its customary loose waves.

Neither of us look bad, but I can't help but wonder if one of us isn't dressed right. If so, it's probably me, and that's really going to undermine this pitch meeting.

The woman shakes my offered hand while giving me a smile that feels almost too broad and enthusiastic despite the air of genuineness in her greeting. "I'm June. I'm the pastor of women's ministries here. I'll be joining you for this morning's meeting, if that's okay?"

"Of course." This ministry would likely fall under this June person's jurisdiction anyway. Although men probably need this kind of assistance as well.

She keeps up a conversation of idle chitchat as we wind through a series of sedately decorated hallways. Many of the office doors are closed, but some of them are open and the small rooms beyond are as differently decorated as a Met Gala red carpet.

One of the offices has a wall covered in tacked up event T-shirts and a chair that looks like a beanbag with legs while another has a modern-looking two-seater sofa set beneath a giant print of a Raphael painting.

Maybe it doesn't matter so much that I'm dressed differently than June is. Maybe the office is a reflection of the variety of people I see on Sunday morning.

The idea calms my nerves enough that I can take a full, deep breath. It might be my first one since I got up this morning.

June leads us to an office in the back corner. It's larger than the others and decorated with quiet elegance in shades of blue and natural wood. There's a conference room off to one side and a conversation area with four chairs facing a round coffee table on the other.

Pastor Brian looks just like he does on Sundays, though he's dressed a little more casually in a Henley shirt and jeans. The deck shoes on his feet are more than a little worn, but the jeans are almost painfully new-looking.

He is seated in one of the chairs, scrolling through something on his phone, but he stands and slides the device into his pocket when June and I enter.

"Amy. It's nice to meet you. I'm Pastor Brian Dennis."

I nod awkwardly. "I know. I see you on Sundays."

"Good, good. How long have you attended here?"

"About a month in person. A month before that online."

"Excellent. Can I get you anything to drink? I've got water, Mountain Dew, and an old Keurig that makes a decent cup of coffee about half the time. Or there's a lot of other options I can get from the break room."

"I'm good. Thanks." My mouth feels dry but I'm still nervous enough to spill a drink all over me and the pastor so I'm not even going to risk a bottle of water.

We situate ourselves in the chairs and Pastor Brian gives me a warm smile. "So, Amy, what can I do for you? You mentioned a ministry need in your meeting request, I think?"

"I . . . yes." I take a deep breath and remind myself I own a business. I'm nearly thirty. And, more importantly, I'm a new creation in Jesus Christ, which makes me valuable, worthy, and important. At least in His eyes.

Now I just have to convince a couple of pastors.

"What I actually wanted to talk to you about was an idea for a new ministry here. I haven't been a believer long, but I've spent a lot of time seeing how people react to each other, particularly when they meet for the first time."

Both of their faces are turned attentively to me and neither appear ready to stop me, so I press on. "Sometimes people who have a lot to offer the world have trouble doing so because they aren't presenting the right impression. I would like to help those people."

Silence falls over the group and I'm suddenly wishing I had that water bottle so that I had something to do with my hands.

June speaks first, her head tilted to the side. "How would you help them?"

I take a deep breath and press on. "Well, I'm a stylist and a clothing designer."

The wide smile from before is gone, replaced with a thoughtful expression that is slowly turning into a frown. "I don't know that the church needs a ministry that tells women they dress poorly."

My eyes slide closed. "I'm sorry. I'm explaining this badly." I shift in my chair and lean forward, suddenly needing them to see my vision, to validate this passion even if it can't become a full ministry under the church. "Let's say there's a woman going for a job interview. It matters what she wears and how she presents herself. Or a mother going to a meeting at school to advocate for her child. Or even someone going on a first date who needs the confidence to show the guy who she really is."

There's no question about June's frown now. It's small to be certain, but if I consider how far her expression had to travel to go from the smile that took up her entire body, the change is extreme.

She's going to tell me I'm wrong. She's going to tell me I've got this whole Christian thing wrong. She's going to tell me that Jason was wrong, and God can't use anything I've spent my life developing and even my career is something He would find horrible.

But she doesn't get a chance to, because Pastor Brian, who I had in truth been essentially ignoring, speaks first. "In order for us to shine a light in certain places, we must first gain entrance."

"I . . ." My gaze swings from June to Pastor Brian. "What?"

He's still looking thoughtful, but there's no hint of a frown or judgement on his face. "As much as we recite the verse that God looks at the heart, that same passage indicates man looks at outward appearance. If we want to position ourselves to show God to others, we must first get them to allow us in the door."

Tension drains out of me as my gaze meets his solemn brown one. "Yes. Exactly."

June's frown lifts a little. "How would we possibly position that as a ministry, though?"

Pastor Brian's eyebrows lift as if passing the question on to me. He seems confidant that I will have an answer.

"It doesn't have to be a ministry that gets a banner in the front lobby. This is something that is more for inside the church than outside. It could be a word-of-mouth kind of thing that the small group leaders share when it's needed."

"You want them to tell the people in their LifeGroup that they're dressed poorly?"

June is definitely not on board with this, so I focus on Pastor Brian. "It's more than just clothes. It's interview skills so they can get a new job. It's etiquette lessons so people aren't distracted by bad manners. It's having the confidence to say no to a date because you don't need a man to feel complete. Maybe it's even having the confidence to say yes because you finally aren't embarrassed to be seen with someone in public."

"And you can give people all those things?" June asks.

"No." I swallow because what I have to offer is probably the shallowest of the list but somehow is still important. "But I know people who can. I've already got an executive who's offered a few hours a month to help with interview skills."

Pastor Brian considers me for a while. "Tell me your testimony, Amy."

I blink. "My what?"

He grins and shifts to sit at an angle in his seat so he can face me more directly. "Tell me the story of how Jesus changed your life."

"I . . . well." I've never articulated my story for someone else. Emma knows everything about me already and even Jason had some extensive knowledge.

But I start talking anyway. It's a bit of a rambling tale at first, because I'm not certain how far back to go. My first-grade art project doesn't seem important but the fact that I felt the need to impress people from an early age seems relevant. I talk about attending an exclusive private high school because my mother wanted me to have socialite friends so she could meet their socialite mothers. I talk about discovering that my twin sister was essentially leading a double life because she felt I would only accept her if she looked and acted in a certain way and I can't say that she was wrong.

Then I talk about how wrecked I was at the thought that I didn't know how to accept my own sister as she was, that when she stopped pretending to be someone she wasn't in order to make me happy I saw a woman who, despite her terrible fashion sense, had a greater sense of self than I did.

My words become a little more stilted as I talk about laying on Emma's floor, questioning the point of everything in life until I realized I wanted to know the God Emma knew. Then I'm talking about the confusion that came when, after accepting a gospel that seemed so simple yet so terrifying, Emma presented me with a list of things I was supposed to do next.

The words spill out then, tumbling over each other as I say things I didn't even realize were true.

"It felt so wrong. I'd spent my life doing what other people told me to do and being who they told me to be and here I was, accepting that there was an all-powerful spiritual being that loves me as I am and wants me as I am and is inviting me into a personal relationship with Him. The last thing I want is more people telling me what to do and say and think."

I'm completely ignoring June now, pulling my legs up beneath me in the chair so I can sit at an angle that directly faces Pastor Brian. "The thing is, I don't know how to be a good Christian. I can't seem to find the rules. But I know how to look professional or elegant or sophisticated or approachable and I know how to present myself in a way that tends to open doors. I know how feeling like I look put together can give me the confidence to do things that scare me."

Pastor Brian's brown eyes stay steady on mine. "And now you want to gift that to other believers."

I take a deep breath, something unraveling in me as he puts the unframed desire that brought me here today into words. "Yes."

"You want to know how to be a good Christian?"

That was not what I came here to talk about, but the man is a pastor so I guess I shouldn't be surprised that he wants to discuss that. "Yes. But . . ." How do I tell him I don't want a person telling me what to do anymore?

"But you want God to tell you what that is. Not me."

Okay. Pastors are spooky. Did God tell him I was thinking that?

"We have a new believers class that will help you learn to do that."

I blink at him. "It's not just going to tell me a list of rules?"

He shakes his head. "No. You'll read parts of the Bible with other new believers and discuss what certain passages mean. There will be a teacher in there who will guide you to certain sections and help you understand context and other information, but her job is to help you learn how to read the Bible and hear God for yourself."

I shift my weight. "And you aren't going to make me go underwater in front of everybody first?"

For the first time, his expression shifts, taking on an amused grin. "Struggling with the idea of not looking put together in front of every-one?"

"Yes." My voice is thin, but I don't want to lie to this man.

He nods. "I think, after you've spent some time in the class and stud-ied the passages, you'll realize that sometimes making yourself vulnerable can actually create a more impactful presentation than perfectly curled hair." He tilts his head a little. "Baptism isn't what saves you or makes you a Christian. It's a symbolic way of showing that you are laying down your own will and letting God be the one who guides your life."

He waits until our gazes meet and says, "It's an act of obedience to Him."

A pang in my chest confirms that what he's saying is indeed true. But I don't know if I'm ready to accept it.

I let my gaze drift to June for the first time in a while and she, too, is looking at Pastor Brian as if she's also having something of an epiphany. The idea that someone can be a minister of the church and still have things to learn is encouraging.

Pastor Brian's description of baptism isn't.

I sigh, debating how much I want this whole ministry thing. All it takes is the memory of Tracy's happy text and Sydney's confident smile to spur me forward. "When is the next baptism?"

"Why do you want to know?"

Isn't the pastor trying to convince me to go underwater and take the new believers class? Isn't that the price of full admission to the church club?

"Because . . ." I drag the word out slowly, trying to read his expression so I can determine the answer he's wanting.

There's nothing. He wears the same expression of nondescript interest he's worn for most of this meeting.

With a sigh, I give him the truth. "Because I am assuming I have to do that before you'll consider my proposition."

He shakes his head. "That's not a reason to get baptized."

"I . . . what?"

"Baptism shouldn't be done in obedience to man. It should be done in obedience to God."

I open my mouth to protest because why does it matter why I do the thing as long as I'm doing what I'm supposed to do?

He speaks first, though. "It would seem, though, that you are working your way toward that obedience with this desire to share your gifts with others."

Gifts? He sees my styling abilities as gifts?

"New faith looks different in adults than it does in children. There are areas of life you've already matured in, which can sometimes make certain areas of your faith immediately stronger than others." He shrugs. "It's not like a child who is still learning how to do everything from keeping their hair clean to keeping a relationship healthy. There are areas of your life that are already strong and simply needed to be shifted toward a godly focus instead of a personal one."

"And that's what I'm doing?"

He shrugs. "Only you know for certain, but that is how it appears to me."

"So we can make a new ministry?"

"I believe that would best fall under June's care."

My heart sinks as I give my attention to June. She did not like the idea when I mentioned it earlier. Even now she doesn't seem thrilled.

"Perhaps we can make it an available resource instead of a self-contained ministry?" She frowns. "I can see the benefit of helping women present themselves in certain situations, but I wouldn't know what to call it as a separate entity. It feels rather like that old show What Not to Wear."

Pastor Brian nods. "That sounds reasonable." His kind brown eyes turn to me. "Do you have other questions or thoughts, Amy?"

Not having to put together something formal releases a knot of tension I hadn't realized was related to the idea. It's replaced by a tumultuous jumble of thoughts and emotions at the consideration that my faith has a lopsided maturity.

Two main thoughts seem to be protruding from the mass of confusion. One, maybe Jason is wrong about whether or not I'm ready to be in a serious, God-honoring romantic relationship. And two, maybe I'm not so opposed to having someone tell me a thing or two about the ins and outs of following Jesus.

Unfortunately, there's only one of those ideas I can do anything about.

With my heart threatening to pound out of my chest, I take a deep breath, and jump. "When is the next new believers class?"

AMY

There have been times in life when I've regretted how busy December can be, but this year, I'm thankful. It keeps me busy enough to avoid Emma, and Mother busy enough to avoid me.

I can't keep avoiding church though, and since my conversation with Pastor Brian somewhat cemented where I want to keep attending, there's no avoiding Emma and, by extension, Jason.

We keep things civil, though, and I try to keep everyone on their toes by varying which service I go to and where I sit. I thought, because the church is so very large, that such tactics would make it so that I didn't have to see either of them, but apparently, if someone is actually looking for you, hiding in the crowd is somewhat difficult.

Which means Emma finds me on the regular, but I've only stumbled across Jason twice all month.

Because he isn't looking for me.

So now, if I happen to see him, I hide.

Like at the Christmas Eve service last night. I saw him holding his lit candle and singing the Christmas carols with a face full of emotion. He'd have had to turn around to see me, though, so it was easy enough to blow my candle out immediately at the end of the service and take myself home to wrap my last presents in front of Julia and Suzanne Sugarbaker and their antics.

I've watched a lot of my comfort show this month. All seven seasons, actually. It usually takes me a few years to go through more than 150 episodes because I only pull out this show when I'm feeling over-emotional.

And lately I've been feeling all the emotions.

This is my first Christmas truly knowing the reason for the season, and it made all the preparations, all the decorations, all the festivities mean so much more.

I stack my family presents into a tote bag so I can lug them over to my mother's house for Christmas lunch. Only one gift remains under the tree. It's for Jason, but I don't know when, if ever, I'll actually give it to him. When I saw it, though, I couldn't resist buying it for him.

It's a bow tie. Black, of course, because he likely only wears a tie when he puts on that tux for his mother, but when you look at it very closely, you can see that the slight pattern on it isn't just made by the weave of the threads or a simple hatch mark pattern. No, the sheen of the tie comes from tiny satin-stitched ones and zeros.

Will I ever give it to him? Or will I pack the tiny gift wrapped in shiny red and green paper into the box of tree ornaments in January?

God knows, but only time will tell me.

I turn my back on the lone gift and get in my car to head to Mother's house.

I smile in true happiness as I unload my tote of gifts and place them under the tree. I don't really care what's in the boxes with my name on the label this year because I've never enjoyed giving this much. Even the simple mug that says Gamer Girl on it makes me happy because I know Emma will enjoy it more than the cashmere scarf I got her last year.

My smile falls as I join everyone for lunch. Emma has her elbows propped on the table, her head in her hands while Carter gently rubs her back and talks to Mother.

"It's going to be a small wedding and we don't want to do a lot of decor, so even if those venues had availability, they're too large and too blank for what we want."

"But a garden wedding in May is so unpredicatable. And soon. You'll need a weather backup plan and there's not enough time to have custom invitations created or find a—"

"I'll just move it inside, then, Mother." Emma's head pops up. "I'm sure my church can squeeze us in. If I'm lucky, they'll already have the decorations for our summer kids Bible school up. I think the theme this year is space travel. We could get married in front of the rocket."

Mother's mouth twists into a puckered frown worthy of the sourest of lemons. "I never know if you're being serious anymore."

I step quickly to Emma's other side and slide into the empty seat. "She's not being serious, Mother, at least not about the rocket ship." Simple is fine, practical, and very Emma but I will not have her getting married in some cardboard children's theme park for the sake of spiting our mother.

I lean toward Emma. "We should go dress shopping soon."

Mother and Aunt Jade both gasp. "You aren't going to make her a custom gown?"

I shrug. "As you said there's not much time. Better to find a good base gown and then I can custom tailor it for her if it's not the gown of her dreams. It's more important for her to get married when she wants than that she wear a custom gown."

"I just don't understand what the big rush is. You haven't even been dating a whole year yet."

Emma opens her mouth then lets it slide shut with a shake of her head before looking at me. "Just let me know when you want to go. My schedule is pretty flexible since I finished making the changes to your app."

I blink. "Changes?"

"Yeah." She rolls her eyes. "Tell me you didn't think I'd let you release something that got such poor reviews in test groups." She bumps my shoulder with hers. "Besides, that design was way too much app and not near enough you. I know how that Look Book works and how you prepare it."

"So . . . it's a digital Look Book now?" I frown, confused and unsure, because I thought Emma hated my Look Book and the process it took to create it. "But I wanted this app to be something, well, something people like you would find helpful."

"It is helpful." She twists to more fully face me in her chair. "You thought I didn't find the Look Book helpful? Oh, no. Now that it's full of clothes I actually don't mind wearing, I use it all the time."

"But you keep sending me pictures of cartoon pajama pants."

"I may have added a few pages."

The delicate clearing of my mother's throat breaks into the conversation and heat floods my face. How could I have forgotten Emma and I weren't alone? I was so focused on helping Emma feel better than I didn't think to shush her when she mentioned the app.

Emma's wide blue eyes and pale cheeks are proof that she, too, forgot Mother and Aunt Jade were there, or forgot they didn't know.

"Darling, what is this about an, er, app?" Mother picks up her martini glass and takes a small sip of the pink cocktail.

"I, uh, well, that is . . ." I sigh. There is no getting out of this without outright lying. I can't finagle it or half-truth it or change the subject. My day of reckoning has arrived.

Which might mean I go into the new year with all of my life completely crushed. Gives a whole new meaning to *new year, new me.*

"I'm making an app that will allow more people to find looks that are fashionably appropriate and beneficial while still catering to their particular fit and fabric needs."

"And budgetary."

I blink at Emma. "What?"

She winces a little as she shrugs one shoulder. "I added a budget element to the backend algorithm."

"That's smart." I emphasize my statement with a nod, thinking of women like Sydney.

Aunt Jade places a hand on my mother's arm as a huff of disapproval escapes her.

"Dear," my aunt says with her eyes shifting from her sister to me, "the boutique has been doing well, but you should have consulted with us before making this sort of expansion investment." Her eyebrows lift toward Emma. "I assume your company is charging her? And it isn't cheap?"

"I got the friends and family discount," I mutter.

Emma smirks and looks at her lap.

Then I sigh, because it's time to face the music. "It isn't coming out of the boutique's budget. It's coming out of mine."

Mother's eyes widen. "You're putting your personal money into it?"

"No. Well, in a way, but no. I'm putting my styling business's money into it. I'm expanding my business. Not yours."

Mother and Aunt Jade frown. "Your business is separate?"

"Yes, I . . ." My chest expands as I take a deep breath and let it out but still everything feels incredibly tight. "I rent my space from the boutique. It's a flat fee every month. And then I work part-time on the sales floor. That's the salary you've been paying me."

Mother stares at me for several moments, clearly taking time to think through the ramifications of my confession. "So, you've been making more money? You're getting more clients and the business is growing?"

"I . . . yes?" I want to glance at Emma to see if she, too, is confused by my mother's response. She doesn't seem upset. In fact, she looks . . . relieved?

"Oh, thank goodness." Mother presses one hand to her chest and she almost slumps into her chair. "I was so worried, especially when you brought in that, ahem, less fortunate client. But if the business is growing enough that you can invest in expansion, then that's a different matter."

This time I do glance at Emma. She's as stunned as I am. "You aren't upset?"

Mother reaches for a dish and begins serving up Christmas lunch. "Why would I be upset? I am a businesswoman, Amethyst. Despite wanting the finer things in my social life, I appreciate a good day's work and a smart head for profit."

"But you wanted to move my desk out into the boutique."

"Because you weren't making any additional money. Businesses need to grow, dear. If they stay stagnant, they eventually fail."

"I . . . so you're okay with this plan? That I keep renting space from you?"

"Of course I am. It's a mutually beneficial arrangement." She turns to Aunt Jade. "You must try these vegetables. They have a divine honey glaze on them."

As the dishes come around, I add food to my plate, but my mind isn't paying much attention. If I was wrong about how my mother would view my business, what else am I wrong about?

I wait until the food's gone around and everyone has murmured approval of the honey-glazed roasted vegetables, before I test more of my familial understanding. "I've been going to church with Emma."

Mother blinks. "You have? Why?"

"Because I talked to her a few months ago and everything she said about her beliefs made sense and fit what I thought was missing in my life, so I . . . changed."

"You're doing the God thing now, too?" She glances at Emma. "Please tell me that doesn't mean you're going to be purchasing a supply of yoga pants now."

Okay, so I wasn't wrong about everything. With a soft laugh, I shake my head. "No, Mother, all my athletic clothing will only be for going to the gym."

She sniffs. "Then I suppose if you're happy, I'm happy." Her fork freezes in mid-air. "But you're still going to attend functions and the opera with me, aren't you?"

"I'm still me, Mother, though perhaps a reprioritized version. I may want to think harder about the charities we support and there will be some artistic endeavors I don't want to attend, but I'm still me. Just . . . the version I was meant to be."

After lunch and an orderly opening of presents where every speck of paper and ribbon is stashed away in a wicker trash can the moment it gets removed from a gift, Emma flops next to me on the couch.

"The version you were meant to be, huh?"

I nod. "I've done a lot of thinking lately, and I know I have a lot to learn, and I'll still make mistakes, but I've come to the conclusion that there isn't any reason to destroy my life and rebuild it. It just needs to be refined. And everything I build or learn or take away or add is going to bring me closer to God."

"That's a pretty smart decision." She pokes at her knee. "And where does Jason fit in that picture?"

I sigh. "I don't think he wants to."

She's quiet long enough that I look up to meet her eyes. Her quiet stare is unnerving. What is it she knows that I don't?

JASON

"I know fratricide is when someone murders their brother, but what's it called when someone kills their best friend?" I grumble as I climb from the car. I'm bigger and stronger than Emma. I could get away from her. She drove us here, but I've got the apps for both Uber and Lyft on my phone. One of them must have a car less than ten minutes away.

"Probably just homicide," Emma says with a shrug. "I don't think they have a special name for it."

"Pity."

"Are you considering fratricide?"

"No." I sigh.

Christmas was strange, at least at first, because I hadn't really talked to Robert since I saw that text message. I had just assumed that because I assured him over and over that Amy and I weren't a thing, he'd chosen to pursue her. And I know that his go-to move isn't showing up with minestrone from a deli.

I couldn't blame Robert. Obviously I see how he could have been attracted to Amy. I couldn't even really blame Amy if she said yes. I had the opportunity to ask her out, to make things official, but I didn't.

Instead I kept kissing her and not asking her out which is, admittedly, a scummy thing for me to have done.

And then Robert said he'd helped her help that woman she'd been buying secondhand suits for, and I realized I'd been a jerk. Again.

Guilt and shame swamp over me, consuming my mind. I should make things right, I know. I just . . . don't know how.

I'm not exactly being the noble and upright guy I'd prefer right now. Yes, I helped fix her app. Once I sat with Stephanie and pulled dozens of ideas out of Amy's brief, the design shifted into something that our preliminary test queries indicate will be quite successful.

There's nothing more I can be for her without changing who I am, and even though I've been fighting some very solid convictions that it might be time to do just that, I can't make those changes for her. They have to be for me. Which means more time before I can ask her out.

If I even get to the place where I think I should.

Fortunately, only my physical presence is needed for this best friend/man of honor duty. Now that Christmas is over, I'm being dragged along to make wedding decisions, but I know Emma well enough to not need an actual opinion. I'll just listen to Emma talk things out until I determine which choice she actually wants, and then I'll select that one.

She leads me into a menswear store and tells the attendant I'm there to get measured.

"I have a perfectly good tux, you know."

"I want you to match the groomsmen, though."

My eyebrows lift. "I thought I was standing next to you?"

Her nose scrunches as her chin lifts. "I haven't decided. Either way, you need to blend in."

"Fair enough." I go in the back to get measured by their tailor and when I come out, Emma's holding up a swatch of blue fabric in front of a display of vests and cummerbunds.

"I don't mind doing something else in the wedding, you know." I run a hand along the back of my neck and resituate my ball cap. "I mean, I understand if Carter's not okay with your plan."

"Stop it. I'm sure." She holds a vest up in front of me, frowns, then puts it back. "I said you could stand up on his side as a groomsman or do the scripture reading or any other number of things and he said that would be ridiculous since without you it would have taken us a lot longer to get our heads on straight."

"I didn't do that much."

"Take the win, friend, and get ready to spend my special day posing with a bunch of girls."

"Are you going to make me carry a bouquet?"

She grins at me. "I haven't ruled it out."

Her smile fades as she runs the small piece of fabric through her fingers. I know the look on her face. She has something to ask me that she thinks I'm not going to like. I have a feeling I know what it is, or at least what it's about. I want to tell her it won't be a problem, that the wedding will be all about her and Carter, so it doesn't matter who else is there.

But I can't.

The words won't form because right now, in this moment, it will matter.

"She's my maid of honor, you know. And the Christmas distraction is over. You'll have to share duties." Her quiet voice is accompanied by a wince and a ball of dread settles into my chest. Emma should be nothing but happy about her wedding.

Time to man up.

After a deep breath and a desperate prayer, I give her a smile that I hope looks genuine. "She can do the whole zip up the dress thing and I'll floof out the skirt when you get to the alter."

Some her tension eases as she shakes her head. "Is that all you know of weddings?"

I give an exaggerated scoff. "As if you know much more."

"I'm learning fast." Her dry tone tells me I haven't fully set her at ease.

Guess I need to be serious for a moment. "Emma, Amy is your twin. Of course she's your maid of honor. Give her any and all the duties you want." I place a hand to my chest. "Honestly, as much as I love you, I'm a guy. I don't care what shade of ivory the tablecloths are or if your bouquet is made of lilies or daisies."

Her eyes widen. "There are shades of ivory?"

I give a solemn nod. "Linen, almond, bone."

Finally, a laugh breaks free. "The fact that you know there's going to be a tablecloth discussion when even I didn't know that is rather hilarious."

"A lifetime of listening to my mother plan events. Seriously, anything you're going to ask me as far as planning goes is just going to be sent to her, so you can cut out the middleman. Just have Amy work with my mother."

My nonchalant, supportive facade cracks at that statement. Amy would be thrilled if she got connected with my mother. Despite the confusion at the Christmas party, once Mom gets to know Amy, she'll love her. Especially after she hears about the ministry she's started that Robert's helping with. It's the sort of thing Mom gets excited about. It won't surprise me if she starts to add Amy to her guest list for large parties, inviting her to meet the other ladies in her society clubs.

Amy will get everything she wanted.

Without having to date me or Robert.

The idea makes me happy, and I don't know what to do with the fact that I still want to help her achieve her goals. They're good goals. She's a good person. And I meant everything I said, even if I should have said it in a better way.

But my heart is also hurting and that means an ugly part of me wants Amy to hurt, too. Even if I was the one holding the knife that metaphorically stabbed me in the heart.

Emma's face screws up into a frown. "I don't know what to say right now."

I raise questioning eyebrows in her direction. "I think you're supposed to be telling the salesclerk whether you want a vest or a cummerbund."

She rolls her eyes at me but pulls a vest off the display rack. It's gray, with a decorative swirl woven through it that closely matches the blue of the fabric. "Vest. Cummerbunds are. . ." Her nose scrunches. "A lot."

"Agreed."

She finishes telling the clerk what she wants, then spends a few minutes discussing how to get the measurements for the other men in the party. I tune it out because my part is done.

My attention drifts to the photos displayed around the store. It's mostly weddings and prom groups, because average people don't have a reason to rent a tuxedo aside from that.

Emma finds me staring at a photo of a couple beneath a tree. They're holding hands and staring into each other's eyes. The bride is blonde, with large curls bouncing down her back.

"She was never really interested in Robert." Emma's tone is quiet and even.

"I thought you weren't getting involved."

"I wasn't, but then the both of you started acting like idiots and left me no choice."

"I'm not being an idiot, I'm being practical."

"But you love each other."

I shake my head. "You've got love on the brain. I hear weddings do that to girls."

She whacks me on the shoulder. "This is not wedding rose glasses—"

"You mean rose-colored glasses?"

"I mean I'm not making things up." She plucks at my sleeve and tilts her head toward the door and starts walking.

I fall into step beside her. "I'm not saying there aren't—weren't—feelings. Amy is very . . ." Smart. Beautiful. Caring. Wonderful.

Ambitious. Calculating.

"Sad."

My feet falter as Emma pushes out the door. "What?"

"Sad. Amy is very sad." She frowns at me. "Are you coming?"

I start walking beside her again. "Why is she sad?"

"She received an invitation to the Pink and Green Ball."

That ball is my mother's largest annual charity event, held at the beginning of March and decorated with a ridiculous blend of hearts and shamrocks. "Isn't that the sort of thing she's always wanted?"

"Yes, but it came from your mother."

"She is the one on the board."

Emma pokes me in the shoulder. "She doesn't want her own invitation. She wants to be your plus-one."

I shake my head. "She doesn't need me right now. Not like that. I hardly know those people anymore. Going with my parents would be a lot better for her."

"That's what I told her." Emma shrugs. "Amy said that was a bunch of cowardly hogwash."

I try to picture Amy actually saying the word hogwash and I can't. "She didn't say that."

"No, she said something about hypocrisy and missed opportunities and you being a blind idiot. I simplified."

Once more, my feet stumble to a halt and I realize Emma wasn't leading me toward the car but to a bakery down the street from the tuxedo rental store. I've been here before to pick up orders for my mother as this is her preferred bakery.

"What are we doing here?"

"Cake tasting."

Normally, that would be one wedding task I'd be more than happy to accompany her on, but right now my brain is stuck on the idea that Amy thinks I'm the idiot for ending things. And what's this about hypocrisy? "What did Amy actually say, Emma?"

Emma opens the door to the bakery and we walk inside. "I didn't catch it all. She was ranting very quickly."

"Try."

We're interrupted by Carter, who was apparently waiting for us in the bakery. If he's free this morning, why wasn't he getting measured at the tuxedo store, too?

After a quick hug and brief kiss, Emma looks up at her fiancé, "Were you successful?"

He nods. "There's a variety of decoration options in the storage room."

"Excellent." Her wide smile turns to me and I'm immediately on edge. "What are you up to?"

She waggles her eyebrows. "Wedding cake."

"I'm aware. But you don't need me here for that. You and Carter are the ones whose opinions matter."

She blinks at me. "I know. But I still have a mission for you."

With her hand once more tugging on my sleeve, she pulls me down a short hallway behind the counter.

I frown. "I don't think we're supposed to be back here."

"I got special permission." Emma walks a little faster. "I didn't want them to have to pull out all the stands and toppers."

"Don't they have pictures?"

"It's not the same. You can look at them all in person and form an opinion while Carter and I eat cake."

"Somehow I think I'm getting the short end of the stick here."

"Being the man of honor isn't always sparkles and roses."

I wince. "I hope it's never sparkles and roses."

She stops with her hand on a doorknob. "I guess that will be up to you."

"How?"

She opens the door and shoves me through. I've barely regained my footing when the door is slamming behind me and an ominous click comes from the doorknob.

"Emma?"

"I will not have my man and maid of honor at odds for my wedding. So you two can learn how to work together." She pauses. "And if my sister and best friend could figure out how much they love each other at the same time, that would be an excellent bonus."

I turn to find Amy watching me with huge, round eyes. A cake topper that looks like a dancing couple is in her hands.

My gaze drops to the doorknob, which has apparently been turned around as the key side is now facing the interior of the supply closet.

I've been locked in this tiny room with the first woman I've cried over since middle school.

And she looks ready to throw that figurine at my head.

AMY

My arm tenses as if in preparation for throwing this cake topper at the idiot's head. It's plastic so it wouldn't do too much damage, but it's still probably not a good idea.

"What are you doing in here?"

He does that thing with his hat where he takes it off and shakes his hair out before settling it back in place. It's ridiculously hot and I don't want to find him appealing right now.

"Allegedly I'm choosing a cake stand but I don't think anyone needs my opinion for that." He sighs. "Pretty sure I'm supposed to be getting back together with you."

"Hard to get back together when you weren't together in the first place." I curl my hand into a fist, pressing my nails into my palm to keep myself from crying. "You made our situation very clear."

"Did I? That's impressive since it was never clear to me to begin with."

"You didn't sound confused a week ago."

"I've been nothing but confused since you came into my life."

The words sting like a hundred bees, and I turn away, giving all my attention to replacing the cake topper to the shelf. More figurines of happy couples fill my vision and I pretend to examine them, even though they seem to be mocking me and such a thing would be a terrible choice for Emma's cake.

Jason groans. "That did not come out right."

I say nothing because truly, what is there to say? Eventually the cake shop owner will want in this closet and will let us out, no matter how Emma convinced them to allow her this favor. More likely it was Jason's mother who arranged it. That makes me hurt even more because how could his mother want me to date her son more than he does?

There's a shuffle of feet and the sound of a crate scraping along the floor and then a warmth invades my space, telling me Jason is within inches. I refuse to turn around. I refuse to give him the satisfaction of knowing I'm devastated. Or the pain. I'm honestly not sure which he would feel or which I would want him to feel.

"Amy." His voice is soft and it almost turns the burn in my eyes into tears. "I'm sorry. I keep saying things wrong around you."

"Maybe that's a sign that you should stop talking."

A soft chuckle escapes him, almost as if the amusement escaped despite his attempt to keep it contained. "You gonna shut me up, then?"

Heat floods both my face and my middle as the implications of that statement settle in my mind. I've read enough books and seen enough movies to know the time-honored way to shut someone up during a romantic argument is to kiss them.

Is he asking me to kiss him? Does he want me to?

I want to.

But I want something real even more.

I turn, pressing my back to the shelf. "Maybe you should try to say what you actually mean instead."

He blows out a breath as he takes off his hat with his left hand and pushes his right through his hair. Then he places the cap back on his head, but this time it's backwards. I've learned this configuration is his serious one, which is completely opposite from the backwards-ball-cap stereotype.

"I like you, Amy. A lot."

"It'd be weird to kiss someone you didn't."

"True." His gaze drops to my lips, and I would kick myself for mentioning kissing if there weren't a shelf of cake toppers in the way. Kissing is absolutely not our problem.

Or maybe it is, but not because we aren't good at it.

"Life has changed a lot for you this past year. You've changed a lot this past year."

"I've changed a lot in the last six months."

He nods. "Right. And . . . that's a lot for an adult to take in. I mean, I guess it's a lot for anyone, but I think we expect to change when we're young."

He isn't wrong. It's been difficult to learn I'm not who I thought I was. At least, not anymore.

"And you're not done changing."

I frown. "Neither are you."

"What do you mean?" He frowns as well.

"Well, it's not like your life hasn't changed in the past six months. You can't tell me that Emma and Carter getting together hasn't altered your daily existence."

"I . . . no. I can't tell you that. The last year has been a lot of change for me as well."

I nod, not entirely sure where I'm going with this but feeling like I'm going in the right direction for the first time in a while.

His hand lifts and his palm cups my cheek, the fingers spearing into my hair. Normally I hate it when someone touches my hair, but it's different when it's him.

"I think that's been my struggle."

I have to blink a few times to get my thoughts back focused on the conversation. "What has?"

"I'm trying to rebuild my life, but I want to shape it in a way that has space for you." He gives a dry laugh. "Hard to do when I keep pushing you out of it."

"You had your reasons, and they weren't selfish ones. You were trying to care for me."

"Instead I hurt you. And myself."

He had. But he'd also been right. I do need to know who I am apart from other people's opinions. I do need to allow God to define my identity apart from stereotypes and others' expectations. But I like what he said about building a life with space for me inside it.

I take a deep breath and throw caution to the wind. While yes, I don't know much about the Bible yet and yes, I've got a lot to learn about how God wants me to act, I think my lack of experience might be helping me see the simplicity of our situation. I've been following Jason's lead because he's been a believer longer, but God is speaking to me, too, which means I've got wisdom to add to this conversation.

"I think there's a difference between letting someone tell you who you are and growing your life to mesh with someone else's. I have a lot to learn. But I don't see that ever changing. God is a big God. Why shouldn't I walk beside you as we both learn more about who He is? Unless you've got it all figured out?"

He grins. "Hardly."

"Then maybe the answer isn't to grow apart from each other and hope that one day we'll fit together like a puzzle piece. That assumes that people stop changing at a certain point in time. What if instead, we tried being in each other's lives, helping to mold each other into a life that finds meaning together instead of apart."

"When did you get to be so wise?"

"Well, a certain somebody once told me that God works through all his children, telling each one different things, because they are the only ones ready to hear it."

"I don't want you to become something for me."

"I don't want to become something for you, either. But I'd like the chance to become something with you."

And then he's kissing me. The shelf presses into my lower back, his hands clasp firm and warm on my hips, and I think a plastic figurine is jabbing me in the ribs. I don't care.

In this moment there is nothing but Jason and the notion that I finally feel safe jumping toward him with all my might.

It takes several coughs and the flashing of the overhead light for us to realize Emma is back.

"Well, I'd say that is progress."

"Go away, Emma." Jason's words are grumbled against my lips, the trimmed scruff lightly scraping my skin.

"Fine, but you really should come taste this cake."

I grin up at him and lay my palm against that scruff, lightly rubbing my thumb along his cheekbone. "We'll be there in a minute."

The door clicks shut and we are cocooned in silence once more.

Jason clears his throat. "What are you doing tonight?"

"Nothing. Why?"

"I'd like to take you on a date. Somewhere that requires I wear a shirt with a collar."

I run a hand along the graphic of his T-shirt. "That'd be nice."

He closes his eyes and takes a deep breath. "I know this is our first date, but . . ."

"It's serious for me, too."

When his eyes open again, they are dark with purpose and desire. "And I'm thinking that maybe we save the kissing."

Disappointment floods me along with an appreciation of the way he wants to protect us, to respect me. "We are really good at that part."

He nods. "It confuses things. Much as I like it, I want us to be built on something more."

"I'd like that, too."

His eyes roam my face before sliding closed as he takes a deep breath and steps backward. "Shall we go try some cake?"

"Yes."

Not wanting to fail at the job of finding Emma a cake topper, I glance over the array of cake toppers and stands once more, trying not to notice how much one particular embracing couple looks a lot like me and Jason. The tuxedoed groom is even wearing a backwards ball cap.

A simple cake topper made of metal twisted into the shape of a dancing couple catches my eye. It's simple and artistic and would look great on a small or large cake. I scoop it off the shelf and hold it up for Jason's inspection. "What do you think?"

He shakes his head. "I think in matters of taste such as this one, I will gladly bow to your expertise."

"Good." I grin and hook my arm through his as we move to the door.

"You know," I say as we walk down the hall to rejoin my sister and Carter. "I got an invitation to the Pink and Green Ball at the end of February. It's pretty exclusive, but I think I could convince the organizers to grant me a plus-one for my boyfriend."

This is a risk, I know, but the truth is my career is going to put me in front of the people he walked away from. It's going to require that I attend events and play a certain part. I'd like to not do it alone.

I'd also like Jason to embrace all the gifts God has given him. Whether he likes it or not, who he is means he can show Jesus to a lot of people that few others have access to. The ball is almost two months away. Surely that's enough time for him to come to some sort of acceptance, right?

He rubs one hand across the back of his neck and winces. I try to hide my disappointment. Didn't we just say that we both had a lot of growing to do? This is just another area of that growth.

"That's gonna be a little difficult," he says, as if he truly regrets telling me no. Maybe we don't have as far to grow as I thought. Maybe he made another commitment? Although I'm surprised he knows which day the ball is on.

Or maybe he just isn't ready for me to call him my boyfriend. I did rather jump into that one. Of course, by February . . . I bring my mind back to the present moment. "Why?"

"Because I also have an invitation to the Pink and Green Ball that already includes a plus-one. I was hoping my girlfriend would agree to accompany me."

I stop as we step into the front of the bakery and turn to face him, unable to keep the happiness from my face. The agreement we made to hold off on the kissing tests my willpower. "Girlfriend, huh?"

His answering smile is crooked and adorable. "You said it first. I'm just trying to keep up."

AMY

Seven Weeks Later

I give Sylvia a wave as I walk through the church foyer, but I duck around a display about raising money to buy car seats for the Pregnancy Care Center so I don't have to acknowledge Jeff. He still weirds me out a little.

Before heading to my new believer class, I stop by the resource closet to drop off a few things a client wanted to donate. I've been given a corner to put up a clothing rack and a set of plastic drawers. It's enough for now, especially since the only stylist is me.

Growing this ministry will be slow and difficult, because it's not just about wanting to help people in a certain way. It's about having the skills to do so.

Robert has agreed to participate, though, by giving mock interviews for the women who are job hunting. He's done three, so far, and all of them said if they can get through a conversation with the Vice President of Precision Businesses, they can handle talking to the manager at the local law office or wherever they happen to be going.

Jason and some of the other people on his staff are helping people clean up their social media or create a basic website, and his mother is going to hold monthly etiquette classes, although she's calling them Personal Presentation Workshops. Pastor Brian has said there will be a lot of other people interested in sharing their skills once we are ready to expand.

I finish hanging the new pieces and slide a pair of shoes into the appropriate drawer before leaving the room. A woman I don't know is pulling a couple of Bibles from the bookshelf on the other side of the room and there's a hint of judgement in her eyes as she watches me straighten a designer suit jacket on its hanger. She doesn't say anything and even gives me a smile as I pass her to leave the room, so I'm sure it was more curiosity than judgement, but I wouldn't be surprised either way.

Even I thought it was ridiculous to think that all my years of fashion training and experience could be useful. But I've seen confidence bloom in the faces of women who look in the mirror and finally see their worth. As much as we want to say that what's on the inside is all that matters, what's on the outside matters, too. Until we're free of these fallible human bodies that are capable of failing us in just about every way, how we present ourselves matters. In the mirror and in the eyes of others.

And I can help with that.

A smile curves my lips as I head down the hall to my classroom. It's only the third week of the class, but I'm finding it helpful to be among other people who feel as clueless as I do. While I'm adding two questions to my list for every one I find the answer to, my confidence that the answers are available is growing. So is my comfort with the idea that those answers may take a while to find and might be difficult for me to understand. If God was small enough for me to comprehend everything about Him, I wouldn't need Him.

"That's a pretty smile. What are you thinking?"

An arm drops comfortingly around my shoulders and pulls me snugly into Jason's side as he walks beside me down the hall.

My smile only widens as I tilt my head back to look up at him. He doesn't wear his ball cap to church, but I can see the indentation in his hair that tells me he had it on in the car on the drive over. As much as I adore the shaggy look on him, he needs a haircut. One hand lifts to run my fingers through the thick strands.

"I know, I know." He groans as he shakes his head, but his grin proves he isn't actually irritated. "I'll get it cut before Friday."

I bite my lip. "Are you sure you want to go Friday? I'll be fine on my own."

His eyebrows lift and he steers me out of the flow of people until we can stop along the wall. "I'm sure. This is important to you."

"But your anonymity is important to you."

"I'm attending as the amazing Amy Trinket's boyfriend, not the powerful Troy Miller's son."

The laugh of incredulity that escapes me sounds suspiciously like a snort, but I'll never admit it. "You don't truly think no one will notice, do you? My mother put it together after all."

"Let them. What's the worst that happens?"

"They start hounding you with invitations and false friendships and flood your company with business designed to get to your father?" I calmly recite all his fears and past experiences as if he might have actually forgotten them. He hasn't, but I wouldn't put it past him to pretend he had for my sake.

"Aside from the fact that I already have a considerable number of trustworthy close friends, it just so happens that, as a thirty-year-old man, I am a little more adept at sorting through false flattery than I used to be. Also, I'm happy to expand my business if needed. Insincere money spends just as well as sincere dollars do, and it allows me to provide more jobs."

His hands squeeze mine before he adds, "As for the invitations, some-one once told me that I could prop open doors that were opened to me to allow others an opportunity."

I wince. "I'm not using you."

"Helping someone I love is a privilege."

There's a suspicious burning in the back of my eyes and I blink rapidly to dispel any gathering moisture that could mess up my makeup. "I love you, too."

He leans down to press a light kiss to the top of my head and then turns me to keep walking down the hall. The warmth of him pressed against my side is both comforting and invigorating.

"I do have a questions about this ball on Friday, though." He's very deliberately looking straight ahead as he walks me down the corridor so I'm certain this question is about to be anything but serious.

"What's that?"

"Well, you know it's been a while since I attended these things."

The corners of my mouth lose their battle and turn up into a slight curve. "I am aware, yes."

He angles his head so that his dark, humor-filled eyes meet mine. "Do I still have to dance with all the young, single ladies?"

I recall Robert telling me why he hid in the information rooms or engaged in so many business discussions and a giggle escapes even as a slice of jealousy rolls through me at the idea of Jason twirling all the ambitious single socialites around the dance floor. I tip my head back to rest on his arm. "Did your mother ask you to do that?"

"Not in so many words, but yes. Actually, it was my dad. In his words, if we were dancing with the daughters, then their fathers felt comfortable focusing on business."

"As it so happens most of my clients are at least middle-aged, if not older."

"So I should ask the grandmothers?" He gives a wince. "They like to pinch cheeks."

And probably had single granddaughters. "Why don't you just stay by my side for this one?"

His arm tightens around my shoulder. "I can do that. I'll gaze at you adoringly like the wives that cling to their husbands' arms. Think I can do a good simpering face?"

I almost stumble at the way he places himself so easily amongst the married people. We've only been officially dating for a month and a half.

The fact that the idea doesn't scare me is terrifying.

He gives me one last hug before I enter my class. I poke my head back out into the hall to watch him saunter toward his own small group. I'll start attending with him when the new believer class ends in March.

And then, eventually, maybe we'll both be attending the premarital counseling class that Emma and Carter are currently going through. A slight shiver passes through me at the thought. Since we've decided the kissing should wait for now and possibly until we take vows, I have a feeling that time may come sooner rather than later.

I push aside the notion as I focus on the class. When I meet up with Jason, Carter, and Emma in the worship center for the service, my brain is scrambling to put all my thoughts about the future in order. Throughout the first song my gaze is snagged by the delicate diamond on Emma's finger and the baptism pool I've yet to be submerged in. Both are symbols of commitment, of a new direction in life, of a confession to the world about a very private decision.

Am I ready for either one of them? Am I possibly even ready for both?

As I focus on the singing, on the words and the way they join everyone in the room in a moment of shared praise, I think the answer just might be yes.

As I've learned in the past few months, though, one absolutely has to come before the other. My commitment to Jesus, to growing in faith, to being the person God made me to be, has to come first. Only then will I be able to build a strong life with someone else.

I remain seated at the end of the service, through the final song, thinking about whether I'm making this decision for me or for Jason. The man in question sits easily at my side, his hand holding mine gently as he sings along. When the notes fade away and people begin to move, I stay seated. Jason stays with me. Emma eases back into her seat on the other side of me. Both of them wait.

And I know the time is right for me. Because both of these people, arguably the two most important people in my life, will love me no matter what. They'll stand with me—or in this case sit with me—no matter what. If I go tell the pastor I'm ready to be baptized, it will be for me. And they won't care if I look like a drowned rat in front of thousands of people or if I'm one of those who slip on their way into the baptism pool and get wet before they're supposed to or if I fumble my words when they ask for me to share what I believe with the congregation.

More importantly, God won't care if my next steps are less than perfect. That's the entire point. I am an imperfect person, and all God asks of me is love and obedience and faith.

Those are things I can give. Jason has shown me that.

Okay, maybe not the obedience part, but if I can love and have faith in another flawed human, I can certainly trust that the perfect Creator of everything is going to follow through.

"I need to talk to Pastor Brian."

Emma starts to ask why, but Jason just nods. "I think he's usually standing to the side of the lobby after the second service to talk to people."

Whether they all know why I want to talk to Pastor Brian or they simply care enough to follow my lead, the entire group seems happy to be slower than snails leaving the auditorium.

Pastor Brian is wrapping up a conversation as we enter the lobby and Jason steers me toward the side of the lobby. It's the first form of pressure he's given me and in some ways, it comforts me, assures me I'm making the right decisions. This man is going to support me where I need it, especially when I'm scared. If this is what obedience means, then maybe I'm willing to consider keeping that word in those someday vows.

The conversation doesn't take long and soon we're leaving the church and getting a table at a local Mexican restaurant. As it frequently does when Emma and I are together these days, the conversation turns to the wedding. They may be planning a simple ceremony with a brief engagement but that doesn't mean I'm going to let it be anything other than fabulous.

Emma dips a chip into the salsa bowl as she scrunches up her nose. "Do we really need centerpieces on the table? They just make it hard to talk to people."

"They don't have to." I pull out my phone and unlock it to open Pinterest. "You're going fairly casual so you don't want the tall ones." Those are the kind I've been looking at because, even though I'm thinking my engagement won't be the yearlong one I used to imagine I'd have, I still want the wedding of my dreams and I think my potential future mother-in-law will have the connections to make it happen quickly. "But there are very short, simple ones that keep it from looking like a conference room." I'm thinking floating candles in low, flat bowls of water or even long stem roses piled elegantly in the center.

Jason is looking over my shoulder as my Pinterest opens and heat floods my ears as the private board I'd made with a selection of ideal engagement rings fills the screen. I quickly click over to my account to find the boards I'd started for Emma's wedding, but the first four options boldly claim to be for a very different ceremony. I've titled them Dream Rings, Dream Dresses, Ideal Reception, and even Honeymoon Locations.

I press my thumb onto the board for Emma's Wedding, but I can't help sending a quick glance Jason's way. Had he seen the rings? The wedding boards?

He grins and gives me a wink but says nothing as he takes out his own phone and asks Carter when he has to go to New York next.

Emma and I talk about the reception until a notification pops up on my screen.

It's from Pinterest. A new user, TechGuyJason, wants to my friend. I go to his account and it's brand-new. Not a single pin or board in sight.

More heat crawls up the back of my neck, but it's not from embarrass-ment this time. I don't know why I was worried. I've always jumped in feet first when I know something is right in my life. It's who I am.

And there's no one else I'd rather be.

Thank you for reading. Want to know more about Emma and Carter and meet one of Amy's odd ex-boyfriends? Check out Pixels and Paint! To get behind-the-scenes bonuses and stay up-to-date on all the latest book news, visit KristiAnnHunter.com and subscribe to the newsletter.

PiXELS AND PAiNT
KRiSTi ANN HUNTER

Acknowledgements

There's an old adage that says to write what you know. It's an idea that works well enough for the beginning writer, but over the years there have been stories I want to tell and concepts I want to explore that aren't my personal experience. Amy's story is one of those.

To all the amazing women who shared their stories with me about coming to Jesus later in life, learning about church as an adult, and having to navigate life moving on, even as it changes completely, thank you. I learned so much more from you than what made it into this book. My faith and my own ministry are better for having met you.

Unending gratitude goes to my friends and family who have supported me, believed in me, and prodded me—sometimes gently, sometimes not—to keep going. There is no way I would still be writing without all of you. To Jacob in particular, thank you for talking story with me and for threatening me when I didn't like this story. Your support means everything.

Finally, thank you to my readers. Since I am truly terrible at marketing, it really is you who helps this book get into the hands of readers. Every time you leave a review, share a post, or tell a friend, you provide a reason for me to write more words. Thank you.

About the Author

Kristi is the award winning author of contemporary rom-coms and light-hearted Regencies from a Christian worldview. A graduate of Georgia Tech, she has always enjoyed exploring how life, love, and beliefs work in the real world to create stories filled with faith, fun, and flirting. She lives with her husband and three children in Georgia where she supports her family, serves at church, and makes way too many visits to Chick-fil-A. Find her online at KristiAnnHunter.com or on some social media platforms under @kristiannhunter.

Also Available

A Noble Masquerade
Hawthorne House Book 1

Lady Miranda Hawthorne has always struggled with the confines of being a proper lady. When the one outlet she allows herself leads her into a world of intrigue around her brother's valet, Marlow, she'll have to decide what to risk for love, family, and country.

Frankly, My Dear Clara
London Dreams Book 1

Mr. Hugh Lockhart has aspirations that involve catching the attention of an aristocrat, but he never thought it would be Miss Clara Woodbury, cousin to Viscount Eversly. As they challenge each others' beliefs and ambitions, will they find a love worth changing their minds for?

See a full list of books available at kristiannhunter.com/bookshelf.

Want some Kristi Ann Hunter merch? We've got that as well. Visit kristiannhunter.com/merch.

www.ingramcontent.com/pod-product-compliance
Lightning Source LLC
Chambersburg PA
CBHW021021310726
48969CB00006B/1488